The Ghost Tracks

Celso Hurtado

This is a work of fiction. Names, characters, organizations, places, events, and incidents are either products of the author's imagination or are used fictitiously.

Published by Inkshares, Inc., Oakland, California
www.inkshares.com

Edited by Adam Gomolin & Ryan Jenkins
Cover design by Tim Barber
Interior design by Kevin G. Summers

ISBN: 9781950301072
e-ISBN:9781950301089
LCCN: 2021943155

First edition

Printed in the United States of America

For Mom, who I wish was still here to read this,
and whose unconditional love made this book possible.

When one is dealing with the authentically paranormal, exercise the greatest of caution, and remain steadfast in your faith, as even the slightest of doubts will leave your soul vulnerable to the truly terrifying.

—John F. Dubois

CHAPTER 1

THEY SAY THAT the first time is the most dangerous. Of course, "they" say lots of things that turn out to be bullshit. Most of them warn, as the curandera had, that he shouldn't be doing this alone. That there should be at least three for the ceremony. It was true that all the literature said so. But . . . he didn't have two other people, which was pathetic enough he supposed. And anyway, he didn't want anyone else here with him. This was his moment, and his alone.

Erasmo surveyed the items laid out on the floor in front of him, still trying to quiet the whispers of doubt tickling the inside of his skull. The random wildflowers he'd picked near the creek looked paltry and limp, not anything like the lush white roses that were recommended for the ceremony. Beside the flowers sat several mostly melted candles he had scavenged from Little Flower. He'd always found it wasteful the way that church threw away perfectly usable items. A small bundle of cedar was next in line, followed by the most important item of all: the offering.

He'd thought long and hard about this last item, endlessly cycling through different possibilities. But the only real option for the offering was the one he wanted to use the least . . . the only one that truly frightened him. He forced his eyes to settle on it now and immediately felt its power. His veins erupted in fire as he studied its contours, his blood seething as it burned through his body. Enough. He turned away, and the effect was broken, his blood cooling almost immediately.

Yes, this was all he needed. Fresh flowers to attract with their beauty and aroma. Candles to entice with their light and warmth. Cedar to protect. And the offering, specially chosen to make his invitation irresistible.

Wait . . . he'd forgotten something. Erasmo glanced around his cramped shoebox of a bedroom, trying to remember where he'd left it. He took the three steps necessary to cross his room and regarded the jagged mountain of books that rested precariously against the wall. One wrong move and they'd all come tumbling down. But what he needed was tucked inside one of them.

He slid out the book that he thought was most likely to contain the note he was looking for, *The Demonologist*, but nothing fluttered loose when he shook its pages. Next, he tried *The Super Natural: Why the Unexplained Is Real*, but it too wasn't the right one. Finally, when he flipped through the yellowed pages of *Ghost Crimes: Based on Actual Paranormal Cases*, a piece of paper with his near-illegible writing scribbled on it slid out and floated into his waiting hand.

Erasmo glanced over the short, repetitive phrases that had taken him so long to perfect. He'd been somewhat surprised to learn during his research that anyone could write their own mantra. That the words themselves didn't hold any particular special power. In fact, the chants' only real purpose was to center people's energy, and he was confident that the words he'd written would serve that purpose just fine.

It was time. Finally, it was time.

Erasmo dug around in his pocket and pulled out a worn book of matches that had only a precious few left. He ripped one out and struck it, the scent of sulfur filling his nostrils. He walked over to the cedar, took a deep breath, and picked it up. This is what the movies and TV shows invariably got wrong. For some damn reason they always burned sage for protection. But sage wouldn't do shit for you. Cedar. That's the good stuff you needed if you really wanted to keep the evil away.

Erasmo's hand trembled as he moved the lit match closer to the cedar. The small flame wavered, threatening to die, but somehow managed to resurrect itself. He held his breath when the fire was less than an inch away. This was it. This would be the official start of the ceremony. This was—

BAM! BAM! BAM!

The knocks on his door erupted without warning. Erasmo's heart jackhammered in his chest, and he dropped both the cedar and the match. This couldn't be right. He hadn't started the ceremony yet. He hadn't even made the offering.

Something was wrong.

Whatever banged on his door must be something from the other side, trying to get in without an invitation. Maybe he hadn't burned the cedar fast enough. Or was it possible that he didn't even need a full ceremony to summon—

"Erasmo, open the door."

Shit.

Erasmo stomped out the match, frantically picked up all the items, and shoved them into his narrow closet. He quickly scanned the room to make sure he'd gotten everything before opening the door. The woman who had raised him his entire life stood in the doorway, wrinkles etched deep into her face, as if someone had taken a finely sharpened knife and carved these bottomless lines into her pale skin. Her wide face, usually cheery and beaming an immense smile in his direction, was now tense and strained, sending a wave of alarm through him.

"I made some food for you," his grandmother said, holding up a yellow, chipped plate. In the middle of the plate sat two steaming chorizo-and-egg tacos, dripping red grease onto the napkins beneath them.

This too alarmed him. The chorizo was the last of their food until his grandmother's check came in, and they were supposed to eat it for breakfast tomorrow morning. He had triple-checked, making sure there would be enough for each of them to have one taco each. But now she'd made them for dinner and was giving them both to him. This made no sense. Despite his unease, the smell of the spicy sausage made his empty stomach rumble in anticipation. Before he could object, she shoved the warm plate into his hands, walked into his room, and gently lowered herself onto his unkempt bed.

"We need to talk," she said, patting the spot next to her.

But Erasmo knew what she wanted to talk about and felt cold tendrils of fear wrap around his chest. He desperately wanted to run and keep running until he was far away from the words that would soon escape her lips. He stood frozen, stupidly holding the plate in his left hand. His grandmother, seeing that he was too scared to move, pressed on.

"The results came back."

His grandmother kept speaking, and Erasmo heard the words he'd spent his entire life in fear of. Each limb shook violently, and tears streamed down his face. Wails squirmed under his tongue, desperate to be born.

After she was done explaining, his grandmother stood up and walked over to Erasmo, fixing her gaze on him.

"Everything's going to be okay," she said, steel in her voice. "I truly believe that . . . and you have to believe it too. Pull yourself together. I didn't raise you to fall apart at the first sign of trouble."

His grandmother then gave a slight smile, a look of resistance flaring in her eyes, and said, "Besides, you know what I say to the cancer growing inside my body?"

He shook his head.

"No sabe con quién jode."

Erasmo looked back at her, confused. His grandmother always thought he understood more Spanish than he actually did.

She gifted him a gentle smile and whispered, "It means . . . you don't know who the hell you're messing with."

After his grandmother walked out, Erasmo set the plate of food down on his nightstand, got on his knees, and pulled two boxes out from underneath his bed. One was a tattered cigar box that used to have a colorful logo on its top. Whatever image had once been there, though, was now an indecipherable mess. The other was a rumpled cardboard box, with the word *Breakables* written on the side in faded black marker. He opened both of them and peered in, even though he'd long ago committed their contents to memory. His eyes lingered on the empty spot in the cigar box, where the item he was going to use for the offering once sat.

After a few minutes, Erasmo carefully slid the boxes back underneath his bed. As he paced around his room, clenching and re-clenching his fists, one singular thought became clear to him: Something was going to have to be done about the news he'd just received. But what? He had no money, and no immediately obvious way to earn some. In fact, he had no marketable skills of any kind. He sighed and dropped his head. A book, one of his favorites, sat by his feet, staring up at him.

The Para-Investigators: 52 True Tales and Concepts of Supernaturally Gifted Investigators.

The beginnings of an idea, a strange but exhilarating one, started to coalesce at the edge of his thoughts. This idea was intriguing, but also potentially dangerous. The more he thought about it, he knew it was probably too dangerous.

He needed some help to think everything through. And there was only one person he trusted enough to help him do that. Erasmo grabbed the keys to his grandmother's battered Civic and headed off to meet his best and only friend.

CHAPTER 2

"HOLY SHIT," RAT said as he pushed up his glasses, tiny eyes dancing behind thick, smudged lenses. "This is by far the best idea you've *ever* had."

"I don't know," Erasmo said, studying his friend's modest but immaculate room. Something was different, but he couldn't quite place what had changed. "Don't you think it's dangerous? We have no idea who might answer something like this. For all we know, it'll be nothing but a bunch of whack jobs."

"*Or* it could be people that really need our help!" Rat almost shouted. He was sitting on the edge of his bed but appeared as if he might burst off it at any moment. "And we can help them. I *know* we can!"

Rat wasn't his given name, of course. That would be Rodrigo. But in ninth grade, some asshole had called him Ratrigo. And unfortunately, because he had more than just a passing resemblance to his rodent namesake, the shortened version had stuck ever since.

"The other thing is," Erasmo said as he paced, "I'm not sure anyone would even trust us to help them."

Rat gave a wide grin, showcasing his yellow, uneven teeth.

"Are you kidding? You're messing with me, right? Dude . . . that's the one ace in the hole we have! Once they know you're the guy from the Ghost Tracks, they won't need *any* convincing that you can help them."

"C'mon, man, not everyone around here believes—"

"Doesn't matter," Rat said, running his hand through the helmet of jet-black, coarse hair that sat on top of his head. "The ones who genuinely need our help will believe it. There are a lot of people out there, like me, who understand the truth. You know what I saw when I was a kid . . . and there are plenty others out there that've had similar experiences. Besides, you were right when you explained it to me. Your grandmother needs money for her treatment. Something *has* to be done. You and I have read almost every book there is on the subject. We knew that we'd use this knowledge one day. This is just a little earlier than we thought. We can do two good things here . . . help your grandmother and help people out there that need it."

Even though the idea had been his, Erasmo now felt a sudden urge to argue against it. What had seemed serviceable in theory seemed ludicrous now that it was out in the open. And Rat's balls-to-the-wall enthusiasm disturbed him too, although he wasn't quite sure why.

But . . . what his friend said was true. They needed to do *something*. At least until he got a callback for one of the summer jobs he'd applied for. Although, in truth, he doubted there'd be much of a market for a high school senior with no practical skills to speak of and no plans for college.

Before Erasmo could voice another objection, Rat jumped off his bed and reached deep into the front pocket of his oversized cargo shorts, his scrawny arm trembling as he rooted around and pulled out a wad of twenty-dollar bills.

"For your grandma."

Erasmo stared at the bills sitting in his friend's hand and willed his lower lip not to tremble.

"But . . . how did you . . ."

"Oh, I sold a few things. Nothing important."

Erasmo scanned the room again, his heart dropping the longer he looked.

"Your . . . your collection is gone."

"Ah, I was meaning to get rid of it anyway."

"But all the years you . . ."

Rat shoved the money into his hand with surprising strength, curling Erasmo's fingers over the crisp bills.

"I really think," Rat said, his eyes flickering with excitement, "that we should get to work on this ad."

Erasmo peered down in disbelief at the notebook, its pages filled with a chaotic jumble of scrawled, illegible notes.

"How is it possible," he asked, "to have been at this for three hours and not have a single thing to show for it?"

"What about the ad I wrote two versions ago?" Rat asked. "C'mon . . . you have to admit that it was pure excellence."

Erasmo flipped back a few pages until he found the offending words.

"You mean this one?"

"*Two badass paranormal experts for hire. We will come over, beat down any ghosts that are bothering you, and mess them up so bad that they'll never come back. We can handle ANY supernatural problem you have. Don't use anyone else but us or those ghosts will get you for sure.*"

Rat mouthed the words as Erasmo spoke them, his face solemn and pensive, as if he were reciting a beautiful stanza of heartbreaking poetry.

"What's wrong with exaggerating a little for effect?" he asked. "Anyway, it's better than what *you* came up with." Rat grabbed the notebook and scanned the pages until he found what he was looking for.

" *'Two individuals who have conducted extensive research into the supernatural available for consultation. Serious inquiries only.'* Dude, I can't tell if it's an ad for paranormal investigators or for some lame-ass research assistants."

"I just don't want to make any false promises," Erasmo said. "What if we run into a situation that we can't handle?"

"Can't handle . . . like what?"

"What the hell do you mean 'like what'? Almost everything we know comes entirely from books and the internet. And the only real experience I've had won't be of *any* help if we're asked to consult on a case involving psychic abilities, or energy manipulation, or any other of the long list of scenarios we might face."

Rat pursed his lips together and shrugged his slight shoulders.

"Well . . . when you put it that way . . ."

"You're not at all worried about this?" Erasmo asked.

"Look," Rat said. "I *know* we can do this. There are people out there right now advertising as experts that don't know a fraction of what we do. C'mon, man . . . do you think they know that they're supposed to research the history of a haunted site extensively before attempting to make contact? Or that they have little chance of actually seeing an entity, because children and animals are *much* more likely to perceive ghosts than they are? Or that the best way to get rid of a spirit is to just ask it to leave, instead of chanting a bunch of stupid bullshit spells at it? I'm telling you, man . . . we can do this. I know we can."

He marveled at how persuasive Rat could be when he wanted. As Erasmo often did, he sent a silent wish out to the universe that one day his friend would be able to speak just as easily and carefree around others. But after all the shit Rat had been through, and all the taunts he'd endured at school over the years, Erasmo worried that it might remain just a wish for a very long time.

In any case, what Rat said was true. He did feel confident in their knowledge, in their understanding of how various phenomena and cases of these types have historically been resolved. And what had happened to him at the Ghost Tracks . . . he knew what it meant, what it *had* to mean.

"Okay," Erasmo said, "you're right. The two of us are definitely a better option than some others out there. I honestly wonder what kind of cases we'd even get though."

Rat tossed the notebook back to Erasmo and walked over to the framed movie poster that hung on his back wall. It was a color print of *The Curse of the Werewolf*, the 1961 movie that his friend adored above all others. Rat studied the titular werewolf, who carried the beautiful Yvonne Romain in his fur-covered arms. Below him, a bloodthirsty mob raged with their torches held high, just waiting for their chance to inflict vengeance on the werewolf for daring to exist.

"Transformation," Rat whispered.

"What?" Erasmo asked.

"Transformation," he said, louder this time. "The departed who have transformed into their next form but haven't let go of their earthly existence. Those are the kinds of cases I want. Spirits who are still here, because they need help moving on to their next destination."

"Well, hopefully," Erasmo said, "we encounter those kinds of lost souls, ones we can actually help . . . and not the kind that want to drive us completely mad until we're a psychotic mess and shoving nails into our eyeballs."

Rat continued to study the poster, adjusting it to make sure its angles were straight and true. He finally turned and regarded Erasmo with a wary look.

"'Nails into our eyeballs . . .'" he said. "You know, my favorite days are when you're a bright, cheerful ray of sunshine."

Erasmo sighed, his already-stretched patience waning even further. This was taking way too long, and he had to get back soon to check on his grandmother.

"I still don't understand," Rat said, pacing around the room, "why we can't just lead off by saying that you're the guy from the Ghost Tr—"

"I told you already," Erasmo said, heat blooming underneath his skin. "I don't want that. If they ask about it . . . if that's what it takes to get them to hire us, I'll tell them then."

Rat clearly sensed that he meant it, and immediately moved on.

"Look," his friend said. "We want to make it clear that we know about this stuff, and can handle any paranormal phenomena . . . so how about this?"

Rat took the notebook from Erasmo and scribbled furiously on it, reading over his words a few times before handing it back.

"Not as exciting as mine," he said, "not as lame as yours."

Erasmo read Rat's scribbles and had to grudgingly agree.

PARANORMAL CONSULTANTS

We are two consultants knowledgeable in all types of paranormal phenomena. Our specialty is displacing spirits from places of residence, but we can consult on any situation that requires expertise on the unearthly. Will discuss our qualifications and fee schedule during first consultation. Serious inquiries only.

"Well," Erasmo said, "it's not exactly what I had in mind, but I don't know that we're going to do better than this."

"No particular reason I'm asking," Rat said, "but are you familiar with the expression 'damning with faint praise'?"

Erasmo's head overflowed with unnerving thoughts as he read the ad again, considering what could happen if they posted it. Probably nothing. In fact, he was growing increasingly certain with each passing second that no one in their right mind would answer it. But if they did get responses . . .

"Give me some time to think over everything before we put this up, okay?"

Rat placed his hand on Erasmo's shoulder and gave a wide grin, which, it shamed Erasmo to notice, made him appear more rodent-like than ever.

"Sure thing," Rat said, his crooked smile growing even broader. "Sure thing."

Erasmo sat on his bed as he regarded the battered laptop, his index finger trembling over the cracked Enter key. He'd spent the last few hours staring at the dim screen, not yet quite able to post the ad on Craigslist. Had it really come to this? Erasmo picked up the stack of medical bills he'd found in his grandmother's drawer and rifled through them. Yeah, he guessed it had.

The message stared back at him, waiting. Erasmo attempted to focus his full attention on the ad but felt a familiar tug at the base of his brain that wouldn't allow it. He glared down at his laptop and ran a search, grinding his teeth as he typed. The various sites that came up, all of which he'd studied countless times before, callously informed him of what he already knew . . . that individuals with his particular history were "at a substantial risk for developmental and behavioral problems."

They also said that people like him were often filled with anger, right to the goddamn brim, like they were a bunch of Incredible Hulks or something.

He'd never understood his relentless compulsion to look up this garbage. What the hell did these doctors know, anyway? Perhaps the simple act of reading about their supposed predisposition to anger *made* people want to break shit and bash someone's head in. Had those asshole doctors ever thought of that?

According to the internet, people like him also carried around a deep-seated hatred for themselves. He thought of this as he stared down at the ad, using one hand to pinch the other, his thumb and index finger plowing deep into his flesh before twisting.

After looking over the ad a few more times, he picked up the laptop and was finally able to upload the paragraph on which they'd worked so very hard. He pressed Enter and leaned back, grimacing as nebulous blotches of scarlet spread over his trembling hands.

CHAPTER 3

WHEN ERASMO WOKE the next morning, he was surprised to find that twelve responses had come in overnight. At first, he was overcome with surprise and genuine excitement. But his stomach churned as he read through them and saw that most weren't serious, instead taking great glee in mocking the ad.

After looking over all the messages, he settled on three to follow up on. He gravitated to these because they seemed to be written by somewhat normal people who genuinely needed help. His flesh prickled as he reread the first of the three messages:

> *Hello. I don't know if you can do what you claim. I don't know if you are someone who is attempting to scam people. I don't even know if you are someone dangerous. But I'm willing to risk all those things on even the slightest chance you can help me. I'm not crazy and I'm not delusional. I am just a person that needs help. Please contact me at the below number if you're genuine. If you're not, please ignore this, and don't prey on the hopes of a desperate woman. Thank you.*
>
> *Nora Montalvo*

Erasmo had thought he'd feel exhilarated to finally put his studies into practice. But now the time had come, now that someone was actually reaching out for help, the only thing he felt was dread spreading through his belly. There was no way to know who had really written these messages. They could very well be from predators who wanted to lure them to a secluded place and rob them, or maybe from disbelieving skeptics who would mock him and Rat as soon as they showed up.

No, he couldn't think that way. They had to at least try. Before Erasmo could talk himself out of it, he picked up the phone and dialed, his eyes squeezed shut as the ringback tone sang in his ear.

"This is Nora," a soft, hesitant voice answered after a few rings.

Erasmo, certain that he'd get her voicemail, was immediately thrown off.

"Hi . . . my name is Erasmo Cruz. I'm calling about the ad."

"Hey," the voice said, now sounding both surprised and nervous. "Thank you so much for responding. But . . . and I hope you don't take offense to this . . . you sound a little young. Do you mind if I ask how old you are?"

Shit.

"Of course not . . . I'm seventeen."

"Oh," Nora said, taking no pains to hide her surprise.

Erasmo was overcome with a deep certainty that she was about to expel a bray of laughter and hang up on him.

"I'd really like to help you," he blurted out, cringing at the eagerness in his voice. "I know I'm young, but . . . I really do know a lot about these types of things." He bit down on his lip hard enough to taste just a hint of copper. "Would you mind telling me what kind of help you're looking for?"

Silence. Erasmo hadn't anticipated how utterly embarrassing this would be. Even though she was a stranger he'd surely never meet, his face burned bright in shame. Right when he'd decided to hang up and move on to the next message, Nora finally broke her silence.

"Okay, Erasmo. This is something I want to explain in person, though. So let's meet. Then we'll see if you can really help me. Any particular place you want to suggest?"

Erasmo had always enjoyed Woodlawn Lake and the park that surrounded it. When he was a child, his grandparents would often take him there; they'd let him feed the ravenous ducks and kick his tattered soccer ball around. He hadn't been there in years, but still thought of it fondly, which was why he chose the lake as their meeting place.

Fat droplets of sweat formed on his back as he walked down the park's jogging path, wondering what the hell he was getting himself into. Thankfully, an occasional stiff breeze blew through the park, providing a small measure of relief.

Erasmo felt a twinge of guilt for not bringing Rat along. He almost had but decided better of it at the last second. His friend was an acquired taste and had a troublesome habit of weirding other people out. The last thing he wanted was to scare their first client away.

As he approached the basketball court where they'd agreed to meet, a small, regal figure captured his attention, her perfectly postured back turned to him. She was wearing a snug baby-blue T-shirt and faded jeans. Lustrous hair fell just past her shoulders in a cascade of amber waves. He kept approaching, and soon he stood directly behind this figure, staring at the back of her head, unsure how to get this person to turn around. What if it wasn't even her? She could be just some girl watching her boyfriend on the basketball court. He stood there, paralyzed, at a loss for how to proceed. The woman must have sensed his tremendous discomfort, because finally, she turned and looked him over, head cocked to the side.

"Erasmo?"

He somehow managed to nod his head up and down to verify that yes, this was indeed his name.

"I'm Nora. Thank you for being on time."

"No problem," he croaked. Every drop of moisture in his mouth had evaporated, replaced with sand and sawdust. He desperately needed a drink of milk.

She stood there gazing at him, her perfectly oval face and fair skin reflecting the sun's warm rays, somehow improving the light just by making contact with it. He was shocked by how young she was, close to his age he guessed. His brain whirred, frantically searching for something to say.

"Well . . . this is a strange way to spend an afternoon," he finally managed to blurt out.

She smiled, but Erasmo noticed that it didn't reach her eyes, which were flat and dull.

"I was just thinking the same thing," she said. Her sad, gray eyes looked into his for a few seconds before glancing away.

"Let's walk while we talk," she said, heading back toward the jogging path. "'Tell your story walking.' Isn't that a saying? I think I heard that somewhere."

They trudged along the gray path for a while in silence, Erasmo desperately wishing that she'd speak first.

"If you don't mind me saying so," Nora finally said, "you look a little different than I imagined."

"Yeah?" he asked, surprised at this. "How so?"

"Well, I thought you might look like a professor type," she said, looking him over, a hint of a smile on her face. "But no rumpled tweed jacket or wire-rimmed glasses that I can see."

"Oh," he said, "you just caught me on a bad day. My jacket is at the cleaners and I forgot my glasses in the car."

She laughed at this, but it was muted, a shadow of a laugh.

"You know, now that I'm actually here with you," Nora said, her slight smile disappearing as she glanced skyward, "it's hard for me to say the words out loud. Part of me just wants to leave without telling you. But I know if I do that . . . tonight I'll be sorry."

"Well," Erasmo said, doing his best to project an air of confidence, "I promise you'll feel better if you just say it. What's the worst that could happen?"

Nora gave a half smile that again failed to spread to the rest of her face.

"You might think I'm crazy, for one."

Tears filled her eyes, magnifying and distorting the left one so that her gray iris appeared unstable. Nora stopped walking, and her head and shoulders slumped toward the ground, as if she were a robot that had run out of power.

"It's going to sound so stupid," she whispered, tears slipping down her face. "I want to tell you. I do. But . . . how do I know you can even help? I don't know anything about you."

Even though Erasmo had known it would eventually come to this . . . that whoever answered their ad would ask this very question, he still found it hard to get the actual words out.

"You ever been down to the Ghost Tracks?" he finally asked, hands shoved deep into his pockets.

Nora looked up at him, her head cocked to one side as if she didn't understand the question. She wiped at her eyes and sniffed.

"The Ghost Tracks? On the south side of town? Um . . . sure, a few times . . . around Halloween I guess."

A dull, throbbing ache now emanated from the base of his skull.

"Do you remember," he began, "about eight months ago, there was an accident that happened down there? There was this—"

"Hold on," she interrupted. "I do remember. That old man on the news, right? And he was saying that . . . wait . . ." She looked him over, studying his face in a way she hadn't before. "Was that you? Were you the one that the old man was screaming about . . . ?"

Erasmo nodded with reluctance, his headache rapidly intensifying. As Nora waited for him to speak, he gritted his teeth, fervently wishing they would snap and crumble in his mouth. Finally, right when Erasmo's nerve was about to abandon him, he haltingly began to tell her what had happened that night at the Tracks.

His gut churned at having to repeat the story, but he had to if this was going to work. Nora seemed confused at first, but then she listened to the unfolding tale with fierce concentration. Relief overcame him when he finally reached the end, his headache almost immediately ebbing away.

Erasmo braced himself for howls of laughter, for protestations that the story couldn't possibly be true, but none came. She stood completely still for a few moments, staring at the ground and deep in thought. Without warning, Nora's head snapped up, her gray eyes locking on his before she spoke.

"There is something inside my little brother," she blurted out.

Erasmo froze. This wasn't quite what he'd expected to hear. A light tickle in the back of his skull warned him to tread lightly.

"Inside him? I'm . . . not sure I understand," Erasmo said. "Do you mean that he has special abilities, or—"

"No, I mean there is some *thing* inside my brother. Sonny has been saying and doing things that . . . Jesus . . . he's only ten years old."

She stared at Erasmo, eyes wide, clearly expecting him to have an answer.

"Can you be more specific? I'm still not sure I understand."

Nora's pale skin flushed, her cheeks burning a violent crimson.

"I hesitate to use this word," Nora said, "but I don't know a better one." Her lower lip quivered as she ran both hands through her thick waves of hair and gripped the back of her head.

"I think my brother is possessed."

Possessed. Interesting, and not what he'd expected . . . but surely wrong. According to all available literature, the number of cases involving a genuine possession are miniscule. The vast majority are almost always the result of undiagnosed mental illnesses. And most other supposed cases are straight-up hoaxes. Erasmo breathed a sigh of relief. He'd be able to help Nora after all.

"I'm not even sure where to start," Nora continued. "A few weeks ago, Sonny began talking to himself, saying strange things. I caught him staring into the bathroom mirror, saying . . ."

Nora paused, her lips pressed into a thin, quivering line.

"He was saying, *'Pig and blood and pyre. Summon the beast that wears fire.'* He kept repeating this over and over again, like a chant. I still don't know what the hell it means. Sonny even *looked* different. He was hunched over, like an old man with a crooked back. And it's getting worse. He's been screaming all kinds of sick and disgusting things lately. My brother would never say those things on his own. *Never.* He . . ."

She trailed off and stared at the ground, her inanimate body casting a cool shadow over Erasmo.

"Are you going to say anything?" she whispered.

Good question, Erasmo thought to himself. He dug his nails into his palms until he felt his skin begin to tear. *Are you?*

"Do you think it's possible," he asked, "that your brother is going through some kind of behavioral phase? Kids like to repeat phrases they hear from friends. Sometimes, they get a kick out of upsetting the people around them—"

A flash of anger pulsed through Nora's face. "Do you think I'd be *this* desperate if it were something as simple as that?" She then fell silent but continued to give him a hard look. After a few seconds though, her face softened.

"Believe me," Nora said, "this is the last thing I want to be dealing with right now. My parents aren't around. . . . Our mom died when I was young, and Dad is living with some whore he met online. If he comes home once a week, we're lucky. I tried telling him about Sonny, but he thinks I'm crazy. It's just me and my brother. He's all I have in this world. And I'm telling you . . . I know that there is something inside of him," she said. "I don't think it or suspect it. I *know* it."

"How can you be so sure?" he asked.

Nora turned away from him, pausing before she answered. "There's something I haven't told you yet," she said.

"What is it?"

"Well . . . I could tell you, but it wouldn't be the same."

"The same as what?"

"Showing you," Nora said. "You have to see it for yourself . . . so that you'll know." She turned back to him, her face blank and unmoving. "Come to my house tonight. Then you'll see."

Nora took his hand and pressed a folded piece of paper into his sweaty palm. Erasmo watched as she turned and walked away, the sound of her steps carried by the cool summer breeze.

That evening, Erasmo stood on Nora's front porch, the dusk sky's violet light casting faint shadows over his body. He couldn't remember a time being this nervous and reminded himself that it wasn't too late to back out. He could just walk down the porch's rickety steps, get back in his car, and go home. He could. But then what? Erasmo took a breath and forced himself to raise his fist, knuckles trembling as they rapped on the wood. To his horror, the door immediately swung open, as if she'd been lying in wait for his arrival.

Nora wore the same clothes from earlier in the day, but her hair no longer fell in perfect, tranquil waves as it had at the park, and the light she'd previously emanated had somehow dimmed.

"Hi," he said, immediately embarrassed at the faint, wavering quality of his voice.

"Thanks for coming," she said, eyes locked on his. Erasmo was unable to meet her gaze, and instead glanced over Nora's shoulder, focusing on the unkempt living room behind her.

"Come in," she said, stepping aside. "Sorry . . . this kid just doesn't know how to pick up." Despite Nora's attempt to blame her brother, almost all of the mess seemed to be hers, as the floor was covered with gossip magazines and women's attire, with only small patches of dingy carpet sporadically showing through. Nora quickly led him through the maze of clutter, steering him into a cramped hallway that had a single pink door on one side and a single purple door on the other. She stood outside the pink door and squeezed her hands together.

"I'm so glad you're here," she said, biting her lower lip. "When I got home from the park, I realized how delusional I must've sounded. But what I'm about to show you will prove everything."

Nora slowly opened the pink door to reveal what could only be her bedroom. He wouldn't have thought it possible, but even *more* of her clothes and magazines were strewn around in here. Jumbles of clutter blanketed the only two pieces of furniture in the room, a twin bed and a small dresser, along with almost every inch of the floor. Pictures of Nora adorned the walls, many of the frames hung at odd angles. Her poses in each were different, but the same beaming smile radiated from every photo.

She motioned for him to sit on the bed, which he did, taking care to move several issues of *Us Weekly* out of the way. Across from the bed sat a flat-screen television, connected to a GoPro. Nora positioned herself in front of the television and began what sounded, to his ears anyway, like a rehearsed speech.

"I know that you must get a lot of unbalanced people making claims that aren't true. I'm *not* one of those people. I've tried to get help for Sonny before, but no one believed me. So, a week ago, I recorded proof that there's something inside of him. I think this will explain everything."

Nora then picked up the GoPro and fumbled with it, pressing buttons until an image of her living room, the very one they'd just walked through, appeared on the television screen. Nora must've been behind the camera, as her voice came through the weak speakers of the television, sounding small and tinny. *"Please God, give me the strength,"* she said as the camera moved through the living room and down the hallway, shaking as it focused on the purple door across from her bedroom.

"For whoever sees this," the tinny voice said, *"I . . . I woke up and heard noises again, coming from his room. It sounds really bad this time. I'm going to try to get him . . . it . . . on camera. So that everyone will know the truth. So that we can get help to force this thing out of him."*

Nora's voice was breathless, almost hyperventilating as she aimed the camera directly at the doorknob. He saw her trembling hand appear in the frame and grab the knob, turning it slowly. Even though the audio coming out of the television's speakers was muffled, Erasmo heard noises coming from the other side of the purple door.

Wet noises.

"Please God . . . be here with me," Nora's voice begged as she finished turning the knob and slowly pushed the door open.

The shrieking started immediately.

Erasmo watched as the camera fell to the floor with a loud rustle, now only recording the side of Nora's bare foot.

"Why?" her voice blubbered on the video. *"Why did you do this? Leave my brother alone!"*

Erasmo found himself unable to tear his eyes away from the video but felt a curious mix of validation and disappointment. The video was interesting for sure, but it was much ado about nothing. The "proof" was merely a recording of the side of her foot, with a lot of screaming in the background. Why would she have thought that this would convince him of anything?

The Nora in the video continued to howl in the background, and Erasmo wondered how much longer he was going to have to stare at the side of her pink foot before the video ended. And what on earth was she going to claim happened in that room? Then, to his great surprise, the image of her foot disappeared as Nora picked up the camera, aimed it into the room, and showed him exactly what had made her scream so very much.

A few minutes later, Erasmo stumbled out of Nora's house, long strands of vomit clinging to his lower lip.

"Wait! Come back!" Nora yelled from behind him, running out onto the front porch. "You can help us!"

For the second time, Erasmo's stomach erupted, this time on Nora's weed-infested yard. He wiped his mouth with the back of his hand and continued stumbling toward the street. He reached the Civic, fumbled the door open, and toppled in before speeding away, not once turning around.

As he swerved through the dimly lit streets of Nora's neighborhood, unsure of which direction he was even headed, a vicious, skull-crushing headache emerged. An image suddenly burst into his head, one of white, swirling powder floating in the night air. He tried to push it away but found himself unable to do so, helpless to prevent his memory from unspooling the familiar scene.

Erasmo gave in, allowing his thoughts to wander to that night. He clenched the steering wheel, his fingers pale and trembling, wishing as he drove that the black night surrounding him would somehow open into a gaping maw and swallow him whole. As he drove, and shivered, and wished for oblivion, a cloud of swirling white powder once again appeared to him, drifting through his vision, so real that he felt the caress of tiny white particles as they fell onto his trembling skin.

CHAPTER 4

ERASMO WOKE THE next morning, sheets soaked with sweat, but unable to remember any specific nightmares he had. Mild sunlight streamed through the window, warming his face as he forced himself to think about what had happened. He was clearly going to have to do something about what he'd seen at Nora's, but he was at a complete loss as to what that might be. The more he turned over each imperfect option in his head, the less appealing each one became. He finally decided that it would have to wait until he gave the situation some more thought.

But damn . . . what he'd seen on the video last night . . . it wasn't like any documented case he was familiar with. Well, there was that one incident in Afghanistan a few years back, but Exco_75 had said that the locals may have exaggerated the specifics of that case. Now that he thought about it, it might not be a bad idea to reach out to his online acquaintance for some guidance.

Erasmo grabbed his phone off the nightstand and opened Instagram. He quickly scrolled through recent posts to see if any of the paranormal and occult pages he followed had dropped anything interesting. As was usually the case, they hadn't. Most of what these accounts posted was strictly amateur-hour stuff: poorly doctored photographs, wildly incorrect claims, and morons waving around EMF gauges and thermal cameras.

Erasmo always laughed a bit when he saw how much useless technology was being used on ghost hunts. He wholeheartedly subscribed to Dubois's idea on what equipment was needed to investigate the layers of reality underneath our own: *One should carry only what a priest, a witch, or a shaman would use; the only indispensable tool is your mind, and its willingness to sense the magic in the world around it.*

Once he finished scrolling through the most recent posts, Erasmo checked to see if Exco_75 was online but was disappointed to see that he hadn't been active for a few days. According to his profile, Exco_75 claimed to be a former priest who'd been excommunicated for experimenting with various occult practices. He now lived in Costa Rica, where he continued his studies. This was what he claimed, anyway. Erasmo had been skeptical at first, but when he'd messaged Exco_75 on a whim and asked a question about the deity Baphomet, his answers proved that the guy really knew his stuff. But for now, he'd have to wait to get Exco_75's insight into what he saw at Nora's. Luckily, he had another trusted resource to consult.

Erasmo put down his phone and reached for the only item he kept on the small shelf above his bed, immediately feeling better once the familiar shape was in his hand. He pulled it down and let his eyes wander over the worn, creased cover of the thick book. Its design was sparse, simply a maroon background with the title centered at the top in a plain, gold font: *A Practical Guide to the Supernatural and Paranormal: The Writings of John F. Dubois.* Its battered appearance did nothing to prevent Erasmo from loving this possession above all others.

He opened it to the introduction and, as he often did, read the three short paragraphs.

Introduction

When faced with unspeakable tragedy, it is human nature to search for answers. I have endured such a tragedy, and after much suffering, my search for answers begins now. Some might say that what I am embarking on is pure madness, but they have not endured the loss that I have.

I am keeping this journal in order to fill it with my findings and investigations. My dear daughter Emma may be gone from this earth physically, but I will not stop until I have found a way to communicate with her spirit, wherever it may be. I will travel to the ends of the earth, and pay any price, if it means learning of a ceremony, or a deity, or even a malevolent demon that would allow me to hear Emma's sweet voice one more time.

If anyone finds this journal, it most likely means that I am dead. If I have filled these pages with useful information, I would be eternally grateful if you shared it with the world. Conversely, if there are dangerous and wicked practices in these pages, please burn this entire book, until only ashes remain.

Respectfully,
John F. Dubois

As far as Erasmo could tell, Dubois's request had been fulfilled. Someone apparently stumbled across his journal at some point and managed to publish it in book form. The printing must've been extremely small though, as whenever he googled the title of the book, there wasn't any trace of its existence. To compound the mystery, its copyright page was missing, as were other random pages.

Erasmo flipped around until he found the section he was looking for. Maybe this would help shed some light on the situation.

Possessions: Demonic and Otherwise

There is a common misconception that only malevolent demons seek to enter and inhabit our physical form. My research has led me to conclude that there are all manners of restless entities, both evil and benign, that seek to take control of a susceptible host.

It is important to remember that the Christian concept of possession being the work of demons, fallen angels expelled from heaven, is not the only interpretation. There are many cultures and religions that believe in the idea of the human body being overtaken by an otherworldly entity, all with their own notions of how such a thing might occur and how to expel it.

For example, the ancient Egyptians believed that individuals could be possessed by nymphs, female spirits of the natural world. In ancient Mesopotamia, exorcisms were conducted by throwing wax figurines of demons into fire. In South Africa, the Xesibe are reportedly affected by a condition called inwatso, where married women are possessed by a spirit and then, amazingly, develop the ability to foretell the future.

But perhaps my favorite example that I have learned of is that of the Gurage people of Ethiopia. From what I understand, a spirit called Awre inhabits the victim and causes extreme lethargy. The local healer is summoned, and, remarkably, he encourages the victim to form a relationship with the spirit. The culmination of treatment is the making of a dish consisting of ensete, butter, and red pepper. The victim's head is draped with a cloth, and he eats the food while surrounded by chanting neighbors. The ritual is over only when the possessing spirit announces that it is satisfied! Truly remarkable!

*One particular non-demonic possession that I encoun-
tered personally took place in New Orleans. I witnessed
firsthand the takeover of a priest, Father Morel, by a
recently deceased child of only eight years. Father Morel
initially resisted this intrusion, his body shaking with great
violence, but finally succumbed. Once she was in control,
the spirit of this young child turned to me and made a
request: to tell her mother not to cry for her, because she
was safe amongst the stars.*

*After she spoke those words to me, Father Morel's body
immediately slumped to the ground, and he awoke minutes later. This filled me with great hope, as this meant it
was possible that my precious Emma could do the same . . .
that she might one day use a living vessel to communicate
with me. I have since tried to replicate this, to have Emma
speak to me through hosts both willing and unwilling, but
I have not yet had success.*

*As far as demonic possession, I have had only one true
encounter with such a thing. I have not yet been able to
chronicle it, as the experience terrified me so that I hesitate
to even put the words on paper. But I will one day, when
my hands stop trembling at the thought of it.*

And he had, as Erasmo knew Dubois's account of the event
was chronicled toward the end of the book.

Erasmo rubbed his dry eyes, desperately needing a glass of
milk, but knew they had run out days ago. He'd have to try to
scrounge up a few dollars to buy some later. First things first.
After last night, no way in hell was he going to respond to any
more messages. He pulled out his laptop, intending to delete
the ad. But he saw right away that there was yet another message, this one from someone named Billy. Erasmo checked his
notes, and they confirmed his suspicion. This was Billy's second

message to him. His first was one of the three that Erasmo had picked to follow up on. He pulled up Billy's original message, which read:

> *Hey there, bud. I could use someone with your particular expertise. Need help with a fairly unique situation. Let's meet up.*
>   *Billy*

Seemed simple enough. The second message read:

> *Hey boss, haven't heard back. Could still use your help. If it helps, I'll pay $100 just to meet up. I promise you'll find it interesting.*
>   *Billy*

Damn. One hundred dollars.

That much money would be a godsend. Uneasiness still slithered in his gut, but the hard truth was this just wasn't an offer he could turn down. After what happened at Nora's though, Erasmo had no intention of going to this meeting alone.

"Dude, I'm so glad you called me for this," Rat said, his tiny eyes darting back and forth with excitement.

As Erasmo navigated the downtown traffic, turning from South St. Mary's onto East Nueva Street, he sensed the coiled tension and electricity emanating from his friend. Rat scratched at his hooked nose as he fidgeted in the passenger seat, the late-afternoon light reflecting dully off his glasses.

"I mean, yeah, am I kind of pissed you didn't tell me that you answered one of the messages? And that you didn't take me to that chick's house? Yes, that licks donkey balls. *But*, I'll let it go, because you came to your senses and did the right thing by bringing me along this time."

They were close to arriving at La Villita. For some reason, Billy had asked that they meet at a small church located on its grounds. The unpredictability of the situation made Erasmo nervous, and he wanted to make sure that they were both on the same page.

"Look," he said, "let's try to quickly answer this guy's questions, get the money, and leave with no bullshit. If we get the sense that he's dangerous in *any* way, we'll just get up and leave. Oh . . . and let me do most of the talking, okay?"

Rat gave no indication that he heard or agreed with what Erasmo had just said, instead gazing out of the window, lost in thought.

He pulled the Civic into a nearly empty parking lot across the street from La Villita and killed the engine.

"Remember," Erasmo said as they got out of the car, "first sign he's batshit, we're out." Rat took in a deep breath and nodded, now looking a little nervous. The two of them crossed Presa and entered the village, their shoes clapping against the cobbled stone street.

As they strolled through the maze of shops, Erasmo marveled at its history. La Villita sat on the south bank of the San Antonio River, and had been the very first neighborhood in San Antonio. It had also been home to Spanish soldiers stationed at Mission San Antonio de Valero, better known as the Alamo. Over time though, the area had devolved into a slum. But in 1939, La Villita began its transformation into its current form, a colony for artists and a home to shops and boutiques. Pottery,

Mexican folk art, sculptures, watercolors, textiles, copperware, and more were sold at the various shops lining the walkway.

Many of the buildings they passed were simple stone structures constructed between the 1820s and 1860s. Others were made of stucco-covered brick with very little architectural detailing. Every time he came here, it gave Erasmo the disorienting feeling of having traveled back in time.

They proceeded down the walkway, occasionally passing small groups of tourists. Given La Villita's long history, it was no surprise that there were plenty of stories about wandering ghosts. Erasmo's favorite involved a group of children believed to haunt the area. They were said to approach pedestrians and appear playful at first . . . until they followed their victims around and chanted the names of demons, huge smiles on their cherubic faces.

Erasmo was lost in thought when he realized that they were standing in front of the Little Church of La Villita. Whoever had named the quaint stone building got it right, as it was the smallest church Erasmo had ever seen.

"Why did he want to meet here anyway?" Rat asked.

"Why the hell not?" a voice asked from behind them.

They turned to see a blond, narrow-faced man with hard features and deep-set eyes, studying both of them.

"You guys the ones that placed the ad?" he asked with a hint of country twang. The man's hands were stuffed into the pockets of an olive-colored canvas jacket. His calm blue eyes shifted back and forth until they settled on Erasmo. "You. You're the leader of this outfit."

"Hi," Erasmo said, extending his hand. "Erasmo Cruz."

"Hey, bud," the man said, shaking Erasmo's hand, his spindly fingers surprisingly strong. "And you?"

"Oh . . . I'm Rat."

"Erasmo and Rat, huh? Well, both you guys got a heck of a name," he said. "Mine's just plain ol' Billy." He flashed an unnatural, strained smile. "Billy Doggett."

"Good to meet you," Erasmo said. "So . . . you have some questions for us?"

"Oh yeah, I do," Billy said, "but how 'bout we go inside and have our little chat in this house of God? That would suit me a little better." Before they could respond, Billy ascended the stairs, his black biker boots clomping loudly on each step.

If anything, the church looked even smaller once you stepped inside. A narrow row of pews sat on each side of the room, divided by a red-carpeted aisle. Behind the altar, set into the limestone wall, a single stained-glass window glowed with late-afternoon light. A cross in the middle of the window burned in fluctuating red and orange hues.

Billy sauntered up to the lectern and motioned for them to sit in the front pew. Unease trickled into Erasmo's belly, but he and Rat slid onto the bench. Billy removed his hands from the abyss of his pockets and placed them on the lectern.

"To answer your first question, I asked to meet here because I plan to visit every church in the city, and hadn't yet had the pleasure of steppin' foot in this one. As for your second, I do have questions, but I'm curious about your credentials for this sort of thing. Someone teach this stuff to y'all? Or do you have personal hands-on experience, maybe?"

Erasmo dug his nails into his sweaty palms and glanced at Rat before answering. "It's a combination of things really. I'm actually known around here for one of my experiences. You ever heard of the Ghost Tracks?"

Billy hadn't, as he only moved to San Antonio the year before. So, in addition to having to tell his own story, Erasmo also had to explain the miracle of the Ghost Tracks as well.

"It's one of our most famous local legends," Erasmo began. "On the south side, in a secluded area at the intersection of Shane and Villamain Roads, are old, seemingly ordinary railroad tracks. This section of tracks looks just like all the others, but us locals know that this block of tracks is extraordinary. In the 1930s, a school bus full of small children stalled on this particular section of tracks. A train came along just at that moment and, unable to slow its massive weight, plowed into the bus, killing every child inside."

Billy started at this, his eyes widening.

"If you were to drive down Shane Road, and place your car in neutral about thirty feet before reaching these tracks, something strange will happen. Your car will move. It will be pushed forward and up a slight incline, until it is safely over the tracks. And what invisible force moved your vehicle up and over the tracks? You've probably already guessed it. The spirits of the dead children. They want to save others from the same fate that befell them, so their tiny ghosts push car after car up the street and over the tracks to safety."

"That's . . . amazing," Billy said as he gripped the lectern tightly, clearly entranced.

"If you ask any San Antonian, they'll easily recite the evidence that supports the existence of these ghost children. For example, if, after you arrive on the other side of the tracks, baby powder is sprinkled over the back of your car, shapes will form in the powder. These shapes will be tiny, scattered handprints. In addition, if you simply drive around, you'll see that the streets in the area are all named after children who died at the tracks. Bobbie Allen, Cindy Sue, Laura Lee, Nancy Carole, Richey Otis. I know it sounds fantastical, but it's true. People come from all over to be saved by the children of the Ghost Tracks."

"That's one hell of a story," Billy said, his face solemn. "And I guess you have some kind of connection to these tracks?"

"I do."

Erasmo then proceeded to give Billy a detailed accounting of what happened that night. Billy stood in silence while the story unfolded, occasionally arching his left eyebrow. When Erasmo finished, Billy stared down at the lectern, stringy hair falling around his face.

"Sounds to me like you're *just* the fella I'm lookin' for," he said, not raising his head. "I mean, damn, I honestly can't believe it. You're perfect. Now I'm going to tell *you* a story. It's a good one, I promise."

Billy paused to clear his throat and run his hands through his hair, as if he wanted everything just right before he continued.

"When I was a kid, we didn't go to church. My dad thought it was all bullshit. To be honest, I never thought that much about it one way or the other. Then I went to college for a year and took an anthropology course. It didn't put God in a flattering light, you know? We spent weeks on evolution, on cavemen, on fossil records, all that stuff. I remember one day this guy in class got all pissed off at the professor, and inside I was laughing at the guy. I mean, what kind of person is going to see all this evidence and still deny the obvious truth? But . . . a few years ago something happened. Something that makes no logical sense but is absolutely true."

Billy took in a deep, shaky breath, thin nostrils flaring.

"I was chosen."

Erasmo's stomach clenched. Damn. A religious nut. This was going to be a problem. He glanced at Rat, who stared at Billy, enthralled.

"Chosen . . ." Erasmo said, trying to hide his annoyance. "You mean by God? He spoke to you?"

"No. At least, not like you're thinking. He doesn't speak in complete sentences. He shows me things. Up here." Billy pointed to his right temple. "And here." Now his finger rested over his heart.

Rat, no longer able to contain himself, blurted out, "Like what kinds of things?"

"Well," Billy said smiling, as if he were happy someone finally asked, "it's going to sound crazy. I mean, it sounds whacko to me too. So I'll just come out and say it." Billy's smile faded before he spoke his next sentence in a half whisper. "He shows me things that haven't happened yet."

Billy paused and raised his right eyebrow, as if he were daring them to question what he'd just said. When it was clear that neither had any intention of doing so, he continued.

"It started a few years back. Small things at first. I knew when I was going to bump into an old friend, for example. But then last year, I saw something that wasn't so small."

Billy released a long sigh and squinted until his shimmering blue eyes were barely visible.

"I saw a man," Billy finally said, "leading a little girl away from her family. I recognized the location too, the parking lot of that H-E-B on Fredericksburg. I was so scared that what I saw would actually happen, I went there every day and waited. Finally, after two weeks, I saw the girl. She'd wandered away and her mother hadn't noticed. When that scumbag made his move, creeping up behind her, I was ready." Billy walked out from behind the lectern and acted out the rest. "I ran over, and I said to the guy, 'Hey, what the hell are you doing?' He looked at me, terrified, and scurried away like the damn rat he was."

Billy smiled, staring at the wall behind them, as if there were a screen on it replaying his heroics exactly as he'd described them.

"You have the sight . . . " Rat whispered. Erasmo turned and glared at him, mentally urging his friend not to say anything else.

"I went straight to the police to tell them about that creep, so they could keep an eye on him. I explained about my ability, that I could help them stop horrible things from happening. But they wouldn't listen to a damn word I said. I understand why. It all sounds so unbelievable. But then, I had an idea."

Erasmo's stomach tightened. Here it comes . . . the reason they'd been called here.

"I figure that if someone documents and verifies what I can do, someone who is an expert in these kinds of things, then they might listen to me. I could go to the authorities whenever He shows me an event, and they could stop whatever terrible thing is about to happen."

"And you want Erasmo to be that guy . . . that expert," Rat said.

"Hell, you're even better than what I was hoping for, Erasmo. People around here know who you are! They'll listen if you vouch for me! I've been looking all over, and the perfect person falls right into my lap. It's divine intervention if you ask me."

"So," Erasmo said, "just to be clear. You want me to follow you around and document your visions coming true? And then tell everyone that you're the real deal?"

"You got it, bud."

"I'm sorry, but I can't help you. That's not really what I do—"

"Wait . . . hold up," Billy said. "You haven't even *thought* about it. Is it 'cause you don't believe me? Is that why you don't want to do it?" Crimson streaks crawled up Billy's neck to his sharp cheekbones. "It's true. All of it. I can show you!"

Damn. This guy had gone from zero to ninety in just a few seconds.

"Look," Erasmo said, "it's not that—"

"I don't suppose," Billy said, "that I have to tell two smart fellas like you about First Corinthians 12:10, do I? It says that God grants special abilities . . . the words couldn't be clearer! Listen to them! *'To another miraculous powers, to another prophecy, to another distinguishing between spirits, to another speaking in different kinds of tongues, and to still another the interpretation of tongues.'*"

Billy clenched and unclenched his fists, the splotches of scarlet in his face now spreading toward his scalp.

"The Bible," Billy screamed, "is *full* of prophets like Ezekiel! It wouldn't make sense for God to stop choosing people to tell his word to now, would it?"

"I wouldn't be of any use to you," Erasmo said, trying to remain calm. "I honestly don't know very much about precognition." A lie, but a necessary one. This guy was clearly unwell and had some kind of bizarre savior complex. Nothing good was going to happen here. Erasmo slid out of the pew, heart hammering, and headed to the door. Rat followed closely behind, his legs visibly shaky.

"Just go then!" Billy screamed from behind them.

They trotted through the village and across the street to the parking lot, occasionally glancing backward. As Erasmo reached into his pocket for the Civic's keys, Billy emerged from the exit and rushed across the street toward them.

"Shit," Erasmo whispered as he fumbled his key into the lock.

"Hurry up," Rat said, a quiver in his voice.

In a quick burst, Billy was on him, grabbing Erasmo's arm and yanking the keys out of his hand.

"You know what?" Billy asked through hard, angry breaths. "You boys are lucky I'm a God-fearing man." He pointed his long index finger at Erasmo. "Especially you."

Billy stared off into the distance, contemplating his next words.

"Even though you don't deserve it, I'm going to give you some advice: Watch yourself. Because when we walked into that church, God sent me a vision. Just for a few seconds, but I saw it, clear as I've ever seen anything. It was you, Erasmo. You were screaming. Screaming real bad. And I could see that you were terrified, although of what I don't know. And . . . there was blood too. So much blood flowing down your screaming face." Billy gave Erasmo a hard look and tossed his keys back to him. "You can believe that or not, but I ain't ever been wrong yet."

With that, Billy turned and walked away, leaving Erasmo to watch him slowly disappear into the shadowy, darkening streets of downtown San Antonio.

CHAPTER 5

WHEN ERASMO GOT home, he expected to find his grandmother in her usual place, settled into her old recliner and watching one of the many novelas she ardently followed. But instead, he was greeted only with a disquieting silence.

"Grandma?"

Erasmo poked his head into the kitchen, but it was still and lifeless. He went back into the living room and stood at the flimsy yellow curtain that separated her room from the rest of the house.

"Grandma? Are you okay?"

No response. *Damn.* He was going to have to go in there. This unnerved him, as his grandmother had a long-standing rule about not going in unless she asked him to. Although, it was hard to see how that rule was going to apply for much longer, as he'd soon be taking care of her.

Erasmo slid the curtain back and was relieved to see his grandmother sleeping peacefully, covered under a pile of blankets. As he studied her face though, his relief soon turned to worry. Was it just a trick of the light, or did her skin now appear as thin as tissue paper, ready to tear at the slightest touch? Was it just his fear of losing this precious woman, or did her bones appear to be emerging from under her skin, giving her face the appearance of a barely covered skull?

His grandmother's treatment wouldn't begin for another few weeks, but even now he shuddered when he thought of how it would change her, and what agonies she'd soon endure.

Erasmo crept to his room and took *A Practical Guide to the Supernatural and Paranormal* from the perch above his bed. He knew the thoughts ricocheting in his head were dangerous ones, but at this point, it was hard for him to give a shit about that when the worst was already happening.

He opened the book and flipped through it a few times until he found the right chapter. Erasmo had read these passages before, but back then they were theoretical. Now he was looking for a more practical use of Dubois's findings.

On the Use of Occult Methods to Cure Disease

Being quite familiar with the desperation one feels when watching a loved one succumb to illness, this topic is of particular interest to me. One of my many regrets is not having known about these methods while my Emma was still alive. It is impossible to know if any of them would have saved her, but oh how I desperately wish that I could have at least tried.

After much research and many interviews, I have come to the conclusion that there are three methods that hold the most promise to genuinely heal the afflicted. Interestingly, they all share one common theme: one must give, in order to receive.

The first method is the use of spells. Over the course of several weeks, I interviewed an old woman in a small town in Connecticut who claimed to be a descendant of one of the first American witches. She repeatedly demonstrated the power to manipulate others by doing nothing more than uttering short incantations and burning various foliage. I personally witnessed this witch cast a spell on a man who spit in her face and called her an abomination. This man was found dead the next morning, having taken a knife and slitting his throat with it.

She provided me with many of her spells, which I have written elsewhere in this journal, but the witch advised that healing spells are the most dangerous and difficult of all. She gave two important warnings in regards to them. First, in order to heal one person, blood must be taken from another. The blood used in these spells must be newly released, and substantial in quantity. Second, never attempt to use a healing spell on someone who has already become one with the spirit world. The results would be monstrous.

The second method involves inviting a disembodied spirit into the diseased body. The afflicted must give himself over completely to the spirit and be at its mercy. There are some benevolent spirits who take possession of a body and cleanse it, absorbing excesses and impurities. These spirits are thought to be healers who have now passed into the spirit world. This is a dangerous course of action though, as a malevolent spirit may accept the invitation instead, and the person you seek to cure may end up significantly worse.

The last method carries by far the most risk but is also the most certain to cure illness and disease. I won't go on at length in regards to it, except to say this: Promising gifts to a demon in exchange for help is a dangerous business. You are likely to lose more than you gain in such a bargain. In the event it is ever truly needed, I have documented elsewhere in this journal the steps necessary to conduct a Black Mass. Be wary though, as the devil is cunning, and full of tricks.

Erasmo closed the book and placed it back on its shelf. A lot to consider, but not tonight. He was worn out and wanted nothing more than to rest. As he settled under his blankets and felt the first wave of sleep gently wash over him, he had only one thought: *I will do anything for her to live.*

When he woke the next morning, Erasmo took stock of his situation. Two attempts. Two disasters. So far, the ad had been a colossal failure. There had to be an easier, less dangerous way to make money, but whatever way that was continued to elude him. He checked his email, but still not one response to his flood of résumés. The thought of selling blood crossed his mind, but he was ninety percent sure that he would pass out and piss himself if he tried. He was frightfully afraid of needles.

Despite what happened at Nora's, and Billy's unhinged meltdown, Erasmo found his thoughts drifting to the third and last message that he'd chosen to follow up on. He took out his laptop and read it again.

> *Hello. I have a few simple questions that I need answered. Assuming you are as knowledgeable as you say, it shouldn't take more than 10 minutes. Will pay on site, preferably at a public place.*
> *Leander Castillo*

Of all of them, this response had seemed the most promising from the beginning. He had to admit that it would be pretty damn weak to give up after two difficult cases and leave the low-hanging fruit rotting on the vine. Just because he'd come across two screwed-up people didn't mean this guy would be. If anything, the laws of probability were now squarely on his side. And the sad fact was he had nothing but time on his hands.

One more. Good, bad, or indifferent, it would be the last one. Then he could at least walk away knowing that he'd given this idea his very best shot.

Erasmo sent a message to arrange the meeting. Leander responded immediately, suggesting some place called Boneheadz at 7 p.m. He also suggested exchanging phone numbers in case plans changed and they needed to contact each other, which Erasmo agreed to. When he called Rat with the news, Erasmo was disappointed when his friend morosely told him that he'd be stuck at Little Caesars all night working a double.

That evening, Erasmo pulled into a nearly empty parking lot and looked the building over. It wasn't particularly impressive from the outside. The only distinguishing features were a large, sloping metal roof, and the word *Boneheadz* displayed in oversized red letters on its wall. He exited the Civic and warily approached the front entrance.

After pulling the creaky door open and stepping into dim, unnatural light, he immediately felt like an idiot. This place was a bar. Of course it was a bar. What else would it be with a name like Boneheadz? Had that registered when Leander suggested it, he'd have offered a different place to meet. But it was too late now, and anyway, there wasn't anyone at the door checking IDs.

He stepped in and surveyed the scene. The space was dominated by a large rectangular bar in the middle of the room. A tall, surly-looking bartender stood by the taps, wiping down pint glasses. Erasmo had no trouble spotting Leander, since there were only three other patrons, and two of them were busy arguing over what Lana Del Rey song to play on the jukebox. This left only the lone man sitting at a corner bar stool, staring at his phone and cradling a maroon drink.

Erasmo immediately saw that Leander was one of those guys who spent a lot of time in the gym and wanted everyone to know it. He was lean but had a rock-solid layer of muscle over his frame. The top button of his lavender shirt was dangerously close to popping off, and his short, spiky hair and pointy leather boots rounded out his douchebag look perfectly.

Erasmo walked up to him and extended his hand.

"Hi. I'm Erasmo Cruz."

Leander's body suddenly spasmed, as if shocked by an electric current. A small yelp escaped his lips as he dropped his phone and almost spilled the maroon drink.

"Oh God, sorry," Leander said, "you scared me." He stood up and grabbed Erasmo's hand, squeezing hard as he shook, bicep undulating under his snug shirtsleeve. "I really appreciate you coming." Leander reached into his pocket and pulled out two fifty-dollar bills. "Is this enough?"

Erasmo's eyes widened. "It is . . . but that can wait until after we talk—"

"No need," Leander said as he shoved the bills into Erasmo's hands. "I'm just glad you came. Do you mind going upstairs to the loft area, though? There are too many people down here."

Erasmo almost mentioned that there were only a few other people in the entire bar, but he was so shocked and relieved that all he heard himself say in response was, "Sure."

They walked over to the short flight of wooden stairs near the bathrooms. As he trudged up to the second floor, Erasmo wondered if Leander was going to ask about his qualifications, and he mentally rehearsed his answer. The two of them settled into a small table by the railing, and for the first time, Erasmo took a good look at Leander's face. He had sharp, proportioned features, but black swollen bags hung under his eyes. Before Erasmo even had a chance to speak, Leander blurted out his first question.

"Can a spirit follow you?" he asked, the words spoken so quickly that they ran together.

"Could you be a little more specific?"

"Like . . . if they wanted to, could they track down a person?"

Finally. Something he could work with.

"Well," Erasmo began, "almost never. Ghosts are usually tied to the specific area they died in, so they wouldn't travel from place to place. Specific objects have certainly been inhabited, like the Tallman bunk beds in '87, and obviously objects can be mobile. But what you're talking about is a ghost following someone over a distance. Like I said, that's pretty damn rare."

Leander took a large swig, then wiped his mouth with the back of his hand.

"You're sure?" he asked, a hint of desperation in his voice.

"Yes," Erasmo said. "I mean, it's not like there've *never* been any cases. There was the Tyng case in Massachusetts. But that was over two hundred years ago."

"Okay . . . I guess that helps," Leander said, but his voice sounded weary and strained.

"Can you give me some background? I think I'd be able to help you more if I knew where this was coming from."

"What if . . ." Leander said after a long pause, squirming in his seat, "what if a spirit wanted to get revenge on a living person? Would this spirit be able to follow if the person they were hunting moved very far away?"

What the hell?

"Well . . . like I said, most are anchored to a specific location. But I guess we should be clear about our terminology. Ghosts don't move from place to place, but other entities can. Poltergeists can follow and torment their targets. Demons do as well. In the extremely rare case of an actual appearance of one, demons are often confused for ghosts, and they can easily travel—"

"Wait, wait . . . go back a second. What's the difference between a ghost and a poltergeist?"

"Well, for one, poltergeists can interact with our physical dimension, unlike ghosts. Second, poltergeists are usually not human in origin. There are different opinions as to what exactly they are. Some say they're a form of energy that a person controls unknowingly. Others say a poltergeist is a type of demon, or some other entity of evil."

"So," Leander said, "a poltergeist can interact physically, but isn't the spirit of a dead human. Okay . . . that's good—"

"Well," Erasmo interrupted, "not always. There are very specific instances when a poltergeist *could* be human in origin."

Leander swallowed hard, his Adam's apple convulsing in his throat.

"Like what type of instances?"

"Three really. The first would be if, when the poltergeist was alive, it was an incredibly evil person. Second, if it lived a traumatic life. And third, if it died in a horrific and disturbing way."

The muscles in Leander's face went slack, and his mouth hung ajar as beads of sweat erupted on his brow.

Damn. It seemed like every piece of information he gave Leander just made things worse. Erasmo reached into his pocket and felt the two bills. He'd been paid to help, not give this guy more shadows to jump at.

"Can I venture a guess as to what's going on?" he asked. "You think there's something in your house, don't you?"

A slow, almost imperceptible nod from Leander.

"I have good news then. You don't have to move to get away from it. If there's anything in your house, it's not going to hurt you, or follow you. In fact—"

"You don't know that!" Leander hissed, a flash of anger in his eyes. "You *can't* know that. And if this is your professional opinion, then you obviously don't know what the hell you're talking about."

Leander finished the remains of his drink in two large swallows.

"I was hoping you'd be of more help," he said, rising from the table. "Thanks for wasting my time." He turned and shuffled down the stairs before Erasmo could muster a response.

Erasmo's stomach clenched, as if it were trying to crush the cluster of shame now blossoming inside of it. He peered down over the railing and saw the evening crowd steadily streaming in. A group of preening loudmouths yelled at the bartender for a round of shots. Erasmo studied their bursting muscles, and their stylish clothes, and the perfect teeth their parents had paid so much for. He found himself longing to pound their self-satisfied, smirking faces with his clenched fists. He wanted to hear the satisfying thuds as he banged his flesh against theirs until they stopped laughing and shut the hell up. He wanted to . . .

Erasmo closed his eyes and took in a deep breath. He listened to the clinks of bottles and the clacking of pool balls and the slow rhythms of the song playing on the jukebox. He finally got up from the table and lurched his way down the stairs, fists balled and shoved into his pockets just to be safe. He stepped out into the early evening and a cool breeze greeted him, stroking his burning face. Erasmo stopped and turned his eyes skyward, standing perfectly still as he watched the emerging moon take its rightful place in the restless, darkening sky.

CHAPTER 6

"ERASMO . . . WAKE UP."

His grandmother's voice floated in from the other side of his bedroom door, its volume—but not its urgency—muted by the thin wood.

His eyelids cracked open, reluctant and sluggish.

"Erasmo, you need to get up. Please."

Why did his grandmother sound like that? He tried to think of what was in her voice that bothered him so, when he realized what the tone most closely resembled.

Fear.

Erasmo jumped off his bed. Was she already getting sick? Did she need to go to the hospital? He yanked the door open, and his grandmother stood in the doorway, eyes narrowed to slits. Her body shook almost imperceptibly, humming with energy, as if she were seconds away from erupting. He'd been wrong. It wasn't just fear in her voice. It was fury too.

He was about to ask what had happened, when a stout, stone-faced woman appeared behind her. With a smooth motion, this woman maneuvered around his grandmother and entered into his bedroom.

"Erasmo Cruz?"

She didn't wait for an answer.

"I'm Detective Torres." The woman turned to his agitated grandmother. "I'm going to need to speak to him alone."

She nodded and backed away slowly, unwilling to turn her back on the detective.

Torres tried to close the door, struggling to push it shut against the crooked frame. She looked young for a detective, late twenties, maybe early thirties. Her small, delicate features seemed at odds with her powerful build.

"Mr. Cruz," she said, turning back to him. "I'm going to ask you a few questions, and I need you to be truthful. Okay?"

"Uh, yeah . . . sure, Detective."

Torres gave him a hard, *don't mess with me* look before continuing.

"How do you know Leander Castillo?"

Leander.

Shit.

"I . . . don't. Not really."

Torres tilted her head toward the floor and nodded slowly, as if she'd expected this answer.

"Tell you what, Erasmo. Let me repeat myself, because maybe it didn't stick in your head the right way. I said I needed you to be truthful."

"That is the truth, Detective," Erasmo said, his heart now thumping steadily. "I don't really know him. Not well."

Torres glanced up and fixed her hard eyes on him.

"You seemed pretty chummy at the bar last night."

The muscles in Erasmo's chest constricted around his heart.

"It was the first time," Erasmo said, trying not to stammer, "we'd ever met. I swear."

"Really . . . first time," Torres said. "Wouldn't have known it from the intense conversation you guys were having. Why were you two even there together?"

"I . . . I put an ad on Craigslist," Erasmo said, cringing at how stupid it sounded, "and he answered it."

"Craigslist, huh? Is that why he gave you money?"

Damn. They must've been at the bar somehow, watching. Erasmo reminded himself that he hadn't actually done anything wrong, and answered the question.

"Yes."

"Look, Mr. Cruz, I'm trying to be nice here, but I need to know what you guys were talking about, or else I'll have to take you in for questioning. And based on her reaction when I told her that I was here to speak with you, I don't think your grandmother would like that very much."

Strangely, instead of fear, or curiosity, or anger, the main emotion burning through Erasmo was embarrassment. First, because this detective was a witness to the tiny, unkempt room he lived in. And second, because of the word he was about to speak.

"Ghosts," Erasmo whispered.

"Sorry?"

"I, uh, placed an ad offering to help people who are having trouble with paranormal phenomena. He had questions about ghosts."

Torres raised her eyebrows in surprise, but that expression quickly gave way to another: interest.

"What kind of questions?"

Erasmo described his exchange with Leander as best he could remember. Torres jotted everything down in a small spiral notebook, which had a Curious George sticker displayed on the back of it.

"That's it? Sure there was nothing else?"

"Positive."

"Okay. Now, I want you to listen carefully. Stay far away from Leander. And if he reaches out to you, don't respond."

"Sure. But can I ask why?"

"He's under investigation."

"Investigation? For what?"

Torres slid her notebook into her pocket and studied Erasmo for a moment before answering.

"Murder."

Erasmo's breath caught at the word.

"What? Are . . . are you sure it was him?"

Torres handed Erasmo her card. "Thanks for the information. It was helpful. If you remember anything else, let me know right away. And I want to be the first call if you hear from him. Understand?"

Torres pushed the bedroom door forward, shoving a few times before it opened wide enough for her to walk through. The detective paused and turned around. For the first time, her face held an expression that wasn't filtered through the prism of her job. The hard contours of her face softened, and Erasmo realized that she was attempting to look friendly.

"Oh, one more thing. Officer Enriquez said to say hello. He wasn't sure if you remembered him or not, but he said he hopes you're doing well."

Torres then turned and exited, the sound of her footsteps echoing throughout the small, somber house.

His grandmother strode in almost immediately, blank-faced and wordless. Erasmo, familiar with this tactic, was usually intimidated into breaking the silence first. But she didn't have the patience to wait for him to crumble today.

"Do you want to tell me what that was about?"

"It was nothing I just know someone she's trying to get information about."

"A bad someone?"

"I barely know him—"

"Stop," she said, her face sagging in disappointment. "I'm old, Erasmo. And let me tell you . . . many horrible things happen when you get old. But one of the worst is that the memories that you most desperately want to fade away, get even stronger. They replay in your mind endlessly, taunting you, now that you have lived long enough to see their consequences. And . . . it's especially hard when those consequences break your heart."

"I know, Grandma."

"Be sure that you do," she said, "because in my life, I've heard every lie, and seen every bad decision imaginable. And if I find out that you are doing *anything* that reminds me of those horrible memories, then you better hope this *pinche* cancer kills me before I get my hands on you."

"I'm not doing anything bad. Promise."

She nodded, appearing temporarily satisfied. Before walking out, she turned to him, her expression both mournful and stern.

"Erasmo."

"Yes, Grandma?"

"Make sure you never, ever forget what's in your blood."

And to this, Erasmo simply spoke the truth.

"That," he said as he dug his nails into his palms, gouging the tender flesh, "would be impossible."

CHAPTER 7

"HELLO?" ERASMO SQUINTED at his clock as he held the phone to his ear: 3:35 a.m.

"Erasmo?" a skittish voice asked.

"Who's this?"

"You have to help me. Please!"

"Leander?"

"She's here! She's here and she's going to—"

Erasmo hung up and turned off the ringer, heart pounding in his ears. He closed his eyes and tried to go back to sleep, but it was a long time before his thoughts allowed him to drift off.

There were three voicemails waiting for him when he woke. He played them and listened as Leander's panic-stricken voice begged for help. Erasmo could only make out random phrases, none of them making any sense.

dancing . . . oh God . . . was dancing . . .

help . . . pink . . . after me . . .

spinning . . . teeth . . . worms

Erasmo found Torres's card lying on his nightstand. He almost dialed the number but found himself hesitant. Leander obviously hadn't been arrested yet. Maybe the case against him wasn't that strong. He listened to the voicemails again, unable to stop himself from wondering what could possibly have frightened Leander so badly.

He reached under his bed and pulled out the two boxes, his fingertips guided by an unseen magnetic force. He opened them and allowed his eyes to float over their contents. He eventually pulled himself away and spent the rest of the morning sipping on glasses of milk and trying to resist the perverse, growing urge to return Leander's calls.

Yes, the cops suspected him of murder, but Leander just hadn't seemed like the violent type. Scared and confused for sure, but hardly violent. And, not unimportantly, he'd passed out those fifties like they were candy.

Money wasn't the only motivation, though. Despite his better instincts, he wanted to know just what the hell Leander was babbling about in those messages. This urge wasn't sane, he knew, but the curiosity gnawed at his gut just the same. What on earth could have thrown Leander into such a panicked state?

He wanted to know.

And he needed the money.

Berating himself even as he did it, Erasmo picked up his phone and made the call.

Erasmo was unprepared for the waves of jealousy that washed over him as he pulled up to Leander's house a few hours later. It was simply a replica of all the other prefabricated homes in the neighborhood: dull vinyl siding, a compact lawn, and non-existent architectural flair. But to Erasmo, it was perfect. He imagined himself one day driving up to a home just like this, his grandmother in the passenger seat beaming with awe and pride at what her grandson had done, what he had. But Erasmo didn't have a damn thing yet. This asshole did instead.

Leander stood waiting for him on the front porch, arms crossed, wearing a gray T-shirt and faded blue jeans. He hadn't bothered to slather product in his hair this time. Erasmo got out of the car and walked over, careful to avoid stepping on the well-manicured lawn. They looked at each other in silence for a few moments before Erasmo spoke.

"Start from the beginning. Tell me everything."

Leander solemnly nodded his head, turned, and entered the house. A blur of neutral colors, fake plants, and family pictures flew by as he followed Leander across the den and up the stairs to a living area. They settled into a plush, chocolate-colored sofa sitting against the back wall.

"It's that girl," Leander started, almost as soon as they sat down. "Sandra Rosales. The one they think I killed. She's after me. I know that sounds crazy, but it's true. She's here, in this house, right now. And not just here." He looked around, eyes wide, as if she might be watching him that very second. "She's following me too," he whispered.

Sandra Rosales. Erasmo should've known this was the murder Torres was talking about. It had been all over the news lately, her devastated parents constantly on TV begging for answers . . . for justice.

"Look," Erasmo said, "you really need to back up. How did this whole thing even start?"

Leander grimaced, took a deep breath, and began.

"I'd never even seen her in person before that night. We met on Tinder and had been messaging a lot, so we decided to finally meet up. I was crazy nervous, but we had an amazing time at dinner. Things were going so well that we decided to have some drinks at the Hangar afterward. On the way there, my cousin Travis, second cousin actually, texted to meet up. I had this uneasy feeling . . . something telling me not to respond. Even though we're related, we'd only recently begun hanging out."

"Why's that?' Erasmo asked.

"Well, we only see that side of the family every few years or so. But I'd bumped into Travis at a bar several months back and had some beers with him. We had a great time and hung out several times since. I mean, I'd heard family rumors about some troubles with the law and stuff like that, but he'd seemed okay. So I went ahead and told him to come out. And when Travis gets there, he's in complete awe of her. Sandra was so smart and charming. She brightened up the whole damn bar. But then . . ."

Leander let out a long breath, his jaw clenched tight.

"He started hitting on Sandra, showing her his tattoos and saying that maybe he'd get one of her someday. I was so damn pissed that I decided to just close my tab, and I offered to bring her back here for a nightcap."

Tears spilled from Leander's swollen eyes. He didn't bother wiping them away.

"But he must've followed us. While I unlocked the front door, I heard footsteps behind me, and the next thing I knew I was waking up on the porch. Hours had passed, and Sandra was gone. I knew right away that that asshole had taken her. I was just about to call the police when I heard screeching tires and realized that they'd found me first."

"But . . . how'd they find you so fast?" Erasmo asked. "How'd they know to even look for you?"

"A homeless guy found Sandra's body in a vacant lot around three a.m. and called the police. She'd been killed by a blow to the back of the head. When the police contacted her friends, one mentioned that she had a date with me that night. I tried to tell them what had happened . . . but my cousin denied everything of course. To make matters worse, the video footage outside the bar shows Sandra getting into my car. The investigation is still ongoing, but my lawyer says I'll probably get arrested soon. The police think I did it. And . . . so does Sandra."

"Sandra? I'm not sure I'm following you."

"Don't you see?" Leander said. "All Sandra knows is that she was on a date with me when her life was taken. Her last memory of that night is of going to my house. The next thing she knows, she's waking up as a spirit, her life robbed from her. It's obvious that she'd think that *I'm* the one that killed her. That's why she's doing this to me now."

"Doing what?" Erasmo asked.

"You know," Leander said, his eyes glassy and distant, "I think I'm going to rest now. Having to relive all this took a lot out of me. Come back tonight. I want you to see for yourself. And when Sandra does appear, you can send her away from here. That should be no problem . . . since your specialty is 'displacing spirits from your place of residence,' right? And while we're waiting, I'll tell you the rest of the story. Oh, and I'll have your money too. Is three hundred enough?"

Erasmo nodded and rose from the sofa to leave.

"I sure hope," Leander said, "that you can do what you claim. Because if you can't, when she comes for us tonight, you're going to wish you'd never placed that goddamn ad."

CHAPTER 8

"SO IS THIS dude a whack job, or what?" Rat asked, slouched in the passenger's seat and gnawing on his fingernails.

"I think he's just jumping at shadows," Erasmo said, the Civic shuddering as he pulled away from Rat's house. "Leander took this girl out on a date and she ended up dead. Of course he's going to feel responsible. Now every time a floorboard creaks, he spazzes out and thinks she's after him."

Rat threw up his slender arms. "Dude, I thought Sandra's ghost wanting revenge was the most believable part of his story! It's the question of whether Leander is the person that killed her or not that's got me curious. His whole 'It was my cousin, I swear' routine sure seems shady. I'm honestly shocked that you even agreed to meet with him again."

"I know . . . but after hearing Leander's story, I honestly believe him. I just don't get the sense that he could have done it." Erasmo gestured to the needle on the fuel gauge, which hovered over the *E*. "Besides, I still really need the money."

"Wait . . . I thought you said this guy lived over by SeaWorld."

"We're going to make a quick stop first," Erasmo said. "Don't freak out . . . but do you remember Nora and her brother—"

"What the hell?" Rat said. "You think it's a good idea to go over there *now*? You do remember what happened last time, right?"

"Of course I do. That's part of the reason I need to go back. Nora came to me for help, and I was completely useless. I've been thinking a lot about her brother. I have to try and convince Nora to get him the kind of help he needs."

"And you don't think she'll just slam the door in your face after the way you ran off?"

"Maybe. But I feel like I have to try. It's not just what I saw on the video either. The other thing I keep thinking about is . . . this kid's like us. His dad isn't really around for him and—"

"Let's just make it quick then," Rat interrupted.

Erasmo nodded and turned onto West Avenue, deciding not to break the uneasy silence that had settled over them. Over the years, Erasmo had learned that if there was one topic that Rat shut down immediately, it was absent fathers.

When they pulled to a stop in front of Nora's house a short time later, he was disappointed to see that the oil-stained driveway was empty.

"They must be out," Rat said. "Let's just get on to Leander's—"

"Wait," he said.

Erasmo studied the yellowing blinds that hung behind the front window. He thought there'd been the slightest flicker of movement.

"I'm going to knock just to make sure," he said.

"It's your call," Rat said. "Want me to go with you?"

"No . . . just keep an eye out, okay?"

It was standing in front of her porch again that gave him second thoughts. Erasmo stood there, slack-jawed, staring at the scene of his previous humiliation. He imagined what he must have looked like, stumbling down the cracked steps, horrified and dripping with vomit. When he'd driven away that night, he was sure that he'd never come back.

But now here he was, walking up the porch steps, again nervous to raise his fist and knock on the door. A violent chill ran through him, his limbs convulsing, as if some invisible entity were attempting to shake some sense into him.

This is a mistake.

He buried this thought and replaced it with another.

The boy needs help.

Erasmo rapped on the door and was shocked when the light shuffle of footsteps immediately approached. As the door slowly swung open, Erasmo's eyes grew wide when he realized that it wasn't Nora who had answered the door.

It was the boy.

A round, grim face peered out at Erasmo, waxen and immobile, as if his skin were made of cheap plastic. After a long, vacant stare, the boy finally greeted him.

"You that guy?" he asked. "The one my sister told me about?" His mouth moved as he spoke, but only slightly.

"Hi, Sonny," he said. "Yeah, she thought I might be able to help. Is she around?"

"No," the boy replied tersely. "There isn't anything wrong with me, anyway, so just go ahead and get out of here."

"Well," Erasmo said, trying to sound conspiratorial, "we're on the same page then. I don't actually think there's anything wrong with you either. Do you know when she'll be back?"

The kid eyed him. He had chestnut-brown hair, just like Nora, but his had been subjected to an unfortunate bowl cut.

"No," Sonny said, his face still expressionless. "Just leave. Please."

"Look," Erasmo said, "I know you don't know me, but is there anything you want to talk about? Or to tell me? I promise that—"

"I said to just goddamn *leave!*" the boy screamed, his eyes suddenly infused with rage, and he slammed the door in Erasmo's face.

Damn.

Well, what the hell did he think was going to happen? This kid didn't know him from Adam. He'd just have to come back when Nora was home.

Erasmo walked back to the Civic as Rat watched him through the smudged car window, a troubled look on his face. When he got in, his friend patted him on the shoulder, his lithe fingers feeling almost ethereal.

"At least you tried," he said.

"Didn't do any good."

"Sometimes trying is all the good you can do," Rat said. "Now let's get the hell on out of here and catch us a ghost."

CHAPTER 9

AS ERASMO NAVIGATED the Civic through Leander's neighborhood, he studied the dusk sky, its fading glow layered with shades of indigo and sapphire. He hoped the elegant beauty of the transforming light was a good omen.

Rat clenched his fists, his arms shaking from the pressure.

"Dude, this is so unbelievably exciting. I mean, sure, this guy could be a crazy psycho who we should not be associating with in *any* way. But still . . . this could be our chance to see a real entity. Tonight could answer so many questions."

"I'm telling you," Erasmo said, "nothing is going to happen." He was about to change the topic when his curiosity got the better of him. "What kinds of questions?"

Rat's head shook, as if the questions themselves were ricocheting violently against each other inside of his skull. "Well, for one, what would this ghost be wearing? Would she be wearing the clothes she wore when she was killed? Or the clothes that she was buried in? Or her favorite outfit when she was alive?"

"All good questions . . ." Erasmo admitted.

"Or the rules," Rat continued, "for where spirits can manifest. Can ghosts only appear where they die, like when a ghost haunts the house they were murdered in? Or can they only appear where their bones are buried? If this ghost *does* appear tonight at Leander's, then that means spirits don't *only* manifest at the location of their death or where their bones are currently buried. It would mean that a spirit could manifest wherever it wants, and *that* would mean—"

"We're here," Erasmo said as he pulled up to the house and parked behind Leander's gleaming black Maxima.

They exited the Civic and approached the front porch. Erasmo wanted to go over the plan one last time, but Rat leaned over and pushed the doorbell before he could.

It hadn't even finished chiming when Leander threw the door open. He was wearing a purple V-neck T-shirt and designer jeans, a sharp-looking ensemble, but looked even worse than he had that morning. If it was possible to lose five pounds in twelve hours, he'd somehow managed it.

"Hey," Leander croaked, his left eye twitching.

"Hope you don't mind," Erasmo said, "but I brought along an associate of mine. This is Rat."

"Hey. You guys come on in." He turned and led them to a tidy kitchen located at the rear of the house. Leander walked over to the stainless-steel refrigerator shimmering in the corner and opened it. "Don't know about you guys, but I could use one."

He turned around holding three Miller Lites. The bottle was in Erasmo's hand before he could say no, its cold slickness against his flesh making him uneasy. He set the beer down on the counter, knowing he wouldn't even open it, much less have a sip. Rat, never one to turn down anything free, had his bottle open and in his mouth before Erasmo could advise him against it. Leander walked to the round oak table in the corner of the room and gestured for them to sit.

"I appreciate you guys coming." Leander drained half his bottle in a series of loud gulps before continuing. "I guess I should just get to it, so that you know exactly what you're dealing with."

Erasmo and Rat slowly leaned forward in unison.

"The first time I encountered Sandra's spirit was the night I came home from being interviewed at the police station. I never actually saw her, but when I was trying to fall asleep, I heard something roaming through the rooms, whispering. I forced myself to look around, and as I was walking down the hallway, I felt it."

Leander stared grimly ahead, his eyes unblinking.

"Her cold breath tickling the back of my neck. I screamed and ran to get away, but I tripped over some shoes on the landing. I could have broken my neck from the fall I took down the stairs. The thing is . . . I know I put those shoes away. *She* did it. *She* put them there so I'd fall down the stairs. I knew I had to get out of the house, so I limped to my car and drove straight to a hotel . . . but guess what?"

"She was at the hotel room too," Erasmo guessed.

"She was! I'd finally calmed down enough to drift off to sleep when I heard noises, scratching noises, coming from the foot of the bed. I told myself it was nothing, but then I felt . . ." Leander's face crumpled at the memory. "Hands . . . cold rotting hands, clawing at my feet. I screamed and tried to hide under the blankets, but then felt them being yanked away, so I jumped off the bed and ran out of the room."

Leander wrapped his arms around himself, his skin now clammy and devoid of color.

"What happened after that?" Erasmo asked.

"I had nowhere else to go, so I came back here. This place seemed as good as any since she was going to follow wherever I went anyway. After that first night, it wasn't nearly as bad. There were still noises in the house most evenings, but no attacks. I knew though, that she'd want revenge at some point, so I figured I'd try moving away, somewhere she couldn't follow, like overseas maybe. But I had no idea if that would even work. So I went online to do some research, and that's when I came across your ad."

"I see," Erasmo said. "What about last night? Why'd you call me like that?"

Leander rose from his chair and paced around the kitchen, taking gulps of Miller Lite every so often.

"I know what I'm about to say will sound crazy," he finally said, "but I swear it's what happened." He quickly drained the remaining contents of his beer and continued.

"Last night I was asleep, but I woke up to strange noises. And this time, the sounds weren't just creaking wood or soft whispers. I figured that this time Sandra was really coming to get me. I was so goddamn tired of being scared though. So, I decided to stop cowering in my bed, to stop putting off the inevitable, and accept my fate. I gathered up the little courage I had and came downstairs, but saw nothing."

Leander stopped pacing and shivered, his left eye now twitching at an alarming rate.

"Then I heard a sound in the living room. I walked toward it, and the closer I got, the surer I was."

"Sure of what?" Rat asked.

"Sure," Leander said, "that there was something in the house with me."

He scratched his right cheek, leaving crooked red welts on his skin.

"I flipped the light switch, but it didn't turn on. Thankfully, I keep a flashlight in one of the kitchen drawers. I walked back to the living room, waving the flashlight all around, trying to find whatever was making the noises. And then I finally saw it. I saw what was in the house with me."

Leander turned to the living room and stared, as if reliving the memory.

"At first, there were just brief glimpses of pink, darting around. But then it stopped, right in the path of the flashlight."

Leander shuffled toward the living room. Erasmo and Rat followed, giving each other an uneasy glance. When they entered, Leander turned to face them.

"I know this is going to sound insane, but it . . ."

Leander grimaced, as if the words sliced his tongue.

"It was a ballerina," he said. "A goddamn ballerina. She wore a pink leotard and a tutu shimmering in the dark. And she was dancing, right here in my living room, on her toes, spinning and twirling."

Leander then began to prance around the room, lurching as he pirouetted and twirled in the air. Loud thumps echoed through the house as he performed an array of off-balance leaps and pivots. Leander finally stopped when he completed an awkward landing in the center of the room, and curtsied, a plastic grin on his face. Erasmo's blood ran cold at this unabashed display of mental instability, and he desperately tried to get Rat's attention. But Rat was transfixed, his eyes never leaving Leander.

"That's just exactly how she did it," Leander said as his grin dissolved. "I was screaming so hard that I didn't even notice at first."

"Notice what?" Rat asked.

He turned to them, his face paper white. "The filth. She was covered in dirt and grime. Fat worms fell from her hair. They crawled all over her skin. And her teeth . . . they were black and rotting. But even in the dim light, I recognized her. It was Sandra Rosales, standing right here in my living room."

"Damn," Rat whispered.

"And that's when I ran outside and called you."

"But . . . why was she dressed as a ballerina?" Rat asked.

"Because," Erasmo said, "she was one. The stories about her all mentioned that Sandra had studied ballet since she was little." After Torres's visit, Erasmo had looked up every article he could find on the case.

"Maybe," Rat said, "it's also because ballet is what she loved most in life, so that's how she's choosing to present herself in death." Rat paused before adding, "Or maybe she just wanted to scare the shit out of you."

Erasmo shot Rat an aggravated look, which he either failed to notice or chose to ignore.

"So now what?" Leander asked. "Just wait for her to show? Or can you try to get rid of her now?"

"I was going to stay a few hours to see if she appeared, but after hearing your story, I don't think there's a need for that," Erasmo said.

"There isn't?"

"No. I can already tell you the following with absolute certainty: I'm not going to be able to remove Sandra's spirit."

"But . . . your ad said . . . well then what the hell are you doing here?"

"I'm not going to be able to chase her spirit away," Erasmo said, "because it's not in this house."

The muscles in Leander's face tensed, and a thick green vein bulged fitfully on his forehead.

"Bullshit!" he yelled. "I saw her!"

"Just give me some time to explain. Let's go upstairs for a minute. Please."

After a few moments of clenching and unclenching his jaw, Leander turned and trudged up the stairs. When they reached the landing, the three of them stood in a circle and stared at each other in silence.

"You said this was the exact spot where you felt her breath on the back of your neck."

"Yeah," Leander said. "I know what I felt, all right?"

"Look up."

Rat and Leander both directed their eyes to the ceiling, staring at it a few moments before dropping their gaze back to Erasmo.

"That doesn't mean anything," Leander said. "I know the difference between cold air from a vent and someone breathing on me. Besides, there were other signs of her."

"Like what? The shoes you tripped over? Look, I'm sure you'd agree that you weren't in a great state of mind that night. Your cousin had just murdered your date, and then you spent all day getting grilled by the cops. Isn't it possible that you came upstairs, took your shoes off, and accidentally left them here on the landing?"

Deep creases formed on Leander's forehead. "I . . . I guess that's possible . . . but what about the hotel room? What about here?"

"But what did you even see in the hotel room?" Erasmo asked. "Nothing. You said hands were clawing at your feet. But did you actually *see* her hands? We both know that you didn't. You feel terrible about what happened to Sandra, and it's messing with your head. It's no surprise that you think she's breathing on you, and grabbing at you, and trying to kill you. If anything, it would be surprising if you *weren't* having an extreme psychological reaction to what happened."

"But she was here. She was dancing. . . ."

"Do you know," Erasmo asked, "when most people claim to see something abnormal?"

Leander shook his head in small, spastic movements.

"It's almost always when they are either drifting off to sleep or waking up from it. What they believe they're seeing is just what you might think: a dream. Or a mixture of a dream and a half-conscious mind that isn't awake enough yet to interpret the world clearly. You were asleep before you came downstairs and saw the ballerina. Your head was clearly still filled with dreams and confused images. And what is it that you'd dream about? The answer is obvious."

"I don't know, man," Leander said. "It seemed *so* real. I'd swear on my life it happened."

"Look, you wanted my help, and *this* is me helping you. You've got big problems . . . too big to waste your time worrying about something that's only going on in your head."

Leander glanced around the room, confused. "I . . . I guess it could've been that way. Everything you're saying makes sense. I really want to believe it, but . . ."

"Tell you what," Erasmo said. "We'll stay up with you for a while, and you'll see that there's absolutely nothing to worry about."

"Okay," Leander said as he exhaled, nodding his head in short bursts. "Okay, that sounds good."

The three of them went back down to the kitchen, where Leander and Rat grabbed a few more beers. An initial awkward silence soon gave way to a steady stream of conversation, no doubt fueled by the alcohol. They talked about the Spurs' play-off chances, and whether Ben Affleck was a good Batman, and their favorite episodes of *Lost*, which they all loved immensely.

"You guys are really cool," said Leander, now on his fifth beer, red beginning to creep into the corners of his eyes. "If I ever get out of this mess, I hope we can hang out sometime."

Rat took this to heart, whipping out his phone and exchanging numbers with Leander, a round of fist bumps sealing the exchange.

As the night went on, Rat and Leander continued to put the beers away, both growing increasingly louder and red-faced as a good-natured argument broke out over who the best wrestler of all time was. This was soon followed by a demand from Rat that Erasmo referee an impromptu WWE match.

"Do you know all the WWE rules?" Leander asked, chuckling.

"Are you kidding?" Rat interjected, cocking his thumb at Erasmo. "This guy knows *everything* there is to know about wrestling. In fact, I've never met anyone who knew more."

Then, with no announcement, the match started. Rat bolted past Erasmo, his arms flailing as he chased Leander around the kitchen and into the living room. Rat jumped on Leander's back, attempting to put him in a choke hold.

"Oh my gosh, folks!" Rat narrated as his slender arms squirmed around Leander's neck. "The Honky Tonk Man is going to win again!"

Leander easily shrugged him off, sending Rat tumbling to the floor. "Wait!" Leander announced. "The Macho Man is not going down that easily!"

A drunken maelstrom of jumping and flailing raged through the house. Erasmo chased behind them, laughing with delight at their antics. After storming through the house several times, a sweaty and grinning Rat finally managed to corner Leander in the upstairs bedroom.

"Okay, ref, get ready," Rat said, brandishing an imaginary guitar. "I'm about to kabong the Macho Man." With that, he took a running start at Leander, who crouched by the bed. Leander attempted to catch him, but they both crashed to the floor in a heap. Leander grinned as he untangled himself from Rat and popped up.

"The Honky Tonk Man is down!" Leander announced. "The Macho Man is going to use his elbow strike!" Leander patted his elbow and prepared to take flight.

"Wait!" Erasmo yelled.

Rat, still on the floor, hadn't moved.

"You okay?" Erasmo asked.

Rat lay on his stomach, face turned toward the bed, completely still.

"Hey!" he yelled. "What's wrong?"

Erasmo looked over at Leander. The drunken redness in his face had drained, and he was now the color of chalk.

Erasmo's knees lit up with pain as he dropped to the floor to inspect Rat. His eyes were open but unmoving, and every muscle in his friend's face was slack. Saliva dripped from his mouth to the shiny oak floor underneath. Erasmo ignored his certainty that Rat's neck was broken and began to shake him.

"Get up!" he screamed.

Rat's body felt cold and limp, like a dead, lifeless dog.

"Call an ambulance!" Erasmo yelled.

Leander remained motionless, attempting to mouth something.

"It was an accident," Leander finally whispered. "I didn't mean to . . ."

Maybe, his desperate mind suggested, he'd landed on something that knocked the wind out of him. Erasmo grabbed Rat and turned him over. His friend's small body gave almost no resistance. Nothing at all lay underneath him though.

Erasmo reached into his pocket to call the ambulance himself and realized that his phone was downstairs. He began to get up, when without warning, his chest exploded in pain. Erasmo looked down and saw Rat's small fists pounding against him. Rat grabbed handfuls of Erasmo's shirt and pulled him down so close that their noses were almost touching.

"Don't leave," Rat whispered.

"What?" Erasmo asked, unsure if he misheard.

"Don't leave me here alone."

"Hey, man," Leander said from behind them, his voice trembling. "What's going on?"

"What happened?" Erasmo whispered to Rat. "You have to tell me. I don't understand."

It was then that he noticed Rat's eyes. They were flicking back and forth at a manic pace. He'd been trying to send a signal, but Erasmo hadn't been paying close enough attention. Rat's eyes were motioning for him to look. But where?

"The closet?" Erasmo whispered. "Did you see something in there?"

Rat shook his head slowly, tears now streaming down his face. He again motioned with his eyes. Not toward the closet. Toward the bed. No.

Under the bed.

His current angle didn't allow Erasmo a good view of whatever Rat was motioning to. It was nothing, he tried to assure himself. Rat had always frightened easily, almost always at threats that were completely imaginary. Still, he at least needed to take a look. Erasmo slid off Rat and slowly crawled over to the bed, his extremities shaking. He started to lower his head, but spasms of fear stopped him cold.

Erasmo cursed his cowardice under his breath. There was nothing under there, he assured himself again. There couldn't be. This situation bore none of the signs of a traditional haunting. There'd been no trauma suffered at this location, and there were no remains buried here either. As far as he knew, anyway. Erasmo inhaled deeply, until his lungs were stretched to their limit, and lowered his head to the floor.

Christ.

There *was* something. A figure. Crammed under the bed.

Erasmo's heart erupted, thrashing frantically, as if it were trying to rip itself apart. Every instinct in his body screamed for him to get up and run, but he resisted. He had to see.

"Hey, what are you looking at?" Leander asked, his voice raw and panicked.

Erasmo studied the figure, feeling his mind break free from its moorings. A distant voice in his head, his grandmother's, pleaded for him to run. But he couldn't pull his eyes away from the figure, away from the silhouette that shouldn't exist but did, away from the layers of sequined ruffles on her tutu, which somehow still managed to sparkle in the dim light.

And then, with a sluggish wriggle, the figure under the bed moved.

CHAPTER 10

"IT'S HER!" ERASMO screamed as he shot up from the floor. "She's here! Everyone get out!"

He grabbed Rat by his shirt and lifted him until his friend was upright and teetering on wobbly legs, like a newborn colt. The two of them stumbled out of the bedroom and down the stairs. After reaching the front yard, they saw Leander in the street, bent over and heaving.

Erasmo's legs loosened, as if they might dissolve into liquid at any moment. He collapsed onto the plush carpet of grass underneath him, feeling the prickly blades stab the side of his face. He inhaled the damp smell of the earth, its musty aroma filling his head. Violently shivering, he closed his eyes and wished for darkness, for ignorance, desperately wanting to push away every trace of what he'd just seen.

Leander had been right all along. There *was* something after him. An entity that was in the very house they'd just run out of. And it had moved. He'd seen that plainly with his own eyes.

But had it moved? Was he sure? Or had his adrenaline just played a trick on him? Now that he was safely outside, he couldn't be sure. But even if it hadn't moved, there'd been *something* under the bed, right?

Yes, there'd been something . . . but maybe not exactly what he had thought.

Erasmo opened his eyes and, summoning a reservoir of power he hadn't known existed, forced himself to rise from the ground. A part of him mourned having to give up the earth's tender comfort, but he had to know for sure.

He glanced over to see Rat and Leander in the middle of the street, hands on their knees, still catching their breath.

"Wait for me here," he said to Rat, and he turned back to the house.

"No!" Leander said, running onto the lawn. "Don't go in there. Something could happen to you!"

"Don't move!" Erasmo screamed at Leander.

His head was clearing now, the fog of terror parting slightly. He turned and ran through the front door, stopping when he reached the foot of the stairs. He looked up but heard and saw nothing.

As he ascended each step, Erasmo braced himself for what needed to be done, trying to summon the same strength that had propelled him off the lawn. He had to go through with this. He *needed* to know the truth. The floorboard beneath his foot creaked as he stepped off the last stair and onto the landing. Leander's bedroom door stood open, inviting him in. He accepted.

Erasmo stared at Leander's bed as he entered, the thought of what lay underneath sending chills coursing through his body. If Leander was right, and there was a spirit bent on vengeance in this house, Erasmo was about to have a very bad moment. And if Erasmo's suspicion was right, well, that was going to be pretty goddamn unpleasant too.

He walked over to the bed, lowered himself to his knees, and closed his eyes. After taking a deep, shaky breath, he slowly reached underneath with his left hand and felt around for whatever might be underneath the bed.

Nothing.

He reached even farther, but his trembling hand grasped only air. He slid his arm frantically in every direction, searching for something, anything.

He'd seen her, goddamn it! Had she left? Had she entered back into the walls of the house, preparing her vengeance? That was the only explanation. Leander was right! She was real and she was going to get them and she—

Then, without warning, Sandra's cold hand brushed against his fingertips. Erasmo shrieked, his jaw almost separating from the violent force his lungs expelled. He yanked his hand away, banging it on the bed frame. His body reflexively shot up from the floor, and Erasmo came very close to sprinting away.

But an insistent whisper in his head stopped him. He had to know.

Bracing himself, Erasmo dropped back to his knees, slowly reached underneath the bed, and found Sandra's hand again. This time, he caressed her cold skin and rigid bones and pulled with all his strength.

And then he saw the terrible truth.

Now Erasmo did allow himself to run, down the stairs, through the living room, and out into the cool night. He grabbed Rat and tried to tell him what he'd seen. But all he could manage was to point his finger at the house and breathlessly pant four words.

"Dead . . . girl . . . body . . . police."

Rat shook his head, face crumpling, and backed away from the house. "Don't say that, man. That's not true. That can't be true."

Erasmo glanced back at Leander, who was now staring at the house and slowly stepping backward. In a sudden burst, Leander turned and sprinted down the street, arms flailing wildly.

"Call the police!" Erasmo yelled.

His lungs burned as he gave chase and quickly gained on Leander. He wasn't going to let this asshole escape. Not after what he'd done. Erasmo closed his eyes and forced his shaking legs forward, hearing only his shoes slap against the pavement and the whistle of his own ragged breath. Now almost close enough to touch Leander, Erasmo leaped forward, arms outstretched. It wasn't until he opened his eyes and felt Leander's limp body underneath his, that Erasmo realized he'd been screaming as he gave chase, but what words he'd been shrieking had already evaporated from his thoughts, never to be remembered.

Torres's jacket billowed around her as she stood glaring at Erasmo, its thin fabric undulating in the night wind.

"Thanks for calling this in and asking for me," the detective said, hands shoved into her pockets. "But what the *hell* are you even doing here? I told you to stay away from him. Instead you're at his house in the middle of the night?"

Erasmo looked away, pretending to take an interest in the activity unfolding on Leander's front yard. Two uniformed SAPD officers stood near the front door, whispering and pointing over at Erasmo, while a burly mustachioed man carrying evidence bags of various sizes trudged toward a police van.

"Anytime you want to give me an answer would be great."

A gust of wind swirled around them and Erasmo shivered. He rubbed his hands together but couldn't seem to generate any warmth.

"I was trying to help him."

Torres rubbed her small, exasperated eyes, then reached into her jacket and pulled out her notebook. "Start from the beginning."

When Erasmo got home, he crept to his room and collapsed onto the bed, every ounce of energy wrung from his body. Despite his desperate attempts to push everything away and drift off into oblivion, persistent, unsettling questions still managed to seep in. Why the hell did Leander keep her body at his house? Did that sick asshole get off on knowing she lay underneath him while he slept? Why was she dressed like that? And why would he even take the risk of inviting them over?

Erasmo closed his eyes. Images of Sandra, which he'd been fiercely shoving down into his mind's dark reservoirs, trying to drown them, floated to the surface. Every detail was ingrained in his memory: her waxen face, the tangles of her onyx hair, each sparkling sequin against her gray skin. When he'd pulled her out from underneath the bed, Erasmo had been horrified to see her left eye gazing off into the corner, as if she couldn't stand the sight of him. Her right eye stared straight and true though, looking directly at him, inquisitive, as if wanting Erasmo to explain how she could have ended up in such a dreadful way.

More images from the evening flooded in. He saw Rat and his tiny frame motionless on the floor. He saw the look of sad confusion on Sandra's gray face. He saw Leander, running in the moonlight. These images floated together in the dark, bleeding into each other, becoming formless splotches and shadows, until somehow, thankfully, he drifted off to sleep.

CHAPTER 11

ERASMO SPENT THE next three days in bed, unsuccessfully trying to convince himself that finding a dead body stuffed under a lunatic's bed wasn't a big deal. His grandmother periodically checked on him, and he cringed when he heard the worry in her voice. She let him be though, and for that he was grateful.

He was sipping some milk and watching *Dr. Phil* when, surprisingly, his phone rang. He'd already spoken to Rat for the day. His friend, dealing with the situation much better than he was, had wanted to hang out. Erasmo was tempted, even swinging his feet out over the floor to get up. But his bed felt like a tar pit, its viscous tendrils insistently pulling him back down, until his body was right back where it started.

The number flashing on his phone wasn't one he recognized. After a fierce debate with himself, he decided to answer.

"Hey, Erasmo. That you? It's me, Billy . . . from the church."

He glared down at the phone, aggravated, as if it had betrayed him somehow.

"How'd you get my number?"

"Well," Billy said, "it took some digging, but you got yourself a unique name. Wasn't that hard."

"Great," Erasmo said. "You calling to yell at me some more?"

"Bud, look . . . sorry I got so upset that day. I really didn't mean anything by it. It's just that this is important to me. I'm trying to help folks that might get hurt."

"It's a bad time right now, Billy."

"Well, make it a good time. This is something you'll want to see."

"Look," Erasmo said, trying to sound forceful, "not one thing about our last meeting made me want to see you again."

Billy exhaled a long, aggrieved sigh.

"Tonight, a teenage kid on the west side is going to get jumped and beaten. If he's not dead when it's over, then it'll be as close as you can get. I'm going to try to stop it, and I want you there so you can see for yourself."

"What . . . ?" Erasmo asked. "You saw this in a *vision?*"

"Yeah, bud, sure did."

"I can't—"

"It's one night, Erasmo. Just come out and see. Then you can decide if you want to vouch for me or not. I need help breaking up the fight anyway. There're going to be three of those sons a bitches beating on this kid. Plus, I have a hundred bucks I can give you just for coming along."

Erasmo knew that he should just say no and hang up the phone. But a perverse, growing curiosity didn't allow him to. The "what if?" questions gnawed at his gut. What if, despite all signs to the contrary, Billy could do what he said? What if this fantastical ability somehow resided in the least likely of hosts? If there was even the tiniest chance that this was true, wasn't it worth an hour of his time?

It had been three days since he'd left his room other than to go to the kitchen or the bathroom. Perhaps this was a good reason to get out of bed, to show himself that he was okay, that he could stop being afraid now.

And the money. He still needed the goddamn money.

Reflecting back on this much later, Erasmo came to under-stand that he'd still been very much in shock from the events at Leander's. He'd been in no shape to make any decisions. No good ones anyway.

The headlights of Billy's decrepit Ford Ranger splashed over Erasmo and Rat as they stood waiting in the empty Boneheadz parking lot. Billy exited his truck and strode toward them, his angular face tense and rigid, as if it were composed of granite instead of flesh and bone.

"Let's go," Billy said, hands shoved deep into the pockets of the same drab canvas jacket he'd worn the first time they'd met. "Don't want to miss nothin'."

Immediately upon setting eyes on Billy, a sense of unease had fluttered in Erasmo's belly. He'd been thinking of this expe-dition as a distraction from his current state of affairs, a game almost. But Billy's expression suggested that he was not mess-ing around tonight. Not one damn bit.

He saw a muscle twitch in Rat's face and wondered if perhaps his friend wasn't feeling so great about this anymore either. Erasmo picked up his old blue JanSport and slung it over his shoulder. He'd brought along a notebook and a few other items, just in case.

Billy insisted that they all ride together in his Ranger. Erasmo reluctantly agreed, but this only fed his growing sense of unease. The three of them piled into the cabin, which stunk of aged sweat. Crumpled fast food bags and empty soda cans covered the truck's floor. The cans and bags swayed and fell around Erasmo's feet as Billy sped out of the parking lot.

"I haven't been this excited in a while," Billy said, sullenly glancing at the rearview mirror. He turned his cold, stony gaze back to the road, his hands turning white from their death grip on the steering wheel. "In fact, it's safe to say that I can barely contain myself."

The three of them sat in an uncomfortable silence as Billy drove them deep into the bowels of the west side. Erasmo was not particularly familiar with this stretch of Commerce Street, which he knew would soon turn into Old Highway 90. After a few minutes, Billy turned left on 40th. The Ranger then meandered down a few streets that Erasmo had never heard of—Eldridge, Guthrie, and a few others—until Billy finally turned and pulled over in front of an empty lot.

"We're here," he said, opening his door.

"Wait!" Erasmo blurted out. The neighborhood had about as many vacant lots as it did houses, giving the street a deserted feel. If there was any trouble, not many neighbors would be around to intervene. "Are you sure this is it?"

"Get out of the truck," Billy commanded.

"I don't know," Rat said. "It doesn't look very—"

"Just get the hell out!" Billy yelled as he exited the Ranger.

Screw it, Erasmo thought. They'd already come this far. He opened the truck's door and stepped out into the quiet street. Rat followed behind wordlessly, eyes tense and alert.

"Prepare yourselves," Billy said, raising his arms to the sky. "You're about to see the hand of God."

It was quickly becoming unfathomable to Erasmo why he'd agreed to this. He reached into his backpack and took out the notebook and pen. He hoped that they'd give the questions he was about to ask less of a *you are completely batshit* vibe.

"How do you know this is where the boy will get jumped?" Erasmo asked.

Billy stifled a smile, seeming to be pleased with this question. "When I saw the vision, I knew *right* away it'd go down here, and I've never even set foot in this part of town. That's part of the vision, knowing . . . feeling . . . where it's going to happen."

"And you feel *when* it's going to happen too?" Erasmo asked. "Most of the literature I've read on precognitives says that the *when* is the most difficult component of a vision to decipher."

"I don't always get the exact day," Billy said, scrunching up the right side of his face, "but this time I did. Not the precise time, though. So let's find a place to settle in, fellas. It might be a little bit before he shows."

Erasmo checked his watch: 8:30 p.m.

"We need a good place to take cover," Billy said, scanning the area. "That way, we can keep a lookout for the kid without getting jumped ourselves."

Meandering around an unlit, deserted street seemed like a bad idea, but Erasmo was at a loss for better suggestions.

"The kid comes from that way," Billy said, pointing east. "Let's head in that direction."

The three of them trudged down the desolate neighborhood, Billy leading the way. "So what are we going to do when we see the kid?" Erasmo asked. "Just tell him to get the hell out of here?"

"Basically," Billy replied. "Tell him it's dangerous and that he should leave. Threaten him if we have to."

"But," Rat said, "if we see some random guy walking and tell him to leave, and he does, how do we know for sure that we actually prevented anything?"

Billy squinted and glanced up at the cloudless night sky, as if he were communing with God that very moment. "This kid is going to be wearing jeans, red shoes, and a green Adidas jacket with white piping on the sleeves."

"Are all your visions," Erasmo asked, "that specific or—"

"Hey," Rat said, squinting into the dark stretch of road ahead of them. "I think someone is coming."

Erasmo scanned the area for movement but saw only pockets of trash and overgrown weeds. He was about to turn away when a massive shadow emerged from the darkness. He watched the dim figure take large, plodding steps toward them.

"Is that him?" Erasmo asked, not liking the panic he heard in his voice. "Is that the kid you saw?"

Billy focused his eyes on the large silhouette in the distance. "I'm not sure. I can't see him very well. . . ."

"I think he's holding something," Rat said.

He was right. It looked like the person approaching them had a freakishly long left arm that hung all the way down to his ankle. As the long-armed person drew closer, Erasmo saw that it was something much more frightening than an elongated arm. The brute walking toward them was holding a baseball bat.

"Let's go," Erasmo said. "That's not your guy, Billy. He's heading straight for us and he's got a bat. We need to leave . . . now!"

"No, wait," Billy said. "I . . ."

Then Erasmo saw a flicker of . . . something . . . in Billy's eyes. Just for a second, but there all the same.

"Let's get the hell out of here," Billy finally said. His words hung in the air for a moment, and then, in unison, the three of them sprinted toward the Ranger. Risking a glance back, Erasmo saw the large man still proceeding toward them, but at a leisurely pace, as if he were a parent who knew his children wouldn't wander too far off.

Erasmo ran faster, his heart thrumming. As the three of them approached the Ranger, he felt an immense wave of relief. But he'd been so intent on getting away, that he hadn't paid any attention to what was waiting for them.

"Wait!" Rat yelled. He pointed his scrawny finger at the Ranger. Erasmo slowed to a jog, panting heavily. He looked around but saw only the truck.

Then, a flicker in the dark landscape.

The cabin. Someone was in the cabin of the Ranger.

Erasmo saw this person clearly now, even though the truck's windshield was caked with grime. The intruder's hair was coarse and black, forming a dense helmet that culminated in a sharp widow's peak on his broad forehead, and a stubby misshapen nose sat snoutlike in the middle of his face. Erasmo stopped cold, unable to take his eyes off the man lounging behind the driver's seat, who sat with both hands on the steering wheel, displaying a wide, crooked grin.

"Shit," Erasmo said under his breath. He glanced over and saw Billy and Rat staring at the truck as well, their eyes large with shock.

Before he knew what was coming out of his mouth, Erasmo asked the obvious question.

"Is this them? Are these the guys that are supposed to jump the kid?"

Billy continued to stare at the truck, unable to pull his eyes away. "Yes," he whispered, "but . . ."

"What?" Rat and Erasmo asked at the same time.

"There's supposed to be one more. . . ."

As if on cue, a gangly wisp of a young man unfolded himself out of the bed of the truck and onto the street. His white T-shirt was too short, barely reaching the waist of his dark blue jeans. He was so tall and spindly, that if his head were just a bit rounder, he could almost pass for Jack Skellington, the Pumpkin King.

They turned around to find their hulking, bat-wielding pursuer now much closer. Erasmo saw that he wore no shirt, and had hairless, milky skin bursting with layers of knotty muscle.

In a flash, the three menacing figures formed a circle around them. Erasmo's heart thrashed, as if it were desperately trying to burst out of his chest and be free of this horrible situation. He curled his hands into fists but didn't even feel strong enough to push them through the warm night air, much less inflict damage with them.

Erasmo turned to see that Rat was faring much better than he was. His friend was moving around on the balls of his feet, shimmying his shoulders, loosening up. He'd gotten into so many scrapes at school, Erasmo knew that Rat was no longer afraid of getting hit, the only possible benefit of the constant bullying he'd endured. Rat's eyes were focused, staring at the Pumpkin King, the one he evidently was going to have a go at. Billy looked fairly calm as well, sizing up the behemoth holding the bat. Erasmo could see Billy turning things over in his head, trying to decide what to do.

"Hey there," Billy finally said.

The shirtless man with the bat looked at the three of them, silently shifting his gaze from one to the other, as if attempting to memorize their faces for reflection later on. His hair was coarse, cinnamon-colored, and cropped close to his wide skull. Every feature was flat, as if his face was made of dough and had recently been struck by a two-by-four. His eyes finally settled on Billy and expanded until they were unnaturally wide.

"The hell did you say . . . *bitch*?"

Erasmo's legs wavered. There was going to be a beating all right, but not of some kid.

His question must've been a rhetorical one, because the Goliath didn't wait for an answer. He raised the bat slowly, until it was over his right, brawny shoulder. Erasmo saw that beautiful grain patterns permeated the wood. He also noticed, with great alarm, that the bat bore maroon blotches up and down its barrel.

"Wait," Billy said. "You don't want to do that. We're just here to help a—"

"You goddamn *stupid* ass," the man said, spittle flying from his mouth. "Don't you see what's going on here? Gimme your wallets. And the keys to the truck."

Nobody moved.

"Give them to me!"

"Leave us alone," Billy said.

Erasmo held his breath. This was it.

"Yeah," Rat said defiantly. "Leave us alone, asshole."

Erasmo watched in horror as the brute took three plodding steps toward Rat, and then viciously swung the bat into his friend's left shoulder. Rat shrieked and crumpled to the ground, his slight frame making almost no sound as it hit the asphalt.

Bracing for an attack, Erasmo turned his eyes to Widow's Peak, who stood just feet away. But Widow's Peak didn't move, instead watching with interest as Rat writhed on the ground. Now that he was outside the cabin of the Ranger, Erasmo saw that Widow's Peak wasn't very tall, and was overweight, with a tapestry of intricate tattoos covering his beefy arms.

"Yeah, Jackie!" the Pumpkin King said. "Get that small son of a bitch."

Jackie. The bat-man's name was Jackie.

"Little guy like you ought to have a smaller mouth," Jackie said. "But you got a big one, don't you? How about I make it even bigger then?"

Jackie flipped his grip on the bat, now holding it by the fat end. He placed his left foot on Rat's chest to hold him still. "Open wide, you little puto." Jackie caressed the knob of the bat against Rat's closed lips, seeking entry. "No? That's okay. . . . I like it better when I have to shove it in anyway."

Jackie pressed down hard, the knob now smashed against Rat's mouth. Rat tried to shove the bat away, but he wasn't strong enough to budge it. His lips turned purple from the pressure, and his screams were reduced to muffled squeals.

Blood. There was blood now. Rat's lips had given way. His teeth were next.

"Stop!" Erasmo screamed, but Jackie did no such thing. He was going to have to take on this monster. Right goddamn now. Erasmo took a step toward Jackie, when a blur on his right jittered past. It took a moment to realize that the blur had been Billy, who was now standing directly behind Jackie, staring at his broad back.

"Hey," Billy said, addressing Jackie's bursting trapezius muscles.

Jackie eased the bat off Rat's mouth and turned to Billy. He looked down at him in annoyance, aggravated at the interruption.

"I told you to leave us alone," Billy said as he reached into his jacket.

Without looking, Jackie flipped his bat in the air and caught it by the handle in one smooth motion. He adjusted his hands, swung back, and . . . did nothing.

Jackie's eyes, which had bulged out in anticipation of decapitating Billy, deflated back to their normal size. The bat trembled, then gently drifted down from its menacing position until the top of its barrel scraped the ground. Jackie seemed to have trouble standing, now leaning on the bat to keep his massive body upright.

It took Erasmo several moments before he noticed the large, crimson slit in the middle of Jackie's stomach. Erasmo turned his eyes to Billy, who stood with his mouth hung open, as if he were surprised that the massive hunter's knife in his hand had actually performed its function. Billy's look of shock quickly gave way to a savage grin, and he then pounced, shoving Jackie to the ground and stabbing him repeatedly, his arm jerking up and down in a relentless staccato burst. Billy's stringy, straw-colored hair hung down around his face as he tore holes in Jackie's chest and stomach. Jackie's massive arms flailed, but struck only air, and his mouth began to make wet, unintelligible sounds. This must have gone on for only a few seconds, but to Erasmo it seemed as if it would never end.

Finally, the Pumpkin King took three long strides and reached Billy in a flash. He raised his long right leg and kicked Billy square in his chest, knocking him off Jackie and onto the street.

Erasmo never heard Widow's Peak make his move. By the time he registered anything was even happening, the world had turned sideways, and the right side of his face was shoved into freshly paved asphalt. Erasmo sucked in the smell of black tar, opening his eyes in time to see Widow's Peak standing over him, his right foot raised.

Widow's Peak's left foot, just inches from Erasmo's face, had on an untied, dazzlingly white Adidas tennis shoe. In that split second, Erasmo marveled at the balls it must take to knowingly walk into a fight with untied shoes. But then Widow's Peak ended that train of thought by bringing his right foot down and stomping Erasmo's head into the ground, causing a sudden and excruciating explosion of pain.

Tiny fissures erupted on the side of Erasmo's face as his flesh scraped against asphalt. He rolled over onto his back, trying to hold his hands up to deflect the next kick that was surely coming, but he couldn't manage even this. His forehead and nose suddenly compressed as Widow's Peak's pristine Adidas now came down squarely on his face.

A swirling constellation of blacks and blues erupted in his field of vision, and sharp stabs of pain penetrated the back of his head. He sucked desperately at the air around him but was unable to draw a meaningful breath. The world lost focus, and just as he was about to drift away into darkness, Erasmo heard a collision above him. Grunts and screams filled his ears, and then two bodies tumbled on top of him, flailing at each other. He felt a small, insubstantial figure wriggling over his body.

Rat.

Even though Rat's shoulder had to almost certainly be broken, Erasmo opened his eyes to see his friend wrestling Widow's Peak, trying to pin him down. Rat's face was a convulsing mask of agony and determination, tears streaking down his face.

"You made a big mistake, asshole," Billy said from behind him.

Erasmo turned to see Billy and the Pumpkin King locked in a circular dance, each one waiting for the other to make a move. Billy held his large, bloody knife out in front of him. The Pumpkin King had no weapon of any kind, but he didn't seem concerned about this in the slightest. Behind them lay Jackie, his massive body blood-soaked and lifeless.

A shriek. Erasmo turned back to see Widow's Peak now straddling Rat, pummeling him, his fists hammering Rat's face and shoulder.

He tried to get up and help, but his legs felt like water balloons. After a few more attempts, Erasmo finally managed to stand, wobbling around a bit before gaining his balance. He glanced around, searching for the bat, but then saw it trapped underneath Jackie's enormous body. Erasmo scanned the area for something else to hit Widow's Peak with . . . a bottle, a rock, a goddamn stick even.

Nothing. He saw nothing. He saw . . . his backpack. Fifteen feet away, behind where Billy and the Pumpkin King were still circling each other, each one tense and ready to explode. His legs wavered as he ran toward the backpack, the street lurching from left to right, as if he were on a suspect ship in the middle of a windstorm.

After several near-collapses, he finally reached the backpack. As Erasmo fumbled with the zipper, another of Rat's mournful cries reached his ears. He managed to get the bag open and shoved his arm inside. A pen, a charger, a notebook . . . where the *hell* was it?

Then his fingertips grazed slick, cool metal. Thank God. He wrapped his hand around the item and ran back, his legs still floundering underneath him. He approached from behind as Widow's Peak bent down and whispered into Rat's ear.

"When I'm done," he hissed, "you'll wish you were never born." He rose from Rat's body, brushing dirt off his jeans. "I'll be back when I finish off your two weak-ass friends."

Erasmo flipped the top of the cylinder open. He'd originally bought it for his grandmother. She had a bad habit of walking to the corner store to save on gas, even though he'd warned her repeatedly that it wasn't safe. He tried to wait until Widow's Peak turned around completely, hoping to spray it into his hateful eyes, but Erasmo panicked and missed, hitting the side of Widow's Peak's head instead.

"Son of a—" He rushed Erasmo and tackled him to the ground, trying to grab the canister away. For once though, a bit of luck was on his side. For just a second, the nozzle pointed directly at Widow's Peak's pockmarked face. Erasmo pressed down, and a glistening stream flew from the nozzle directly onto Widow's Peak's nose and forehead. He made a strangled gasp and fell off Erasmo and onto his back, wiping furiously at his face as hacking coughs erupted from his mouth.

Erasmo shot up and ran over to his friend. "Are you okay?" he asked, peering down. "Can you move?"

Rat nodded and slowly extended his right hand. Erasmo took it and pulled his friend up. He was about to lead Rat back to the Ranger, when a strangled grunt arose from behind them.

Erasmo turned, scanning the area where Billy and the Pumpkin King had been circling each other, but they were gone. No. Not gone. They were on the ground.

And Billy was killing the Pumpkin King.

There were already at least four stab wounds that Erasmo could see, and Billy's right arm was raised, about to inflict another one.

"Billy!" Erasmo yelled, running to him. "C'mon, let's get the hell out of here!"

Billy either didn't hear him, or didn't want to leave, because his response was to bring the knife down directly into the Pumpkin King's gut. A wheeze escaped from the King's mouth, along with a spray of blood. He raised his gangly arms to fend off Billy, but they flailed aimlessly, as if they were twigs thrashing in a violent maelstrom. Despite the Pumpkin King's current butchered state, Erasmo was still surprised when the dying man began to sob, his quivering lips pulling back to reveal small, perfect teeth.

Erasmo reached Billy and grabbed hold of his arm. "Stop! You're killing him! We need to get out of here before someone—"

But Billy shoved Erasmo away, hard enough to make him fall backward and land on his ass. Billy ran his fingers through his hair, tucking a sweep of it behind his left ear, and raised the knife again.

"Please," the King gurgled through the blood in his mouth. "We weren't going to hurt you. We were just—"

Billy punched him in the face, preventing the King from finishing his thought. Billy's thumb caressed the knife's black handle before raising it once again and bringing it down into the King's blood-soaked sternum.

"Billy!" Erasmo screamed. "What the hell are you doing?" He rose unsteadily, about to move toward Billy again, when he realized the canister of pepper spray was still in his hand. He placed his finger on the nozzle, aimed it at Billy, and was about to press down. But then . . . something miraculous occurred.

A voice floated in from the darkness.

"Hey . . . are you guys okay?"

A lithe silhouette glided toward them.

Billy turned away from the King, his face streaked with blood, and addressed the approaching figure.

"We're fine," Billy said. "These guys jumped us, so we had to protect ourselves."

"Okay," the voice said. "I heard all the fighting so called the cops. They'll be here any minute."

Billy and Erasmo exchanged a glance, and then both nodded in silent agreement. Erasmo walked over to Rat, grabbed his good arm, and led him to the Ranger. Billy rose from the Pumpkin King and followed, sheathing the bloody knife inside his jacket.

"Hey, aren't you guys going to wait for the cops?" the voice asked.

Erasmo helped Rat into the cab, being careful not to touch his bad arm, while Billy slid into the driver's seat and started the engine. He pulled the Ranger forward slowly, the crackling static of tires against asphalt filling the cab.

Erasmo glanced around but couldn't find the Good Samaritan. Perhaps he ran away. Which, surveying the scene,

Erasmo couldn't blame him for. His stomach dropped at the Samaritan's absence, out of disappointment or relief he couldn't say.

But then, the Samaritan was suddenly there, appearing out of the darkness on their right as the truck rolled forward. The three of them stared at the Samaritan, turning their necks in unison to keep their eyes on him as they passed.

The boy looked confused, his green Adidas jacket fluttering in the wind as he studied the three passing men. He must have been frightened when he saw them staring back, their eyes wide, because the boy slowly backed away from the truck as it rolled by, his crimson shoes flashing in the muted light.

CHAPTER 12

ERASMO DIDN'T FIND out the truth about his parents until he was fourteen. His Uncle Javier, with a steady stream of blood-freezing statements, had finally told him what no one else could ever bring themselves to.

The fact that it was his uncle who'd divulged the information he'd sought for his entire life was somewhat surprising. In general, Erasmo had always tried to avoid his uncle, as Javier clearly detested him. It sure seemed like that, at least. A frigid, tense look passed over Javier's face whenever Erasmo walked into the room, his uncle's eyes gliding right over him as if he weren't even there.

He never lost too much sleep over his uncle's lack of warmth toward him, though. Erasmo honestly didn't have much to say to him either. Back then, when Erasmo's grandfather was still alive, Javier used to come by every Sunday. During these weekly visits, Erasmo always hid in his room, silent, not wanting to experience another of his uncle's contemptuous looks.

Because of their uncomfortable relationship, Uncle Javier wasn't exactly the person Erasmo wanted to turn to for answers. But too much time had gone by, too many questions had gone unanswered. It seemed like each year of his short life had brought a new and terrible understanding of his situation. Like in kindergarten, when he'd been shocked to find that not everyone was being raised by their grandparents . . . that, in fact, it was quite a strange arrangement according to other kids. Or when he was ten, and it had occurred to him for the first time that his beloved grandparents might be lying when they said they didn't know the whereabouts of his parents, and why they'd never been around.

So, at fourteen, after years of dodges and deflections from his grandparents, he was desperate for the truth. And since it seemed like his uncle didn't give one shit about sparing his feelings, he thought that Javier might be apt to just come out with it. And if his uncle didn't want to talk about Mauro Cruz, well . . . that was too goddamn bad.

After much internal debate, Erasmo decided this confrontation should take place at his uncle's house. He didn't want his grandparents interrupting, and he certainly didn't want Javier to hold anything back, which he might do if they were around.

So, on an overcast Saturday morning, Erasmo announced he was going over to his buddy Martin's house. He spent a lot of time there, so he was fairly certain nothing about this would arouse suspicion. Erasmo stood in Martin's driveway and waved goodbye as his grandfather's truck drove away, the rusted F-150 producing a dissonant symphony of creaks and squeals as it lurched down the road. When he could no longer see the truck, Erasmo turned and began the walk to his uncle's, which was only six blocks away.

He spent most of the walk attempting to sooth his blistering nerves. Erasmo had never dropped in on his uncle like this before and was braced for any conceivable reaction. Hostility, annoyance, ambivalence—everything was on the table. But it didn't matter. He was not going to leave without an answer.

His uncle lived in a small corner house that he rented, its exterior covered with peeling, avocado-green paint. Erasmo's pulse accelerated as he approached it. The maroon Ford Taurus his uncle owned was parked at an odd angle in the driveway, its windshield coated with a murky film of tree sap. His legs trembled as he walked through the overgrown yard and up the cracked stairs to the porch.

The front door loomed over him, its stripped, ashy wood daring him to knock on it. His heart refused to slow and, in fact, thrashed in his chest even more violently than before. Erasmo inhaled deeply, sweet oxygen flooding his brain.

"You have to do this," he whispered to himself. "You have to."

His heart slowed, but just a little. He could do this. He was going to do this. He—

Click. Before Erasmo fully realized what was happening, the door cracked ajar and then slowly swung open.

His Uncle Javier, who by all accounts looked exactly like Erasmo's father, stood in the doorway, puffy-faced and unshaven. His eyes were inflamed, and multiple foul odors from last night's festivities wafted from him. His uncle stood there and looked him over, as if Erasmo were someone he'd never seen before. Javier then sighed and gazed over Erasmo's head, as if he were addressing someone standing behind him.

"Thought this might happen one day," his uncle said, eyes slowly blinking. "I . . . I didn't know when you'd be ready. Come in."

Erasmo walked into his uncle's house and, when he emerged ten minutes later, was no longer the same person. He stumbled through the front yard, his gut a lurching mass of spasms. Before he could even make it to the street, his stomach clenched violently, expelling all of its contents. Acid scorched his throat, and the stench was horrible, but somehow the stink felt appropriate on him.

Erasmo plodded up the street, clumpy strings of pink liquid hanging from his mouth, and managed a small, gurgling laugh. He had always been so sure that the answers he'd sought would free him. The joke, as usual, was on him.

Even though Uncle Javier had not spoken for very long, he'd answered every question Erasmo had about his father. Erasmo was overwhelmed with the sensation that what he'd learned in those few minutes was too massive to fit safely inside his head. As he stumbled home, his temples felt as if they were bulging outward from the strain of containing everything he'd ever wanted to know about Mauro Cruz.

As the three of them fled in Billy's Ranger, Erasmo's head again burst at its seams with an overload of terrifying, disorienting information, reminding him very much of that terrible morning at his uncle's. Erasmo wasn't sure what he was more in disbelief of. That two of their attackers were in all likelihood dead, or the fact that they were now running from the scene. Getting away as quickly as possible had seemed like the obvious thing to do, but the farther they drove, the more his brain began to function again. They were leaving the scene of a murder. No . . . it's not murder if it's self-defense, right? They just had to tell the police what happened. That kid had shown up, and he could tell the cops. . . .

His chest clenched. The kid got a good look at them and could give the police their descriptions. *And* he'd seen the truck. Shit, for all they knew, he could've taken a picture of the Ranger's license plate. The cops were about to be greeted by two dead bodies and the news that three suspects had left the scene. Suspects they'd undoubtedly be searching for.

"We have to go back," Erasmo whispered.

Billy stared forward wordlessly as he drove, while Rat's eyes remained glassy and distant.

"We have to go back!" he yelled.

"No," Billy said, his dispassionate eyes remaining fixed on the road.

"We have to!" Erasmo said. "Those guys could be dead! Look . . . it was clearly self-defense. But if we run, it looks like we did something wrong. The police—"

"No," Billy said. "They were just a couple of bangers. The cops won't look too hard."

"It's not only your decision," Erasmo said, trying to stave off full-blown panic. "Me and Rat—"

"You and Rat nothing. *I* did most of the work saving us, so *I* say if we go back or not. And I say we don't."

"But—"

"Rat here knows what's up—don't you, Rat?" Billy said. "Let's ask him. Do you want to go back and talk to the cops?"

Erasmo wasn't sure Rat would even be able to respond. His skin was as pale as his dark skin would allow, and he gingerly held his right shoulder, as if he were afraid it would fall right off if he let it go.

"Hell no," Rat said with surprising strength.

"Well, that settles it," Billy said. A streetlamp cast warped ovals of light on Billy's blood-streaked face as the truck turned onto Culebra. "Besides, I think I've proven now that you should listen to me. The boy was there, just like I said he'd be. You can no longer deny that I'm doing the Lord's work."

There it was, the other unsettling development that didn't quite want to fit inside Erasmo's brain. The undeniable reality of this boy's existence remained protruding from the top of his skull, as if it were unruly straw bursting from the top of a scarecrow's ravaged head.

As they drove, Erasmo felt the adrenaline slowly drain from his cells. His limbs now felt as if they were barely attached to his body, and he was genuinely unsure if he could make them do anything at all.

"Just take us back to my car," Erasmo said, barely able to hear his own words.

And Billy did just that.

Erasmo drove Rat straight from the parking lot to University Hospital. The doctor who examined him, a hefty Indian gentleman, explained that Rat had suffered a nondisplaced fracture of his humerus and prescribed some hydrocodone. The doctor flashed a suspicious look when they explained that Rat fell off a ladder. But he looked exhausted and didn't seem to really care how Rat got his arm all mangled up.

"Try not to fall off any more goddamn ladders," the scowling doctor said as he tucked Rat's arm into a sling.

After dropping Rat off and finally getting home, he tiptoed into his grandmother's room. Erasmo was alarmed to find her shivering, even though she was buried under blankets. He grabbed a quilt from the closet and added it to the mound already covering her. Erasmo sat on the bed, stroking his grandmother's hair, until she finally stopped shivering. He then tiptoed to his room and collapsed onto the bed, immediately falling under.

Erasmo woke the next morning still feeling sluggish and hazy but immediately pulled down *A Practical Guide to the Supernatural and Paranormal* and found the chapter he was looking for. He still didn't believe that Billy was a seer but wanted to read Dubois's thoughts on the subject.

On the Power to Foretell the Future

After the death of my daughter, I desperately wished that I had known well beforehand that one day she'd fall ill. Then, I could have done everything within my power to try and change her tragic destiny. The ability to see beyond time is truly the ability to bestow life and death itself. As such, I set out to find individuals who possess this remarkable power.

Unfortunately, sorting the crystal-ball-gazing charlatans from the truly gifted is of utmost difficulty. The vast majority of supposed precognitives are simply attention- and money-seeking fakes. There are no valid methodologies to ascertain if an individual has this ability other than the most obvious: if their predictions indeed come true.

Throughout history, there have been many who have claimed the power to prophesize, but few who could. Even the famous prognosticator, Nostradamus's supposed success at predicting future events is a deception . . . one conjured by his vague proclamations and deliberate misinterpretations by translators of his work.

Perhaps the only true prophets to walk this earth are described in the Bible. God himself spoke to them, and they in turn spoke for him. But any person who claims to hear God's word in the present day would surely be thought mad. As they should be, for who would truly be worthy of hearing His divine words?

I myself experienced this inability to tell fact from fiction. I heard whispers of a self-professed seer in a small Greek village offering his services for a modest price. I traveled there and, after inquiring about him, was immediately ushered by reverential locals to his small abode. A teenage boy opened the door, held his hand out, and gave his price. I placed the amount in his palm, and he then

studied my face and said the following: "You wish to com-
municate with that which you should not. This is a fool's
journey you have embarked on. The only thing you will
find is your own untimely death."

His words at first shook me to the core. But, as I stood
there considering the situation, I realized that he had gone
back inside with the money and had left me with nothing
but unprovable words. I won't know if this teenage boy
can truly foretell the future until I learn the manner of my
own death, a truly grotesque thought indeed. As such, the
only words I can offer on this topic, obvious as they may
be, are simply this: Be wary of those claiming to know the
unknowable.

Erasmo sighed and placed the book back on its shelf, wondering what had become of the mysterious Greek boy. He
apprehensively turned on the television and spent the rest of the
day monitoring every local channel. In a state of near-constant
panic, he was certain that at any moment a breaking news
flash was going to announce a manhunt for three suspects in
a double murder. Finally, KSAT 12 ran a story on their 5 p.m.
broadcast about a stabbing on the west side of town. Erasmo's
heart leaped as he saw footage from the scene and recognized it
immediately. The reporter mentioned how neighbors had heard
screaming, and then solemnly gave the names of two victims,
but it was her last statement that left Erasmo dumbfounded.

"Both stabbing victims are in critical condition but
expected to fully recover."

He stood in front of his small television, shaking wildly
with relief. They hadn't died. And there was no mention of any
suspects. Was it really possible that everything would be okay?
He grabbed his phone to share the news with Rat and was terribly disappointed when the call went straight to voicemail.

Over the course of the next week, Erasmo suffered from terrible nightmares and spent most of his time curled up in bed. He periodically called Rat to check on him, but his friend never answered and hadn't returned any messages. While this concerned him, it was completely understandable. Not only was Rat in substantial pain and doped up from the medication, but also it must hurt like hell for him to talk with those busted-up lips. Erasmo decided to stop calling for a while and give Rat some time to heal.

But on the tenth day with no contact, as late afternoon gave way to early evening, Erasmo's worry built to an unbearable level. His instincts continued to tell him that Rat just needed time to recover from the trauma. People like them just weren't cut out for this sort of thing. But still . . . ten days and not a word from him. He decided it wouldn't hurt to take a drive to Rat's and check in, just to be sure.

He gulped down two glasses of milk and then showered, instantly feeling less like a zombie once the scalding water hit his skin. Erasmo sucked in the rising steam, feeling its warmth spread through his nose and settle into his lungs. As he stood under the showerhead, enjoying the fat drops of water pelting his face, it was hard not to feel a bit better.

While the memories of their assault still deeply unsettled him, the truth was that no permanent damage had been done. The three of them were involved in a brutal fight, that was true. But everyone involved was either okay or would be soon. He suspected he'd still be having nightmares for a long while, but it could've been a lot worse.

Erasmo dressed and stepped outside for the first time in over a week. The sun descended into a sky suffused with gray, somber light. Walking to the Civic, he was surprised at how good it felt to be out of the house, to have somewhere to go.

He spent most of the ride over desperately hoping that Rat would be home, and that his mother wouldn't be. Elisia Martinez had always been cordial to him, but Jesus was she harsh with Rat. Ms. Martinez was a tiny woman, and Erasmo often wondered how so much ill temper could be contained in such a small frame. She was always on Rat for one thing or another. And Ms. Martinez didn't give a damn if there was anyone around to witness her withering assaults on Rat either. Erasmo always left their house wishing that she'd make more of an effort to hide her disappointment with how her son had turned out.

Since his father wasn't around, Rat had to endure the full force of his mother's rages all by himself. Erasmo had attempted to bring up the subject of Rat's father a few times over the years, but he'd always been politely shut down. In fact, Erasmo could not recall one instance in which Rat had mentioned his father, even in passing. For his part, Rat never once asked about Erasmo's own uncomfortable parental situation. Erasmo had always found it odd, since this seemed like a topic they'd naturally bond over. But he also instinctively understood that, sometimes, acknowledged but silent suffering was better for a friendship.

The Civic shuddered as it jerked to a stop, still several houses away from Rat's. The blue Corolla Ms. Martinez drove was nowhere to be seen. But strangely, there was another car sitting in the driveway: a black, glistening Nissan Maxima.

One of Rat's relatives? Didn't seem likely. Was someone visiting? That couldn't be it, since Ms. Martinez wasn't even home. Could someone be visiting Rat? Even more unlikely, as Erasmo knew with certainty that he was Rat's only real friend.

But the gleaming Maxima stood in the driveway, nonetheless.

Ten days since he'd heard from his friend.

Erasmo shut the engine off, slunk down into his seat, and waited.

Three hours passed, and not a soul came out of the house. Just an hour into his "stakeout," Erasmo had given serious thought to just leaving. There could be plenty of explanations why this car was parked in the driveway, all of them perfectly innocuous. Except, the longer he sat there, the more he was sure: Erasmo had seen this Maxima before. He knew this car. But from where? The answer to this riddle flitted around his brain, a butterfly that refused to land, its wings tickling the innermost ridges of his cranium.

Erasmo closed his eyes and tried to conjure a memory that might help. Instead, he was greeted with an image of Rat, crying in agony as he desperately fought off Widow's Peak. Erasmo felt an overpowering surge of gratitude and admiration whenever he replayed this memory. Not many people could have endured that much pain and still gotten back up to fight. Rat had been *so* incredibly brave when things got crazy. Both times really, because when the shit hit the fan at . . .

And then Erasmo knew. He knew who owned the shiny black car in the driveway, and who was inside with Rat that very second.

So he didn't leave, and instead Erasmo sat in his car and stared at the small house Rat and his hateful mother lived in, his stomach roiling as it simmered in its own bubbling acid.

He didn't understand this. He didn't understand anything.

It took another hour for the two of them to finally emerge from the house. Erasmo didn't blink as they descended the three steps from the porch to the front yard. He didn't move as Rat slid into the passenger side of the car. And he didn't breathe as Leander started his Maxima, backed out, and drove away, his car somehow still managing to glisten in the faded, pale light.

CHAPTER 13

IT DIDN'T TAKE long to realize that tailing a car was not as easy as it looked in the movies. Leander made his way onto I-10 West, and already Erasmo was having a difficult time keeping up with him. He tried to hang back a few car lengths to blend in with the other cars. But before he knew it, the Maxima was out of sight. He stomped on the gas pedal, desperate to catch up, feeling the Civic's engine rattle as it struggled to obey him. Erasmo whipped his head around, searching the evening traffic as it pulsed around him, but didn't see the Maxima anywhere.

His fists erupted in pain as he pounded the steering wheel, and he now pushed the Civic even faster. A Suburban, a Jetta, an old Cavalier. No Maxima. A torrent of questions rushed through his head. What the hell was Rat doing with Leander? And how was Leander not in a jail cell right now? And where the hell could the two of them possibly be going together? Now he wouldn't know the answers to those questions because he was too goddamn incompetent to tail a car without losing it.

With the Maxima nowhere in sight, there was nothing left to do but turn around and go home. He could drive by Rat's house tomorrow and wait . . . see if Leander showed again. Maybe he'd get lucky. Maybe. He sighed, checked his blind spot to get over to the exit lane, and what he saw turned his blood cold. There, slightly behind him and to his right, was the Maxima.

How did they get behind him? Leander had been so far ahead. . . .

Idiot. In his rush to catch up, he must've sped right past them.

Erasmo snapped his head back and laid off the gas until he was a few car lengths behind them. A sigh of relief escaped his lips. It hadn't appeared like they'd seen him.

An insistent, lucid part of him argued for turning around and going home. He could just ask Rat about all of this tomorrow. Erasmo wanted to believe that his friend would tell him the truth about what was going on, that he'd answer every question about this insanity. But Erasmo couldn't be sure that was really true. Not after seeing this.

They were now approaching the I-10/410 interchange. Erasmo's eyes burned, as he was afraid to blink even once for fear of missing a turn signal. Sure enough, Leander's blinker now flashed insistently in the evening light, and he merged onto NW Loop 410. After a few minutes, Leander exited on Bandera Road and turned right, with Erasmo following close behind. Every muscle in his body was clenched. Even his bones felt as if they were under immense strain. Erasmo took a deep breath, unsure how long his nerves would be able to endure this.

As it turned out, he didn't have to wait long to find out where Leander and his friend were headed. Erasmo's eyes jerked in their sockets when he saw the Maxima slow down and casually turn right, into the parking lot of InTown Suites.

Deciding it was too risky to follow Leander directly into the parking lot, Erasmo kept going and turned into a Walgreens next door to the hotel. He was thankful to find the drug store almost deserted. After pulling into an empty space, he killed the engine and looked over at InTown Suites.

The Maxima was also parked, but no one had exited. Could they have seen him following and stopped to investigate who'd taken an interest in them? Or were they meeting someone and just waiting for this other person to show?

Five minutes dripped by, and as far as Erasmo could tell, nothing happened. His vantage point wasn't great, as Leander and Rat were parked on the far side of the hotel parking lot, as far away as they could be. He could still see them, though, two shadows flickering in the dormant car.

And then, without warning . . . movement. Not from the car, though. From somewhere else. There. The door to one of the suites stood open, from a room on the third floor.

Before Erasmo could fully process what was happening, a figure emerged from the room and dashed down the stairs. It was too dark, and the figure was too far away for Erasmo to get a clean look. He had no choice: He was going to have to get closer. He started the Civic, guided it to the parking lot exit, and turned left onto Bandera. The three men quickly came up on his left. Erasmo drove as slowly as he could without drawing attention to himself.

Leander was out of the car now, talking to whoever had come down the stairs. But he was also standing right in front of the guy, making it impossible for Erasmo to get a good look.

Even driving slowly, it didn't take long for Erasmo to pass them, still no closer to finding out who this third person was. There was a cross street up ahead that he could use to turn around, but it wasn't for another hundred feet or so. He'd have a much better view coming from that direction, as he'd be in the lane closest to the hotel. It must've taken only seconds to reach the light and perform a U-turn, but to Erasmo it seemed as if an eternity had passed. In his heart, he was sure they'd be gone by the time he turned around and reached them.

They came up on his right and Erasmo's heart dropped when he saw Leander getting back into the car. The stranger stood by the rear driver-side door, waiting for Leander to unlock it.

Erasmo was close now, but the stranger's back was to him. The figure reached forward and opened the Maxima's door, about to get inside. *Damn.* He wasn't going to get a good look. But then, perhaps as a small measure of restitution for the many breaks that had never gone his way, he got lucky. Before the stranger entered the back of the car, he turned his head, and Erasmo saw that he was no stranger at all.

Erasmo's lungs refused to draw breath. He felt untethered, weightless, dangling upside down over a raging river, about to fall in. This was not right. There was no explanation for any of this. With a considerable amount of effort, he turned into the Walgreens parking lot for a second time and parked the Civic at a drunken angle, straddling two spots.

Erasmo watched as Leander patiently waited to turn out of InTown Suites. Finally, the Maxima swung out of the parking lot and passed in front of him, a constellation of infinite stars dancing on its body. Even through the heavy tint, he saw Rat, his hooked nose appearing even larger than usual due to the large grin on his pockmarked face. He saw a glimpse of Leander, who looked somber and, Erasmo thought, a little scared. The third man he couldn't see but knew was in there. Sitting inside that car's soft, leather belly sat one Billy Doggett, no doubt contemplating the fluctuating, uncertain future.

CHAPTER 14

DESPITE THE FOG of shock and confusion enveloping his brain, Erasmo managed to realize that he still needed to follow the Maxima. His compromised mental state made the drive surreal and indefinite, an endless series of random stops and turns. The other vehicles on the road were hazy apparitions, unreal and unimportant. He paid no attention to where they were heading, his sole focus on following the shimmering black vessel carrying his friend.

He felt his brain lifting up strands of information and trying to tie them together. How could Leander and Billy possibly know each other? And Rat should want *nothing* to do with either one of them. What was he doing in the same car as those lunatics? Erasmo was so numb that he now no longer cared if they saw him; he made almost no effort to hide the fact that he was following them.

They were now on a residential street, somewhere on the south side of town, when Leander pulled over to the curb. Erasmo eased the Civic to a stop about six houses away from them and killed the engine. His entire body tensed, waiting for their next move, but no one emerged from the Maxima. Erasmo realized that he had no earthly idea what he was going to do if they did.

Ten minutes slowly crept by with no movement whatsoever. He had initially assumed that they'd come to this neighborhood to meet someone. But perhaps they were doing the exact same thing he was: waiting.

His suspicion was proven correct, as an hour passed with still no activity. Erasmo scanned the mundane, cramped houses in the neighborhood, wondering which one they were staking out. Distressing pangs in the left side of his belly reminded him that he hadn't eaten since lunch, and his bladder complained with increasing urgency.

Another thirty minutes stretched by, and Erasmo seriously began to question if he'd be able to make it for much longer. He laid his head back and closed his eyes, fervently wishing that something would just happen already. And then, without warning, it did.

A low grumble approached, and headlights splashed over the street. A battered red Mustang pulled up to the house that sat directly across the street from where Leander was parked. The Mustang's door thumped closed and a large figure exited, clomping up the porch stairs in a rush.

After a moment, the driver's side door of the Maxima opened, before quickly slamming shut again. Erasmo heard yelling from inside the car, and it rocked up and down, almost imperceptibly, as if there were lovers inside instead of three insane men.

A few seconds later, the yelling subsided, and the Maxima's engine hummed to life. He watched as the car sped off, recklessly careening through the neighborhood. Erasmo started the Civic and pulled into the road. Nothing to do now but head home. He trembled and ground his teeth as he slowly navigated the deserted, lightless streets, spending the entire drive home wondering what on earth had become of his only friend.

CHAPTER 15

THE NEXT MORNING, Erasmo woke with a dull ache in his stomach. He sat in his bed, eyeing the overcast sky peeking through his window, and mulled over what he'd seen the night before. Still unable to make any sense of it, he forced himself out of bed and into the kitchen, hoping that some milk might soothe the pain in his gut.

As Erasmo poured, he thought of Rat, and how happy he'd looked to be in the company of those two dangerous, unstable men. A shudder convulsed through him, leaving him limp and clammy. He must've looked as pathetic as he felt.

"Is it that bad?" his grandmother said from behind him.

Erasmo turned to her and almost said that he was fine, but then blurted out the question squirming on his lips.

"Have you ever discovered," he asked, "that you didn't know someone as well as you thought?"

His grandmother was silent for an uncomfortably long time. Tears welled in her eyes, and she gave him a wistful look.

"More times than I care to remember." After wiping her tears away, she continued. "Erasmo, you're going to find that you can only ever truly know yourself, and even that is mostly an illusion. People are often too terrified to admit to

themselves their secret desires . . . why they want to either constantly reconstruct or destroy themselves. It can take a lifetime
to understand the truth about yourself."

"But if you know someone *really* well—"

"That's your first mistake, Erasmo, believing that such a
thing is even possible. You'll never know what lies in the dark
corners of other people's hearts. Worry instead about what lies
in the dark corners of yours."

A sad smile formed on her weathered lips.

"Your grandfather's favorite saying was: 'De músico, poeta,
y loco, todos tenemos un poco.'"

Erasmo stared at her blankly.

"It means," his grandmother said, "that we're all a little bit
crazy." She had the usual gleam in her eyes that shone whenever
his grandfather came up. "But here's the trick. Even though
you can never truly know anybody, if you think that someone is truly worth it, take the risk and love them anyway. If
their heart is just too dark . . . too damaged, you'll know soon
enough."

She came over and hugged him, and he immediately worried at how much weaker her embrace was than usual.

"I'm going to visit Margaret for a while," she said, and
then shuffled out of the room, leaving him alone to stew in his
thoughts.

The gravel crunched under Erasmo's feet as he trudged through
his neighborhood. He was too restless to stay cooped up all day
and worry about his grandmother and whatever the hell Rat
was up to. So he'd decided to make the trek to H-E-B while
his grandmother was away, to save her a trip to the store later.

The neighborhood was strangely quiet. Usually there was a lot more activity. Young children clad only in diapers wailing in their front lawn. Older folks leaning on the rusted chain-link fences that divided their tiny yards as they chatted with neighbors. The school dropouts strolling down the street, trying to look tougher than they actually were. But not today. The unusual stillness made him nervous.

But then the quiet was broken by a low grumble approaching from behind. Experience had taught him to never look directly at a passing vehicle when walking through the neighborhood. As the car got closer, he turned his eyes away from the road and toward the small houses that lined the street.

"Erasmo!" a voice called.

His heart froze, and a gleaming black car stopped next to him.

"Erasmo Cruz!"

The voice. It was . . . familiar. He'd heard this voice before. But where? Unable to restrain himself, he turned, his eager eyes seeking out the driver.

And what they found was the hard, resolute face of Detective Torres.

"Get in, will you?" she said. "Got a few questions I need to ask."

He stood in the warmth of the afternoon sun, unable to move. What could she possibly want to talk to him about? He frantically cycled through possibilities but was at a complete loss.

"You know . . . the longer you stand there with that scared look on your face, the more I'll suspect you've been up to no good."

These words got him moving. Erasmo opened the car door and apprehensively slid into the passenger seat.

"Where you headed?"

"Just going to H-E-B, Detective."

"That's a little bit of a walk, isn't it?" Torres said as she pulled forward. "I can take you."

She glanced at Erasmo, holding the look for a few moments before returning her eyes to the road.

"So," she finally said, "I could use your help with something. Wanted to pick your brain about Leander."

"Leander? What about him?"

"There are," Torres said, "a few complications in the case. He keeps insisting that his cousin did it . . . that his cousin put Sandra's body under the bed to frame him."

"Seems pretty unlikely," Erasmo said.

"I agree. But the thing is . . . this Travis guy is by all accounts pretty disreputable. On top of that, Leander has a solid alibi. A neighbor claims that he saw Leander passed out on his front porch around 2:30 a.m. or so. He thought Leander came home drunk, didn't make it inside, and was sleeping it off. According to the neighbor, he doesn't know Leander very well, so he just let him be. Seems strange, but nevertheless, it matches up with Leander's account of the night. Given all that, we just wanted to make sure we hadn't missed anything."

"Okay," he said. "That makes sense."

"Mainly, I just wanted to double-check if there was anything else Leander might have said about his cousin . . . any details you might've left out."

Erasmo thought it over but was at a loss.

"Nothing comes to mind. He said they weren't particularly close, that Travis showed up to the bar that night and kidnapped Sandra from his house later on. Then the cops showed up and told Leander that her body had been found, and she'd been killed by a blow to the back of her head. That's it."

"All right," Torres said, a disappointed look on her face. "But if you remember *anything* else, make sure to let me know immediately. Okay?"

They sat in silence for a few moments as Torres drummed her fingers on the steering wheel. Erasmo's heart dropped as he realized there was clearly something else on her mind.

"So . . ." she finally said. "The incident at the Ghost Tracks . . ."

Shit. Cold sweat seeped from Erasmo's skin, and his teeth clenched involuntarily at the mention of the Tracks.

"I remember seeing it on the news," Torres continued. "That was last October, right?"

"Yeah."

"Do you mind . . . I mean . . . would it be out of bounds to ask . . ."

"You want to hear about what happened that night," Erasmo said for her.

He was surprised to see a sheepish expression spread over her usually stern face.

"I do, yes. Out of personal curiosity, not a professional one. I mean, I know what everybody says, but I was curious about what *really* happened."

Flutters filled Erasmo's stomach, as they always did when he was about to tell this story.

"If it's not something you're comfortable talking about, I understand," she said.

"No, Detective, I don't mind telling you."

Erasmo closed his eyes, inhaled deeply, and allowed his mind to drift back to the night his life changed forever. After a few moments, he opened his eyes, gazed out of the window, and began to recount the miraculous story of the young man who was saved at the Ghost Tracks.

CHAPTER 16

WHEN HE WAS a junior, Erasmo's sociology class spent a few weeks studying folklore and superstitions. The class was taught by Mr. Regalado, a mustachioed gentleman who resembled a mole and drank an endless supply of Hawaiian Punch. He'd advised them in between sips, his tiny eyes surveying the class, that their semester projects could be on anything they wanted, as long as it was at least minimally connected to the course's subject matter. Given that Halloween was coming up, Erasmo knew right away what the subject of his project was going to be.

Erasmo had ventured down to the Tracks on a brisk October evening. He'd wanted to get a few pictures and quotes for his project. Erasmo imagined that a photo of white handprints on the trunk of a car, with amazed track-goers gawking in the background, would work wonders for his grade. He'd even brought a bottle of baby powder with him in case any of the visitors forgot to bring their own. Erasmo stood at the L-shaped intersection of Shane and Villamain and looked for approaching headlights, but saw none, and was surprised at how deserted the Tracks were.

He decided to take some pictures of the area while he waited. Erasmo placed the bottle of baby powder down on the road, surveying the scene to determine what angle might work best. A weak shimmer of moonlight provided the only illumination, but its rays couldn't fully penetrate the corner of darkness the tracks sat on. He decided to just point and click and hope for the best. His phone's flash mixed with the moonlight to ignite the tracks, exposing the rusted metal rails embedded in gray, worn asphalt.

It was then that he first heard a murmur in the distance. An engine. He scanned both roads, but no headlights approached. The sound quickly drew closer, its grumble both muscular and threatening. Erasmo continued to search for the glow of oncoming headlights but saw nothing.

This turned out to be his mistake. He'd been looking for headlights when there were none. A 1997 Ford F-150, painted moonlight blue (he would find out later), roared down Villamain with its lights off. Finally spotting the hulking shadow speeding toward him, Erasmo picked up the baby powder and jogged out of the intersection to the side of the road. The power emanating from the approaching engine vibrated the air around him. His stomach clenched as he realized that the truck wasn't slowing down. In fact, it was picking up speed. Erasmo inched even farther away from the road. From where he was on Villamain, the truck would shoot right by him, miss the left turn onto Shane, and wreck into the brush.

The driver must have seen the approaching dead end though. Erasmo watched in horror and disbelief as the truck swerved, tires wailing, and ended up aimed straight at him. He turned and began to run, but his legs felt weightless as he furiously pumped them. Warm air from the truck's engine tickled the back of his calves, and Erasmo released a throat-shredding shriek. He had a vision of the truck devouring him, his body pulled under its smoldering mass of steel, his head crushed into bony pulp. He gathered himself and leaped away from the truck's path, his limbs contorting to brace for the fall. The back of Erasmo's head exploded as it hit the metal of the tracks. Vacillating white orbs bloomed in his vision, obscuring the night sky. Sounds of wrenching steel and exploding glass reached his ears as he lay on the tracks, its twin metal bars digging into his back.

Erasmo tried to get up but immediately collapsed back to the ground, his arms and legs a tangled mess. The white orbs grew bigger as they swirled and pulsed in his field of vision. His head felt as if it were an expanding balloon, each engorging throb bringing his cranium closer to bursting. Then, thankfully, a pleasant weightlessness settled in. He floated toward the emerging stars, the swirling orbs expanding until welcome oblivion overtook him.

But, as he drifted into the ether, an alarm sounded deep in his damaged head. A familiar sound approached. It was the static hum of rubber on asphalt. A car was coming. He tried to force his eyes open, but his eyelids only fluttered helplessly. The driver of the car wouldn't see him in the dark. The approaching tires would roll right over the tracks and his flaccid body.

Erasmo twisted himself in an attempt to roll over onto his stomach. Arcs of sharp pain shot through his back, but he'd somehow managed to turn over, as his stomach and chest were now pressed against the coarse asphalt. Oddly, his body felt as if it were still turning, as if he were in space and trapped in a slow, continuous rotation because there was no gravity to prevent him from doing so. The sound of the engine, this one much less monstrous than the truck's, was closer now. He gritted his teeth and told himself that he wasn't spinning endlessly. No. He was facedown in the middle of the street about to die.

Erasmo brought his elbows up to his side and pushed in a desperate attempt to crawl. No movement. A pale glow from the car's headlights spread over him. He tried again, his knees grinding into the asphalt, and this time managed to move forward a few inches. The car was close now. Soon it would crush him.

It was then that he felt tiny, probing fingers on his body. At first they were hesitant, as if doubtful of his tangibility. But then they suddenly hardened, and he could feel the unnatural strength behind the miniature grips that took hold of him. His body jerked forward, the asphalt scraping against his skin. He was about to cry out in pain, but then his body lurched again.

Erasmo's mind reeled. Could this be happening . . . or was he unconscious on the side of the road, dreaming? Or perhaps he was at this very moment lying crushed under the car, and this illusion was his mind's final spasm of consciousness? Even as Erasmo felt himself being dragged along, he wasn't entirely sure. But then voices . . . children's voices . . . gentle and lyrical . . . whispered all around him. The words flowed together, a tapestry of soothing intonations. Listening to them, he knew.

This was real.

Erasmo prepared for another hard jolt across the asphalt, but, when he opened his eyes, realized that he was now safely on the side of the road. He turned his head and saw an old Corolla, splattered with rust, slowing to a stop in front of the tracks.

"Grandpa! Did you see that?" a voice yelled from inside.

A figure emerged from the car and shuffled over to him. Erasmo tried to speak, but his mouth wouldn't move. The man, his silhouette frail and bent, spoke instead.

"Padre nuestro, que estás en el cielo. Santificado sea tu nombre. Venga a nosotros tu reino. Hágase tu voluntad en la tierra como en el cielo. Danos hoy nuestro pan de cada día.

Perdona nuestras ofensas, como también nosotros perdonamos a los que nos . . ."

No longer able to resist the pull of oblivion, Erasmo allowed the soothing words and silent breeze to carry him away before he could hear the end of the old man's prayer.

Light. It burned past his retina and into his concussed brain. It was as bright as the sun. It was the sun.

"Sir, can you tell me your name?"

A woman. He couldn't see her because the sun covered the world. The sun was the world.

"Sir, are you able to tell me what your name is?"

"Mauro."

"Your name is Mauro?"

No. That was not his name.

"Erasmo. My name is Erasmo."

"Okay, Erasmo. Can you tell me where it hurts?"

With no warning, the sun is extinguished, gone before he can say goodbye.

His vision wavered before finally focusing on a broad-faced woman, her black hair pulled straight back into a knot. The uniform she wore was heavily starched and devoid of even one wrinkle. Erasmo yearned to tell her that he loved her, but managed to hold the words back. In her hand she held a penlight.

"My head. My head hurts. And my back."

She nodded, her onyx hair flashing in the moonlight.

"Looks like you have a concussion. We should take you in to get checked out. Losing consciousness is nothing to play around with. You—"

"Señor . . . help . . . por favor."

He recognized the old man's voice. For the first time, Erasmo got a good look at him. Long, meandering wrinkles sat deep in his skin, and he wore his silver hair combed straight back. Despite his age, knots of thick muscle bulged from his forearms. Erasmo thought his weathered exterior made the old man look simultaneously fragile and tough as hell.

The EMT looked over her shoulder at the old man. He was standing behind her, flanked by two teenagers. One was a long, handsome boy. The other, a fair-skinned girl with a stunned look on her wide face.

"Please, sir. I already told you, he needs space."

"Lo tocaron," the old man said to the EMT.

Erasmo glanced around, searching for the truck that had almost hit him. Its front end was crushed against some trees, smoke still pouring from under its crumpled hood. Two other EMTs worked on a large unconscious man a few feet away from the wrecked truck.

"Lo tocaron," the old man repeated to the EMT before turning to Erasmo, his eyes wide with wonder. The old man slowly got down on his knees. "Lo tocaron. Por favor, has sido tocado por de la mano de Dios. Mi nieto está muy enfermo. Por favor, ayúdalo. El te salvó. Ahora que has sido tocado por la gracia de su espíritu, puedes salvar a otros. Por favor."

Erasmo stared at the old man, unsure what to do. Despite his name and the dark shade of his skin, Erasmo spoke almost no Spanish.

"Sir, I'm going to have to ask you to back away and give us some space," the EMT said.

The old man paid no attention to this request. Tears fell down his face, traveling down the gullies etched in his cheeks.

"Los fantasmas de los niños te salvaron. Fue por una razón. Salva a mi nieto. El es un buen muchacho. Está enfermo de sus huesos. Por favor."

The hard look on the EMT's face softened as she peered down at the old man.

"You don't understand what he's saying, do you?"

Erasmo didn't have to respond.

"He wants you to touch his grandson."

"Why would—"

"He thinks that if you touch him, his grandson won't be sick anymore."

Erasmo studied the kneeling man, as if the sight of him would somehow clarify what she'd just said. "I still don't—"

The old man spoke again, this time in English. "You touch by God." He pointed at Erasmo with a long, crooked finger. "The little chil'ren . . . they save you."

The news crew arrived soon after, surely speeding over once they heard there'd been an accident at the Ghost Tracks. The reporter, a slender woman who strode confidently through the scene, caught the old man just as he was getting into his car to leave. Erasmo watched, stunned at what unfolded next.

The reporter began to interview the old man, while the teenage boy served as a translator. The boy's voice was clear and even, not intimidated by the lights or the moment. He was calm and reserved when conveying his grandfather's description of coming upon the scene, but robust and animated when he described Erasmo, unconscious, being pulled off the road by tiny, invisible hands. The reporter could scarcely contain her glee.

Erasmo was still under examination by the EMT when the reporter first arrived, so she'd left him alone, snatching the old man instead. But when the EMT gave Erasmo the okay to leave, the reporter still waited for him, talking excitedly into her phone. He tried to quietly slink off, but she immediately whipped around and came running, her large, hairy cameraman plodding closely behind. Erasmo sprinted to the Civic, stupidly looking back and giving the cameraman a good shot of his face. The reporter yelled questions at him, only giving up when he scurried into his car and started the engine.

He still wasn't sure why he hadn't just stopped and talked to the reporter. Probably because he was still in shock and hadn't even begun to process what had just happened to him. The urge to run, to just GET THE HELL OUT OF THERE, had been so powerful. That night and all of the next day, viewers of KSAT 12 News watched as the old man and his grandson described the miracle at the Ghost Tracks. The news segment concluded with a flourish: video of Erasmo fleeing into his decrepit car and speeding off, the Civic's taillights disappearing into the night.

The story became a mini-sensation for a few days. Most people laughed it off, to be sure. But there were many who took it to heart. Almost all his classmates approached him, wanting to hear his firsthand account, wanting to know just how many tiny hands he'd felt pulling on his body.

Thankfully, the attention died down after a few days. But now even eight months later, many in San Antonio still remembered, and marveled at, the inexplicable story of the young man who was saved at the Ghost Tracks.

"Wow . . . so pretty much the same story everyone around town tells, huh?" Torres said as she pulled into the grocery store's parking lot.

"Yeah. Although, you're being kind in not mentioning that a lot of them laugh when they tell it."

Torres nodded her head, and Erasmo appreciated that she hadn't attempted to deny the truth.

"You know how it is," she said. "Not everyone's a believer."

"How about you, Detective? Do you believe?"

Torres was silent. She slid on a pair of aviator sunglasses she'd produced from her jacket pocket, as if this would shield her from the question.

"Can I ask you a different question then? Do you believe *me*? The story I just told you?"

Torres's silence continued, but she then released a long, weary sigh.

"This job doesn't make it easy to believe, Erasmo. The things I see every day . . . Christ. But I can truthfully say this. I *want* to believe. I want to believe you so bad that it hurts."

"Tell you what, Detective," Erasmo said, flashing Torres the most genuine smile he could muster. "I'll just have to believe enough for the both of us."

With that, he opened the car door, stepped out into the pleasant afternoon light, and watched as Torres violently gunned the engine and sped off, tires shrieking, as if she were being pursued by something mad, and fierce, and terrible.

CHAPTER 17

WHEN HIS GRANDMOTHER returned a few hours later, Erasmo immediately hopped in the Civic and headed over to Rat's. He'd already called him three times with no response. There was no question about it. Rat was straight up avoiding him.

When Erasmo arrived, he saw there were no vehicles in the driveway this time, so he jumped out and jogged through the front lawn. He pounded on the door, his fist immediately smarting from the force of the blows.

No answer. He thumped on the door again, even harder this time. Still nothing.

Erasmo walked back to the Civic, slid in, and waited. This time, he was prepared to wait all damn day if he had to. But his resolve proved to be short-lived, as after three drudging hours passed with no sign of either Rat or his new friends, Erasmo could no longer stomach just sitting there. He took a few moments to berate himself for his shamefully weak constitution, and then started the Civic to head home.

But head home to do what? To lay in bed and dissect the many ways the ad had been a terrible mistake? To ponder the fact that he still was an unemployed embarrassment? To agonize over the fact that his only friend was now inexplicably hanging out with deranged lunatics?

He sighed, pulled his phone out, and scrolled through its meager list of contacts, his usual ritual when he was morose and lonely. He examined the list, knowing the futility of this exercise even as he continued to scrutinize the names. It was as if he expected to find some new entry on the list, one that he'd somehow forgotten about. Instead, the same names stared back at him: cousins he rarely spoke to, acquaintances from school, and old coworkers from various odd jobs he'd held.

Then, to his great surprise, Erasmo did see a name he hadn't scrolled over hundreds of times before. It was the name of someone whose face sometimes flickered through his head as he drifted off to sleep. Even with all the strange things that had happened lately, his mind still constantly wandered back to that evening, mulling over what he'd seen at her house. But what did the events of that night really mean? Nothing, other than that a boy, a child, needed help.

Late-afternoon sunlight spilled through the car window and spread over the screen of his phone, washing the name and number out, making them almost impossible to read. It was almost as if the brilliant star had inexplicably taken an interest in his affairs and was warning him not to go.

He didn't listen.

This time, her car was in the driveway. Erasmo hurried through the yard and up the porch steps, raising his hand to rap on the door before he could change his mind. But then, without warning, it flew open before he could even knock.

Nora stood in the doorway, perfectly still, her gray eyes large and expectant. The plain blue sundress she wore swayed around her as she finally gestured for him to enter. Once inside, they both wordlessly took a seat on her sofa, an aging avocado-green behemoth that looked comfortable but was actually hard as hell.

Erasmo was certain that she'd want to talk about her brother right away, but instead, Nora only sat there on the ugly sofa and gazed at him in silence.

"How have you been?" she finally asked.

This one question was the only encouragement he needed to pour his scared, lonely heart out to her. He breathlessly divulged to Nora every ghastly event of the last several weeks. She listened while he explained about Leander, and Sandra's body, and Billy, and the fight, and Rat, and seeing all of them together.

Erasmo understood that this was complete madness, sharing these secrets with her. He barely knew this woman. As he rambled on, unable to stop himself, Erasmo was certain that she was completely disinterested, only listening out of sheer politeness. Why would Nora possibly want to hear these insane stories about people she didn't even know? From a person she barely knew? But he didn't care. It felt so good to tell someone, to make those terrible events real by speaking the words out loud, to validate to himself that these things had actually happened, that they weren't all just apparitions in his head.

And Nora proved to be the perfect audience. She interjected at all the right moments, clarifying portions she found confusing and asking about points of the story he'd inadvertently left out. Her intense eyes remained locked on his own as details and explanations and descriptions poured out of him. She seemed genuinely fascinated as he spoke, which was a new experience for him. The flood of words slowly turned into a trickle, and then dried up completely until Erasmo sat in silence, embarrassed at his outburst.

"Well," Nora finally said, "at least now I know you'll be useful the next time I get into a gang fight."

It took Erasmo a few seconds to register that she'd made a joke . . . that she was being playful. For some reason, this seemed incomprehensible to him.

"Oh yeah?" he asked after composing himself. "You get into lots of gang fights?"

"I sure do," she said. "In fact, I have one scheduled for next Thursday. You available?"

"Actually, I believe that day I'm busy changing future events again. But next time for sure though."

She laughed, genuinely and unguarded, the pureness of her voice causing a twinge in Erasmo's heart.

The conversation then turned to Nora. She was open and forthright as she told Erasmo her own secrets, big and small. About how she'd never really recovered from her mother's death. About the hurt she felt at her father never being around. About how she loved the rain so much more than the sun. About how she'd wanted to be a news anchor since she was a little girl but had no money to study broadcasting.

"But that's not going to stop me. I'm going to find a way."

"I can totally see you on TV," Erasmo said, meaning it.

Nora's cheeks flushed a deep red.

"Do . . . do you really think so? Are you just saying that? You don't have to . . ."

"No, seriously. I bet the viewers at home would hang on to your every word."

"How do you know, Erasmo? You haven't even seen my skills yet. But I do have them! Check this out. Try not to get too freaked out about all the talent you're about to see on display, okay?"

Nora held up three fingers and counted down to zero. She then placed an imaginary microphone to her lips and began.

"Good afternoon. This is Nora Montalvo, and today I'm interviewing noted paranormal investigator Erasmo Cruz."

"Uh . . . thanks for having me."

"Our viewers would like to know if you're as cool a guy as you seem, or if it's all a front?"

"Oh, I would say that I'm *mostly* cool . . . but I can't rule out the possibility that there might be a small, tiny, insignificant percentage of me that is, in fact, not cool."

"Fair enough. It's my understanding that you know someone who might be able to tell the future. Any chance he can help our weather guy be right for a change?"

"Well, I can definitely see about putting in a word."

"Great! Last question. Our viewers at home would really like to know your current relationship status."

"Oh . . . I don't have anyone in my life right now."

"Well, Mr. Cruz," Nora said, smiling at the imaginary camera, "I wouldn't be so sure about that."

As she signed off to her viewers, Erasmo's body felt as if it were floating above the sofa. In fact, he questioned the very reality of what he was experiencing. Erasmo knew without question that this conversation was actually happening. But nevertheless, it felt like too close to fantasy to be true. He kept reminding himself that, to Nora, this was simply a friendly chat, nothing more.

"I'm glad you came by," she said. "I'd been hoping to hear from you."

Erasmo was stunned. Could this be true? The notion of Nora spending even a single stray thought on him seemed too fantastical a notion to even entertain.

"I had been wanting to get in touch," he finally said, "but after what happened . . ."

"We don't have to talk about it. That was my fault. I shouldn't have . . ."

"No, you should have. That's the entire reason I was even over here that night. In fact, I . . . I do want to talk to you about Sonny. I think that—"

Nora gave a soft smile, reached over, and squeezed his hand.

"I do want to talk about how to help Sonny," she said. "Just maybe not today. Is that all right?"

"Sure, okay." He was uneasy about putting off the conversation but didn't want to push back too hard either.

Shortly after, Nora announced that she had to go pick up Sonny from summer school. "He freaks out if I'm not there exactly on time," she explained.

Erasmo extended the farewell as long as he could, but eventually he found himself standing at her door, hesitant to walk out of it.

"I really enjoyed . . ." he fumbled.

"Give me a hug before you go."

Nora stepped forward and placed her head on his chest. Erasmo felt her arms reach around him, and she pressed her body against his. For a few seconds, he just stood there, arms at his side, helplessly lost. He finally managed to recover, raising his trembling arms and placing them around Nora.

"So," she said, her voice muffled against his chest, "do you have any plans for tomorrow?"

On the way home, Erasmo almost ran off the road twice, his head too filled with Nora's splendor to pay attention to something as mundane as driving in a straight line.

"Thank you," he whispered to the universe. "Thank you."

The next several days were a fervid, intoxicating blur. Every morning he'd go over and learn new and wonderful things about Nora. She slept with her toes pointed down, like a ballerina on her tiptoes. She knew almost every song by The Cure by heart and would happily recite the lyrics on request. She had a scar on her left knee from when she tried to jump rope while wearing roller skates when she was ten.

Nora took him to some of her favorite places around the city, and he quickly fell in love with her energy and zeal. She was enthusiastic about everything big and small, from the perfect barbacoa taco at the taqueria by her house, to the way the sunset looks from the trails of Eisenhower Park. The force of her energy made him burn with excitement too. He'd never felt this alive before. But it was more than that.

For once, he didn't feel broken.

Nora was especially excited one morning when she announced that they were going to get pan dulce.

"Just so we're clear, I don't take just anyone to my favorite panadería. But you'll be happy to know that you made the cut. Also, you should be aware that I'm *highly* suspicious of anyone who walks into this place and doesn't order at least one concha."

When they arrived at the bakery, he watched with admiration as Nora walked in and effortlessly charmed the older couple behind the counter. Her finger danced in the air as she pointed out an assortment of polvorones rosas, empanadas, and thick slabs of pink cake.

"He'll order the rest while I head to the bathroom," she said. "I'm checking your bag when we get home," Nora whispered as she passed by.

As Erasmo studied the sweet breads, he noticed that the man behind the counter stood unnaturally still, and that his eyes were studying his face. The old man didn't look at all familiar. Why would he be staring—

"Mr. Cruz," the man said, almost in a whisper. "My wife. Her hands are bad, from severe arthritis. Would you mind . . ."

The woman, thin and fragile, held her hands out to him. They were purple and gnarled and swollen.

"It . . . doesn't work that way," Erasmo said. "They saved me, but I can't fix her."

"Please," the man said, tears now in his eyes. "They've touched you with their power. If you touch my wife, maybe it will somehow help her. Please."

Damn. The last thing he wanted was to give them false hope. But, at the same time, he couldn't think of a single reason not to at least try.

Erasmo took her hands in his, touching her so gently that their skin barely made contact. He closed his eyes and desperately wished for her good health. When he released her and opened his eyes, they were smiling at him, both making the sign of the cross. When Nora returned, they insisted that the bread was free.

"Can't even leave you alone for a few minutes," she said as they left, her mouth full of cake.

After almost a week of spending time together, Nora told him to just unlock the front door and walk in when he arrived, using the key she hid under a dingy fiberglass bulldog that sat on her porch. This gesture, the trust it showed she had in him, almost moved Erasmo to tears.

"Are you sure?" he asked.

Nora paused before responding.

"Do you know why I've invited you over here every day this week?" she asked.

This question took him by surprise, and he was unsure how to safely answer it.

"No," he said.

"I don't claim to have the power to see future events, like Billy. But there are some things that I *can* see. And one of those is the person you're going to become."

"I'm . . . not sure I understand," Erasmo said.

"Well," Nora said, "most people you come across in life, you know right away that there is nothing to them, that they have no potential. You, Erasmo, are not like that. When I open the door every morning, I see someone who is becoming the person he is supposed to be, who is growing into himself. As special as you are right now, you are going to be so much more. And I just might want to be along for the ride."

Nora walked over, her eyes never leaving his, and wrapped her arms around him. By the time the embrace was over, Erasmo knew that he would forever be in her service, if she was generous enough to allow it.

He walked out of Nora's house that afternoon wanting to conquer the world for her. He was going to quadruple his efforts to get a job. And Christ, he couldn't have her riding around in his grandmother's piece-of-shit Civic. As he strode through her patchy lawn, he resolved to claw his way through every man, woman, and child who even remotely stood in the way of providing Nora the life that she wanted.

During this time, Erasmo continued to call Rat constantly, leaving messages that went unreturned. He also drove by his house several times a day to see if Leander's car was parked there, hoping to confront them. But he'd neither heard nor seen a damn thing from Rat. Erasmo thought about his friend constantly, even when he was with Nora.

When he'd mentioned Rat to Nora, she'd said, "If he felt that he needed your help, he'd return your calls. I love that you are so concerned about your friend, but if he wants to make mistakes with his life, don't let him drag you down with him."

Adding to his general sense of unease, he still hadn't confronted Nora about her brother. Erasmo had been waiting for her to bring up Sonny, but for some reason she hadn't yet. He promised himself to have the conversation with her the next day and live with the consequences of whatever happened.

The next morning, as Erasmo drove to Nora's, he furiously attempted to find the right words to say to her. But was there a good way to tell someone you cared deeply for that she'd made up a fantastical story to explain away her brother's illness?

Despite driving as slowly as possible, he arrived at her house still completely unsure of what to say. He trudged up the porch stairs, his hands balled into sweaty fists. Before he could retrieve the key from under the bulldog, Nora opened the door, greeting him with her usual radiant smile. She wore faded jeans and a snug Beatles T-shirt that displayed all four members—Paul looking as handsome as ever. She walked out and enveloped him in a warm hug that made him want to give her the world. But she didn't want the world. She wanted something else.

Nora took his hand and led him inside, depositing him on the sofa. Before he could bring up Sonny, she whipped out her phone, walked over to the window, and struck a pose.

"I was just taking my good morning pic," she explained. This was something he'd learned Nora did every morning without fail.

Erasmo watched as Nora took a slew of selfies, effortlessly morphing her facial expressions across the emotional spectrum. She took great care to make sure her shirt was visible in each shot.

"Not sure if I want to post a serious Nora pic or a silly Nora pic on the Gram today," she said. "What do you think the Beatles would prefer if they could weigh in on this?"

"Hmm . . . well, I'm fairly certain that they wouldn't care one way or the other."

"Agree to disagree," she said. "They seem like thoughtful fellows who would be more than happy to help out a young lass in need."

"Is that so? How many of their songs do you know? Can you even sing any?"

"I could unleash an amazing display of vocal talent and sing 'Sgt. Pepper's' for you, but I think you're already captivated enough with me as it is."

A brief moment of silence presented itself while she added a caption to whichever of the many photos she'd chosen to post.

"I want to talk about Sonny," Erasmo blurted out, desperate to get the conversation over with as soon as humanly possible.

Nora's hands froze on her phone, which she then slowly slipped into her pocket.

"Okay, good," she said. "I . . . didn't want to rush you. I figured you'd need some time to research our options."

Research. The truth was that he needed to do zero research to discover what he already knew. Sonny wasn't possessed. He was ill. He had to be.

Even in genuine cases of possession, the *vast* majority are of the diabolical vexation type, which is usually caused by people being idiots. Morons who mess around with séances and spells, who either don't know what they're doing or don't have the gift, falling victim to opportunistic entities. There's no way a kid as young as Sonny was messing around with that stuff.

It couldn't be diabolical obsession either, when the possessed are subjected to horrible visions and sinister voices in their head. That's just not what he saw on the video.

That only left diabolical possession, the rarest of all. And the odds of this were so miniscule that it was laughable, especially considering that mental issues were almost always the cause of the abnormal behaviors blamed on diabolical possession.

No, he didn't need to do any research. What he needed was to find the strength to tell Nora the truth, and to get Sonny real help.

"It's been a little better lately," Nora said, speaking at a rapid clip. "He's never had any episodes during the day, and most evenings he's perfectly fine. But on the nights that it does happen . . . it's bad. Nothing like what was on the video, but still horrible." She chewed the fingernail on her left thumb and paced around the room. "The good news is that we know what's wrong with Sonny. All we need to figure out now is how to get rid of it. When all of this first—"

"Nora," Erasmo said, trying to interrupt.

"—started, I went straight to the archdiocese for help. I thought that they'd send a priest over to investigate, to try and cast it out somehow. But the father I talked to just sat there shaking his head and said that they 'no longer conduct those types of ceremonies.' But I know that's complete *bullshit*! He just didn't believe me! He thought I was some kind of goddamn crackpot!"

The sudden flash of anger in her voice startled Erasmo, blistering his already-frayed nerves.

"So," Nora said, "the last couple of weeks I've been mulling it over, and I was thinking that maybe *you* should go talk to them. After all, I'm sure they saw the news stories. The priests over there must know who Erasmo Cruz is."

"Nora, I really don't think that . . ."

"But last night," she continued, ignoring him, "I had *another* idea. Now I'm thinking that it'd be even better to skip the archdiocese altogether and go straight to the local media."

"Wait . . . the media?"

"Yes!" Nora exclaimed, pacing faster now, her cheeks flush. "If we can bring enough attention to what's happening to Sonny, it would put pressure on the Church to help him. I mean, they can't ignore news stories about a kid that desperately needs their help, right? And the news people would talk to you, wouldn't they? Because of what happened at the Tracks?"

"Nora, please—"

"I know in my heart that they'll listen to you. I mean, after that experience you had with the children . . ."

"Nora!" Erasmo yelled, startled at the volume of his voice.

She stopped mid-pace and turned to him, her left eye twitching.

"I have to say something," he said, "and when I do, I want you to hear me out. Can you promise to do that?"

Nora gave no answer. Erasmo proceeded anyway.

"There is definitely something wrong with Sonny, but not what you think."

The muscles in Nora's jaw flexed, tense sinews strained and bulged beneath her porcelain skin.

"I know exactly what's wrong with him."

"No," Erasmo said. "I'm afraid that you don't."

"I absolutely *do* know Erasmo! And so do you! You saw it!" Nora's features contorted into a mass of fractured creases. "There is nothing else it could be!" she screamed as tears slipped down her face, leaving shimmering trails in their wake. "Nothing!"

"But Nora, there *are* other explanations," Erasmo said, his gut churning uncontrollably. "Explanations that make much more sense."

"Like what?" she yelled. "That he's *sick* . . . that there's something wrong in his head *mentally*? That's bullshit!"

"Nora . . ."

"*Screw you*, Erasmo!" Her face was a deep scarlet now, blood surging beneath her translucent skin. "You said you could help us! But you're a liar! I should've known . . . just a big goddamn liar with a stupid internet ad. Did that accident at the Tracks even happen? Or is that just another lie you tell people?"

She walked up to Erasmo, tears still falling from the tiny slits her eyes had shrunken to, clenched fists high above her head. He braced himself, certain she was going to bring them down directly onto his face. Her features were screwed up into a wretched expression, as if something were attempting to eat her from the inside out.

"You saw it!" Nora screamed. "You left here crying like a little bitch! And now you're going to tell me that it's not real? That my brother is sick in the head? Get the hell out of here! I'll find someone else to help us. You're useless. I can't believe I actually let you touch me."

Erasmo stood frozen, unable to fully process what was happening, while Nora's fists remained trembling in the air. It was clear that she desperately wanted to pummel him, and he doubted that she'd show self-restraint for much longer.

"Why are you still standing there like an idiot? I said to get out!"

Erasmo genuinely attempted to turn around, to move his legs so that they'd carry him out of the room. But his limbs didn't respond to any of the directions he gave them. Nora grabbed his arm and yanked him toward the door.

"Get. The. Hell. Out." Nora's lithe hands shoved him out of the house. "Leave! And when you hear about Sonny being helped, that he's better, don't show your stupid face wanting to apologize. I won't care!"

Erasmo stood limply on the porch and stared out at the sparse lawn. He braced for more yelling, but none came. Instead,

Nora gently sobbed behind him, which he found infinitely more disturbing. "You saw it, Erasmo," she whispered.

He descended the stairs, his skin now clammy and trembling. She was right. He'd seen it, and had run out of her house, down those very stairs, dripping with his own bile.

"You saw it," she whimpered again.

He'd seen *something* that night, but now that some time had passed, was he even sure of what it had been? The truth was the lighting of the video hadn't been very good. In fact, at first, he had a hard time making out anything at all.

Erasmo remembered sitting on her bed, straining to get a clear view of what was happening on the television screen. He'd gotten up and walked over to it, hoping to see a little better. In the video, the room Nora had walked into, Sonny's room, was dark, and the camera only picked up vague outlines in the shadows.

When Erasmo got closer to the television, he could make out a figure, Sonny presumably, sitting on his bed, hunched over. The boy was shaking his head back and forth, as if he were vigorously saying no, the force of his head movements so strong that his gangly body swayed from side to side.

During brief pockets of silence in the video, when Nora wasn't screaming, Erasmo could hear wet, slobbering sounds in the background. He'd inched closer to the television and then saw that Sonny was hunched over even farther, as if he were studying his lap intently. The boy's head began to whip back and forth again, this time the movements so powerful and vicious, it looked as if his neck might snap in two. What was he . . .

Wait. His lap. There was something on the boy's lap.

Standing in front of the television, his mouth agape, Erasmo began to waver. Sonny had something in the room with him. By then, Erasmo could see the outline of a figure, one that had been there the whole time. There was something on Sonny's lap, and he was eating . . .

Without warning, a brilliant flash appeared on the video. Nora must have turned the room's light on. Erasmo could then see exactly what Sonny was doing, and this time his legs did give way. He fell on his ass, his eyes still locked on the screen, unable to stop watching even as the contents of his stomach roared up his throat and onto the floor.

The intestines were the worst part.

Sonny had one dangling from his mouth, a massive, wrinkled worm undulating between his teeth. He was gnawing on it, trying to rip the slimy tube open so that he might feast on its contents.

"Why?" Nora had screamed in the video. "Why did you do this?"

Sonny pulled the intestine out of his mouth and threw it at Nora. The camera jostled as she tried to dodge the glistening projectile.

"I LIKE MEAT, BITCH," the boy answered in an impossibly deep voice. He buried his head in the carcass's gut and rooted around inside of it. When Sonny's face rose, his skin glistened scarlet, a thin web of veins stuck to his right cheek.

"Echo . . ." Nora had sobbed on the video. "Echo . . . oh my God. Please, please, stop doing that to him . . ."

The golden retriever's coat, surely once shimmering and luxuriant, was now matted with his own blood. He lay belly-up on Sonny's lap, his body shaking as Sonny continued to rummage around his insides. Erasmo had watched as the dog's head lolled on screen, his long pink tongue hanging out of the side of his mouth.

"He was a good boy. Leave him alone . . ." Nora's words were barely intelligible through her sobs.

Sonny stopped gyrating his head inside Echo's belly and slowly brought his face up. The boy's eyes did not look straight ahead. Instead, they were turned far to the left, as if he were trying to see something beside him without turning his neck. He reminded Erasmo of a ventriloquist's dummy whose operator was not very skilled. Then Sonny broke out in a large grin, the corners of his mouth turning impossibly high, and his eyebrows arched as far as they could go, revealing the tops of his eyeballs.

The bloodstained lips, the quivering tissue stuck in his teeth, the web of veins dangling from the corner of his mouth . . . and worst of all, that joyous, maniacal grin. These ghastly images finally compelled Erasmo to scramble off the floor and run out of Nora's house that night, swearing to himself as he fled that he'd never go back.

A deep, bone-shaking chill snapped Erasmo out of the memory. He trudged across the yard, still in a state of shock at how horribly his conversation with Nora had all gone. All he'd wanted to do was explain to Nora that her brother was sick and needed help. But she was right . . . about everything. He was, without a doubt, cowardly and useless. Being so viciously cast away from her was what he deserved.

When Erasmo finally reached the Civic, he turned for one last look at Nora, but she'd vanished inside, surely too disgusted to stand his presence any longer. He stood perfectly still for a moment, seeking the sun's comfort, but the early-afternoon light did nothing to warm his cold, trembling skin.

CHAPTER 18

OVER THE NEXT few days, Erasmo spent a lot of time with the boxes underneath his bed. He caressed their contents, studying them intently, despite the fact that he'd pored over their details countless times before.

This is finally the right time, he thought. His bones were telling him to just do it; so many of his questions would be answered once and for all. Erasmo touched his pocket and felt the lump that rested inside. It was newer, not like the objects inside the boxes, but it went with them. A package deal so to speak.

The more Erasmo wallowed in his pathetic state of affairs, the stronger the urge became to go through with it. Tonight was the night. He was sure this time. But when? It was only 9 p.m., and that seemed to him a little early for such things. He decided to have a glass of milk and wait for a bit, just in case.

In case of what though? In case Nora, by some cosmic miracle, reached out to him? She wouldn't, of course. Deep down he knew that. The hate in her eyes as she threw him away had been too clear to believe otherwise.

Erasmo reached for the shelf over his bed and pulled down his favorite book. Reading Dubois was as good a way to pass the time as any. He vaguely remembered an entry about a soothing incantation, which would be helpful right about now. It didn't take long to find it.

On the Use of Spells to Alleviate Suffering

The aching, unceasing hurt one feels when suffering a deep loss is enough to drive even the strongest person truly mad. Unfortunately, I have learned this from experience. As I have so far been unsuccessful in making contact with my daughter's spirit, I've now turned my attention to healing the excruciating void in my soul.

My research recently made me aware of a bruja, a witch in Oaxaca, Mexico, who professed to know an incantation that helps those afflicted with great suffering. This sounded exactly like what I needed. I traveled there and met with the woman I'd heard about, who was gaunt but immensely powerful. She assured me her spell worked, but that the price was too high, and I was better off living with my sadness. I was unrelenting though, and finally she gave me the list of ingredients to collect, and the incantation itself.

It took days, but I gathered what was needed. The toughest to obtain was the innards of a human eye, but I am not easily deterred. The witch told me that I needed to swallow the combined ingredients at midnight, under the moon, and chant the words she gave me.

That night, I swallowed the foul concoction and fervently sang to the moon in a language I didn't recognize. Soon, I began to hear whispered words all around me. A soothing voice spoke in a beautiful timbre.

And it told me to do terrible things.

I saw visions of myself hunting men, women, and children . . . lessening my pain by inflicting it upon these innocents. I felt the strange words in my mouth and the potion in my gut combining to change me, to unleash a monster that was now only barely restrained.

I cannot lie. This was an intoxicating feeling. The weight of my sorrow had finally lifted, and all I had to do to keep it away was birth more sorrow into the world.

But is this what I wanted my life to be? A monster unleashing the very pain that had consumed me? Could I go down a path that meant giving up any chance to encounter Emma ever again?

No. My quest must continue.

I ceased the incantation, the words dying on my lips, and forced myself to relieve my stomach of its vile contents. The soothing voice and the terrible images disappeared, and my grief immediately rushed back in to fill the void.

I sometimes think of the spell, yearning for the relief it gave me, and often whisper the words underneath my breath. A list of the ghastly ingredients is still tucked away in a safe place. Best to be prepared.

One never knows what the depths of desperation might bring.

Erasmo closed the book and slid it back onto the shelf. He found the story fascinating, but it was of little practical use to him. Except . . . there was something in Dubois's story that pricked his heart, that quickened the blood in his veins, but he couldn't pinpoint exactly what.

He lay down on his shallow mattress and drew the blankets over him, curling into a fetal position as chills coursed throughout his body. Between the constant worries about his grandmother's health and being rejected by Nora so thoroughly, he'd slept very little the last few days. It felt good to lose himself in the comforting darkness underneath his blankets. A breeze whispered outside of the window. His consciousness tumbled downward, the outside wind providing a soothing soundtrack to his descent.

Erasmo gave in to the dark, and inside of it was an image, a beautiful one of him and Echo. The dog was alive, and leapt at Erasmo, deliriously happy to see him, licking his face with that bright pink tongue. He felt the dog's love for him, and felt the same love swell from his own heart in return, and knew that he'd give his life to keep this animal safe. In fact, he would kill someone if he had to. . . .

A buzz surrounded him, loud and insistent. Erasmo erupted from underneath the sheets.

Nora. Was it her?

He grabbed his phone and held it for a moment, unable to look at the screen. After closing his eyes and saying a silent prayer to whoever might be listening, he glanced down.

Erasmo was startled when he saw the name. It wasn't Nora, but his disappointment was tempered by pure shock.

Rat.

He stared down at his phone for a few moments, and then checked the time. 1:45 a.m. Why the hell was he calling so late? Terrifying thoughts flooded his head, each one worse than the last. Erasmo closed his eyes and answered the call, certain that nothing good was on the other end of it.

"Hey," a thin voice said. "It's me."

Erasmo said nothing. A strong gust of wind rattled the walls around him, the cheap wood creaking under the strain.

"I need to meet you," Rat said. "Tonight. Right now."

"I've been trying to get ahold of you," Erasmo answered after a long pause. "For weeks."

"I know. I didn't want to talk to you until I was sure. Until it was the right time."

"And the right time is almost two in the morning on a Thursday?"

"Actually, yes," Rat said. "It's exactly the right time."

Erasmo hesitated, unsure how much of his hand to tip.

"Will you be alone?" he asked.

"I know this is all really strange," Rat said, "but just come meet me and I'll explain everything. It *has* to be right now though."

Given the company Rat had been keeping lately, Erasmo was perfectly aware he shouldn't even consider going. But Rat was the only real friend he'd ever had, and Erasmo already knew that he was going to get dressed, run out to the Civic, and drive like a maniac to his friend. He had to try and help, if such a thing were still possible.

"Where?" Erasmo asked.

"Jim's. I'll be out front."

Rat didn't have to specify. They only ever went to the one on Fredericksburg and Hillcrest. It was public, so that made Erasmo feel slightly better.

"Okay. I'll be there."

"Thanks. But be fast, okay?"

With that, the line went dead.

As he drove to the diner, heading up Zarzamora toward Fredericksburg Road, Erasmo was surprised to find that he wasn't scared. He was anxious to help his friend and prepared to fight if the situation called for it, but he wasn't scared. In truth, he had very little to lose. Especially considering his plans for the night.

Erasmo turned onto Fredericksburg and soon passed Woodlawn Theatre, its ancient, vertical neon sign rising defiantly into the night air. As he drove to the diner where he and Rat had spent so many hours together, his thoughts drifted to the beginning of their friendship.

Rat had been the instigator. In the middle of their freshman year at Lanier High School, he'd approached Erasmo in the library one day, asking him about the book he was reading, *Ghosts Among Us.* They took to each other instantly. Of course, having no one else to talk to during lunch certainly helped forge their new bond. The two of them began to spend every lunch period together in the library, quickly discovering their many shared interests. Since then, they'd been virtually inseparable. Until the last few weeks anyway.

Erasmo saw Jim's in the distance now, its large red letters announcing to whoever might be hungry at two in the morning that it was open for business. There didn't appear to be many patrons at the diner. But of course, there wouldn't be at this time of night.

He pulled into the large back parking lot, slid into a spot, and killed the engine. Erasmo glanced around but saw no sign of Rat. In fact, there was no sign of much of anything. A dusty Dodge Neon sat a few parking spots away, its front windshield a complex web of delicate cracks. The only other vehicle in the lot was a hulking, caramel-colored, four-door pickup that sat in the back aisle farthest from the diner, about seventy feet away. The old truck was backed in, its grille sparkling in the night, as if smiling and eager to show off its gleaming metal teeth.

He texted Rat that he'd arrived, but several minutes passed with no response. Erasmo debated whether he should get out of the car. He wanted Rat to know that he was there, in case his friend was watching from a distance. On the other hand, he didn't exactly love the idea of standing around in an empty parking lot in the middle of the night.

In the end, he was too anxious to just sit there and wait. He decided to go in the diner and take a look, make sure that Rat wasn't waiting for him in one of the booths. Erasmo jumped out of his car and walked across the lot. He was just about to step onto the sidewalk that ringed the diner when he jerked to a stop.

Something had moved.

He scanned the large lot, but the entire area was still and silent. The filthy Dodge Neon and the truck in the back aisle were still the only vehicles there. He must have been . . .

A flicker registered in his field of vision, and this time Erasmo saw where the movement came from. His stopped heart tumbled into his belly as the truck's engine erupted, its growl filling the night air. Harsh white light burst from the truck's headlights, splashing Erasmo and exposing him to the night.

He tried to make out who was in the driver's seat, but the headlights blinded him. The truck's engine roared again, even louder this time. He heard the mechanized power of the engine, and faint images of swirling white orbs flickered in his head.

Erasmo's eyes began to adjust to the light. He could make out a figure now, hunched forward, gripping the steering wheel with both hands. This figure's right hand moved to shift the truck from Park to Drive. He saw the outline of a face. And then, with a suddenness Erasmo was not prepared for, realized that he was looking into Rat's small, black eyes.

"No," Erasmo whispered.

Its tires wailed as the truck lunged forward. If Erasmo didn't move, the massive vehicle would mow him down where he stood, crushing his bones under its enormous weight. Time slowed to a crawl as he observed every detail of the old Ford speeding toward him. The rotation of its massive tires hypnotized him. He catalogued each sparkle of light gleaming from the truck's metal body. He observed the determination in Rat's pointed face as he gunned the engine.

Erasmo wasn't sure when he made the decision, but he knew he wasn't going to make an effort to get out of the way.

The swirling orbs continued to flash through his vision. Some things were just meant to be and couldn't be cheated. His only regret was that he'd never find out why his only friend had done this to him.

The truck closed in with terrifying speed and would soon crush him. Erasmo closed his eyes and waited, wishing for it to be quick, wondering what exactly he'd feel. The coolness of the metal bumper on his skin before it tore through his body? The hard groove of the tires' tread as it rolled over his face? He let out a long breath, expelling every wisp of air inside of his body, and prepared for the impact.

Instead though, a terrific screeching seared Erasmo's eardrums. He smelled the noxious fumes of burnt rubber but felt nothing. He opened his eyes to find the truck in front of him at a drunken angle, the driver's side presented to him. Rat yelled at him through the window, his small eyes bulging.

"Get in!" Rat screamed. "Hurry!"

Erasmo stared inside the cab, stunned, completely unsure what to do.

"Get in, Erasmo!" A thick green vein pulsed in the middle of Rat's forehead. "Please!"

Everything about this was wrong. He felt it. Wherever this truck was headed, it was nowhere good.

"Get out of the truck and come with me," Erasmo said. "Whatever they told you, or whatever they're making you do, it's all bullshit. We can just leave—"

Just then, steely fingers, bristling with strength, grabbed the back of Erasmo's neck. Erasmo struggled as his assailant forced him to walk around to the other side of the truck, where he was thrown into the open passenger-side door. His torso now lay in the cab, but his legs stuck out, flailing aimlessly.

"We don't have time for this shit," the person abducting him said as he shoved Erasmo's legs into the cab and yanked him upward until he was sitting more or less upright. A hand reached into his pocket and took his cell phone before the door slammed shut.

Erasmo turned to see who had manhandled him and was not surprised that Billy's angular face stared at him through the window. His kidnapper then climbed into the back seat, directly behind Erasmo, a half grin forming on his lips as he did so.

"Hurry up, Rat! Go!" another voice said from the rear.

Erasmo turned to see who had screamed this order to his friend and saw Leander, grim-faced, slapping his hand on the back of the driver's seat.

Erasmo's head snapped backward as the truck jolted forward. They careened through the parking lot, made a sloppy right onto Hillcrest, and were soon sailing down the road with no other cars in sight.

"You okay?" Rat asked, glancing briefly at Erasmo before returning his attention to the road.

"What the hell is going on?" he asked.

No one cared to provide him with an answer.

"Where are we going?" he asked, with more urgency this time.

"Settle down there, bud," Billy said. "We're doing you a favor. You just don't know it yet. You're about to be in for a show."

"Show? What the hell are you talking about?"

The engine's grumble vibrated through the cab, as if it wanted to be part of the conversation.

Erasmo turned to Leander, who sat still and expressionless in the back seat.

"And you? What the hell are you even doing here? Shouldn't you be in jail?"

Leander peered down, almost as if the question shamed him. "Well," he said, "the law's pretty strange as it turns out. What they charged me with, abuse of a corpse, is actually only a misdemeanor. And I have an alibi for the actual murder itself, since a neighbor saw me unconscious on my porch that night, so they had to let me go while they keep investigating."

"That's when he called—" Rat started.

"No," Erasmo interrupted, pointing to Leander. "I want to hear it from him."

"I called Rat when they let me out," Leander said after a long sigh. "I was desperate. I figured if I could just talk to you two, maybe you'd still help me."

"Help you with *what*?" Erasmo snapped, a surge of heat rising in his chest. "What are we supposed to do about a murder investigation and a dead body under your bed? Last I checked, neither of us has a goddamn law degree."

"There was no one else to call," Leander said softly. "And . . . I knew of a way you could still help me." Leander had lost even more weight since the last time Erasmo had seen him, his skin now sallow and clinging to his bones.

"I didn't steal that girl's body and hide it in my house," Leander continued. "It's like I told you before . . . my cousin Travis killed her. It had to have been *him* that put her body under my bed."

"Bullshit," Erasmo said. "Why the hell would he risk doing that?"

"To make it look like I'm the one who murdered her, obviously," Leander replied.

"The police *already* thought that you were the one who murdered her!" Erasmo yelled.

"Travis didn't know that!" Leander said, eyes wide. "For all he knew, I had spilled my guts and they were about to knock his door down and arrest him. And even if I did kill her, which

I didn't, why on earth would I leave her under my bed like that?"

"Because you're a sick asshole, that's why," said Erasmo.

Leander ignored this and continued. "Knowing that Travis was still out there, after what he did to Sandra, gnawed at me constantly. I was terrified that he might hurt someone else but wasn't sure how to stop him. Then I had an idea."

"He wanted *us* to help stop Travis," Rat blurted out, unable to contain the words any longer. "He called and asked if we could follow Travis around, watch his house, that kind of stuff. You know . . . make sure he wasn't hunting around for another victim."

"That's right," Leander said. "And I thought that, in the process, the two of you might come across some information that would help get me out of this mess. I figured if you could find some dirt on him, like if he's into drugs or beating on a girlfriend, maybe, then that would make the cops look at him a little harder."

"That's why I agreed to help," Rat said. "Travis wouldn't be able to hurt anyone else because we'd be following him. It would give us a chance to gather information that might help Leander, *and* we'd make some cash. It sounded like a win for everybody."

Erasmo turned to Rat and glared at him. "Why the *hell* did you even talk to him? You were there! You saw Sandra and what he did to her."

Rat stared forward, his expression blank, smoothly finishing a left turn before answering, "Didn't you hear what he said? His cousin was the one that did it. Leander is completely innocent."

His sweet, naive Rat. True believer to the end.

"So first," Erasmo said, "he wants us to get rid of a spirit that's haunting him. And then, while in jail for being in possession of a *corpse*, he wants us to follow around his cousin, who he blames for the murder. These are not the actions of a sane individual! Can't you see that?"

"I knew," Rat said, "this would be your reaction. That you'd say Leander definitely killed Sandra, that he was crazy, that it was too dangerous. So I just went ahead and did it myself."

Erasmo's mind churned, thoughts tumbling over themselves, his heart picking up speed. "Rat," he whispered, "where are we going?"

"Hold your water, buddy," Billy said. "He's getting to my favorite part of the story."

"I was watching Travis's house one night," Rat continued, "and was worried that maybe I'd missed something. I couldn't stake out his house twenty-four seven, so there were large chunks of the day where God only knew what that asshole was up to. I sat in my car, wishing that there was some way to know exactly *when* he was going to do something bad, so I wouldn't miss it."

The spit in Erasmo's mouth dried up and his stomach turned over on itself. A grotesque understanding settled over him, and he now knew exactly where the four of them were headed.

"Then I realized that maybe there *was* a way," Rat said.

"No," Erasmo said. "Stop this truck right now. Rat . . . Billy can't do what he says. He's a goddamn lunatic. Don't you remember what he did to that guy who jumped us? He would've *killed* him if that kid hadn't showed up! God wouldn't give that kind of power to a murderer!"

Rat continued, as if Erasmo had said nothing at all.

"I got his email address from the Craigslist response you forwarded to me. When I messaged, Billy said he'd be happy to help, but only if you were there to see, so that you could tell everyone about his gift. And he's right, Erasmo, people need to know what he can do."

"He can't do *anything*!" Erasmo said, his entire head now pulsating. "He's manipulating you. How can you not see that?"

"He was right about that kid with the red shoes," Rat said.

"There was some *other* way he knew about that!" Erasmo replied, almost screaming now. "It wasn't because he had a God-inspired vision."

"Well then, how? How did he know?"

Erasmo searched for the words but had no clear answer to give. All he knew was that every fiber in his being told him it wasn't possible that Billy had the sight. Maybe it was his inherently violent nature. Or perhaps it was his constant references to his supposed ability, as surely a true messenger of God would be humble and restrained. Or it may even have been the way Billy seemed to be taking great glee in whatever awfulness was about to happen. Whatever the reason, his bones were screaming at him that it just couldn't be true.

Erasmo then had a terrible thought, one he couldn't push away. Was he knowingly turning a blind eye to the genuine possibility of a seer, just because he detested the package it came in? Billy had foreseen the beating, and the boy with the red shoes. Erasmo had been so caught up in all the events that happened afterward, he'd refused to let this sink in. Is it possible his gut was wrong, and he was missing the obvious truth? No. There were too many things that just didn't add up, that didn't feel right. He was correct about Billy. He had to be. If he couldn't at least trust his instincts, then he truly had nothing.

"So the three of us began going to Travis's house," Rat continued, "and parking across the street to see if Billy felt anything. The first few times we went, Travis never came home. But the third time we waited outside, he did show up. That son of a bitch hadn't even walked from his car into the house when Billy saw a vision clear as day." Rat paused and turned to look at Erasmo, the muscles in his face pulsing, as if there were eels crawling under his skin. "Travis is going to kill another woman."

"Let me out," Erasmo said, barely audible even to himself.

"I wanted to stop Travis right then," Leander said, "to get out of the car and put an end to him. But Billy held me back, saying it'd be better if we caught him in the act. All we'd have to do is be there when it's about to go down, and then call the police. They'll come, see it for themselves, and arrest him. Then he'll be stopped forever."

"And you'd be completely in the clear," Erasmo said. "How convenient." He turned to Billy. "And you. Do you still really think I'm going to peddle your bullshit for you? And that anyone would actually give a damn even if I did say you had a gift?"

"Look, I'm just trying to help," Billy said, gazing out the window. "Unless you want this murdering son of a bitch out on the street. People finally knowing what I can do is definitely an added bonus though. That's why I wanted you here tonight. Plus, your boy here," Billy added, gesturing to Rat, "wouldn't do this part of it without you. You will *not* be able to deny what I can do after tonight. And if you still do, then you and I are going to have a serious problem."

The first caress of genuine panic flitted across his heart. He now recognized the neighborhood the truck was accelerating through. They were getting close.

"Rat," Erasmo whispered, "please."

Rat's face twitched, but his eyes remained fixed on the road. "I want to help save this woman. I want us to see the miracle that's about to unfold."

"There's nothing to see!" Erasmo pleaded. "It's not real!"

"Well," Rat said, "if you really believe that, then you're about to be in for quite a surprise."

Erasmo then understood that there was nothing he could do except wait to arrive at their destination. He considered making a run for it once the truck stopped, but there was Rat to think about. He couldn't just leave him to the demented whims of these lunatics.

"We're going to make it," Billy said, his eyes now closed. "You took so long to show up, I thought that we might miss the whole thing. But I can sense that it hasn't happened yet."

There was a confidence in Billy's declaration, in his entire demeanor really, that unnerved him. What was it Billy knew that they didn't?

"Well," Erasmo said, "are you going to tell me what you saw in this vision?"

Billy opened his left eye and regarded Erasmo warily. "Been waiting for you to ask, bud," he said, his other eye now popping open as well. "Wouldn't be much of an event anticipation if I didn't tell you what event we were actually anticipating, now, would it?"

Billy rolled his shoulders and stretched out his arms, as if his body needed to be warmed up to tell the story properly. He gave each of them a solemn look before proceeding.

"Well . . . sometime tonight, a young woman is going to visit Travis. She'll be wearing a purple dress, with silver high heels, like she just came from the club. She'll go inside, and then Travis is going to do to her exactly what he did to Sandra. Afterward, he'll wrap her up in a blue plastic tarp, throw her into the trunk of his Mustang, and speed off."

The truck turned one last time, and before Erasmo could mentally prepare himself, it slid to a halt, the engine reluctantly wavering before it fell silent.

"What do we do now?" Rat asked.

Billy glared out of the window, silent and lost in his own head as he studied Travis's small, lightless house.

"How do we know when this is supposed to happen?" Erasmo asked. "How do you even know for sure it's tonight?"

"Leave him alone," Leander said. "Can't you see he's concentrating?"

No one spoke for a few minutes, until Billy finally said, "I didn't know it would be tonight. Not when I first had the vision a few weeks ago." He took his eyes off the house and now scanned the street in both directions. "I've been coming here every day since and waiting, hoping to get a stronger sense of when it would be. And then a few hours ago . . . I felt it. Travis intends to murder this woman tonight."

"For the vast majority of true precognitives," Erasmo said, "events that they predict usually occur shortly after seeing them. But this vision came to you weeks ago. Why are you so out of line with the normal time frame? And what makes you sure it's going to be right now? Maybe it won't happen for another five hours. Or maybe—"

"Do you have to goddamn question everything?" Billy asked, eyes narrowed to slits. "Some things just *are*. Do you ask how salmon know to swim upstream? It's inside them, a part of them . . . an insistent whisper, *commanding* them to fulfill their purpose."

"I don't know," Erasmo said. "Everything about this contradicts the usual paradigms. Eighty-five percent of reported precognitive activity involves a loved one. But not you, Billy. No, you're having visions of complete and total strangers. People who—"

"Shut the *hell* up!" Billy said, spittle flying from his mouth.

With that, a dreadful silence fell over the cab, and the waiting began. Each of them scanned the street constantly, searching for even a hint of movement. A tense, uneventful hour passed, with not a single vehicle driving through the neighborhood.

"No one is coming," Erasmo finally said. "Are we really going to sit here all night, waiting like idiots?"

Just then, as if summoned by his words, a wave of cool light erupted from behind them, splashing through the cab. A car had turned onto the block. Erasmo's throat constricted as he swiveled his head to look. All he could see, though, was the harsh, blinding light emanating from the car's headlights.

"Here we go," Leander said.

The car approached slowly behind them. As it crawled closer, Erasmo saw that it was a maroon Chevrolet Malibu. He held his breath as the car approached Travis's house, and he let out a relieved sigh when it didn't come to a stop. Instead, the Malibu meandered past both the house and the truck, continuing down the dark street. Erasmo felt a surge of relief when the car's taillights disappeared in the distance.

"Man, I really thought that was it," Leander said, sounding shaken.

"I don't know . . . ," Rat said. He was peering out of the windshield, his small eyes searching.

"What is it?" Leander asked.

"Didn't you see the driver? It was a good-looking woman."

"It's dark," Erasmo said. "It could have been a four-hundred-pound Hawaiian guy for all you know."

"No, man . . . I saw her," Rat said. "How many attractive women are going to be driving down this exact street at this hour?"

"But she didn't stop," Leander pointed out.

Erasmo saw his chance.

"I bet we scared her away," he said. "She saw four shady-looking guys parked in a truck at three in the morning and decided not to get out. We've already changed things just by being here!"

"No . . . it's still happening," Billy said. "I feel it."

"Rat's right!" Erasmo said. "How many good-looking women are going to be driving past here at three in the morning? It's over. We stopped it. Let's get the hell out of here!"

"She was driving pretty slow," Rat said. "Maybe she was looking for the right address. . . ."

Erasmo's heart stopped as he saw light spread across Rat's face. He looked down to see the same illumination against his own skin, and soon its glow spread over the entire cab.

"She turned around," Rat whispered. "She's coming back."

CHAPTER 19

NO ONE SPOKE. The only sound in the night air was the rustle of tires against asphalt, growing louder each second.

"Get down!" Billy finally hissed. "She'll see us!"

Without thinking, Erasmo responded to the command and slunk down as far as possible. He looked over to see Rat hiding as well. A look of shock covered his friend's face, as if, despite all of his professed faith in Billy, he couldn't believe this was actually happening.

Erasmo listened carefully as the Malibu approached. He closed his eyes and willed the car to just keep going, to keep drifting down the road and not ever come back. But then he heard the Malibu roll to a stop, and cold stabs of panic penetrated his belly. The car's engine shuddered off not far from the truck.

"Call the police," Erasmo whispered.

"Let's make sure it's her first," Billy said.

"Call them *now*," Erasmo said, shaking his clenched fist.

They heard a car door close. The distinct clicks of high heels against pavement drifted into the cab.

Erasmo's head pounded in rhythm with his heart. This couldn't be happening. But was it? Was it *really* happening?

Only one way to know for sure. He slowly crept up to the door's window, eyes closed, waiting until his nose was pressed against the glass to open them.

The woman was absolutely riveting. Chestnut hair fell in lustrous waves down her strong, sensuous back. Her plum-colored dress shimmered and undulated around her, the wind playing with its sheer fabric. Silver two-inch heels, glittering in the night, carried her to the entryway. After a brief pause to adjust her dress, she rapped on the front door.

This wasn't real. There was *no* way it could be. But despite his psyche's feeble protestations, the young woman continued to exist, checking her watch as she waited on the porch.

"I'm calling the police," Rat said, taking his phone out.

"No," said Billy. "It's too soon. If the police come now, all they'll find is the two of them talking."

"Then how are we supposed to know when to call?" Erasmo asked. He was thankful that at least a part of his mind was dealing with the task at hand, while the rest of it flailed, searching for a glimmer of understanding.

"Why would you even *want* to call the police?" said Billy, tauntingly. "I thought you said that nothing was going to happen. I guess there'd be no need to call the police then, right?"

"Well," Erasmo said, "something is obviously going on, although I don't know what the hell it is." He grasped for even one reassuring thought but found none. "Let's say that something really is about to happen," Erasmo said. "How are we going to know when to call the police?"

"I've given that some thought," Billy said. "We have to go in there."

Erasmo almost objected out of habit but held back while he considered his options. Just making a run for it was out of the question. He had to stay for Rat and the woman in the plum-colored dress. And if the four of them just remained in the truck, God only knew what would happen inside that house. Billy had been right so far; he had to acknowledge that and worry about the implications later.

"Let's get out of the truck, quietly sneak into the yard, and look into the windows," Erasmo said. "If we can see them, see what's happening, then we'll call the police when . . . if . . . things start going downhill."

Billy grunted, clearly surprised at Erasmo's suggestion. "Good idea. I like it."

The four of them got out and walked across the street, single file. When they reached the middle of the yard, Billy motioned for Rat and Leander to check the right side of the house. Billy and Erasmo crept over to the left side, immediately seeing two large windows that sat ten feet apart from each other. A white linen curtain hung in the first window, obscuring their vision of anything inside. However, the second window's curtain hadn't been completely closed, and a sliver of the room behind it peeked through. Erasmo turned his head at different angles but saw only glimpses of a perfectly made bed and a sturdy oak dresser.

"Do you hear anything?" Billy asked.

Erasmo strained but could only hear the light breeze whispering around them. He was about to suggest they join Rat and Leander on the other side of the house, when Billy reached out and pushed the window upward.

"No!" Erasmo whispered. "It's too dangerous!"

"We'll be able to hear better if it's open," Billy said as he shoved harder, splotches of crimson blossoming on his face. But the window must've been locked, as it refused to budge even an inch.

A deep sense of relief ran through Erasmo, but it proved to be short-lived.

Billy walked back to the first window and inspected it. Erasmo followed him, hoping fervently that this one too was locked. Billy rubbed his hands together and shoved up as hard as he could. Erasmo's stomach dropped when the window slid open with no resistance at all.

". . . ass like that."

A wave of dread spread through Erasmo, freezing him in place. This didn't mean anything, he desperately tried to reassure himself. It could be consensual. A late-night visit to a friend with benefits. Happened all the time. He strained to hear more but there was only silence. Until finally, in a breathless voice, Travis spoke.

"Don't move. . . ."

"No, please . . . you don't have to . . ."

"Shut up!"

Wet, raspy, gagging sounds now.

"Call the police!" Erasmo said.

Billy looked at him with wide eyes, betraying either panic or excitement, Erasmo couldn't be sure. With no warning, Billy sprinted away from the window, heading back toward the truck.

Leander and Rat came running, drawn by the sound of Billy sprinting through the front yard. Both were ashen-faced and twitchy.

"Where's Billy going?" Rat asked, voice shaking. "Is it happening?"

Erasmo watched as Billy reached the truck, realizing for the first time how bad their situation looked. Leander, already under suspicion by the police, was now at the scene of another assault. Erasmo and Rat, who were with Leander when a body was found under his bed, were *again* with him at another crime scene. After being expressly told to stay away from him. And now Billy, the only reason they'd come here, was about to get into that truck and speed off, leaving them with no good explanation as to what they were doing at this house, other than to say, "The guy who brought us here said he could tell the future, Officer."

But, to Erasmo's surprise and relief, Billy did not get into the truck and roar off. Instead, he reached into the bed, pulled out a long object, and sprinted back to them.

"No time for the police," he said, running past them. When Billy reached the open window, he stopped and turned, caressing Jackie's bloodstained bat. Erasmo was shocked to see it again. Billy must've taken it when they were running back to the Ranger, after the boy in the red shoes had shown up. "I got this. Y'all stay out here."

Erasmo walked over to the window and positioned himself behind Billy, who looked back at him in surprise.

"You wanted me to see, didn't you?" Erasmo asked. "Let's see it then."

Billy reached out and pushed the curtain aside, revealing a tiny, immaculate bedroom. Billy climbed in first and then turned to Erasmo, taking his hand and pulling him in.

"Stay out here and call the police," Erasmo said to Rat and Leander once he was inside.

They stared back at him through the window, openmouthed.

As Billy and Erasmo moved through Travis's small bedroom, the unmistakable sound of ripping cloth reached their ears.

"No!" the woman screamed, sounding as if she'd spoken through a mouthful of water.

The altercation seemed to be happening toward the front of the house. They sprinted out of the bedroom and down a short hallway, emerging into the living room.

And there they were.

The young woman lay sprawled on a threadbare sofa, her beautiful plum dress ripped away. Travis was on top of the woman, his meaty hands holding her down, pants pooled around his ankles. He snapped his thick head around at the sound of their entrance. This movement caused the muscles in Travis's broad, tattooed back to flex, his latissimi dorsi expanding as if they were wings readying for flight.

He was a big son of a bitch. His face, bulbous and burned deep brown by the sun, registered no sign of distress at the sight of two strange men running into his living room. Instead, Travis took his hands off the girl and turned to them without even bothering to pick his pants up.

"You assholes just made a big mistake," he said, his dull eyes surveying them as he spoke.

"The police are on their way," Erasmo said. "You still have time to run. Just leave her alone and go."

Travis seemed to give some thought to this as he pulled up his jeans and buckled his belt, his eyes never leaving them. "Who the hell are you?"

"It doesn't matter," Erasmo said. "You're running out of time."

He approached the two of them. As Travis did so, he stretched his massive arms out to his sides and made circular motions, warming his muscles up. Then he casually reached into his back pocket and pulled out a large folding knife, its oak handle thick and well worn.

Erasmo's heart stopped beating, and he found himself unable to move his limbs.

"I don't give a *damn*," Travis said as he got closer, unfolding the finely edged blade, "who the hell's on their way. Tell me why you're here."

Erasmo could think of nothing to say, no explanation, that would prevent Travis from slicing him and Billy up, an event he suspected was only seconds from happening. He desperately wished for the approaching wail of sirens but heard only the sound of his own strained breathing.

"Please," the woman begged, "you don't—"

"Shut up!" Travis said, turning to her. "I'll be done with them in a minute."

And then all hell broke loose.

In a sudden burst, Billy darted past him, heading straight for Travis. Erasmo watched in a mixture of relief and horror as Billy, bat cocked behind his head, swung viciously at Travis's face. The bat connected with a dull thud that resounded throughout the room. Travis's thick head snapped to the side, and his body crumpled to the floor in a limp jumble of muscles and tattoos.

Despite his shock at the suddenness and brutality of what had just happened, a wave of relief coursed through Erasmo. He released the breath trapped in his lungs and found himself able to move his limbs again. It was over. All they had to do now was sit tight and wait for the police to show up.

But Billy was just getting started. He loomed over Travis, who lay on the ground with his extremities splayed in uneven, awkward positions.

"Uwwwgh . . ." Travis mumbled.

Billy glared down at him, jaw muscles flexing. He held the bat upright in his left hand, as someone would hold an umbrella in a light drizzle. Billy's eyes slowly swept up and down Travis's body.

A chill caressed Erasmo's spine. "Billy?"

Suddenly, Billy's eyes widened, and his arms shook, as if he were being charged with a massive amount of voltage.

"Billy, what's wrong, man? Are you—"

Before Erasmo could stop him, Billy lifted the bat high and with a throaty grunt brought it down directly onto Travis's face.

"Hey!" Erasmo screamed. "What the hell are you doing?"

Billy proceeded to bombard Travis with blows, each one cracking bone and ripping flesh. It was only after Travis's face had been hammered repeatedly that Erasmo finally overcame his shock and ran at Billy, tackling him. As they lay tangled on the floor, a shrill wail reverberated through the house.

The woman. She stared at the bloody mess that was left of Travis's face. Her hands clawed at her scalp, grabbing fistfuls of luxuriant hair.

"It's okay," Erasmo said, getting off the floor and walking toward her. "We're not the bad guys here. He was hurting you. The cops will be—"

But, before he could finish, the woman bolted from the sofa, threw open the front door, and bounded down the steps, wailing. Erasmo stood frozen, listening as her screams slowly dissipated into the night.

Rat and Leander then burst through the door, coming to an abrupt halt and almost falling over each other when they saw Travis and what little remained of his head. The two of them wore identical wide-eyed, slack-jawed expressions, as if they were intentionally mimicking each other.

"Oh my God," said Leander, the words almost too faint to hear.

"He was going to kill her!" Billy yelled, still on the floor clutching his bat. "He was attacking her, just like I said!"

Leander and Rat turned their horrified faces to Erasmo, who found himself unable to speak.

"Tell them, Erasmo," Billy said. "Tell them what he was doing!"

"What happened?" Rat said, clearly in shock, his eyes drifting from the mass of bloody meat on the floor to Billy and back again. "You said all we had to do was show up and wait . . . that the cops would handle everything."

"There was no time," Billy said. "He was attacking her, and then pulled a knife on us. I *had* to do it."

"But," Rat continued, "his head . . . I don't . . ."

"Billy did that to Travis," Erasmo said, finally finding his voice, "because he *wanted* to, not because he had to."

"That's bullshit!" Billy screamed. "The only reason that woman isn't being assaulted right now is because *I* brought us here. You don't understand anything! I'm fulfilling my purpose. When Travis was lying there on the floor, God showed me what was to come. I saw everything. Travis was never, *ever* going to stop hurting people. It wouldn't have been right to let him go on living."

Rat and Erasmo shared a long, mournful look. For the second time in just a few weeks, they were faced with the dilemma of whether to flee the scene of a crime or stay and face the repercussions. But this one was different. Someone was dead. Not hurt, or maimed, or possibly dead. Just straight-up dead. Rat looked as if he'd rather be anywhere else in the world than where he currently stood. His lips quivered, and his small eyes filled with tears.

I'm sorry, he mouthed as a large drop rolled down his cheek.

Erasmo considered how the conversation would go when the police arrived. He imagined them trying to explain why they were even there, and how Travis had ended up with half his head bashed in. The girl, who could have helped verify their story, was long gone.

And there was something else to consider. Billy wasn't entirely wrong. They *had* saved this woman. Erasmo had no idea if Travis would've continued brutalizing women if he'd lived, but he *did* know that Travis attacked someone tonight. Does that mean he should be lying dead on his living room floor? Well, it meant that when you play with fire, sometimes you get half your head taken off with a baseball bat.

"Let's get the hell out of here," Erasmo finally said.

The four of them sprinted out the front door and through the lawn. Erasmo and Rat jumped into the front of the truck while Billy and Leander clambered into the back seat. A nervous whine escaped Rat's throat as he fumbled in his pocket for the keys.

"Hurry up, Rat," Erasmo said, certain they'd hear the blare of sirens at any moment.

"I told you," Leander said, his voice quietly floating through the cab.

"What?" Erasmo asked.

"I told you," Leander said again.

"Hurry up!" Billy screamed at Rat, who'd finally managed to pull the keys out of his pocket.

Erasmo turned around to find Leander staring directly at him, a hint of a smile on the corner of his mouth.

"I told you it wasn't me," Leander said as the truck's engine roared to life. "I didn't murder anyone. It was that son of a bitch all along."

CHAPTER 20

AS ERASMO EMERGED from deep sleep, a panorama of disorienting visions floated through his head. Images of small, wet mouths, and bloodstained teeth, and maggot-infested meat had ravaged his dreams, and he now woke in a gloom of confusion. Erasmo wasn't even sure where he was until seeing his own dingy mattress. He shook his head, sat up, and checked his phone: 4:45 p.m.

Jesus. He'd slept most of the day. At least the five o'clock news would be on soon. He turned on the TV and changed it to KSAT 12.

Erasmo's throat felt as if it were coated with dirt. He shuffled out to the kitchen and poured himself a large glass of milk, immediately feeling better as it washed over his arid throat. He thought of calling Rat but quickly dismissed the idea. He needed time to think everything over before talking to any of them, even his friend. There were just too many problems to consider, the main one being his presence at the scene of a fatal beating.

But his thoughts were elusive, fluttering moths, and the flame they kept returning to was Billy Doggett. Billy, who had now twice predicted dramatic events that impossibly came true.

In fact, if Billy hadn't let his bloodthirst get the best of him, his plan would've more or less worked. But now, they couldn't tell *anyone* about what Billy had foretold and what they'd stopped from happening, at least not without incriminating themselves in a murder. Erasmo felt a slight twinge in his chest as he thought of another prediction Billy had made . . . the only one that had yet to come true.

You were screaming. Screaming real bad. And I could see that you were terrified, although of what I don't know. And . . . there was blood too. So much blood flowing down your screaming face.

He tried to focus on the most immediate concerns. Had they left anything behind that could tie them to the scene? Had they touched anything in the house? No one had worn any gloves, and there'd been no time to wipe the place down, so their prints could definitely be a problem.

His phone's ringtone floated into the kitchen. Erasmo sprinted to his bed and stared down at the screen. Leander.

"Hey, that you?" Leander asked, voice shaking.

"Yeah," Erasmo said, "what's going on?"

"The cops were just here. A detective."

Erasmo's heart shriveled into a frail husk.

"What?"

"I'm freaking out over here, man! She asked me when I last saw Travis . . . and where I was last night! I mean, she didn't arrest me, so maybe they don't have anything, right? Maybe she was just fishing—"

A series of sharp knocks erupted from his room's back door.

"Mr. Cruz! Open up. It's Detective Torres."

Time itself seemed to slow down, the detective's words stretching out over an indefinite, horrifying duration. The police were here for him. They knew.

"I need to talk to you. Now!"

Last time, Torres had come through the front to get to his room. Now she was knocking directly on the rear door that opened to their backyard. Had she been worried that he would try to run? After hanging up the phone, Erasmo took a deep breath, walked over to the lopsided door, and opened it. Detective Torres stood there, grim-faced. Her notepad was already flipped open, as if she were expecting to write something of note immediately.

"Hey," Erasmo said, attempting to appear confused by her presence.

Torres entered, but just barely. She stopped two feet inside the room and stared at Erasmo, her hard eyes unblinking.

"I know you weren't expecting me," she said tersely, "but I need some answers." Whatever friendliness she'd shown him previously was now entirely gone.

"Sure . . . no problem, Detective."

Torres looked to the ceiling and gazed at it, as if she were searching for answers in the cheap plywood. "When was the last time you saw Leander?"

"Leander?" he asked, his mouth impossibly dry.

"Yes, you know. Leander. The guy you met with at Boneheadz. The one we told you was suspected of murder. The one with a dead girl under his bed. That guy. Leander."

How the hell did Torres know? Or *did* she even know? Leander could be right. Maybe she was just fishing. There was no way anyone could've seen them at Travis's. It had been so dark. Right? Erasmo clenched his roiling stomach and rolled the dice.

"You told me not to see him again after that last incident, Detective. I haven't."

Torres pulled her eyes away from the ceiling and focused them on Erasmo. "I also asked you to stay away from him the first time I came here, and you sure as hell didn't listen then."

She returned her eyes to the ceiling, as if she couldn't bear to look at him. "I'm going to ask one more time. When's the last time you saw Leander?"

A desperate urge to run overtook Erasmo. He wanted nothing more than to shove Torres out of the way and flee, far away from her and this house. But that was impossible. There was nothing to do now but press forward.

"Like you just said, Detective, he kept a dead girl under his bed. Why on earth would I see him again? Yeah, I was trying to help the guy, but that was before I knew how screwed up he was. If you remember, we were the ones who called you about that body in the first place. I'm kind of shocked that you'd think I'd see him again, honestly."

Torres nodded her head, deliberate and knowingly, before responding.

"Tell you what," she said, "let me ask you something easier. Where exactly were you last night?"

Erasmo had anticipated this question from the moment Torres had stepped into his room, but hearing the actual words still knocked the wind out of him. Cold sweat erupted from his pores, slickening every inch of his skin. It was far too late to back out now, so he steeled his nerves and delivered another massive lie.

"I was just here in my room last night, Detective," he said, fixing a perplexed look on his face. "I was exhausted . . . spent the whole evening sleeping."

"Sleeping?"

"Yeah, didn't go anywhere at all. Started reading for a bit and then just drifted off."

"Well, damn," Torres said, her steely eyes fixed on Erasmo, "you must be one tired son of a bitch then."

The temperature in his room couldn't have been more than seventy degrees, but Erasmo felt as if he were in a sauna. Plump drops of sweat threatened to slip down his forehead, practically announcing his guilt. He wiped at his brow, the act itself an admission of his distress.

"Sorry?"

"I mean . . . you slept all last night, yeah?" Torres asked. "Went to bed early and all?" The detective made a show of looking Erasmo up and down. "And you *still* took a nap in the middle of the afternoon?"

"A nap? I don't . . ." Erasmo stammered.

"You've got lines all over your face," Torres said. "Not to mention a pretty bad case of bedhead."

"Oh . . . yeah. I haven't been feeling great the last couple of days," Erasmo managed to say, focused on keeping every word steady. "I think I might've picked up a bug or something." And before he could stop himself, he added, "Sleeping isn't against the law, is it?"

"No," Torres said, sharply and with no hesitation. "It's not." She then turned so that her back was to Erasmo. "But obstruction of justice certainly is."

Erasmo froze. His muscles tensed as he waited for the detective's next words. But Torres allowed him to stew in the silence for a long, excruciating moment.

"You're aware of this, right? That impeding a criminal investigation is something you go to jail for?"

"I am," Erasmo said, attempting to quell his rising panic, "but I'm telling you, I was here asleep."

"I see," Torres said. "So you weren't at Travis Castillo's house last night with three other guys?"

Shit.

Erasmo's legs lost their strength and almost gave out underneath him. But he managed to steady himself, swallow hard, and continue.

"No . . . why would I possibly have gone there? Like I said, I was here the entire night. I'm not really sure what else you want me to tell you."

"Well," Torres said, glaring at him, "you could tell me why one of his neighbors saw four guys running from Travis's house last night."

She walked closer to Erasmo, until the detective's solid frame was just inches away.

"And why one of the guys fits your *exact* description. While you're at it, maybe you can also explain why the neighbor said that one of the other guys looked just like your little friend Rat too."

And there it was. They *had* been seen. For a few moments, Erasmo considered just plopping down on his bed and telling Torres everything. And he almost did, his mouth opening to utter the words. Except . . . that neighborhood had been so damn *dark*. It just didn't seem possible that anyone could've gotten a good look at them. He was certain of it. So certain, that he inhaled deeply and took one last gamble.

"So, this person saw our faces?" Erasmo asked in an incredulous tone. "Or did he just describe us generally? I mean, you know that there are other short Hispanic dudes in San Antonio besides Rat and I, right? Shit . . . that's almost half the damn city." He debated with himself before adding, "Then I guess you should take me in so the witness can identify me, since they got such a good look and all."

Torres stood with her eyes cast down, looking as if she were trying to remember something she'd forgotten. After a few seconds, she sighed, slid the notebook into her jacket, and showed her palms to Erasmo.

"Okay," she said. "Let's talk."

And just like that, Torres dropped the formal, adversarial demeanor, casting it off as easily as if she were sloughing off a heavy overcoat.

"I have no idea how much you already know, but Travis is dead. His front door was wide open all morning, and a neighbor finally went in to investigate. Found him with his head bashed in."

Erasmo wasn't sure how he was supposed to react to this. Well, how a person who *wasn't* hiding something was supposed to react. Surprised? Horrified? Uncaring? He tried for an expression that conveyed both shock and disturbance.

"I don't know for sure if you were there last night or not. I think you might've been, but I can't prove it. And honestly, I'm not entirely sure how much I even care one way or the other."

Erasmo felt a strange mixture of relief and abject confusion at this statement. Was Torres trying to trick him into admitting something?

"It's my job to try to solve these things, you know. I get a big pat on the back every time I bring someone in and say, 'This is the guy. Right here. He did it.' The funny thing is though . . . a lot of times . . . they don't care if the guy you bring in did it or not, as long as he's a poor excuse for humanity and we can close a case. Don't get me wrong, we don't go out and frame guys or anything like that. But if you bring a guy in and it's obviously better for everybody if he's off the streets, a lot of times it's a 'close enough' type situation." Torres paused, studying Erasmo for a few seconds before continuing. "Do you know why I'm telling you this?"

Erasmo shook his head.

"We found an item in Travis's bedroom. An earring . . . one that Sandra wore the night she was killed. When her body was found, the one in her left ear was missing. We're running some tests on the one we recovered at Travis's, but we're pretty sure it's a match."

Erasmo remained silent, unsure what to say to this.

"I think there's more to this case than it seems. *Way* more. But as of now, the case of the young, beautiful murdered woman is solved. Our bosses are happy. Of course, there's a whole new case, the case of the bludgeoned-to-death tough guy. But guess what? No one gives a shit about that case, especially because they wouldn't want to dig deeper and find out anything that might contradict Travis's guilt. This was a dangerous guy, and our city is better off without him around. No need for further investigation. Close enough. And if he got taken out by four guys who bashed his head in, all the better."

Torres shoved her hands into her pockets and shrugged.

"But for me . . . I don't really feel that way. I think we should find out *exactly* what happened last night and why. And I'd like to know how the one piece of evidence that blew the case open was conveniently right there out in the open, like it was just waiting to be found. But . . . I don't run the department. I came here on my own because I wanted to see if there was anything you wanted to get off your chest."

Erasmo remained silent, and Torres nodded her head in acceptance as she opened the back door.

"Look, I don't know what happened last night, but let me leave you with this. Whatever it is that you're involved in . . . stop that shit right now. And be smarter about who you keep company with. I hope I never have to see you again, Erasmo."

With that, Torres stepped out into the backyard. Erasmo quickly closed the door and locked it, then collapsed onto his bed, shaking furiously. Crackling sounds floated in from outside as Torres stomped away, her feet crushing dead leaves and brittle twigs. The noises faded, until soon, Erasmo could hear nothing at all but the delicate, muted sound of his own trembling body.

CHAPTER 21

THE DAY AFTER Torres's visit, Erasmo's nerves were still blistered and raw from the encounter. He was having a hard time wrapping his head around the fact that he'd been questioned, by an actual detective, about his involvement in a murder.

He was also slowly digesting the fact that Leander had apparently been telling the truth this entire time. His whole insane story, from the unhinged murderous cousin to why Sandra's body was planted under his bed, all of it unbelievably true. He wanted to call Leander right after Torres left, but his brain had been too overloaded reinterpreting the events of the last few weeks to handle a conversation. It wasn't until the next morning that he felt clearheaded enough to call.

"Hey!" Leander said. "What the hell? You hung up on me and—"

"That detective showed up here too," Erasmo said. He proceeded to tell him the entire story.

"Wow," Leander said afterward. "I'm glad you were too smart to fall for her bullshit. I called Rat right after you hung up on me and warned him too. He freaked out and said that he was going to hide at his cousin's in Austin for a few days. It seems like Torres is just going to let everything go though."

"So that's it?" Erasmo asked. "You're in the clear now?"

"Looks like it. Got a call from the DA's office this morning, telling me that the 'abuse of a corpse' charge had even been dropped. Assholes didn't even apologize."

"And Billy?" Erasmo asked. "Have you heard from him?"

"Yeah," Leander said after a long pause. "He's called a few times, but I haven't picked up. Just don't have it in me to talk to him again. All I keep thinking about is Travis's face . . . what Billy did to it. I know we're probably better off with him dead, but the fact that Billy had it in him to . . ."

Erasmo knew what he meant. In the last few days, images of the bloody, flattened mess that used to be Travis's head sporadically flashed in front of him. It was as if that horrific sight had been a lightning bolt, its afterimage seared into his retinas.

"I'm just glad you're no longer a suspect," Erasmo said.

"I . . . I've been given my life back," Leander said. "Look, I know things got pretty rocky there for a while. But what matters is . . . I asked you for help, and now I've been cleared. So from the bottom of my heart, thank you."

Erasmo was stunned at this. Whenever he considered the events of the last few weeks, all he managed to see was an endless series of colossal misjudgments. Was it really possible that some good had come of it all? Even the slight possibility of this offered a welcome sliver of comfort.

"And this isn't goodbye either," Leander said. "Once you've gone through some serious shit like this with someone, it's friends for life. See you soon."

And before he could say anything, the line went dead, and Erasmo was left staring blankly at the phone.

Of the many horrible events that he'd been a part of recently, it surprised Erasmo to discover that the worst part, by far, was being alone at the end of it all. He was unnerved by the suffocating nature of the loneliness that now overcame him.

Every cell in his body revolted at his current state of solitude, clamoring for and demanding the presence of another human being. All of these bizarre happenings had been so surreal that he'd begun to feel only barely tethered to reality, and now he needed someone to ground him before he floated off into the waiting sky.

If he could just talk to someone about everything he'd seen. The woman in the plum dress, Travis and his bludgeoned face, Billy being right yet again . . . people and events he needed to diminish by speaking about them in the cold light of day. But there was no one. He certainly couldn't tell his grand-mother. She needed every ounce of her strength to fight off the rogue cells attacking her body. The last thing he wanted to do was burden her with his crap. And poor Rat was traumatized enough without Erasmo making him relive all of it.

Which was how, despite every effort to dissuade himself, he once again ended up on Nora's front porch. Erasmo stood there and swallowed hard, hands shaking as he rapped on the door. He listened intently, but only silence emanated from the house. Erasmo knocked again, harder this time. His heart bounced in his chest when the sound of footsteps finally approached.

He prepared for the door to open, but then . . . nothing. Was she on the other side, small teeth gnawing on her thumb-nail, trying to decide what to do? Or perhaps that was just wishful thinking. Most likely, she was backing away from the door quietly, desperate to avoid him. Another thirty seconds passed. The only thing that kept him from leaving was the dis-tant hope that she'd at least come out and tell him to go to hell. Then at least he'd get to see her face one last time.

After another minute, he'd given up on even that and turned to leave, when miraculously, the door creaked open. Nora stood in the doorway, perfectly still. Her hair was a tan-gled and matted mess, as if she'd just woken up, even though it was almost noon. A wrinkled gray nightgown hung from her frame, various stains discoloring the front of it. She remained silent, her face unmoving and unreadable.

Erasmo searched for something to say. He had a whole speech prepared, but after seeing her, every word of it fluttered out of his head. Then, right when he was on the verge of outright panic, Nora did something unexpected: She began to sob.

He stood paralyzed, unsure what to do. Words seemed not enough, but he couldn't imagine presuming to touch her. Erasmo stood there with what must've been an alarmed look on his face, until finally, she spoke.

"I missed you."

Those three words knocked the wind out of him. Not even in his most fevered, optimistic fantasy had he imagined that Nora wanted to see him. Erasmo walked across the rickety porch and enveloped her in his arms, scared that she would dissolve into swirling wisps of vapor. But her warm body pressed against his own. This was real.

"Thank God," she said, her voice muffled.

The next few minutes were a haze of tears and stammered apologies. "I was too embarrassed to call," she explained. "I thought you'd never want to talk again. I didn't mean *any* of those things. It's just . . . I lose my head sometimes when I get angry."

"No," he said. "I told you I'd help and didn't. You had every right to be mad."

He began to tell her what had happened at Travis's, every single detail. But, despite his urgent need to unburden himself, Erasmo stopped himself. He trusted her completely, but now that he was about to speak the words, involvement in a murder just seemed too much to put out there. Besides, her mere presence had already soothed his blistering nerves. He was comfortable sharing at least one piece of news though.

"Do you remember Leander, the guy who—"

"Of course," she said. "How could I forget?"

"Well, it turns out he didn't do it after all. There won't be any charges against him."

"Oh my God . . . that's wonderful!" Nora hugged Erasmo so tight that he had trouble drawing a breath. "I knew it," she said, a satisfied smile on her face.

"What?" he asked, perplexed.

"Don't 'what' me. You did it! You helped him."

Erasmo wanted to set her straight, to explain that he hadn't done anything at all. How, in fact, he'd been stupendously wrong about Leander. But as Nora looked at him with such affection and admiration, the words dried up in his mouth.

"Tell me! How did you prove it wasn't him?"

"Well . . . I can't really say."

"You're right! Something like that should be kept secret. The important thing is that you helped him. I *knew* I was right about you!"

Had he not been so busy frolicking in her attention, Erasmo might've seen where Nora's intentions were headed.

"I know that you doubt yourself . . . but see how you helped Leander? You've been touched for a reason. Thank God you're back. Sonny's been in a bad way. Worse even than before. But you're here, and now you can go back to helping him."

Over the next few days, Erasmo spent every available moment either with Nora or trying to figure out what he was going to do about Sonny. Even before showing up on her doorstep, he'd already decided to do and say whatever was needed to keep Nora in his life. Unfortunately, now he had to *actually* do something. But what? How on earth was he supposed to help a child who needed professional psychiatric help?

His head ached from constantly generating ideas only to reject them seconds later. The situation would have almost been funny, if the thought of losing Nora again weren't so horrifying. In the end, after three straight days of wringing his brain out, he settled on the best plan he could think of.

"I'm ready to try and help Sonny," he said one afternoon over a lunch of chicken salad sandwiches, trying to sound as casual as possible.

She placed the sandwich down and fixed her storm-cloud gray eyes on him. "I've been hoping . . . praying really . . . for you to finally say that."

"I'm going to attempt to drive the entity from Sonny's body," Erasmo said. "Force it out of him, and away from here."

He was shocked when a look of displeasure flashed across Nora's face.

"You mean . . . like an exorcism?" she asked, brow furrowed.

"Yeah," Erasmo said, "more or less."

"But . . . you're not a priest."

"Well, no . . . but . . ."

"I thought only priests could do exorcisms."

Erasmo said nothing as he tried to hold back the look of annoyance threatening to emerge onto his face. He had just assumed that Nora would be over the moon at *any* attempt to help Sonny.

"Yes, typically that's true," he said. "But the fact is the essence of the ritual is the words that are spoken, not who happens to say them. I promise you, if there is a demon inside your brother, it won't know, or care, if I have a degree in divinity or not. Underneath his vestments, a priest is just a man; he has no more mystical power than you or me. All this beast will know is that a powerful force is attempting to expel it from Sonny."

Erasmo could see by the dull look on her face that Nora was both disappointed and unsettled by this idea.

"But . . . priests do perform the ritual sometimes, right?" she asked. "Haven't even some popes conducted them?"

"Yes," Erasmo said. "Pope John Paul conducted three: one in 1982, one in 1984, and one in 2002. Pope Benedict did a few as well. And under Pope Francis, more priests are being trained as exorcists than ever. But the Church is of the opinion, and rightfully so, that performing the ritual is very dangerous, to both the possessed and the exorcist. A major exorcism can only be carried out by a priest with a bishop's approval, which is *very* difficult to get. That's why I'm offering to do it. But if you don't feel comfortable with that, then you should just ask the church for one."

A pained expression flitted across her face.

"You already know," she said, staring at the floor, "that they turned me down."

"Well," Erasmo said, "then it doesn't sound like we have much of a choice."

"I told you, they only said no because they didn't take me seriously. But you . . . they'll listen to you, because of what happened. . . ."

"What . . . you mean at the Tracks? I'm sorry, but they won't. No one at the archdiocese would even know who the hell I am. And even if they did, do you think they're going to risk their reputation for me? Some guy who shows up with a story about railroad tracks and ghost children? It's *never* going to happen. And we're not going to the media either, if that's what you're about to say. You asked for a plan to help Sonny, and I've given you one. *That's* the plan I'm willing to try."

Nora glared at him, the thin, veiny skin around her eyes twitching in arrhythmic spasms. She began to speak but stopped after the first syllable, appearing to think better of whatever she was about to say.

Erasmo added what he hoped would be the coup de grâce. "Feel free to contact the church again if you want to. But even when they do consider performing the ritual, it's their standard practice to conduct a complete battery of psychological exams to rule out mental illness."

He studied her face for any visible reaction to this but saw only the briefest flicker in her eyes.

"Fine," she said. "But I want it to happen soon. I'm going to rest now. Please leave."

With that, she stiffly got out of her chair and shuffled down the hallway, leaving Erasmo alone with a growing horde of restless, unnerving thoughts.

CHAPTER 22

WHILE HE WAS doing some research on an exorcism in Guatemala that Exco_75 had once mentioned, Erasmo's phone buzzed in his pocket. His stomach clenched when he saw the name on the screen.

Billy. Damn it. He'd allowed himself to hope that this psycho would never call him again. In fact, he'd been optimistic that Billy had just up and left town altogether. After all, he'd committed a murder, and there wasn't any real reason for him to stay in San Antonio. Erasmo almost let it go to voicemail but figured it'd be better to know what Billy wanted.

"Hey there, bud . . . you still alive and kickin'?" Billy said, his drawl somehow more pronounced than before.

"Hey, Billy. You up to speed on Leander's situation?"

"Sure am. It's my understanding that our friend is completely free and clear." The self-satisfaction was hard to miss.

"Yeah," Erasmo said, "everything worked out, and I'm glad it did. But I should tell you, I'm done with all that. I'm moving on."

"Moving on?" Billy laughed. "Like what . . . gettin' a regular job? You know, I actually think that might be a good idea for you, Erasmo. I don't think you quite have the stomach for this sort of thing."

"You're a hundred percent right, Billy," Erasmo said. "I made a mistake when I ran the ad. That kind of life isn't for me. Good luck to you, though."

"Now," Billy said after a long pause, "just hold up a sec. Before you take that job selling insurance or some shit, you and me got unfinished business."

"Actually, I think we're all done. Like I said, I'm moving on."

"Now, Erasmo," Billy said. "Haven't I shown you what I can do? Haven't I proven it to you? *Twice?*"

"I'm not really sure what happened, to be honest," Erasmo said. "All I know for certain is that every time I'm around you, someone ends up getting beaten with a baseball bat."

"What the hell do you mean, *you're not really sure what happened?*" Billy asked incredulously. "You know exactly what happened. I knew things that I shouldn't have." Billy's voice started to rise, but he caught himself, and his next words were deliberate and measured. "Look, Erasmo, I know we can't tell people about what happened with those thugs or with Travis. But I really think that those two events should give me the benefit of the doubt. For what I'm about to tell you, I mean."

"I already told you, I'm out."

"What kind of coward are you, Erasmo? How can you not believe what your own eyes have seen?"

"I don't—"

"Just listen, damn it! Someone else is going to get hurt. I saw it. The visions are coming faster now. I'm not sure why, but they are. This time, it's a young boy."

"A . . . young boy?"

"Yeah," Billy said. "He's going to be taken in the middle of the night. I don't know from where I wasn't shown that part.

But I did see where he's going to be taken to. It's an area with lots of trees, over by one of the missions. Close to that stone bridge–looking thing . . . the one with arches underneath it."

"The aqueduct? Over on the south side?"

"Yeah, that's the one. Look . . . I need your help. I have to stop this from happening, but I don't think I can do it by myself."

"I already told you, I'm not going on any more of these, Billy."

"Why? Because you think I'm wrong?"

"I just—"

"What if I'm *right*? And I can't stop it by myself? How are you going to feel when that little boy's guts are hanging out of his belly, draggin' all over the ground while he tries to crawl away from the sicko that sliced him open? Because *that's* what I saw. How are you going to feel then?"

Erasmo found himself in the remarkably strange position of arguing against basic rationality. Billy had been right both other times. However it was that he knew, there was no arguing with the fact that Billy's predictions had come true and had helped save two people. And now, for the third time, Billy claimed to have seen something terrible that needed to be prevented. The logical thing for Erasmo to do was to help him stop it, or at least show up and make sure that Billy was finally wrong.

But it wasn't logical. He still couldn't bring himself to believe that God would invest this sacred ability in such a flawed, violent person. Surely there was an explanation for Billy's foreknowledge of these events. Erasmo just hadn't been able to figure it out yet. But did *how* he know really matter? Wasn't the pertinent thing that he *did* know? But what did

Billy expect him to do? Be at his beck and call, strolling into violent situations until one of them got killed?

"This will be the last time I'll ask you to do this," Billy continued, as if reading Erasmo's thoughts. "After we save this boy, I'll spend all my time finding a way to make the police believe me and have them deal with all this from now on. Shit, I don't want to be in the middle of this craziness either, Erasmo. You think I liked having to do that to Travis? I haven't slept through the night since. But after what I saw, I just couldn't let him . . ."

"But what if you were wrong?" Erasmo asked. "What if Travis was never going to hurt anyone else? You killed a man because you saw some illusion in your head—"

"I *know* what I saw. And I haven't ever been wrong since this whole thing started. Never. If I was wrong even one time, then I'd just crawl into a hole and kill myself, because that would mean my gift was taken, that God didn't believe in me anymore. And that . . . I couldn't live with. But it ain't ever happened, and I don't know why I'd be wrong now."

"I just don't—"

"Look, man, I know your heart's not in this. I know you think that I've tricked you somehow, that I'm not really seeing these events. But I don't have time to find someone else that can help me stop this son of a bitch. Whatever happens, I promise this will be the last time I'll come to you."

A small boy, running for his life in the black night, begging for his parents. Erasmo closed his eyes and made the only decision that would allow him to sleep that evening.

"When?"

"Not sure yet," said Billy. "I'll call you when I get a better sense of it."

Erasmo was about to hang up when Billy added one more thing.

"Oh, and just a word to the wise. Don't you be leaving me hanging. That's something I'd *strongly* recommend against." And with that, the line went dead.

After the events at Travis's house, Rat had hightailed it to Austin to stay with his cousin for a while. Since then, Erasmo's only communication with him had been a few text messages. The first one came shortly after Torres's visit.

with gabe in austin just 2 be safe. don't wanna have to lie to a detective. this is some crazy shit, huh? will call when I get back.

The next message came a few days later, after Erasmo had sent three unanswered texts.

still here in austin. will head back in a few days. I'm okay.

Erasmo had been so immersed in all things Nora that he hadn't worried too much about his friend's absence. But he did suspect that Rat was having trouble dealing with everything they'd gone through. Someone with a sensitive heart like Rat was surely going to have a hard time processing the brutality of what he'd witnessed. Erasmo figured that getting away for a while would be good for his mental well-being.

But as he lay in bed preparing for the next day's ceremony, Erasmo decided that it had been too long since he'd spoken to his friend. He grabbed his phone and dialed.

"Hello?"

"Hey!" Erasmo exclaimed.

"Dude, just got back in town today," Rat said. "You must have ESP or something."

A smile stretched over Erasmo's lips. "Are you messing with me? You're messing with me, right?"

Rat laughed, staccato and high-pitched, a sound Erasmo was relieved to hear.

"Damn, can you believe everything that's happened?" Rat asked after a long pause. "I mean, I genuinely can't wrap my head around it. We have now been around not one, but *two* dead bodies. Not to mention our fight with actual gang members."

Erasmo desperately wanted to tell him about the exorcism he'd be performing soon but decided to save it. His friend seemed freaked out enough already.

"Look," Rat said. "I need to tell you something."

"Okay," Erasmo said, a sense of unease settling into his gut.

"I don't even know how to begin," Rat said. "I guess I should start with . . . I'm sorry. I should've told you what I was up to with Billy and Leander. I knew you wouldn't go along with it, but I shouldn't have kept it from you. When I called you that night to meet up at Jim's, I honestly thought that you'd just come with us. But you didn't . . . and when I saw Billy shove you into the truck, I knew I'd messed up. I just really wanted you with me when we saved that girl and cleared Leander's name. But that was a mistake, and I'm sorry I put you in that situation."

Rat began to sob gently, a sad, feeble sound that made Erasmo's chest tighten.

"And even though I called you in the middle of the night, surely sounding like a lunatic, you came running to help. No one else would have done that for me. Thank you."

Erasmo rarely cried, as he'd done enough of that as a child. But now, he was surprised to feel tears stream down the side of his face. He wiped them away, and none followed after.

"No sweat, man. But I have to tell you something."

"What?" Rat asked.

"Just that . . . if you ever call me for help in the middle of the night again, I'm going to tell you to go screw yourself."

Rat burst into laughter, and the tightness in Erasmo's chest eased.

The two of them said their goodbyes and promised that they'd hang out soon. Erasmo now turned back to his research, focused. All he had to do now was conduct this damn ceremony and help Billy one last time, and things could finally go back to normal.

CHAPTER 23

"I HOPE YOUR skin doesn't burst into flames."

Erasmo ignored his grandmother's comment, pushed open the double doors, and walked into the massive church as she trailed behind him. As far as he could tell, his grandmother had attended mass at the Basilica of the Little Flower at least once a week since she was a child, without ever missing. This made her disappointment in his nonexistent church attendance all the more acute, and she never missed an opportunity to remind him.

They stopped in front of a marble font, the engraving on its base reminding all congregants that it had been donated by the actress Barbara Stanwyck. Erasmo dipped his fingers into the cool water and hurriedly made the sign of the cross. His grandmother, wearing a simple black dress, glared at him, outing him as an imposter to anyone paying attention.

They walked down the aisle and chose a row toward the front, settling in next to a young couple whose faces beamed with love and unrestrained hope. Before he could stop it, a thought escaped the black, bubbling recesses of his subconscious. The rogue thought whispered to him, insistently wondering if his parents had ever shared even one moment as pure as the one on display in front of him. He already knew the ugly answer though, and his stomach turned in on itself, gnawing his insides, punishing him for allowing such a thought to surface.

Erasmo glanced around the church, and, as always occurred on the rare occasions he visited, was taken by the graceful elegance that surrounded him. The impossibly high ceiling, the stone pillars, the ubiquitous arches, the stained-glass windows glowing with intricate details, all somehow managing to soothe him. His eyes continued to move around the room, then settled on the altarpiece that loomed over the white marble altar. Winged angels flew on thick, billowing clouds, forming an arch around a cross that emanated radiant beams of light. Despite himself, Erasmo could almost feel the power flowing from it.

Perhaps his favorite feature of the basilica was also its most understated. His eyes found the gray, marble bricks that lined the walls, a single name carved into each of them. His grandmother had told him that, because Little Flower was constructed during the Great Depression, money had to be raised to complete it. The people whose names were carved into those marble bricks had donated at least twenty-five dollars during a time when every penny was sacred. He'd always liked the idea of that sacrifice being permanently celebrated and whispered a few of the carved names under his breath.

"Mass is about to start," his grandmother said. "Try to pay attention. You might learn something."

And start the mass did, with all the usual Catholic pomp and circumstance. He did honestly try to pay attention but found it almost impossible to do so. He'd only agreed to come for two reasons, and listening to this priest's questionable interpretation of the Bible wasn't one of them.

The first reason was that his grandmother was due to start her treatment in earnest this week, and she'd requested that he attend. Given the circumstances, he would do anything to bring her even the slightest bit of contentment.

The second reason was that Erasmo intended on doing something that he hadn't done since he was a child: say a prayer.

He glanced over at his grandmother, her gnarled hands clutching the rosary that she carried everywhere with her. He wanted to ask her if the countless prayers she'd said during her lifetime had made even the slightest difference. They certainly had done nothing for his father.

Erasmo closed his eyes, intending to ask God for the only thing he wanted, but the words refused to coalesce in his head. He tried again, but still they would not come, the thoughts turning to sludge before he could will them into existence.

He knew damn well why, of course. And it wasn't only because his many childhood prayers had gone categorically unanswered. No, there was an even bigger problem. If he opened his mind to God and begged Him to spare his grandmother's life, would he not be betraying everything he believed and knew to be true? Because there was a cold, hard fact that he could not resolve: The Church did not believe in wandering spirits.

From their perspective, dead souls simply went to either heaven, hell, or purgatory. They did not lurk in old Victorian houses, or creep around deserted cemeteries, and most definitely did not haunt railroad tracks on the south side of San Antonio. He knew with certainty that the Church was completely incorrect about this, and yet here he was, eager to beg God for His mercy.

Perhaps he was thinking about this all wrong. After all, most everyone he'd ever talked to about this subject had absolutely no problem both attending church *and* eagerly discussing the time they'd encountered a spirit of some kind. Although, he didn't know if this made them wholly uneducated in church doctrine or simply blasphemous.

Another possibility, he considered, was that God in fact did allow for the existence of spirits on earth, but that us humans had just screwed up our interpretation of his word. It certainly wouldn't be the first time that had happened.

Whatever the case, he had to put aside his own bullshit and do what he came here for. He closed his eyes again, cleared his mind, and attempted to talk to God.

Lord . . . I know you haven't heard from me in a while. The last time I can remember is when I bombarded you with unanswered prayers when I was little. I don't hold those against you. I know now that I was going about it the wrong way. . . . I was asking something for myself. While it's true that I was only asking for something that no child should ever have to beg for, nonetheless, it was selfish in nature.

What I'm asking for today, though, is not for me but for this beautiful woman sitting next to me, who is truly one of your servants. Your knowledge is boundless, so you already know that she is sick, and what it is I'm asking for. You also know what I'm about to offer, but I will ask anyway. God, please spare my grandmother. She does not deserve the slow, tortuous death she is facing. If a soul is necessary to replace hers, please take mine. I freely offer it. I understand that my soul is not nearly as valuable as hers, but it is all I have to offer. I ask for nothing else, just this one monumental mercy. Amen.

Erasmo opened his eyes as the priest continued to drone on. For some reason he'd expected to feel something, to sense a difference in the air around him. But he felt nothing, as if his conversation with God had in fact not happened at all. But he'd done what he came to do and felt comfort in knowing he had made his appeal to the highest authority. He sat back, took his grandmother's hand, and listened as the impassioned priest sternly warned his congregants of the many dangers of bearing false witness.

As Erasmo and his grandmother descended the steps outside Little Flower, she placed her hand on his shoulder, a telltale sign that she wanted to have a serious talk.

"Do you know why I wanted you to come today?" she asked.

"I . . . because your treatment is about to start?"

"Kind of," she said, crinkling her eyes. "Erasmo, I don't know what's going to happen . . . where we'll be a year from now. At some point, we're going to have to talk about what happens if—"

"No!"

"Listen," she said, "this is something about you that's worried me for a long time. Many times, I have seen you refuse to look trouble directly in the eye. If there's one thing I can promise, it's that running from hard truths only causes more pain and heartache."

They crossed Zarzamora, his grandmother stopping when they reached the sidewalk. She looked up at him, a pensive look on her face.

"The reason that I made you come today," she said, "is that I wanted to pray for you."

"Pray . . . for *me*?"

His grandmother turned and pointed to the north tower that rose majestically from the roof of the church. Atop this tower stood a large bronze statue, gently reflecting the afternoon sunlight.

"St. Therese of Lisieux," his grandmother said, "is so revered that they built this entire structure as a shrine to her. Do you know why the church is called Little Flower?"

"Because," Erasmo said, "she thought of herself as 'a little flower of Jesus.'"

"That's right," his grandmother said, pleased that he knew this. "She believed that being a beautiful flower in the garden of life was enough. That growing, and giving love, and bringing peace was enough."

She moved her eyes from the statue and set them on Erasmo, taking his burning face in her rough, trembling hands.

"And it's true, Erasmo," she said, her eyes sparkling at him, full of faith and love and power. "It's absolutely true."

His grandmother let go of his face, turned, and gingerly walked toward the Civic, her black dress fluttering in the warm afternoon breeze.

CHAPTER 24

ERASMO SAT HUNCHED over on his bed, studying the two books laid out in front of him. He needed additional preparation for the exorcism but wasn't entirely sure which book to begin with.

He picked up the one his fingers naturally gravitated toward and opened *A Practical Guide to the Supernatural and Paranormal.* While still confident that Sonny was not truly possessed, it surely wouldn't hurt to reread Dubois's account of his only experience with a fallen angel.

A Demonic Encounter

Some years ago, an associate with similar interests brought to my attention an alleged case of demonic possession in Romania. Ordinarily, I would have balked at such a long trip, but then my associate said something that gave me a start.

He claimed that the young man in question was possessed by the demon Amdusias.

The news excited me, as this was a powerful demon indeed. Amdusias is a great duke of Hell, who rules over twenty-nine legions of demons. Surely the opportunity to encounter a being so powerful was worth the long, arduous trip.

I hastily made the trek to the town where this afflicted man was rumored to be located. As soon as I inquired about him though, the locals scurried off, unwilling to even meet my eye. On my third night there, one lone woman approached and said that the person I sought was located deep in the belly of the forest. She was the boy's mother and begged me to help him.

She led me to the edge of town and pointed the way. I followed a dirt path lit only by weak moonlight, until it ended, and then found myself wandering in complete darkness. I almost gave up hope and turned around, when I saw him. He was a frail young man, clad only in filthy pants, cowering against a tree. I called to him, but he began screaming, begging me to go away.

When I entered that forest, the sky had been empty, but now dark clouds loomed overhead, thunder and lightning rumbling within them. This was when fear first crept over me, as I knew that Amdusias was thought to control thunder. Soon rain pelted my skin, and I saw that the young man had risen.

Before I could speak, he began to scream in agony. I glanced down and saw that his hands and feet were transforming into claws, his bones cracking and breaking to take their new hideous shape. But even worse was his face. I watched in utter disbelief as the middle of his forehead pulsed and bled, until finally a long, pointed mass of bone emerged and grew from his skull. It took me a moment to recognize what it was.

A horn.

He glared at me, eyes glowing, his horn dripping with blood. It was then that this creature screamed at me, the sound a deafening mixture of thunder, and animal savagery, and blaring trumpets. This unnatural, malevolent sound sent me running from the forest, begging for my life, until I finally emerged back into town.

I am ashamed to say that when faced with a truly powerful entity, I was too terrified to even speak. It is important to note that his appearance and demonic bellowing were not the only reasons that caused me to run. What truly frightened me was that, while in his presence, I felt my very thoughts beginning to unravel.

After this terrible, unnerving experience, my only counsel in regard to confronting a true demon from Hell can be distilled down into one simple word.

Run.

Reading Dubois's encounter with this demon never failed to send chills up Erasmo's spine. At least, Erasmo assured himself, he didn't have to worry about anything like that happening tomorrow. He then picked up the other book, a slim volume titled *The Rite of Exorcism: English and Latin*. Erasmo was familiar with the rite, as this was a topic that had always held great interest to him, but he wanted the words fresh in his mind. He opened the book and was soon immersed in faith and ritual and magic.

Several hours later, his head swimming with long, elaborate prayers, Erasmo slid the two books inside his backpack and triple-checked its other contents: his grandmother's cross, four handcuffs, their respective keys, and the small bottle of chrism, which was a mixture of oil and balsam used for church rites. Not a lot, but it was all that he needed. Erasmo placed his backpack by the door and slid into bed, hoping for a quick descent into sleep. It was important that he rest well. After all, tomorrow was going to be quite a day.

CHAPTER 25

HIS HEART FLUTTERED as he paced around Nora's small porch, waiting for her to come to the door. As Erasmo scanned the dimming sky, he was disconcerted to see that the sun had a strange quality to it, appearing blurry and nebulous, as if it were a smudge in an otherwise perfectly rendered sky. He watched with unease as the sun continued its leisurely departure, knowing it would soon take whatever light was left in the air with it.

It was 8:30 p.m., the exact time he'd told Nora to expect him. He would have strongly preferred to do this in the morning, but the renowned exorcist Father Thomas had said in interviews that he always started the rites after 8 p.m., and if it was good enough for a master exorcist, then it was good enough for him. He knocked again, and this time the door swung open.

The boy stood in the doorway, rigid, muscles pulsing under his waxen face.

"Sonny!" Nora called from inside. "Is he here? Let him in, please."

The boy glared at him, his eyes narrow and tense, but the he finally stepped aside.

Nora awaited them in the kitchen. He'd expected her to look nervous, to have sallow skin and dark bags under her eyes from a restless night's sleep. But she was clear-eyed and radiant, practically bursting with excitement.

"Thank you for this," she said, beaming.

He ached to hold her but settled for giving a faint smile and replying, "Sure, no problem." After an awkward pause, he added, "If it's okay, I'd like to go ahead and get started."

Nora nodded. "Does it matter where?" she asked.

"I'd prefer his bedroom," Erasmo said. "That's where he spends most of his time, right?"

Another nod from Nora. She turned and led them through the living room, Sonny following behind her. Now that he had a better look, Erasmo saw that the boy had a wiry, athletic build, bristling with youthful strength. He wore a sweater and jeans, just like his sister. He even walked like her, with measured strides and head held high, as if they were descended from a line of forgotten royalty.

When they were almost to his room, Sonny turned and regarded him with dull, vacant eyes. It was a look he'd seen before, this dead-faced expression, one that sent chills convulsing through Erasmo's spine.

He closed his eyes, trying to shake away the memory. But when Erasmo opened them, he stumbled backward in horror. Sonny's lips and teeth were now smeared crimson, and webs of veins hung from his chin. His curled, ruby-red tongue dripped with a glistening stream of blood and saliva. And worst of all, the child's soulless eyes leered hungrily back at him.

"Nora . . . I can't. I . . ."

She turned to him. "Is everything okay?"

Erasmo closed his eyes again, clamped his teeth together, and willed the image in front of him to change. When he finally

dared to look, he saw both Nora and a clean-faced Sonny staring back at him, both clearly confused.

"Sorry . . . everything is fine. Let's just go ahead and get
started."

Erasmo followed them into Sonny's bedroom and looked
over the small space this child lived in. Nothing appeared different since the video had been taken. The twin bed was still
there, right in the middle of the room. A set of drawers made
of shiny, thin wood sat against the right wall, and a crooked
desk with an aging desktop sitting atop it was pushed against
the left one. The room was void of decoration or personality of
any kind. Erasmo realized that Nora and Sonny were watching
expectantly, waiting for him to say something. He summoned
his prepared speech and began.

"There are a few things I want to make clear before we
get started," he said. "There are real risks involved with this
ritual. A true exorcism is a fight, a brawl in which the exorcist
tries to forcefully evacuate the presence from the body of the
inhabited. This can get very ugly, and there's a risk of physical
harm for all of the parties involved. Also, keep in mind that
exorcisms are often not successful. Sometimes, the entity is just
so powerful that it's impossible to force it out. And even if it is
vacated, the presence often just reinhabits the body as soon as
the exorcist is gone."

Nora looked at him, her brow furrowed. "But there's a
chance that it will work, right?"

"Well," Erasmo said, "because of my experience at the
Tracks, I believe that if there's a presence in Sonny, it will
respond to me. That's not very common, but because I've
already interacted with other entities, I hope that—"

"Wait a goddamn minute," Sonny said, his prepubescent
voice sounding strangely adult. "You think that you're about to
talk to a demon, but *I'm* the one in this room that needs help?"

"Sonny!" Nora yelled as she glared at him, furious.

Erasmo forced a strangled laugh out of his throat.

"Well, that's a fair point, Sonny."

The three of them studied each other in awkward silence. Erasmo already didn't like how this was going so far, but there was nothing to do but press on.

He opened his backpack, reached in, and pulled out the bottle of chrism that he'd mixed himself. It hadn't been blessed by a bishop, but it would have to do.

"Let's start." He began to anoint the windows and door with the chrism while Nora and Sonny watched intently. When he was done, he reached into his backpack again.

"This next part is for safety." He looked at Sonny as he produced the handcuffs from the bag. "I'm going to have to restrain you. These are just to make sure that you don't hurt yourself or your sister."

"Or you," Sonny said.

"Or me, that's true. We don't know how this thing is going to react when I start the rite. It may not take kindly to me attempting to communicate with it."

"This is all such crap," Sonny said, glaring at the handcuffs.

"Sonny," Nora said through gritted teeth, "I don't want to hear any of that. You promised me you'd try this. Please. Do it for me."

The boy stared at his sister for a moment, disgust on his face, but then shuffled over to his bed and plopped down on the mattress.

Erasmo gave the handcuffs to Nora, whispering, "It might be better for you to do this."

She took them from his hands, her eyes trained on Sonny. "Lay down, kiddo. No worries. I'll make sure nothing happens to you."

Sonny lay down with no further protest and closed his eyes as he allowed Nora to slip the handcuffs over his wrists and ankles. The boy grimaced as she attached the cuffs to the bedposts.

This was really going to happen, Erasmo thought, marveling at the unreality of it all. He walked over to the side of the bed and looked down at Sonny. Seeing the boy with his limbs spread apart and chained to the bed incited a terrible churning in his gut. Sonny's eyes remained closed and his body appeared relaxed. In fact, the kid looked downright serene.

"I'm going to start. Allow your mind to drift. Don't fight if you feel the presence taking over, okay?"

Sonny opened his eyes and looked at Erasmo as if he'd just politely requested that the boy flap his ears and start flying. A flush of heat erupted in Erasmo's chest, and a thick vein in his forehead began to pulse heavily.

He removed his grandmother's weathered cross from his backpack, along with *The Rite of Exorcism*. Taking a position at the foot of Sonny's bed, he closed his eyes and breathed deeply, searching for the part of himself that he now needed, the spark in his soul that the ghost children had responded to.

Erasmo's mind drifted, and it happened upon a memory. He was a child, sitting on a chair in front of a window, tears streaming down his face. He was furious, and heartbroken, the loneliest boy in the world.

Yes.

This memory helped unlock his power. He felt the thrum of celestial energy growing within him, expanding and magnifying his senses. His skin tingled, as if there were spirits caressing his flesh at that very moment.

He had found it. He was ready.

"*Ecce Crucem Domini!*

Fugite partes adversae!

Vicit Leo de tribu Iuda,
Radix David! Alleluia!"

The energy coursing through his body continued to grow. This felt natural and right. He was not scared. If anything, he now felt emboldened. Could it be that he'd finally found his purpose . . . his true calling?

Erasmo glanced at the boy and saw that his eyes were wide and unblinking, perhaps startled by the suddenness of the prayer.

He then began the ceremony in earnest, reciting the Litany of the Saints. The invocations came haltingly to him at first. But by the time he got to Psalm 53, he was locked in a groove, the words flowing from his lips.

When it was finally time to address the demon directly, his heart sped up, and the energy inside him pulsated in time with the words.

> *"I command you, unclean spirit, whoever you are, along with all your minions now attacking this servant of God, by the mysteries of the incarnation, passion, resurrection, and ascension of our Lord Jesus Christ, by the descent of the Holy Spirit, by the coming of our Lord for judgment, that you tell me by some sign your name, and the day and hour of your departure."*

There was no visible reaction from Sonny, who lay motionless, as if he took no notice at all of Erasmo and his commands. He continued, undeterred, soon reaching the part of the rite he suspected might finally prompt a reaction from the boy. He reached into his backpack and pulled out the vial filled with holy water he'd taken from Little Flower.

"May the blessing of almighty God, Father, Son, and Holy Spirit, come upon you and remain with you forever."

He then sprinkled the holy water on Sonny, taking care not to get any in his eyes.

And still not even the tiniest sliver of reaction from the boy.

Erasmo continued to press on with the ritual, not pausing until it came time to attempt expulsion of the demon.

"Therefore, I adjure you every unclean spirit, every spectre from hell, every satanic power, in the name of Jesus Christ of Nazareth, who was led into the desert after His baptism by John to vanquish you in your citadel, to cease your assaults against the creature whom He has formed from the slime of the earth for His own honor and glory."

Erasmo glanced over at Nora, who stood entranced, hanging on every word. He turned back to Sonny and was surprised to see a difference in his appearance. The muscles in the boy's face had gone completely lax, and his mouth hung open, a bead of drool forming on the corner of his mouth. His eyes were lifeless and stared upward, unmoving. If Erasmo didn't know better, he'd have sworn the kid looked catatonic.

"Depart, then, impious one, depart, accursed one, depart with all your deceits, for God has willed that man should be His temple. Why do you still linger here? Give honor to God the Father almighty, before whom every knee must bow. Give place to the Lord Jesus Christ, who shed His most precious blood for man. Give place to the Holy Spirit, who by His blessed apostle Peter openly struck you down in the person of Simon Magus; who cursed your lies in Ananias and Sapphira; who smote you in King Herod

because he had not given honor to God; who by His apostle Paul afflicted you with the night of blindness in the magician Elymas, and by the mouth of the same apostle bade you to go out of Pythonissa, the soothsayer. Begone, now! Begone, seducer!"

Erasmo peered down at Sonny, only to see that his lifeless expression had not changed. He was about to turn to Nora when he saw movement . . . a flash in Sonny's eyes, like the flicker of a light bulb about to burst to life. There it was again, as if the calm in his eyes had briefly parted to reveal a maelstrom underneath.

The boy's mouth now twitched and jerked, as if something were trying to escape from his throat. Erasmo's flesh prickled as a chill spread over his skin. He turned to Nora, who apparently had seen nothing, because she only gave him a weak smile in return. He pivoted back to Sonny, only to find the momentary storm in his eyes gone, and his mouth completely still.

Erasmo studied the boy, but there were no further flickers or twitches, just an expressionless child. The boy's eyes . . . for just a second, he could've sworn they had looked different . . . like someone else's entirely.

Shit. What now?

"I don't think this is going to work," Erasmo finally said. "If there's a demon inside Sonny, I can't force it to manifest against its will. Often, these presences will only emerge when no one else is around, which is why they often take control of the possessed at night. And this one might be clever enough not to show itself when someone in the room is trying to persuade it to leave."

A throaty, violent laugh erupted from behind Erasmo. He whirled around and saw Sonny writhing on the bed, each limb jerking in spasms as he howled in delirious laughter.

"Nora!" the boy bellowed, his face turned up to the ceiling. "Can you believe this moron?" Sonny's face turned crimson as he struggled to catch his breath, unable to stop himself from erupting in laughter. "What a dumbass!" he yelled breathlessly.

A burst of heat enveloped Erasmo's head, and he forced himself to look at Nora. Her face was frozen, confused, trying to process what was happening. But then the muscles in her face fell and rearranged themselves until they held only one unmistakable expression. Disappointment.

Erasmo's face burned even hotter now, radiating intense waves of heat.

"Nora . . ." he started but was unsure what to say next.

"What a loser!" Sonny screamed. "Nora . . . who do I sound like?" The boy proceeded to mimic Erasmo, his words brimming with derision. *"I command you unclean spirit . . . begone . . ."* Sonny promptly fell into another bout of relentless laughter. "What a joke! This asshole watches too many movies."

Nora began to say something but stopped herself. Her facial muscles rearranged themselves yet again, this time falling into a look even worse than disappointment.

To Erasmo's horror, Nora now looked at him with outright pity.

"Nora, tell this loser to get the hell out of here!"

"I . . . I . . ." Erasmo stammered, frantically trying to think of anything that might salvage even a little of his standing with her.

"Hey, dumbass, are you going to let me off this bed or just stand there with that stupid look on your face?"

Erasmo tried to detach his gaze from Nora's, not wanting to see the pity in her eyes any longer, but he found himself unable to make even the slightest motion.

"I think we should stop," Nora finally said. "This obviously isn't working."

"Okay," he said, the word barely a whisper.

Erasmo turned back to Sonny. The boy had a smirk on his lips, and his eyes were now serenely closed. He was obviously enjoying the moment.

"Any day now, douchebag," Sonny muttered under his breath.

Erasmo felt a sudden, overwhelming desire to sink his fists into this child. He could almost see himself, a crazed look on his face as he pounded the boy repeatedly and with great viciousness, until he was too exhausted to raise his fists back for even one more blow. The momentary vision was so real that he actually felt Sonny's tender flesh quiver under his striking knuckles.

Instead of beating this child though, as his humiliated heart desired, Erasmo reached into his pocket, grabbed the handcuff keys, and began taking them off. He glanced down at Sonny as he unlocked the last one, slipping it off the brat's limp right wrist. The boy's eyes were still closed, but his obnoxious smirk had faded away.

"You can get up—"

Sonny's hands shot out, grabbing fistfuls of Erasmo's shirt. The boy's eyes pulsated wildly underneath his eyelids, and his mouth twitched in violent spasms. Sonny was slowly pulling him downward. Erasmo tried to tear the boy's hands off him, but . . . Jesus . . . the kid was unbelievably strong.

"Let me go!" Erasmo yelled.

Sonny had a death grip on his shirt and kept pulling him lower until their faces were almost touching. Sonny's eyes suddenly flew open, straining against their sockets. He opened his quivering mouth and spoke.

"Can you smell my stink?" Sonny asked, his voice now somehow deep and raw.

And Erasmo could. Even as he frantically tried to pull away, he could. A putrid gas emanated from the boy's mouth, the smell of sickness and rot.

"You'll have to tell me," Sonny said in his new, guttural voice, "what it feels like to be eaten." The boy gave him a crazed smile, baring his small white teeth. "I've always wanted to know."

Sonny's throat produced a rumbling growl that rose from deep inside his body. Suddenly, Erasmo felt the bottom of his shirt lift up, his belly now exposed.

What the hell? Was he . . . oh God . . . he was going to . . .

He pummeled the boy with his fists, the very thing he'd yearned for just moments before, but Sonny wouldn't let go. Instead, the boy effortlessly withstood the blows as he maneuvered his face…

Christ . . . he was trying to get his mouth . . .

Erasmo swung even harder now, but Sonny was squirmy. He couldn't get a clean hit on the kid. The boy was relentless, ferociously shoving his slobbering mouth toward his stomach. Just as Erasmo prepared to strike another blow, he felt small, wet teeth fasten themselves onto his belly. He brought his fists down again but it was too late. Erasmo could only shriek as the boy, with an unmistakable grin on his face, began to rip his tender skin from his body.

CHAPTER 26

ERASMO SCREECHED AS the boy gnashed and ground his flesh. He pounded the top of Sonny's head, but the boy would not open his mouth and free him. Instead, Sonny began to viciously jerk his head from side to side. Uncontrollable panic now overtook Erasmo as he felt his skin begin to rupture.

As he clawed at Sonny's eyes, hoping to blind him for even a moment, Erasmo felt it. With a sudden burst of excruciating pain, his warped, tortured skin gave way and ripped apart. He screamed as brilliant, luminescent orbs appeared in his vision, swirling in front of him. Erasmo glanced downward and saw a scarlet piece of meat dangling from Sonny's grinning mouth. Sonny jerked his head up, flipping the piece of Erasmo back and into his open mouth, just as a ravenous dog would. Sonny looked up at him with a wide, pleased grin as he chewed.

"Mighty tasty," the boy said in his deep voice, lips smacking as he enjoyed the meat.

A piercing wail reverberated through the room as he staggered backward. It was Nora. She stood screaming in the corner, her right hand curled over her stomach, as if it were her who had just been eaten.

"Help me," Erasmo croaked.

Nora continued to scream, blotches of red spreading over her face.

"Call for help," Erasmo said, louder this time.

"I . . . I can't do that," Nora finally managed to blubber. "They'll take my brother away."

"Please . . ." Erasmo begged. His vision blurred, and his head felt weightless. Unconsciousness would overtake him soon. He turned and saw Sonny still happily chewing and smacking on the meat, his pale face streaked with Erasmo's blood.

Feeling the sticky wetness of his shirt plastered against his skin, Erasmo forced himself to look down. Blood rapidly spread over the blue T-shirt he wore, his abdomen the epicenter of the eruption. The blooming stain reminded him of a pattern in a Rorschach test, except this one grew and changed the longer he stared at it. A sudden movement on the floor forced his eyes off the drenched shirt. It was Sonny, now crouched down by the foot of the bed, his muscles tensed as he prepared to pounce.

Oh God.

Sonny was going to eat him again.

A whimper escaped Erasmo's lips. No longer able to stave off the inevitable, his legs gave way and he collapsed to the floor, landing on his back.

"Nora . . . please," he moaned. "Help me."

Nothing from the woman he loved. Not a goddamn word. She continued to cower in the corner, her eyes wide and unbelieving.

He had to get up. Right now. Erasmo placed his hands on the floor and tried to push, but his arms felt unsubstantial, as if they were made of smoke. He tried again, grunting and moaning, but his body refused to move.

A quick, catlike motion out of the corner of his eye caught his attention. He jerked his head and saw that Sonny had leaped and was now in the air traveling toward him. Erasmo picked up his right leg, coiled it, and kicked as hard as he could. His leg felt limp, as if it would fold in upon itself if it made contact with anything more substantial than air. But he was relieved to hear a loud *whoomp* when his leg connected with the boy's chest.

Sonny stumbled backward and fell to the floor. The pain in Erasmo's stomach was now sharp and continuous, as if he were being repeatedly stabbed with a jagged knife. He forced himself not to think about the grotesque scene that surely lay under his shirt and concentrated on only one thought: He had to get out of this house.

Erasmo tried again to get up, this time bending his body forward as if doing a sit-up, but the side of his belly exploded in retaliation. He glanced over and saw Sonny slowly pushing himself up from the floor. It wouldn't be long before the boy attempted to taste his flesh again. Trying to ignore the pain, Erasmo steeled himself and shifted his weight to his right side. Planting his left leg for support, he pushed against the floor, straining with everything he had to get upright. Then, after almost blacking out from the pain in his gut, Erasmo opened his eyes to a miracle. He was standing. Hunched over and on wobbly knees, but standing, nonetheless.

"Where are you going?" Nora asked, as if her brother wasn't currently stalking him as prey. "You can't leave. I . . . I can take care of you. I have some gauze here somewhere. . . ."

"I'm leaving, and you can't stop me," Erasmo said. He'd tried to sound forceful but was alarmed at the sluggish quality of his voice. He turned and lurched desperately toward the hallway, certain that Sonny was about to pounce again at any moment. After the first few agonizing steps, Erasmo was sure he was going to faint. But as his vision blurred and his legs wobbled, he thought of the piece of himself that was now traveling down the boy's throat, and his legs steadied as the world snapped back into focus. He shambled through the hallway and headed for the front door. He listened for Sonny's footsteps but heard only the faint plops of his blood spattering on the threadbare carpet below.

Erasmo almost cried with relief when he made it to the front door and leaned against it to rest. He had never been as tired as he was at that very moment. The creak of a floorboard whispered behind him. He turned to see Sonny emerging from the hallway, his face smeared with blood. He walked toward Erasmo with no discernible expression, the dullness of his pale face interrupted only by streaks of crimson and his shimmering gray eyes. Erasmo reached for the brass doorknob and turned it. To his horror, nothing happened. He twisted again and still it did not move.

"You may not leave," Sonny said as he approached. "Being eaten by one such as I is a great honor, and I am not yet done feasting."

Erasmo frantically jerked the knob in both directions, but still the damn thing wouldn't budge. He closed his eyes, preparing to fight off this crazy child-thing one more time. But when he opened them, he saw his mistake. There was a small oval knob that unlocked the door, located underneath the doorknob, that he'd forgotten about.

He whirled around and saw that Sonny was now almost on top of him, his blood-coated tongue stuck out, as if he could not wait even one more second to have another taste. Shrill screams filled the room. Erasmo wondered why Sonny would make such strange noises before realizing that he was hearing the sound of his own terror-stricken cries. With trembling hands, Erasmo tried to turn the small oval knob to unlock the door, but his hands were slick, and it slipped right through his fingers. He tried again, with the same result, and now felt the sickening heat of Sonny's presence just inches away. Taking a breath, he turned the small knob one more time, and his heart jumped at the sound of the lock clicking open. Erasmo threw open the door and lurched down the porch and through the yard, tears welling in his eyes when he finally approached the Civic. He flung the door open, dropped into the worn driver's seat, and fumbled his key into the ignition.

It was only then that he glanced back. The door stood open, but no one came running after him. Tears of relief rolled down the side of his face, dropping onto his shirt and mixing with his blood.

Erasmo pulled away from the house. His vision was dim and blurred, but whether from blood loss or weeping he didn't know. After a few blocks of swerving unevenly all over the road, he pulled over to the curb and parked. He had to see. He needed to know just how badly his body had been maimed. Erasmo took a deep breath, grabbed his soaked shirt with both hands, and pulled up. He stared down at his wound for what seemed like a very long time, his eyes lingering over the mutilation, in wonder at the complete and absolute strangeness of having been eaten.

CHAPTER 27

THREE WEEKS. It had been three full weeks since Sonny had tried to eat him. His flesh prickled at even the thought of the boy, and his hand reflexively gravitated to his stomach. After he'd left Nora's that horrible evening, Erasmo had driven himself to University Hospital. He had explained to the emergency room nurse that he'd been in a fight with a crazy drunk who'd bit him. The doctor, a stern heavyset woman with a purple birthmark on her right cheek, asked him a shitload of questions about what happened, but Erasmo stuck to his drunken fight story. Finally, she'd given him something for the pain that worked wonderfully. The fiery pangs in his stomach cooled, allowing the doctor to examine and clean the wound.

"You were lucky," the doctor had said. "The wound is wider than it is deep. The patch of skin that was torn off consisted primarily of the outermost layer of the epidermis, what's called the stratum corneum. Now, there was some underlying tissue that was taken with it, but this could've been a lot worse. I bet the shock of having a bite taken out of you was just as unnerving as the pain from your actual wound, if not more so." She'd peered farther into the wound, spreading it open with her gloved hand. "Right now, your biggest risk is infection. I'm going to give you amoxicillin clavulanate to prevent that, but you need to keep a close eye on it." The doctor had snapped her gloves off and looked at Erasmo with sympathetic eyes before continuing. "I'm not going to lie to you. Without cosmetic surgery, the scarring is going to look pretty bad. But the wound itself will heal just fine as long as you keep it clean and dressed."

When Erasmo had returned home from the hospital, he'd snuck into his bedroom through the back door, so that his grandmother wouldn't see what kind of shape he was in. Over the next few days, he'd waited to leave his room until she had either fallen asleep or had gone to the store. And when she'd brought plates of food to his door, he would take them, quickly ask the usual questions about how she was feeling, and then disappear back into his room. Suspicion seeped from his grandmother, but she said nothing.

Erasmo's exhaustion had been constant, as the injury wouldn't allow him to sleep well. He'd tried to rest, but as soon as his body shifted even slightly, pain erupted from the wound. After several days, the deep ache in his stomach finally began to lessen, until one morning he awoke to find that the pain was tolerable.

While Erasmo's body healed, his thoughts often turned to the exorcism. He contemplated the savageness of the being that attacked him and spent hours reading through his many books on the subject. There were constant nightmares of the ravenous look in the boy's eyes while he chewed and smacked on raw flesh. And after turning everything over in his head countless times, Erasmo had been able to come to only one inescapable conclusion.

He had been so very wrong.

There *was* a demon inside of Sonny.

At first, he suspected it might be the creature Makalos, servant of the greater demon Magoth. The meaning of Makalos's

name is "wasted" or "gaunt," and his obvious need for sustenance would account for the hunger that clearly burned inside
of Sonny. He was almost convinced.

But then he remembered the Rabisu.

These are fallen angels that have transformed into vampiric
spirits. They are known for lurking in dark corners, attacking people, and seizing their souls. The Rabisu are sometimes
referred to as a "lurking demon" and "the croucher." Erasmo
closed his eyes and saw Sonny, crouched on the floor, blood
smeared on his face, ready to pounce. A shiver erupted from
deep within him.

Erasmo also read that when the Rabisu taste blood, their
hunger for it becomes absolute and unstoppable. And that's
when he knew for sure.

One of these creatures was inside of Sonny.

And he sure as hell was going to do something about it.

Erasmo knew where he'd gone wrong. He had committed
the greatest sin there was. He hadn't believed. He never genuinely considered the possibility that he was face-to-face with
the rarest of all paranormal phenomena. He'd held back, not
fully investing his energy, not harnessing his gift as he should
have.

And he wasn't going to make that mistake twice.

Erasmo was healed now. At least, healed enough for what
he had to do. Tomorrow he was going to wake up, drive to
Nora's house, and brawl with the fallen angel that was inside of
Sonny. And he wasn't going to stop until it was fully expelled
from the boy's body.

And if it refused to leave, and ever wanted Erasmo to stop
trying to drive it away, then that demon was just going to have
to kill him.

In the morning, Erasmo gathered his supplies and headed to Nora's. He hadn't called her, as he didn't want to give the demon any forewarning of what it was about to face.

He'd been deeply disappointed that, in the weeks it took to heal, Nora hadn't called him even once. The unsettling image of her standing in the corner of Sonny's room and ignoring his pleas for help played in his thoughts constantly. But despite Nora's refusal to help him that night, or even check on his well-being since then, he somehow still missed her terribly.

After arriving, he saw right away that her car wasn't in the driveway. Erasmo wasn't sure if the sigh that escaped his lips was one of relief or disappointment. He got out of the Civic and rapped on the front door just in case but heard nothing.

He was just about to step off the porch when a breeze stirred up the air, and a terrible stench suddenly walloped him. It seeped from the house . . . a horrid, putrid stink that made his stomach reflexively convulse. He turned and ran back to the door, banging on it as he called out for Nora. Still no movement from inside. Erasmo tried the doorknob, but it held firm. As he turned, frantically looking for anything that would help him break in, the fiberglass bulldog caught his eye. He walked over and peered down at the scowling beast.

Did she still keep it under his right paw?

He slid the small statue over, and there the key was, exactly where he'd last left it. Erasmo picked up the key, inserted it into the lock, and turned. He felt both relief and panic as the bolt retracted with a solid *thunk*.

When he stepped into the house, a wall of gut-convulsing foulness greeted him. Erasmo retched and stumbled backward, gagging in violent spasms.

Jesus.

Something was rotting in here.

He steeled himself and forced his way into the fog of decomposition. Not sure where to begin looking, he held his hand over his mouth and headed to the kitchen. Perhaps the stink was just from some old food that was left out. Nora wasn't very particular about cleaning up, so maybe that's all it was. Sure enough, the stench intensified the closer he got to the kitchen. As he stood at the entrance, his stomach twisted, bile flooding his throat.

Crumpled cans of Dr Pepper scattered noisily around his feet as Erasmo entered the room. He shuffled past the grimy stove, on top of which sat a battered metal pot containing the rotting, viscid remains of ancient macaroni and cheese. His eyes wandered over the crooked stacks of plates that covered every inch of the countertops. Various moldering, congealed foods caked the filthy dishes, and small clusters of flies busied themselves gorging on the putridness.

A hint of motion caught the corner of his eye. Erasmo turned, at first seeing only a plate of decomposing roast, but he recoiled as he looked closer and saw a swarm of maggots slithering through the rotting meat.

Erasmo walked to the refrigerator, which his assaulted sense of smell told him was exuding a terrible stench. It stood in front of him, the stainless steel smudged with blurred fingerprints. He gripped the handle tightly but couldn't force himself to open it.

He should just leave. That would be the safe, sane thing to do. Just get the hell out of there. He didn't have to see what was inside this refrigerator, to find out what was giving off such a horrid odor. Christ. How could Nora live with this smell?

Sonny's voice echoed in his head.

I like meat, bitch.

Was that what was waiting for him behind this door? Rotting sustenance for the demon inside Sonny? Had she been feeding it?

Erasmo continued to hear the boy's voice as he held his breath and pulled, needing to know just how badly he'd misjudged everything.

The door swung open. A warm, rancid fog billowed out of the refrigerator and enveloped him. He noticed right away that the refrigerator wasn't even on. His eyes darted around its contents, jumping from shelf to shelf. A half-full gallon of gray milk stood directly in front of him, the thick, gelatinous clumps floating inside making his stomach lurch. Next to it, broken, rotting eggs sat festering in an open carton. And there was indeed meat, but just of the ground beef variety, shriveled and black, like tiny, decomposing worms. There were also numerous bowls and plates covered with tinfoil. He thought about what decaying meats and jellified liquids might be lying underneath the crumpled aluminum, and his stomach clenched again.

Erasmo slammed the door shut and studied the refrigerator. It didn't appear to be leaking anything. As far as he could tell, the refrigerator looked perfectly fine. Why would she just leave it like this? He went around to check the back, and what he saw shocked and baffled him. The refrigerator's power cord lay on the floor like a lifeless snake, not plugged into the wall at all.

He took in a breath of putrid air and his stomach rebelled again. If he stayed in there much longer, he'd no longer be able to stave off his urgent need to vomit. Erasmo trotted out of the kitchen, into the living room, and headed for the front door. He turned the knob to leave but stopped himself. Why would Nora possibly leave food rotting in the refrigerator like that?

Could something have happened to her? Then, despite himself, he had a thought that truly terrified him.

Perhaps she had left.

Nora could have just packed up a few bags and gone. Taken Sonny to live somewhere far away, where she thought they could outrun whatever was inside him. He let go of the knob and turned around, eyeing the living room for clues, although, given the mess, it would've been difficult to spot them even if there were any.

He thought of how Nora often liked to talk about her plans while she lay in bed, making lists of all the places she wanted to visit, her eyes sparkling as she conjured the future. Could she have left something behind that would tell him where they might've gone? Surely a few minutes looking around her bedroom wouldn't hurt anything. It would be worth enduring the foul air just a bit longer to find out if she had really left, and where he might find her. He turned and walked to her bedroom, sidestepping mounds of clothes as he did so.

The door to Nora's room was slightly ajar, squealing as he nudged it open farther. The room was surprisingly clean, for Nora anyway. Even though there was old mail strewn about the grimy wood floor, he'd seen it in worse shape. He picked up various envelopes from the floor and studied them. All were bills, most past due.

Erasmo rummaged through a pile on top of her dresser, finding a mix of makeup, coupons, and receipts. He wasn't even entirely sure what to look for. It's not like she was going to leave a note saying where they'd gone.

He pulled open the top drawer, feeling a pang of guilt as he did so. Panties of all colors overflowed from the cramped space. His hand rifled through them, searching for anything that might be hiding between their satiny folds, but found nothing.

The drawer underneath was crammed full of socks, no pairs bundled together. Erasmo wondered how long it must take her to find even one matching pair in this sea of lost companions.

He then opened the bottom drawer, and his eyes lingered over what sat inside. It wasn't clear to him what he was seeing. At first glance, an unremarkable, crooked pile of magazines sat in the corner of the drawer. But as he studied them further, it was clear that they weren't ordinary magazines. He picked up the top one, stared in astonishment, and flipped through its pages, each one more disturbing than the last.

Erasmo reached into the drawer and gathered up the rest of the magazines, which were all in the same, chilling vein as the first. This revealed a pile of envelopes that had been hidden underneath the magazines. There were eight of them, bound together by a ragged piece of twine. He placed the magazines back in the drawer and picked up the envelopes. Without fail, every piece of mail Nora had ever received in his presence immediately ended up either on the floor or in the trash. But not these. Erasmo read the return address on the top envelope, and his lungs stopped pushing air out of his body.

This had been a mistake. Erasmo no longer wanted to know where she might've gone. In fact, he didn't want to learn any more about Nora than he knew at that exact moment. He wanted to leave, to walk away from these magazines, and the letters, and the stink that he was certain had worked its way into his skin. And he would have, had it not been for Sonny. He had to think about Sonny.

Erasmo tugged on the strand of twine, his heart picking up speed. The small knot came undone, and the envelopes loosened from their tight formation. He shuffled through them, the return addresses different, but for all intents and purposes, the same.

Shivers racked Erasmo's body as he fumbled one of the envelopes open. The letter inside was typed, a form letter from what he could tell, but its neat and professional appearance didn't lessen the monstrousness of what its contents might mean.

Dear Ms. Montalvo,
We regret to inform you . . .

He opened more envelopes, dropping each letter after a quick glance. They were all the same. Erasmo read the last one and then let it flutter to the ground, rejoining the others. The full implications of the magazines and the letters detonated around him in mind-bending explosions. As he stood frozen, terrible realizations slowly settled on him, as if they were snowflakes drifting down wistfully from a gray, ominous sky.

He found himself unable to move, completely unsure what to do next. All that he *really* had were some questionable items in a drawer. He knew what they hinted at, but he would need more. He would need . . .

Erasmo walked over to Nora's closet, slid open the mirrored door, and surveyed the scene. Piles of garbage bags stuffed with clothes leaned on one another in unstable formations. Clutches and handbags spilled from the top shelf. And in the few crevices of space left, various shoes were crammed in haphazardly. It would be difficult to find anything in this chaos.

He stood on his tiptoes and felt around the back of the top shelf, finding only more purses and what felt like mounds of scarves. He knelt down and shoved the garbage bags around, hoping to find what he was looking for buried among them. Nothing.

Where could it be? Maybe the garage. She liked to keep all kinds of random things in there. He was almost to the door when his gut whispered to him, stopping him in his tracks. The TV was in here. And she'd probably want to keep it close by. This room was the obvious, natural storage place. He decided to take another look around, but there just weren't that many hiding places in here, especially since he'd already looked in the drawers and closet.

Erasmo regarded the bed, with its gray, rumpled sheets and mismatched pillows. It lacked a headboard and didn't have much going for it in the way of comfort. But there was one attribute the bed did have: plenty of room underneath.

He walked to the edge of the bed and fell on his knees, as if to offer prayer. After taking a deep breath, he felt around underneath, grimacing as his fingertips skimmed thick layers of dirt and tangled strands of hair. He swept his arm side to side, moving down the length of the bed as he did so. Erasmo was almost to the end, and about to give up, when his fingers touched something cool and supple. He grabbed and pulled, his eyes widening as a tan leather bag slid from underneath the bed. And not just any kind of bag.

A GoPro storage bag.

He rose from the floor and placed it on the bed. Erasmo stared at the bag as his heart pounded, not wanting to unleash its contents, but knowing he had to. His hand shook as he took hold of the gleaming zipper and pulled.

His heart jumped. There it was. The GoPro from the first night he came over. The one she'd used to show him unthinkable perversities. He slid it out of the bag, along with the HDMI cable next to it. Erasmo walked over to the TV and plugged the camera in.

It felt unnatural in his hands, as if he were holding a small, decomposing animal. He had to watch the video again, Erasmo knew that with certainty now. But the knowledge that it was necessary wouldn't make it any easier to suffer through those images. The first time he'd seen the video, though, he hadn't been prepared for its grotesqueness. Things were different now. He was different now. And this time, he knew what he was looking for.

A single thumbnail appeared on the screen. He clicked it, and immediately Sonny's savage face appeared on the television, his mouth covered with a sheen of glistening blood. This was the exact part that was playing when Erasmo vomited and fled the room. Nora must've turned it off before she followed him outside, and the video hadn't been played since. Sonny continued to grin at him through the screen, veiny globs of flesh stuck in his small teeth. The boy was talking now, surely saying something vile, but the volume was too low to hear what it was.

Erasmo saw what he was looking for almost immediately, cursing himself for not noticing the first time. But what did this all mean exactly? He turned back to the camera bag and rummaged through it, finding only a few straps. He then eyed the side pouches. Erasmo unzipped the first one, only to find two rechargeable batteries. He tried the second pouch, and there they were.

SD cards.

They could be videos of anything of course. But he knew that the one he needed was in there. It *had* to be. Erasmo took out the SD card already in the GoPro, and Sonny's crazed face thankfully blinked out of existence. He inserted a different card and held his breath.

This time, there were lots of videos on the thumbnail screen. He chose one randomly. It was Nora sitting on her sofa, wearing a snug black dress. She smiled flirtatiously and laughed before speaking directly to the camera. Erasmo found the volume button and turned the sound up.

". . . and I just turned twenty-one. I really enjoy hiking and other outdoor activities. I do have a wild and crazy side. I mean, once you get a few in me, watch out! Anything can happen! Let's see . . . what else? I'm single and don't have any kids of course. Oh, I also enjoy dancing!"

Nora continued to divulge her interests, but Erasmo had heard enough. He went back to the home screen and selected a different video. It was the same: Nora showing off her body in a formfitting dress as she mouthed a slew of lies. This video started at the beginning though, and he heard who it was intended for. His thoughts raced as he took out the SD card, attempting to interpret what he was seeing. As disturbing as these videos were, it wasn't the footage he was looking for. He selected another card and inserted it into the GoPro, taking a moment to brace himself.

There was only one thumbnail on this card. Erasmo selected it, and his mouth fell open when he saw the image that appeared on-screen. His heart ceased beating, unable to generate even a flicker in his chest. Sonny filled the television screen again. Just as in the other video, he sat on his bed, his face smeared with blood, a gutted, lifeless dog lying on his lap. But this time, the boy wasn't grinning.

He was crying.

"Please," Sonny sobbed, "I don't want to. Please . . ."

A voice floated in from off-screen, calm and reassuring. "Sonny, you *have* to do this. I told you, it won't even take long. We just need to get a few good shots. And when we're done, you can have whatever you want. Didn't you want that new *Zelda* game? We'll go get it as soon as we finish. I promise."

Sonny, terror in his trembling eyes, was now barely intelligible. "Buuuh . . . buuuht . . . it's Eh . . . Echo. I . . . luh . . . loved him. . . . Pleeassse . . ."

A change in tactics by the off-screen voice. "DO WHAT I SAID, SONNY! JUST GODDAMN DO IT!"

The source of the commanding, enraged voice now appeared on-screen. Nora, wearing a white T-shirt streaked with spurts of blood, walked up to Sonny and grabbed a fistful of his thick hair.

"DO I HAVE TO DO EVERYTHING FOR YOU?" Nora shoved Sonny's face down, rubbing it in Echo's open abdomen. "DO I?"

She finally let go of her brother's hair. The boy's bloody face rose from the dog's entrails, his blubbering even worse than before. Nora stepped back behind the camera.

"NOW PUT YOUR STUPID GODDAMN FACE IN HIS STOMACH AND LEAVE IT THERE!"

And Sonny did.

Edited. The video Nora had shown him that first night had been edited. He'd seen it clearly on the second viewing: brief jumps that were easy to miss if you weren't looking for them. And here was the original video, in all its unadulterated atrocity.

A creak whispered behind him. Erasmo's body stiffened, every muscle clenched tight against his bones. His heart convulsed as he slowly turned his head, and his eyes fell upon a familiar figure.

Nora, her face still and cold, stood in the doorway. She studied Erasmo with her shimmering gray eyes before turning her gaze to the television screen. After a few seconds of glaring at the video, she turned her pale face back to him.

"I wasn't sure," she said, entering the room, "that I'd even be able to get enough good footage." Nora approached the television and studied the images flashing across it. "He was being such a damn baby, you know? I mean . . . people around the world eat raw meat all the time. What, he can't chew on some for two damn minutes?" She shook her head in disgust, as if aggravated all over again. "Well," she said, looking at him expectantly, "aren't you going to say anything?"

Erasmo, who was still trying to process both the monstrousness of the video and the fact that Nora was now in the room with him, couldn't find his voice. He was overwhelmed with shock at what Nora had done, and crippled with sorrow at what this poor child had suffered. He had a sudden memory of the boy, trying to chase Erasmo away when he'd visited.

I said to just goddamn leave!

Tears blurred his vision as he realized that Sonny wasn't being a jerk to him that day. Sonny had been trying to save him.

Nora glared at the letters scattered on the floor. "Those idiots," she said, picking up one of the rejection letters and looking it over, "wouldn't know a good story if one bit them on the ass. I mean . . . I tried to make it easy for them. Attractive young woman, handsome young brother who might be possessed . . . what more do they want? I mean, they're paranormal reality shows, not a production of Shakespeare."

She dropped the letter and flashed a smile at Erasmo. "I'm kind of glad you found out," she said. "Perfect timing actually. I finally heard back from the one show that has some sense, *Unexplained Phenomenon*. They're very interested. A production crew is coming down in a few days to watch the tape and talk to Sonny. If everything goes well, there'll be a whole episode just about us."

"But Sonny . . . what you did to him . . ."

"What I did to him? Christ . . . he got a little bit of blood on his face and had to make some faces. Big deal. He's already forgotten about it! And that dog he was blubbering about was already on his deathbed anyway."

Erasmo felt his shock beginning to give way to anger and revulsion. "All of this . . . just so that you *might* come out on a cable TV show that nobody watches? You put your brother through this to be on TV for five *goddamn* minutes?"

Nora smirked and proceeded to talk slowly to Erasmo, as if she were explaining the situation to a confused toddler. "Well, you see, it just takes *one* appearance on television to get noticed. Just *one*. Which show it is doesn't even matter. And I was told by a producer that these paranormal shows are by far the easiest to get on. Don't you see? If someone important is watching, they'll take one look at me and want me for their project. I *know* that if I can just get seen, *anything* could happen. Anything. But after all these rejection letters, we needed something to give us an edge, so I made this video. And it finally worked."

Blood rushed through Erasmo's veins, filling his ears with a swirling hum as his head pounded relentlessly. First Billy had fooled him, and now this. He'd been so wrong about so many things. But not now . . . now he understood.

"Those stupid ghost shows weren't even your first choice, were they?" he asked.

The muscles in Nora's face tightened.

"Like I said, it doesn't matter what show—"

"I saw those pathetic submission videos you sent . . . *Big Brother*, *Love Is Blind*, *The Amazing Race*, you tried them all and got rejected, didn't you? You even lied about your age. What? You couldn't wait a few more years to become a big star?"

Nora shook her head at Erasmo's ignorance. "I was just trying to give myself a chance, that's all. Maybe get noticed by the right producer. As I'm sure you've heard, those Hollywood types aren't exactly shy about offering work to attractive young women."

There was no reason to stay, as Erasmo was now certain of what needed to be done. Except . . . he still had so many questions. Questions he knew would gnaw at his bones over time, like perpetually famished rats. And this would be his only chance to mine her warped brain for answers, as Erasmo knew they were never going to be in the same room again. Any answers she might give wouldn't change anything; he was fully aware of that. But the certainty of that knowledge didn't prevent the question from tumbling out of his mouth.

"Why did you pretend to like me?"

Nora placed her hand daintily over her mouth, unsuccessfully attempting to suppress a giggle. "Oh, Erasmo, you're not going to cry, are you? Because it kind of looks like you are. Is that even what you really want to know? I bet what you're *really* asking is if I was even pretending at all. Do you want to hear me say, *Oh, Erasmo, you've got it all wrong. My feelings for you are real.* Is that it? Look, you're a nice enough guy, although I must say, terribly needy. It's just that my sights are set really high. Higher than anyone in this shit town, that's for sure."

Erasmo remained silent for a long moment, and then whispered, "I wish that you'd never answered that goddamn ad."

Nora's brow furrowed as she considered this. "You know . . . it's kind of a funny thing. I truly believe that it was fate for us to meet. You believe in fate, don't you, Erasmo? The only reason I was even on Craigslist was to look for modeling jobs, since these stupid shows had all passed on us. But then I stumbled across your ad and couldn't believe what I was reading. I realized that if I could get someone like you to join up with Sonny and me, then these producers would take us seriously. But first, I had to convince you that there was *actually* something inside Sonny, so I decided to show you the tape we'd made. But that didn't go very well, did it?"

Erasmo's head pounded as questions continued to ricochet in his skull. "But . . . if this was just about those television shows, then why did you want me to contact the Church about an exorcism?"

Nora exhaled a long sigh, now seemingly bored with answering his questions. "When you told me what happened to you at the Tracks, who you were, my wheels began to turn. I started to think even *bigger*. Can you imagine all the attention we'd get from an exorcism done by the Church itself? That would be *national* news, even better than being on those stupid shows. But you wouldn't go for it. I could tell that you didn't *really* believe Sonny was possessed. That's the only reason I went along with your stupid idea to do the exorcism yourself. I thought that maybe if you saw proof up close and personal, you'd come around. I thought it'd be an opportunity to really convince you."

"*Convince* me? He bit a goddamn *hole* in my stomach!"

"Well, to be fair, that's not really how I envisioned that whole thing going. I told him to just bite you a little bit. I had no idea he'd take out such a large chunk and that there'd be so much blood. I was as shocked as you were."

"But his breath . . . it smelled so bad. . . ."

"His breath? I'm not sure . . . oh wait . . . that's right. I thought it'd be a nice touch if Sonny threw up all over you, so I made him eat some spoiled eggs before you came. But that little asshole couldn't even manage to get *that* right."

"This whole time," Erasmo said, studying Nora as if seeing her for the first time, "it was *you* who needed help."

"Oh, *I'm* crazy? It's crazy to want to better yourself? It's crazy for a beautiful young woman to want to be discovered? It's crazy to want a better future? This is *not* supposed to be my life, Erasmo. IT'S NOT! How am I supposed to get noticed if I have to spend the prime of my life taking care of my brother? I'm supposed to be somebody, but Sonny is *ruining* it! The least he can do is help me get the life I'm supposed to have. I don't think that's crazy at all."

Erasmo was stunned at Nora's complete lack of shame over what she'd done. Her casual dismissal of the mental and physical torture she'd inflicted on Sonny sent a wave of fury coursing through him. At that moment, Erasmo wanted nothing more than to make her suffer for her sins. He found himself desperately wishing there was a corpse in the room, so that he could have the satisfaction of forcing her to eat every scrap of its dead flesh.

Nora must've noticed a change in his demeanor, as her tone softened, and she extended an olive branch. "Look, the producers of *Unexplained Phenomenon* are coming to interview us in a few days. You can *still* be a part of this. It'd be such a great story! We can say that we're dating and tell them about your experience at the Tracks. I bet they would *love* that! We'd get on the show for sure. You might even get your own episode. And then from there—"

Erasmo walked over to the dresser, reached into the bottom drawer, and pulled out the stack of magazines. "And from there, what? You think *this* is going to happen?"

Nora flinched when she saw the magazines, as if she were more embarrassed by them than the video of her shoving Sonny's face into a bloody carcass.

Erasmo held up one of the magazines. It was a tattered edition of *Us Weekly* with Kim Kardashian on the cover. Except, it wasn't completely her. The body was unmistakably Kim's, her curves spilling out of a white bikini. But her head had been cut off, and Nora's smiling face had been haphazardly glued on. The effect was alarming, as Nora's head was out of proportion to Kim's figure, and her smile was slightly crazed. The words *Kim Kardashian* had been scratched out, and *Nora Montalvo* was now scrawled over them.

"You think this is going to be *you*?" Erasmo asked as he shook the magazine. He ripped out page after page, staring at them incredulously. Pictures of Nora's face, in assorted shapes and sizes, were glued onto every taut, airbrushed body in the issue. Her name was scrawled everywhere, with jagged arrows pointing to her various faces in case it wasn't obvious enough who the star of the magazine was.

"You think your name is going to be in the news?" He threw the magazine at Nora's face. "Well, that's the only damn thing you got right."

Erasmo grabbed the camera bag and shoved the GoPro into it.

"No, wait . . . you can't take that! I need it to show the producers next week. Everything is ready to go. I've even made the house smell bad so I can tell them that he—"

Erasmo walked past her, his muscles tensed as he emerged into the hallway. He was ready to force his way out if she made even the slightest move to stop him.

"Wait! Erasmo!" She was frantic now, an urgency in her voice that hadn't been there before.

He hurried through the living room to the front door, exhaling when he finally wrapped his hand around the doorknob. Nora ran out of the hallway, her face filled with confusion.

"Why are you taking the videos? What are you going to do? I thought you *cared* about me!" she screamed, her large eyes shimmering.

"You're going to get what you wanted," Erasmo said as he pulled open the front door and stepped outside. He stopped and looked over his shoulder, taking one final glance at her pale, frightened, beautiful face. "You're finally going to be discovered."

CHAPTER 28

ERASMO SAT ON the floor of his bedroom, staring down at the beer, desperately wishing to take a sip. He imagined placing the cold bottle to his lips, slowly tilting his head back, and shivering as waves of exhilaration coursed through him. He continued regarding the bottle but felt no closer to picking it up.

He reread the note he'd spent the last hour writing, even though each line was already burned into his memory.

> *To Whom It May Concern,*
> *Enclosed you will find a video of a woman named Nora Montalvo abusing her brother. Please investigate accordingly. She has committed a crime, is not in control of her mental faculties, and is not a fit guardian for this child. Thank you.*
> *A Concerned Citizen*

Erasmo placed the letter and SD card into a manila envelope addressed to the SAPD. He walked to the back door and stepped out into the black night. As he trudged to the mailbox, a chorus of dogs howled at the pregnant moon. He wondered with dread what story Nora was going to spin to the police.

That the video was a joke? A tasteless prank? Or perhaps she'd say that she was an aspiring filmmaker simply testing out some ideas. Nora was adept at weaving stories, and this worried him. He placed the envelope in the outgoing mail and stared at it for a long moment.

Please, Erasmo thought. *Just let me get this one thing right.*

He walked back to his room and settled onto the floor, once again staring down at the perspiring beer.

At some point over the last few days, Erasmo realized that he was on the verge of doing it, of finally acting out what he'd only imagined so many times before. Wasn't that why he'd asked his neighbor to buy him this beer . . . so that he could have one for the first time in his life? So that he could get drunk, and then . . .

But so far, he hadn't even been able to place the bottle to his lips. It was all the years, he knew. All the years spent terrified of what might happen if he allowed alcohol or drugs into his body. He'd read that addiction lurked in the genes, and God knew he was carrying around some bad ones. But even now, when there was every reason to have a drink given his plans for the evening, Erasmo still couldn't bring himself to do it.

He was as alone as he'd ever been, and the foreseeable future didn't offer much hope. The only two people that gave a shit about him were an outcast that no one else could stand and a grandmother whose remaining time was rapidly disintegrating. And Nora . . .well . . . that was a wound that would never heal.

If being alone, and rejected, and deceived were the only things burdening him, then maybe he'd be able to weather the storm without resorting to this. But it was so much worse than that, wasn't it?

Because he had learned the worst possible truth.

None of what he believed was real.

Not a goddamn thing.

Leander hadn't been chased by a ghost. He'd only been scaring himself, simple bumps in the night magnified by his shame into fraudulent terrors. Sonny had not been possessed by a demon. He just had the misfortune of being related to a selfish, unhinged sister. And Erasmo Cruz, the boy who was saved at the Ghost Tracks . . . well, he could finally admit the truth now, couldn't he?

That was the biggest lie of all.

He could see that now. That he'd never really been quite sure of the events that night. That he'd woken up in a stupor, scared and confused, with very few memories of what had actually happened. But he'd wanted to believe it so bad, *needed* to believe, so it had become true to him.

The old man had kept yelling, insisting that he'd been saved by the children, telling him that he'd been touched by God. Hadn't it felt so good to hear those words? To entertain the notion that what the old man described was exactly what had happened? To believe that he was special enough to be saved?

But looking back, he could see that the deceit hadn't ended there. No . . . he'd eagerly glossed over important facts about the very Ghost Tracks themselves, hadn't he? When he researched them more and read that the stretch of road leading to the tracks actually declined, not inclined, accounting for why the cars rolled forward, it had been so easy to dismiss. Same with the revelation that the streets around the tracks were actually named after the developer's grandchildren, not after the children who had lost their lives. He'd even been able to brush off the fact that the handprints found on the cars were actually the owners' own handprints, simply made visible by the baby powder.

In truth, there had been only one revelation about the children who died on the Tracks that had threatened to puncture his cocoon of self-deceit. The most surprising one of all.

There were no children who had died on those tracks.

There never had been.

Now, there was a bus full of kids who had died on some railroad tracks. That did actually happen. Just not in San Antonio, Texas.

It occurred in Salt Lake City, Utah, in 1938.

San Antonio did, however, provide its citizens with daily coverage about those kids in Utah, until somehow, San Antonio had adopted the story as its own, and the legend of the San Antonio Ghost Tracks was born.

But even this fact had not swayed him. The old man had seen what happened. *Why would he lie?* Erasmo would ask himself. There were other reasons to believe. Hadn't those tiny hands felt so real? Couldn't he feel them even now, when he closed his eyes and transported himself back to that night? *It had to be true,* he'd told himself.

And there had been one last deceit he'd wanted to keep alive, hadn't there? A story he had spun for himself as soon as he'd gotten home from the Tracks that night, sweaty and exhausted. A hope at first, and soon a firm belief, that he'd been saved by those children not out of chance but by design. That they'd been sent by a spirit from the other side to help him.

That they'd been sent by his father, who wanted to do in death what he never did in life: protect his son.

But now, he could no longer carry any of these lies in his heart. The truth was that there was nothing extraordinary in this world. There was no magic waiting for him once his life was over. And there was certainly no afterlife, where he'd thought he would finally have a chance to meet his parents.

He'd even convinced himself that, because of what happened at the Tracks, it was possible for him to interact with his dead father. That he had the ability to summon spirits. He'd been positive that he would be able to lure Mauro Cruz back into the physical realm using only three things: his innate ability, a properly conducted summoning ceremony, and an offering of what his father loved most in the world.

A cheap bag of heroin.

But he could let those fantasies go now. He should actually be grateful to Leander and Nora for forcing him to admit the ugly truths he'd been shielding himself from. Erasmo finally picked up the beer and held it to his nose, the smell of the alcohol immediately making him light-headed.

The hole inside of him had been clamoring for so long now, and until tonight he'd successfully resisted trying to fill it, mainly because he knew what it would do to his grandmother. He knew perfectly well that voids such as the one that sat in the middle of his being, sucking at his essence, couldn't actually be filled. But he also knew that didn't stop the afflicted from trying. They threw all kinds of things down its gullet . . . alcohol, betting slips, sex . . . just to make it shut up for a few hours. It was hard to make yourself go away, to cover up your deformed, rotted underpinnings, even for a short time. But it could be done, couldn't it?

Forget the beer. He was ready to get on with the main event.

Erasmo reached underneath his bed and grabbed the cigar box, carefully pulling it out. As he prepared himself, he glanced around the dim room that he'd lived his entire life in. Its uneven measurements and ill-fitting components were a part of him, ingrained into his very cells.

His father had lived in this room as well. When Erasmo was eight, his uncle had mentioned this casually one day, as if he were saying nothing more important than that they needed milk from the store. Erasmo had been dumbfounded. His father had slept, and read, and breathed in this room. From that day forward, the bedroom had taken on an entirely different dimension, transforming into mysterious and hallowed ground.

Erasmo's father had done more than just sleep and read in this room of course. His uncle had made that abundantly clear. His uncle was the one person who hadn't held back. When Erasmo came looking for answers, Javier had stood there and delivered them. He had shown absolutely no qualms about giving Erasmo the truth. Too much truth as it turned out. He'd long thought that he wanted to know everything, every microscopic tidbit of information, about his father. But by the end of that visit, he sat in silence, hoping that Uncle Javier would just shut the hell up.

Hearing about the constant arrests was one thing. Same with being told that his father was routinely found passed out in public. But did he really need his uncle to tell him about the times his father was caught prostituting himself in back alleys? Uncle Javier at least had the decency to look away when he told Erasmo how much his father had charged the johns.

Ten dollars.

Erasmo's fingers conjured a dull drumbeat as they tapped the cigar box.

Growing up, it had been clear from their absence that his parents had chosen *something* over him. He'd often passed the time while looking out the front window, waiting for them, wondering what exactly it had been. He had walked into Uncle Javier's house that day in search of an illuminating answer, and instead came out with a soul-deadening one.

The cigar box creaked softly as he opened it, the contents inside lying exactly as he remembered them. The small plastic bag sitting in the center of the scattered items hadn't been easy to obtain, but a neighbor had finally come through for him.

When Uncle Javier told him what had become of his parents, what they'd chosen over him, Erasmo knew that one day he'd be staring down at the contents of this box. He'd heard, of course, how powerful it was. He had read many accounts of the initial euphoria, and then how you came to need it, until it became the only thing you cared about. He had to know for himself though. He had to feel what his parents felt. What his father felt. He wanted the same blissful sensation running through his veins. Unlike most families, he and his parents never had the chance to bond together over shared experiences. He meant to rectify that tonight.

Erasmo desperately needed this event to be spectacular. He wanted the prick on his skin to be followed by warm sunshine gliding through his veins, igniting his blood with bliss and jubilation. He wanted to see rainbow waves of light bend the living world into glorious and incomprehensible compositions. He wanted to feel the pores of his skin open and quiver with delight, waves of electricity pulsing through his trembling flesh.

That's what he so desperately wanted. Because if that wasn't what he felt . . . if it wasn't the glorious rapture he'd always imagined . . . if it was just about some junkies getting high for a cheap thrill . . . well, if that's all his parents traded him for . . . he might just kill himself tonight and be done with it.

Erasmo reached under the bed and took out his other treasured box, the cardboard one. He wanted to have one last look before filling his veins, certain it would get him in the proper mood. He looked down at the meager contents, only two items, relics from another person and another time. When he was twelve, he'd begged his grandparents for whatever they had of his father. They'd grimaced and wrung their wrinkled hands and told him repeatedly that there was nothing left. But after months of continued pleading, they'd finally given him this box on the day he turned thirteen.

Erasmo reached in, withdrew a yellowed scrap of paper, and looked over the blocky, oversized word written on it. He'd read this word thousands of times. As far as he could ever tell, it appeared to be a fragment from a shopping list. But its function was unimportant. What *was* important was that his father had made those crooked lines and held this piece of paper in his hands. Erasmo read the word again, as if for the first time.

MILK

A dog-eared magazine stared at him and begged to be picked up. He listened. His favorite part of the cover had always been Hulk Hogan's expression. It was terrifying, reminiscent of a feral animal, his mouth pulled back in a triumphant howl as he sat on Andre the Giant's back.

Erasmo's eyes wandered to the top of the cover and read the name of the magazine that his father had found important enough to keep as one of his few earthly possessions.

Wrestling Superstars.

There had been one other item in this box. The item most responsible, in his estimation anyway, for the events of the recent weeks. The book had once lain at the bottom of this box but was now perched on the shelf above his bed. He'd read the book *so* many times, hoping to glean some morsel of insight into his father's nature. Why had he read it? Was he a believer? Or had he read the journal only to laugh at its claims? Perhaps reading material was scarce and this was all that happened to be on hand. It was impossible to say. But his father, for whatever reason, had been interested enough to read it, and this fact alone was enough to endow the book with mystical qualities. It had compelled Erasmo to explore this topic further, reading every book on the subject that he could find. He glanced at the shelf.

A Practical Guide to the Supernatural and Paranormal: The Writings of John F. Dubois.

As he suspected, basking in the pathetic nature of these items had indeed put him in the right mood. It was time. He'd long ago done the research, and everything he needed was assembled in the cigar box: a spoon, a vitamin C pack for the acidic solution, a lighter, a rubber hose, and of course, the H.

Erasmo heaped a sizable portion onto the spoon, added water and the vitamin C, and began to cook it. As the eager flame leaped from the lighter and spread itself against the spoon's rapidly blackening bottom, a sense of relief and assured-ness fell over him. He was finally doing it.

After a few minutes though, worry began to set in. In the movies, the solution always seemed to turn into a clear liquid right away, but the concoction he was brewing still looked lumpy and cloudy. He spent several minutes staring in confusion at the bubbling liquid. But then, to his great relief, everything finally looked as it should. As far as he could tell anyway.

Erasmo beheld the spoon and felt the power emanating from the drug. His entire life had unfolded in its haphazard manner largely because of it. His parents hadn't been the only ones who had been hooked, of course. He closed his eyes and imagined his trembling infant self, screaming for the very relief he now held in his hands.

Erasmo's hand trembled as he placed the lighter down and grabbed the syringe from the cigar box. He'd worried about spilling some of the drug, but the syringe sucked up every last drop.

The plastic tube bit into Erasmo's lower bicep as he wrapped it around his arm. The tension was uncomfortable, but he forced himself to pull even tighter. He didn't want the injection to fail because of something as stupid as not being able to find a vein.

He picked up the loaded syringe and glanced down at his arm. As it turned out, he needn't have worried. A plump green vein throbbed under his skin, like a fat, undulating caterpillar. Erasmo scanned the room and wondered where his father had taken the needle. He closed his eyes and tried to imagine the scene.

Erasmo didn't have any clear memories of seeing his father in person. In fact, he only had a few old pictures to rely on. But underneath his closed eyes, he could see his father's wiry frame, hunched over as he slid the needle into his arm, its slender shaft disappearing into the tracks scarring his flesh. Erasmo saw this happening but couldn't make out exactly where.

But the more Erasmo thought it over, the more he realized there was a spot in the house that had been calling to him all along. A spot that was perfect to feel pure oblivion cascade over him. A spot that was perfect to give his life away.

He walked into the kitchen and grabbed a battered plastic chair sitting in the corner. It was the same one he'd always used during his childhood vigils, and it was the one he needed now.

When Erasmo was young, he both loved and hated the small, cloudy front window he now approached. In the mornings, it was all love. He'd run to it and eagerly sit in his chair and wait. Today was always going to be the day. His parents were going to come ambling up that small, sparse yard, desperate to see him. As the day progressed, though, love of that window gave way to ambivalence and, by nightfall, was reduced to nothing but hostility. Until the next morning, anyway.

He gently placed the chair in front of the window and saw that it looked at home in its old post. His arm now throbbed from the lack of circulation. He needed to hurry. A slight moan rose from the chair as he settled in.

The vigils by the window had come to an end after his talk with Uncle Javier. There had been days immediately afterward when he still wanted to sit in his chair and wait, when he told himself that his uncle had been wrong, that the body the police found was really someone else's. But these lies to himself must not have been convincing enough, as his battered psyche soon tried a different tactic. He'd felt his thoughts morphing, stretching toward the idea that he had never even spoken to Uncle Javier. The door to his uncle's house had gone unanswered that day. That's what happened. He could still keep the flame of hope alive. All he had to do was allow it to live.

The gloom that had enveloped him since leaving his uncle's cleared a little when he entertained these thoughts, and he'd so desperately wanted to keep traveling down that rabbit hole. But Erasmo had been terrified of what it would mean if he indulged these delusions. Would he permanently cease to know the difference between the truth and his self-deceiving inventions? So after a few days, he forced himself to clear his eyes and embrace the truth. Erasmo's parents had both been hardcore heroin addicts. His father was dead, found under an abandoned house years ago. His mother, who had given birth to him while she was in jail, never wanted him and left the state with her new boyfriend as soon as she was released.

Some of the answers his uncle gave only led to more questions. Had his father been alone when he died? Had he known that his life was slipping from his body? Had he been scared as he lay trembling underneath that house? Uncle Javier said that his father's corpse had been so decomposed when they found it, that the cause of death couldn't even be determined.

Erasmo hated his father, a hate so fundamental to him that it felt as if his very bones were made of it. Every Father's Day, every time an acquaintance asked about his parents, every time he was subjected to even the slightest indignation related to his parentage, the hate swelled from his cells and enveloped him in totality. But despite all of that, Erasmo desperately hoped that his father hadn't been scared and alone when he died underneath that house.

The throbbing vein in his arm called to him, whispering in rhythm with his heart. It was ready and waiting in its plumpness.

His only regret was what this might do to his grandmother. Even now, just the thought of her almost persuaded him to drop the syringe. But would she really want him to endure this pain? Wouldn't she want him to find some comfort? And if anything happened to him, he knew Rat would take care of his grandmother as if she were his own family.

It was too late to stop now. He was so close. He wanted the relief. He needed it.

The tip of the needle trembled as he held it over his forearm, a fat drop of the H clinging to it, a preview of what would soon be coursing through his body. He pressed the sharp point against his bulging vein and felt his skin give way as he began to depress the plunger.

But then, something happened. A miracle? Of course not. There was no such thing as a miracle. A sign? There was no such thing as a hint from the heavens either. A happenstance of chance? It must be.

His pocket vibrated again.

Erasmo placed the needle down on his lap and pulled out the buzzing phone. It wasn't a number he recognized. He briefly thought about letting it go to voicemail, but curiosity seized him.

"Hello," Erasmo said, his voice thin and shaky.

"Hey, man, it's Billy. You okay over there?"

Billy. Erasmo was stunned, unable to answer, or even process, this question. Billy was calling at this *exact* moment to ask if he was okay? How did he know—

"Hey! You there?" Billy asked, sounding agitated.

"Yes."

"You all right? You sound like you're out of it."

"Yeah . . . I'm fine," Erasmo said.

"Listen, get dressed. Right now."

"What? Why? I . . ."

"It's happening. Tonight. Right now."

"Wait . . . what's happening? I don't understand. . . ."

"Get in your car and get to the aqueduct! The boy is being taken right now!"

CHAPTER 29

THE AQUEDUCT. It would be deserted this time of night. So, if in fact there was a kidnapped boy, and a monster that wanted to mutilate him, it was a location that made sense. The park that contained the aqueduct was near Mission Espada over on the south side, which was still fifteen minutes away. He merged onto I-37 and gunned it, keeping a lookout in his rearview mirror for cops.

Given the outcomes of his last two encounters with Billy, Erasmo had come better prepared this time. He reached into the pocket of his hoodie and felt the cool metal of his grandfather's switchblade.

When he was alive, the old man would often mention to Erasmo how the battered knife was his weapon of choice back when he was a young hell-raiser. His grandmother kept it around for strangely sentimental reasons. He'd occasionally catch her admiring the weapon and reminiscing, her eyes glazed over with happenings from long ago. He knew where his grandmother stored it and had decided to borrow it for this occasion.

While Erasmo was grateful to have the switchblade, he suspected there was little chance that he'd actually be able to use it to defend himself. With any luck though, he wouldn't have to find out.

Soon, he was on the access road to 410, turning onto dimly lit Espada Road. He drove slowly past small houses that reminded him of his own neighborhood. Finally, he saw Billy's truck parked on the side of the road and pulled up behind it. As Erasmo exited the Civic, Billy got out of the Ranger and jogged over to him, a grim look on his face.

"They should be here soon," Billy said. He was wearing a black baseball cap pulled tight over his forehead, the bill almost completely covering his eyes. "Let's walk the rest of the way. This is far enough from the park so that sicko won't notice our cars when he gets here." Billy shouldered a knapsack. "Don't know about you, but I came prepared."

The two of them trudged down the side of the dark road in silence until they reached the fence that lined the edge of the park, which consisted only of short wood posts strung with wire.

"I saw it," Billy said. "He's going to take the boy over there, into that wooded area." He gestured over to the thick swath of trees that sat behind the aqueduct. "The kid will be wearing a gray T-shirt. Let's find a hiding place while we wait for them to show."

They stepped over the short fence and into the park, which Erasmo hadn't been to in years. Billy made a beeline for the aqueduct itself, stopping only when he stood in front of the structure that the park was built around. "It just looks like a small bridge," he said, his words tinged with disappointment.

"It kind of is," Erasmo said. "You can't really see it from where we're at, but on the top of it is a channel where the water flows. And that channel is held up by these big arches," he said as he gestured to the two limestone arcs the aqueduct sat on. A jagged dirt path cut under the left arch, the smaller of the two.

The larger right arch accommodated a meandering creek that ran underneath it.

"So it's a bridge for water?" Billy asked.

"Yeah, basically. It helped keep the water flowing to Mission Espada," Erasmo offered, surprised by how much he remembered from his grandfather's talks on the various missions. He added a line the old man had liked to use. "Those Spaniards were some engineering sons of bitches."

Billy said nothing to this and continued to look over the aqueduct.

"It looked bigger in the vision," he finally said. "We're going to have to go under that big arch on the right, the one with the creek running under it. That's where he's going to take the boy through."

Erasmo shivered as he eyed their path but nodded that he understood. "As soon as I see trouble, I'm calling the police," he said as they descended the broad steps that led down to the bottom of the arches.

"That's the plan," Billy replied. "But if this asshole is doing something to that kid, or even if he's *about* to do something, we're going to have to stop him ourselves. Be ready."

Erasmo reached into his pocket and caressed the knife as they stood in front of the large arch, peering in. Clusters of haggard trees, rotting sheets of leaves, and still, black creek water awaited them. Erasmo turned back and glanced at the park, with its inviting benches and neatly manicured grass. It was as if they were about to enter an entirely different world.

"Keep to the left," Billy said. "There's enough land here on the side to keep our feet out of the creek."

Erasmo took a breath and entered into the opening, overcome with a sensation of being swallowed as he did so. They soon emerged on the other side and found solid footing along the creek bank. Leaves crackled and twigs snapped under their feet as they made their way deeper into the dark underbelly of the park. Erasmo was alarmed to see the land rising steeply on both sides of them. He studied the terrain to his right, which now slanted upward at a distressingly sharp angle, and tried to assess the likelihood of being able to scramble up it successfully. It was possible, but he wouldn't want to bet his life on it.

"How much farther?" Erasmo asked. "Every inch of this place looks exactly the same. How can you tell from your dream the exact spot we should even be looking for?"

Billy stopped cold, almost causing Erasmo to collide into his back.

"That's a good place to wait," Billy said, pointing to a cluster of emaciated trees a few feet away. "They'll give us some cover."

Billy unshouldered his knapsack and placed it on a layer of wet leaves, glaring at Erasmo as he did so. "I don't have dreams, you know," he said.

The tone of Billy's voice, the simmering intensity in those few words, provoked an eruption of flutters in Erasmo's stomach. "Dreams? I don't—"

"You asked how I could tell from my *dream* what spot we should be looking for. I don't dream . . . never have."

"What are you talking about?" Erasmo asked.

"Dreams are some bullshit that's rattling around in your head while you sleep that don't make a lick of sense," Billy said, his voice trembling. "I don't have those. What I *do* have are visions of events that have not yet happened, but most certainly will. Does that sound like a dream to you, boss?"

"I guess when you put it that way, they're two very different things."

"That's right, Erasmo, two *very* different things. You want to know another difference?" Billy asked in a raised voice, as if he were a preacher just beginning to warm up. "These visions are given to me so that I can help . . . so that I can stop evil things from happening. Does that sound like just a dream to you?" Billy's eyes narrowed until they were thin, angry slits peering out from under the bill of his cap.

Erasmo remained silent, not wanting to piss him off any more than he already was. But Billy curled his bony hands into fists and strode toward Erasmo, his feet kicking up soggy leaves as he did so.

"I asked you a question. Does it sound like a bullshit dr—"

Erasmo whirled around. "I heard something. I . . . I see movement," he lied, hoping to distract Billy for a moment. He pretended to peer through the spindly trees in front of them. "What color shirt did you say that kid would be wearing?"

"Green," Billy said, not bothering to scan the area as Erasmo was pretending to do. "He'll be wearing a green shirt."

Erasmo felt the bottom of his stomach fall away. He reached into his pocket and folded his hand around the knife.

"That's not what you said when we got here. You said he'd be wearing a gray T-shirt. Gray. Not green."

Billy remained perfectly still and then exhaled a long, wistful sigh.

"I did say that, didn't I?"

Erasmo fingered the knife's switch, unsure whether to trigger it or not.

"There is no kid, is there?" Erasmo asked.

Billy turned his face skyward and studied the heavens, his sharp features dimly lit by the pale moonlight.

"What are we doing out here, Billy?" Erasmo asked, heart jackhammering in his chest. "Is this about me helping you? Because I can't even if I wanted to. No one would believe—"

"It ain't about your damn help. I just wanted to be alone with you, out here in the darkness, without an audience. That's all. Nothing wrong with that, is there?"

Erasmo continued to finger the switch but was too uncertain of what was happening to actually pull the knife.

"I knew it was all bullshit," Erasmo said.

"Watch out now," Billy replied. "I never said that. There *is* a boy who's going to be kidnapped. Just not tonight. The visions are real. My mission is real."

"Bullshit," Erasmo said. "Look . . . since you have me out here, at least tell me the truth. How did you do it? How did you *really* know those things were going to happen?"

Erasmo was ready to pull the knife if he came even a step closer, but Billy stood perfectly still as he exhaled a sigh and shook his head, apparently at the inconvenience of having to deal with such an idiot.

"You don't get it," Billy said. "You just don't get it. I see events that are supposed to happen. And then they happen. That's it."

"That's it? And they just happen exactly the way you see them?"

A slight grin broke out on Billy's mouth. "Well, not always *exactly*. Sometimes they need just a little bit of help."

Erasmo's blood ran cold.

"A little *help?* What the hell does that mean?"

"It means that God is telling me that He wants these things to happen. That's why the events are in my head, with every detail burned into my brain. If they don't happen by themselves, that means He wants me to . . . help things along, that's all. So I do."

"Wait . . . are you telling me," Erasmo said, his head now loose and weightless, "that you see these things in your head, and then you *make* them happen?"

"This is too big for you to understand, Erasmo," Billy said. "I could try to explain, but you'd never comprehend it."

"Billy, is *that* what you're telling me? Did you make those things happen *yourself*?"

"Let's see, how can I dumb this down enough for you?" Billy said. "If I see it in my head, then it *has* to be there for a reason. Why would He choose me and show me the way and *not* want me to act on the vision He's given? That wouldn't make any sense, now, would it?"

"You . . . you made those horrible things happen," Erasmo said, his entire body now shaking uncontrollably.

"*God* made them happen. I was just chosen to—"

"You're not chosen," Erasmo said, his voice weak and unsteady. "You're just a delusional psychopath."

"Don't you say that!" Billy yelled, eyes bulging. "You don't know *anything*!"

An avalanche of questions overwhelmed Erasmo, questions he desperately needed answers to. "But how did you get that woman to show up at Travis's house? How did you know what she'd be wearing?"

"I knew you weren't the fastest draw, but damn, Erasmo," Billy said, flashing a large, toothy grin. "All it took was one phone call to an escort service. They're real accommodating as it turns out. Those whores will dress up in whatever you ask if the price is right."

Erasmo tried to back away from Billy, to create enough distance to make a run for it, but his legs refused to move.

"I told her to knock on the door and tell Travis that she was sent over as a present. I knew if that pretty young thing showed up on his doorstep in the middle of the night, that sick asshole would lose control and do the rest."

"But *why*?"

"I told you, Erasmo," Billy said, as if it were perfectly obvious. "Because I saw these things in my head, and they hadn't happened yet. And it's *impossible* that God would have given me a false vision. So, I helped it along a bit."

"But . . . the fight . . . those guys?"

"Same thing with those stupid thugs. That neighborhood was where I'd park my truck and sleep when I had nowhere else to go. Every evening, I saw that kid in the Adidas jacket walk by like clockwork. And then one night, I had the vision of him getting beaten. But after a few weeks, it *still* hadn't happened. God's will had to be served, so I picked some random neighborhood guys, told them what the kid looked like, and paid them some money to jump him. But those idiots took it too far. They jumped *us* instead. Those assholes thought they were going to steal from *me*." Billy flashed his teeth. "But I showed them, didn't I?"

The part of Erasmo's brain that was still working urged him to keep Billy talking until he could think of a way to get out of this.

"None of this makes any sense, Billy," Erasmo said as he scanned the ground for large rocks to throw. "You said God showed you those visions to prevent bad things from happening, but nothing good came out of anything that we did."

"How can you say that?" Billy asked, incredulous. "A murderer who didn't deserve to live getting taken out *is* something good. It's what God wanted. Don't you see? That's why He gave me that vision in the first place. And those violent street thugs getting what they deserved is a good thing too. And don't forget about that kid in the jacket. You can't deny that we saved him."

"*Saved* him? You hired those guys to *beat* him!"

"No, man," Billy said. "He was never in any real danger. Those guys were supposed to run off as soon as they saw us coming. It was supposed to be a win for everybody. The vision would have been manifested, which is what God wanted. The kid wouldn't get beat by the *real* thugs anymore, since we changed the future. And you'd see proof that I'm a vessel of God and would help me spread the word."

"You're insane," Erasmo said, studying the steep land around him for possible footholds. Maybe he *could* just scramble up the incline, but not with Billy trying to drag him back down. "Don't you see that the kid was *never* going to get jumped? You just saw a random image in your head and thought that it actually meant something. It didn't. We made absolutely no difference."

"You're wrong, Erasmo. That kid takes a completely different route to get home now. We saved him by changing his future. We could've saved even more people if you'd helped me, but you just didn't want to believe."

"Right," Erasmo said, now clutching the knife harder, "as if anyone was *ever* going to believe that you can really tell the future, even if I did back you up. You're as stupid as you are crazy."

"Well," Billy said, "there's an awful lot of folks around here who believe that what happened to *you* was real. Besides . . . you know how people are." Billy peered up at the black sky and sighed before continuing. "Half these idiots will believe absolutely anything."

A rising gust of wind swept through the trees, their branches swaying back and forth helplessly. Billy took off his cap and ran a steady hand through his matted hair before he spoke again.

"You know, there isn't one vision I've had that hasn't come true."

"That you haven't *made* come true, asshole," Erasmo said.

"The semantics of it don't matter," Billy said. "The fact is every vision that has been placed in my head, I have seen played out in the actual world. I ain't ever been wrong yet."

Billy pulled his cap back on, reached into his knapsack, and withdrew an item that Erasmo couldn't make out.

"Every vision," Billy said, as he switched the object from his left hand to his right. It caught a glimmer of moonlight, and the brief moment of illumination was enough to stop Erasmo's heart. A knife. Billy was holding a hunting knife, its fine, serrated edge gleaming in the dim light.

"Except one," Billy said.

Erasmo turned to run but immediately stepped on a large, jagged rock and tumbled to the ground. He scrambled to get up but in his panic only managed to grab wet clumps of dirt. He felt Billy's hand snatch the back of his hoodie and yank him upward. Erasmo tried to break free, but Billy placed his left arm around Erasmo's waist and pulled him close, as if they were lovers. This illusion was shattered when Billy curled his wiry arm around Erasmo's neck, placing him in a choke hold.

"Do you remember?" Billy hissed in his ear.

Erasmo did. In fact, the words had never quite stopped whispering to him since he'd first heard them. *You were screaming. Screaming real bad. And I could see that you were terrified, although of what I don't know. And . . . there was blood too. So much blood flowing down your screaming face.* At that moment, struggling to draw a breath, Erasmo knew Billy Doggett was once again going to be entirely correct about the future.

"Let's see now . . ." Billy said as he felt around Erasmo's forehead. "The cut needs to be just right, exactly where He showed me. That means I need to start just about . . . here."

Erasmo thrashed his body wildly, bucking his back like a bronco trying to throw off his rider. But Billy's arm pulled even tighter against his throat, and soon Erasmo's lungs were on fire, pleading for even a wisp of oxygen. His vision darkened, and now his head felt as if it wanted to separate from his body and float away, a sensation both familiar and alarming.

Erasmo continued to flail and writhe. But wasn't this what he'd wanted? To drift and float away until he slowly dissolved into nothingness?

The cool blade of the hunting knife brushed against Erasmo's forehead. It was just the tip but enough for him to feel the extent of its sharpness. All Billy had to do was flick his wrist, and half of Erasmo's face would peel right off.

"Hold still," Billy said. "I need to get this just right."

Erasmo wondered how long it would take for someone to find his body out here, rotting, with a curiously maimed face. It was a horrible thought, but at least he'd have relief. The void inside of him would close forever. It wouldn't be long now. This, he thought as his lungs screamed in his chest, was what he wanted.

But if that were true, then why was he still thrashing and clawing?

Erasmo's vision wavered, and the world went completely black for a moment before immediately blinking back in. He pulled at Billy's arm, trying again to somehow wrench it free, but his hold was too strong.

Was this what it had been like for his father at the end? Had he known what was happening to him, as Erasmo did now? In his last moments, had his father spared even a small thought for the son he was leaving behind?

Pressure continued to build under his face, which felt as if it might burst at any moment. The world went black again, and from somewhere deep in his flickering consciousness, Erasmo heard his uncle's raspy, tired voice.

When they found him, there wasn't much left. His body had decomposed, and the animals had gotten at him too. It was like . . . they found him, but he wasn't even there.

Through the haze, three thoughts rose and whispered to him.

I am here.
I am here, and I am not him.
I am not him.

Erasmo reached a convulsing hand into his pocket and felt two objects. His hand clenched the one made of steel.

He felt Billy's body tense at the sound of the blade unfolding. Erasmo brought his right arm up over his head before bringing it down as hard as his weakened body would allow. He felt only the slightest bit of resistance as the knife plunged into Billy's right thigh.

Erasmo felt immediate relief as the enormous pressure on his trachea lessened and then disappeared completely. Without Billy holding him up, Erasmo crumpled to the ground, his lungs burning furiously. Even though his neck was no longer being crushed, he still couldn't get enough oxygen. It was as if his throat were made of putty, and Billy had squeezed hard enough to mold it shut. He sucked at the air around him but couldn't breathe enough to cool the fire in his lungs.

Billy stood still, staring down at the object protruding from his leg, as if he couldn't comprehend what it was and how it could've possibly gotten there. He looked at Erasmo, the muscles in his face slack with shock, and then back down at the knife, drawing the connection between the two.

"Son of a bitch," he hissed, limping toward Erasmo, grimacing as he dragged his right leg behind him. "You're still going to bleed. All over your goddamn face."

Erasmo tried to stand but could manage only a wobbly position on his hands and knees. He looked over his shoulder to see Billy limping toward him, only a few feet behind. Erasmo turned and began to crawl away furiously, sharp pebbles and twigs digging deep into his palms.

"I got you, asshole," Billy croaked.

Erasmo's left side exploded in pain. He collapsed to the ground and rolled over onto his back, realizing that Billy had kicked him with his good leg. Erasmo curled into the fetal position, expecting a torrent of blows to rain down, but none came. Instead, Billy straddled him, grunting in pain as he sat on Erasmo's chest.

"Don't you get it?" Billy said as he shifted his weight, trying to find a comfortable position on Erasmo's body. "I've seen it, so it *has* to happen. It *has* to. Because if it doesn't, then that means I'm not chosen at all, that I'm not special, and that *can't* be true."

"You aren't chosen, Billy," Erasmo said. "You just saw my face at the church and conjured a strange image of it. I bet you probably have *lots* of strange images floating through your head. They're not visions of the future. They're just things that you *want* to do. That's why you make these things happen . . . so you can act out your dark fantasies. That's all this is. Please. You don't have to do this."

"You're wrong," Billy said. "You *have* to be. Because if what you're saying is right, and God hasn't been giving me these visions, then that means what I've always feared is true."

Billy placed his hand over Erasmo's mouth and leaned in close.

"That would mean," Billy whispered, "that I'm crazier than a shithouse rat."

Billy leaned back and grinned at Erasmo, his eyes bursting with delight. "Now don't move."

He stared intently at the top right corner of Erasmo's forehead, slicing his hunting knife through the air several times in succession. Erasmo felt his insides droop and loosen, as if everything inside of him had liquefied.

Practicing.

Billy was practicing the stroke he was going to use to carve his face open, because he needed to get it just right.

Erasmo jerked his head back and forth, but Billy held his head down. He looked around for something, anything that could help, and then he saw his possible salvation. It was so close he almost missed it. The switchblade still stuck out of Billy's thigh, its black handle almost invisible in the dim light. He grabbed for his grandfather's weapon, but his arm was pinned under Billy's knee, and he couldn't extend it far enough to reach.

"Stop struggling. I see it now. Exactly where you need to bleed."

Billy placed the tip of his hunting knife on Erasmo's forehead.

Not like this. Please. Not scared and alone. Not like him.

"Right."

Billy began to draw the blade downward.

"Here."

Erasmo jerked his left arm forward with all of his strength, freeing it, and found his hand next to the knife's handle. He grabbed it, felt its coolness, and twisted as hard as he could. Billy unleashed an amazing howl and toppled off him, clutching his leg.

Erasmo reached into his pocket. It was still there.

He got up, willing his legs to straighten and bear the weight of his shivering body. Erasmo watched as Billy struggled to his feet, grunting like a boar, the right side of his jeans drenched a deep shade of maroon.

"You don't understand . . ." Billy began.

"I know," Erasmo said, pulling the syringe out of his pocket. "You keep telling me, Billy."

Erasmo ran toward him and dove at his legs, tackling him to the ground. Billy struggled to get away but seemed to have lost some of his strength.

Erasmo straddled him, taking a millisecond to enjoy the reversal as Billy wriggled underneath him like an undulating cocoon. It had to be now, while he had the chance. He yanked the cap off the syringe and placed his thumb on the plunger. Erasmo stabbed the syringe at Billy, aiming for the carotid artery in his neck. It was going to go in too, right on target, until Billy's hand shot up and snatched Erasmo's wrist.

The needle trembled, only a few inches away from the pale, dirty skin of Billy's neck. Erasmo pushed down with all the strength he had left, the needle so very close to penetrating flesh. Billy fervently pushed the syringe away, fear showing on his face for the first time.

Erasmo's arm shook and burned as he struggled to maintain the pressure, but still the needle did not move forward. He wouldn't be able to keep it up for very much longer.

Erasmo felt behind him with his left hand, grabbing and searching. There was only wet denim and slick flesh, but then finally it was there, brushing against the side of his hand. Erasmo grabbed the handle of the blade and dug it deep into the meat of Billy's thigh. Billy let out an immense wail, and the resistance against Erasmo's arm dissolved to nothingness.

He shoved Billy's face to the side, exposing the straining cords in his neck. Erasmo sunk the needle in and depressed the plunger, not stopping until every drop of the drug had been expelled.

Erasmo wasn't entirely sure why he'd even brought the syringe with him. It had seemed easier to just throw it in his pocket than spend time hiding it in his room. And a part of him had considered how nice it might be to just shoot up out here, huddled under the shadows, cool grass against his face, with only the stars as a witness to his surrender. After all, his father hadn't been found inside and whole; he'd been found decayed and unrecognizable, mixed in with the earth itself.

But that no longer mattered.

The effect on Billy was immediate. Every muscle in his body relaxed in unison, and his eyelids dropped slowly until only a white sliver of his sclera was visible.

Erasmo leaned down and whispered into Billy's ear. "Good news, Billy. I'm going to call the cops and tell them all about you, just like you wanted. My advice to you is to get the hell out of town, and don't ever come back. Ever."

Erasmo rose and turned to walk away.

"You don' unnnerstan . . ." Billy mumbled.

"I know, Billy," Erasmo said as he stumbled into the night. "I know. You ain't ever been wrong yet."

CHAPTER 30

ERASMO DIDN'T ACTUALLY call the cops, of course. He knew they wouldn't believe one word of his story. And he certainly wasn't eager for the police to take a closer look at Travis's death, given that he and Rat had both been at the scene. He just hoped that the threat was enough to scare Billy away permanently.

As Erasmo lay in bed, morning light creeping into his room, he continued a debate he'd been having with himself the last few days: whether to tell Rat the truth about Billy. He'd initially resisted the idea. What good could possibly come of it? But there was still the chance that Billy might reach out to Rat, and his friend should know to stay as far away from that guy as possible.

He picked up his phone and dialed.

"Hello?"

"Hey," Erasmo said. "We need to talk. Can you meet?"

"Yeah," Rat said after a long silence. "Actually, there's something I've been wanting to talk to you about too. I just wasn't sure when the right time would be. I'll take this call as a sign that the right time is now. Come over."

Erasmo opened his mouth to ask what the hell Rat was talking about, but the line disconnected before he could get the words out.

Thirty minutes later, Erasmo stood on Rat's porch, lifting his fist to rap on the door. But before he could, it swung open, and he had to suppress a gasp at Rat's appearance. His friend looked even more emaciated than usual, which Erasmo hadn't thought possible. Rat's skin was waxy and sallow, its dull complexion somehow managing to dampen the light around him.

"Let's go for a ride," Rat mumbled, grabbing the keys from Erasmo's hand. "I'll drive."

Erasmo began to protest, but Rat was already walking to the Civic, his oversized T-shirt flapping in the air behind him. Rat was buckled in and had the engine going by the time Erasmo slid into the passenger side.

"Where we going?" Erasmo asked as Rat backed out of the driveway.

"It's a surprise."

"A surprise? Dude, I've already had enough of those to last a lifetime. I'm not sure I can take another one."

Rat didn't acknowledge this, and only stared ahead as he drove through his neighborhood.

"Actually," Erasmo continued, "that's why I wanted to talk. There are some things that I've found out. Terrible things. We really messed up with Billy."

"How so?" Rat asked, his tone only slightly above a whisper.

Erasmo told him everything. When he'd finished, his friend sat completely still, both hands on the wheel, his face unreadable.

"Well," Erasmo asked, "aren't you surprised?"

"Yeah, I am," he said. "I guess it's just a little harder to shock me now, after everything we've seen." For the first time,

Rat took his eyes off the road and looked over at Erasmo, his thin lips a flat, unmoving line.

"As for Billy himself, well . . . people do crazy things when they're trying to find their place in the world," Rat said. He gave Erasmo a weak smile before adding, "Or if they don't have a place at all." He then turned back to the road, his half smile disappearing. "I'm relieved you're okay, though. Billy didn't know who the hell he was messing with."

The two of them sat in silence as Rat drove up I-10, heading to the north side of town. The weekend traffic was light, so it didn't take long to reach 1604, which Rat wordlessly merged on to. Erasmo was surprised when, shortly later, Rat flashed his blinker to exit on Stone Oak Parkway. He felt his impatience growing, wanting an explanation as to what they were doing way the hell out here. The Civic now turned onto Canyon Golf Road, and Erasmo's eyes widened as he gaped at the elegant houses he was in the midst of. The sizes of the front lawns alone stunned him. His grandmother's entire house would fit into just a corner of many of them.

"Who do we know that has enough money to live out here?" Erasmo asked.

Rat continued to navigate through the opulent neighborhood, finally gliding to a stop in front of one of the properties, a two-story behemoth constructed of tan stucco and white stone. Erasmo couldn't imagine the cost for the house's landscaping alone, given the varieties of neatly manicured greenery that lined the expansive lawn. He didn't have to get out of the car and survey the view to know that his poor Civic looked comically out of place.

Rat killed the engine and immediately slid out of the car. Erasmo watched as his friend jogged onto the lawn and rushed down a long stone path that led to the entrance. Erasmo jumped out and chased after his friend. When he caught up to him, he found Rat staring silently at the mammoth oak door safeguarding the home.

"It doesn't look like anybody is here," Erasmo said, noting that there were no cars parked on the property. Rat looked at him with sad eyes, fished into his right pocket, and held up a silver key for display. He inserted it into the lock and twisted, stepping through the hulking doorway while waving at him to do the same.

Erasmo entered, his grimy tennis shoes squeaking against the foyer's maple floor as he followed Rat. The hallway entrance opened into a vast, open area dominated by a massive stairway in the center of the room. Ornate stonework surrounded them, with pillars and arches everywhere he turned. The ceiling reached seemingly impossible altitudes, with glistening chandeliers hanging high above them.

As Erasmo glanced around, marveling at the abundance of both sheer space and heartbreaking beauty, he could scarcely believe that people actually spent their lives in houses like this. He had an urge to bound up the stairs and explore, to slink into the hallways that branched out in front of him and stare in wonder at the many delights.

Rat turned left, passing underneath one of the ubiquitous stone arches. Erasmo followed him down a hallway and then into a living area, which housed a leather sectional, plush armchairs, and a massive stone fireplace in the corner. The walls were covered with a multitude of family pictures. Rat stood by the fireplace, surveying a few of the photographs hanging above the mantel. His face was wrinkled with disgust, as if he were studying pictures of freaks, instead of portraits of a serene family basking in proper lighting and good fortune.

"Who are they?" Erasmo asked as he strode up to one of the pictures to get a better view. This image was of a middle-aged couple and two eager boys, presumably the inhabitants of this

house. The gentleman was dark, lithe, and balding, a small tuft
on the top of his head the only proof that he'd once possessed
hair. The woman was striking, even to Erasmo, who was not
particularly attracted to white women. Both the boys were in
their early teens and reed-thin like their dad. But they sported
unruly, overgrown hair, as if attempting to preemptively stave
off the future.

"Take another look," Rat said, his eyes now fixed on a vaca-
tion photo of the sun-drenched family in a rapturous group
hug, their feet buried in blinding-white sand. "Anything look
familiar to you?"

Erasmo studied the man. There actually had been a twinge
of familiarity when he first saw the photo. Was it someone he
once knew? Erasmo squinted at the picture, editing the man's
features. If the slightly large nose was instead even larger . . . if
the mildly protruding ears instead jutted out even farther . . .
he would look kind of like . . . actually, he would look a *lot*
like . . .

"Rat," Erasmo said. "Is this . . ."

"Yeah," his friend said, turning away from the photos.
"It is."

"I didn't even know he lived in town, or that you even knew
where he was. You never really talk about him."

"Well, I didn't know much about him until a few years
back. My mom had always told me she didn't know where he
was, that he'd fled long ago to someplace far away. Imagine
my surprise when the Bexar County Appraisal District website
listed an address for him right here in town. A pretty nice one
too." Rat raised both his arms skyward to illustrate the point.
"He owns his own business, repossessing cars for banks of all
things."

"Wow," Erasmo said. "So, we're here to hang out with
him?"

"Hang out with him? Oh no, not at all. He doesn't even know I'm here."

"Oh, well, that's cool of him to give you a key so that you can come over and relax in style whenever—"

"No, he didn't give it to me," Rat said, glancing downward. "I stole it."

Tingles crept up Erasmo's spine. "Stole it? Rat . . . what the hell are we doing here?"

Rat lifted his eyes to meet Erasmo's.

"Something wonderful."

Erasmo's heart fluttered, as if it had lost its rhythm and could no longer find it.

"Dude, you're scaring me—"

"A few years back," Rat said, "when I found out he lived here, I came over and knocked on the door. I knew that it was a mistake even as I was doing it, but I had to see, you know? A small part of me wondered if my mom had lied to him the same way that she'd lied to me. I thought that maybe if he knew that I was *so* close by, he'd want to see me. One of his sons, my half brother I guess, came to the door. I still remember the look this kid gave me, like I was a mangy dog looking for scraps or something. He called out for his dad and I just stood there, panicking. I honestly thought my heart was going to explode. Finally, my father stepped into the doorway."

Rat paused, his eyes glistening and distant.

"He looked like me. Well, I looked like him I guess I should say. I know I should've expected the resemblance, but it was still a shock to see a different version of myself." The muscles in his face tightened as he added, "A better version of myself." Tears began to spill down Rat's cheeks, dropping soundlessly onto the plush carpet below. "My father just stood there, looking at me. And I could see right away that he knew who I was . . .

what I was. But still, he didn't speak. So I stood on that porch and waited, desperate for him to say something."

Rat wiped furiously at his eyes with the back of his hand. "And then he finally did."

Erasmo had a fairly good idea of what he was about to hear. He wanted to tell Rat to stop, that he didn't want to know the rest, but he couldn't find the words so he just continued to listen as his bones filled with dread.

"He said that there was nothing for me here. That my mom was a crazy whore and that whatever she told me was nothing but lies. That he wasn't"—the words caught in Rat's throat as his face trembled—"that he wasn't my father. Then he yelled that I shouldn't ever come back." Rat pointed his finger sternly, reenacting his father's manner. "Or he'd call the police to take me away."

Erasmo had no idea how to respond to this. He felt terrible for his friend, certainly. And he wished that Rat had shared all of this with him before now, instead of choosing to carry the burden alone. But there was also an alarm going off in the back of his head, growing persistently louder. It emanated from one central question, a question he'd already asked, but for which an answer remained blurrier than ever.

What the hell were they doing here?

Rat, as if he sensed that very question hanging in the air, began to answer in soft, measured words. "I've been wanting this for so long but was never quite sure about the timing." He turned his back to Erasmo and drifted to the other side of the room. "But then you had the idea for the ad, and I knew. It was a sign. A sign to move forward."

"Move forward?" Erasmo asked, trying to stave off panic. "With what?"

Rat stopped to study yet another photo, caressing the mahogany frame with his spindly fingers.

"Transformation."

The cold, serene manner with which his friend said this word sent a shudder coursing through Erasmo.

"Transformation? What are you talking about?"

"I . . . have a lot to explain," Rat said. "Let me get through it all, and then you'll see clearly. I guess I should start with this."

He slowly reached under his shirt and pulled a revolver out of his waistband.

"What the hell . . ." Erasmo said, holding his hands in front of him as he took a step backward.

"No!" Rat yelled. "C'mon. It's not for you. Never for you."

"But . . . then why . . ."

Rat raised the gun, planted the muzzle directly against his temple, and gave Erasmo a gentle smile. "It's for me, of course."

"No!" Erasmo screamed.

"Calm down," Rat said, lowering the gun. "It's not time yet. I want to explain first."

"Look, man," Erasmo croaked, his heart pounding in arrhythmic spasms, "you're scaring the shit out of me."

"Why are you scared? There is nothing to fear. We should welcome death. It's a beautiful transmutation, from a repulsive existence to an ethereal one. And I'm ready to experience my rebirth."

"Rat, you're not going to do this. There is so much for you to live for—"

"That's a *goddamn* lie, Erasmo! And you know it! I understand why some people, like my father and his kids, want to squeeze every possible moment out of their delightful existence. But for someone like me . . . it's better to just get on with finding out what wonders the next life might hold."

"No, man, that's not how it works," Erasmo said, his voice sounding thin and unsteady to his ears.

"It doesn't? How the hell do you know?"

"Rat . . ."

"Do you know why I'm doing it here, in this house?"

Erasmo had been wondering that very thing. Why go through all the trouble to do it here, of all places? But now . . . now it was obvious.

"I think I do," Erasmo said.

"You see!" Rat exclaimed, a thin smile on his lips. "It makes sense to you too! That's how you figured it out. It's the most logical thing in the world."

"You think you're coming back as a spirit," Erasmo said.

"I *am* coming back," Rat said, resolve dripping from his words.

"And you think that if it happens here, then you will come back. Right here."

"Right here," Rat agreed.

"And your spirit will live in this house."

"Goddamn right it will."

"Rat . . ."

"It's as good a place as any, isn't it? And I won't stay here forever, just long enough to give my father a few . . . nightmares, that's all." Rat broke out in a wide, quivering grin. "And, who knows, his goddamn brat kids may get a few spooks too."

"My God," Erasmo whispered. "You're just as insane as they are."

This dissolved the smile from Rat's face, replacing it with snarled lips and bared teeth. "Don't you say that to me! I'm not crazy! What I'm about to do is *real* and *true*. I AM going to come back. Don't you understand? What happened to you at the Tracks was my *inspiration* for all this! I know that if those children can come back, and exert their will on this side, then I can too."

"Rat, this is bullshit!" Erasmo screamed. "I know why we're *really* here. You just don't want to live anymore! That's all this is. You're trying to dress it up as some kind of wondrous transformation. But the truth is that you hate everything about yourself and can't stand the hurt anymore and want to give up. It's as simple and common as that!"

Rat raised the revolver and jammed it against his temple.

"You're wrong," he said, the skin on his gaunt face twitching as he spoke. "So very wrong. As you're about to see."

Erasmo watched in disbelief as Rat's bony finger curled around the trigger.

"Please!" he said, sliding forward. "Don't!"

"STOP!" Rat screamed. "You come any closer and I'll pull the trigger."

"I can't let you do this," Erasmo said, tears now streaming down his face.

"I'll do it if you don't stop right NOW!"

There was no more time. Erasmo took in a deep breath, gathered his legs under him, and leaped toward his friend. Rat stumbled backward, but Erasmo managed to grab his ankles and tackle him to the floor. Erasmo's eyes closed as he braced for the gun's report to fill the room and shred his eardrums.

But to his shock and immense relief, the only sound he heard as they lay tangled on the floor was that of his own breathless panting. Erasmo scrambled up from the floor and saw the revolver lying a few feet away. He reached down and curled his hand around its wood grip. Rat lay on his back, looking up plaintively at Erasmo, his lips quivering.

"Why did you do that?" he wailed, tears filling his narrow eyes.

"I had to," Erasmo said. "You're my friend . . . and I just don't have enough of those to start losing any."

Rat continued to weep as he pushed himself off the floor, his eyes never leaving Erasmo's.

"This isn't *your* decision to make. I want this!" His small fists trembled. "I *want* this!"

"Man, the thing is, I don't think you do," Erasmo said. "Otherwise, you wouldn't have brought me here. You could have done this a hell of a lot easier without me around to stop you."

Rat shook his head furiously, sending drops of tears flying in every direction.

"No, man, I brought you here because I wanted you to see me. The new me. After I changed."

"Rat, please . . ."

"Not everyone can see the transformed. But *you* can, and one day you're going to see my new—"

"NO!" Erasmo yelled. "You're not going to do this. Not today, not ever."

"And why the hell not?" Rat asked.

"Because I'm alone too!" Erasmo yelled. "And I don't want to be even more alone than I already am. We're in this together. Isn't that why we've been friends all this time, because we're the same? Because we see ourselves in each other? Well, you can't just leave that." Erasmo placed his hand on his friend's trembling shoulder. "You can't just leave me."

Rat's chest heaved as he wiped at his face. "You don't understand . . . how bad it is. . . ."

"Man, but I do," Erasmo said. "My parents threw away the life we should have had together. They threw *me* away. For nothing. I'm not sure exactly what I believe anymore, but there is one thing I'm holding on to. I do believe that things are going to get better. For both of us. They have to."

Erasmo tossed the gun on the sectional, then extended his arms around Rat and held him. It was the first time he'd ever done so. Rat's body felt airy and inconsequential, as if he were hugging an empty shirt on a hanger. Weak and muffled sobs pressed against his chest. Erasmo leaned down and whispered into Rat's ear.

"The universe owes you and me a few, and that's a debt I have every intention of collecting on."

Erasmo let go of Rat, stepped back, and extended his hand to him.

"We're going to make a pact," Erasmo said, "you and me. Right here. And this house is just the place to do it."

"A pact?"

"Yeah, a pact. You know what a pact is, don't you?"

"Yeah . . . I just wasn't aware anyone over the age of eight made them anymore."

A joke. Good.

"Well, we're going to make one now."

Rat took a long, wary look at Erasmo's waiting hand. Finally, he shrugged his shoulders, reached out, and grasped it. Erasmo peered directly into Rat's eyes, which gazed back at him with both suspicion and curiosity.

"We've had a rough start, no doubt, but that's over now," Erasmo began. "There's a lot of life still in front of us, and all the grievances that have been holding us back don't matter anymore, starting right now. We're not going to have a substandard existence because of some bullshit that happened a long time ago. There are lives out there for us . . . wonderful and peaceful lives. We just need to believe that we deserve them and have the guts to go out there and take them for ourselves. That's the pact. Right there. You in?"

Rat's face contorted, and it appeared as if he might start crying again, but no tears came. His friend closed his eyes, and his body trembled, but he tightened his grip on Erasmo's hand. When he spoke, it was in a gentle whisper.

"I . . . I'll try."

"That's all I can ask," Erasmo said, embracing Rat again, wishing to the stars that his friend's pain would one day be eased. "That's all I can ask."

CHAPTER 31

HE SPENT THE next few weeks attempting to process what Rat had wanted to do . . . what he'd wanted his new existence to be. All Erasmo could see when he closed his eyes was his friend's sure and certain face as his finger curled around the trigger.

As much as he loved Rat, he was wary of him now, in a way he never imagined he would be. Still, they talked every day, and at certain times he seemed like the same old Rat. It had been shockingly easy to fall back into their normal routines, as if nothing had happened. But the truth was never far away, a persistent, dreadful whisper in his ear.

Erasmo constantly debated with himself over what to do about Rat's mental health. He wanted to bring up the idea of counseling, but there was no telling how Rat would react. Inevitably, he always ended up deciding to just wait and monitor the situation. If even the slightest downturn in Rat's demeanor became obvious, he would have no choice but to broach the topic. Or worse, go to Rat's mother and demand that she step in and do something. It was drastic, but too many atrocities had already happened, and he didn't want to be responsible for any more.

The strange truth, though, was that despite his constant worries about Rat, he felt closer to his friend than ever before. Erasmo now understood that seeing someone at their absolute lowest point was a form of magic, inextricably binding the sufferer and the observer together in a lifelong union, even through time and space. Their interactions were now clear-eyed and brutally honest, the experiences they'd shared and what they knew about each other rendering any bullshit pointless. Erasmo had been heartened by their recent conversations, as the pact was a frequent topic of conversation.

"It's weird," he said to Erasmo one evening as they prepared for an all-night movie marathon. "In some ways, finding out about my father actually helped. I mean, look at everything he has. He's smart. He's got business sense. I keep wondering if those qualities are lurking around somewhere inside of me too, and I think I'm going to try and find out. Part of the pact, right?"

"Part of the pact," Erasmo agreed.

"Now . . . why don't you go get us some snacks? It would be an absolute crime to watch *Aliens* without Doritos and a tall glass of Big Red in hand."

"My friend," Erasmo said as he grabbed his keys, "that's the smartest thing you've said in quite some time."

He pulled into the lightless, empty parking lot of Primo's Grocery and killed the engine. As he stepped out of the car, a loud *clang* echoed from behind him. He jerked around only to see nothing at all.

Calm down, dude. There's no one out there. It's all over.

Erasmo briskly walked into the store and gathered enough of the usual junk food to last the night. He'd read earlier that some anti-inflammatories might inhibit the spread of certain cancers, so he grabbed a couple of aspirin bottles too. After chatting with the cashier about the Spurs' lackluster season, he gathered the bulging bags and strode back to the Civic.

As he loaded everything into the back seat, he heard a soft, rustling noise behind him.

Damn, get ahold of yourself, man. You're jumping at shad—

CHAPTER 32

IN A CONFUSED haze, Erasmo sat in the dark, half-conscious, desperately trying to hold on to the thoughts flickering through his ruptured head. There were many of them, but they proved to be slippery and elusive. After a few moments of squinting into the darkness, he finally managed to capture one. It was a useless thought, though, which wouldn't help a goddamn thing. But it was the only one he'd been able to extract from the morass in his head, and so he was forced to consider it:

How the hell did I end up here?

Erasmo shifted in the chair, feeling the ropes dig into his chest and shinbones. The back of his head was wet and misshapen, and it throbbed so hard it felt as if a crazed animal were trying to escape from his skull.

The sound of gentle scraping whispered behind him. He jerked around, his eyes frantically searching the dark for whatever might be lurking in its black belly. Sweat dripped into his right pupil. It should sting, but he felt nothing.

"Who's there?"

The only response to his question was a powerful gust of wind that shook the walls of whatever makeshift prison he was in, and the faraway rustle of branches and leaves shivering against each other.

Erasmo clenched his eyelids shut and forced himself to breathe. He couldn't panic. He had to think. But his head still hurt so bad. . . .

Another faint, slow scraping sound, this time directly in front of him.

"Please!" he screamed. "This is a mistake!"

No response, not even the wind this time.

He was no longer able to prevent his body from shaking uncontrollably. And if he didn't keep his shit together, Erasmo knew he'd soon begin screaming into the darkness, as the urge to do so was now compelling and powerful.

He took a deep, slow breath and tried to remember.

It had been so dark in the parking lot. It could have been anybody. Anybody at all.

Erasmo inhaled a lungful of stale air as the ropes bit into his limbs. Every one of his muscles ached from being tied to the chair for so long.

A sound drifted from the darkness, very close this time. A boot brushing against the concrete floor perhaps. He strained his eyes, but the shadows revealed nothing.

"Please! Untie me! There's been a mistake."

Erasmo tried again to jog his memory. He remembered hearing something in the store's parking lot. Erasmo had turned, but . . .

He wasted a few moments attempting to convince himself that this was just some kind of robbery but knew that it wasn't true. Whoever went to the trouble of taking him desired a pound of flesh, and it was certainly going to be extracted. Of that, Erasmo had no doubt.

His thoughts were slow and clumped together, like hand-fuls of mud. Despite the discomfort of his strangled body, and the haze enveloping his head, ideas began to form in the muck.

This must've been planned, maybe well in advance. Whoever took him had been watching, following him. This person must be strong too, having been able to knock him out with just one blow and drag him away.

And he was tied up. Did this mean his abductor wanted to do things to him? Horrible and painful and grotesque things? This person, whoever it might be, was going to come in here and hurt him. He was going to . . .

Wait. He felt something. Air, a slight breeze, on the back of his neck. Perhaps there was an open window or a hole in one of the walls. If he yelled, maybe someone would hear. . . .

But then Erasmo had a realization, and his bladder released liquid warmth all over his thighs. The air wasn't a breeze at all. It was a breath, tickling the tiny hairs on the back of his neck. A hoarse voice whispered into his ear.

"You're a damn liar."

The voice moved, circling him and repeating the words, his cadence flat and monotone.

"You said it wasn't real."

The figure continued to circle him in the dark, and then Erasmo, who was very close to unleashing the shriek that had been building in his chest, felt a warm breath caress his face.

"But you were wrong," the voice whispered, "and now you're going to help me . . . or I'm going to peel your face right off your goddamn skull."

Erasmo heard a click, and a circle of illumination erupted above him. The brilliance of the light blurred his vision as his eyes struggled to adjust. The man stood directly in front of him, but Erasmo couldn't quite make out his face. He had a baseball cap pulled low. And he was holding something. A knife. Jesus. A large, serrated knife.

"Please . . . this is a mistake!" Erasmo blinked furiously as his eyes began to acclimate to the light. "I'm not who you want. I can't be!"

The figure reached up and slowly slipped off his cap. It took Erasmo a few moments of staring into the crazed face in front of him to realize that he did know this person. In fact, there was no question who the man standing in front of him was. Cold wisps of fear spread through his belly as he now understood that, despite his protests, he had been so very wrong. This wasn't a mistake at all.

"It's still happening," the man said in a trembling voice, taking a position behind Erasmo. "All of it."

A wiry hand grabbed Erasmo's hair and, without warning, snapped his head back, exposing his throat.

"But now you're going to make it stop."

Erasmo felt the tip of the knife slide around his neck in abstract patterns.

"Please," Erasmo said, "what I told you was true. I—"

"Don't lie to me!" the man screamed. "You promised it wasn't real!"

And this Erasmo could not dispute. He had, in fact, promised the man standing behind him, pressing a knife against his throat, that very thing.

"And if it isn't real," Leander Castillo said, pressing the knife down harder, "then why the *hell* is she still after me?"

Erasmo tried to speak, but no words came. What words would there be? Leander was clearly mad and, as he saw now, must've been from the beginning.

"*Tell me!* Why is she still after me? Oh, no answer?" Leander said. "Well, maybe this will make you more talkative."

Before Erasmo had a chance to beg for his life, Leander deftly repositioned the blade and slashed his face from the top of his right brow to the bridge of his nose.

Erasmo screamed as thick blood poured down his face in waves. He tried to speak, to plead for his life, but his throat only produced shrill, incoherent sounds.

"Make her go away!" Leander shrieked, tears streaming down his face. "Make her go away like you said you would!"

Leander now appeared in front of Erasmo, red-faced and screaming, spittle flying from his mouth.

"I *did* kill her! Is that what you need to know? It was an accident, I swear to God, but I killed her. Now make her stop following me!"

Erasmo shrieked again, swallowing his own thick, warm blood. He closed his eyes and was somehow able to shut out the horror erupting around him. Leander's screaming continued, but it was distant now, a hum in the background, almost unimportant.

He thought about his father, who died alone and never lived a real life. He thought about Rat, whom he would die for. He thought about beautiful Nora, and how when he first saw her, his heart swelled and warped into something different than it had been before. The humming continued in the background, insistent and with even greater urgency now.

Behind his closed eyes, an expanse of space and time spread out before him. Images from his past and present flickered in and out of the darkness. Erasmo's grandmother, cooking atole de arroz on her decrepit brown stove. His faltering grandfather, throwing a wobbly football to him on his eighth birthday. His third-grade class, euphorically singing "We Wish You a Merry Christmas" the last day before winter break. He mourned for these memories, knowing they would soon whisper out of existence.

The screams he had been ignoring were frantic now, and Erasmo felt the tip of the knife dig into his throat. The blade pierced his skin, tickling his Adam's apple and releasing a single drop of blood that trickled down his neck.

Death would arrive soon, and as the inevitability of this settled over him, he felt something unexpected. A small piece of his subconscious, buried under a black ocean of fear and uncertainty, broke free from its constraints, yearning to rise to the surface. He reflexively shoved it down, but it continued to ascend.

He'd never been able to recollect much of what happened that night at the Tracks; he'd relied on the old man's story as his own. The story he wanted and needed to believe. That's the tale he trotted out whenever anyone asked. But where were his own memories of that night?

Now that Erasmo was so close to death, could his mind finally bear the weight of the truth that he'd buried for so long?

A cloud of white powder erupted in front of him.

Erasmo was transported to that night. It was almost as if he were truly there, instead of bound to a chair, hemorrhaging blood in an unkempt shack. The black sky with scraps of clouds floating across it. The goose bumps on his flesh as the wind fluttered across his skin. His head pounding while his body lay limp on the side of the road. He heard someone coming, running through the dark to him. Erasmo could only make out a silhouette. It was that of a short, stout man, wearing a hat of some kind.

"Are you okay?" a breathless voice asked.

Erasmo couldn't answer. He genuinely didn't know.

"Sir! Are you okay?" Louder this time, the voice streaked with fear.

The man produced a long cylindrical item, almost dropping it.

"Wait a minute," he said, struggling with the object. "Let me . . ."

A burst of blue light shot from his hands, and Erasmo saw right away that he was a cop. A young, plump one, breathing heavily. The name on his right breast read: *Enriquez*. He continued to fumble with the flashlight, almost dropping it, before finally getting it under control.

"You okay?" the officer asked, aiming the harsh beam directly into Erasmo's face.

"Yeah . . . I think so," Erasmo answered as he slowly sat up. "My head just hurts. There was a truck. I jumped to get away from it and landed on the tracks. Hey, can you lower that light? It's bothering my eyes."

"Oh," Officer Enriquez said, sounding embarrassed. "Sure, sorry about that." He lowered the beam away from Erasmo's face and onto his body. "An older gentleman and his family called in the accident. They seem pretty messed up by the whole thing. When I got here, they just pointed in this direction and wouldn't say a word. I thought you'd be pretty mangled up, to be honest. An ambulance is on the way, so . . ."

The officer froze and the muscles in his face went slack, his jaw lowering until it hung fully open.

"Hey," Erasmo said, "is everything . . ."

Officer Enriquez's eyes widened as he took a step backward. Erasmo whipped his head around, bringing fresh stabs of pain to his neck. But when he scanned the area behind him, there was nothing there, only the narrow road and suffocating darkness. He turned back to see that the officer's stunned expression hadn't changed. Erasmo studied his eyes and tried to follow their path. That's when he realized the officer wasn't looking behind Erasmo at all. Officer Enriquez was staring at Erasmo himself.

A chill shot through him. His injuries must be worse than he thought. Erasmo forced himself to look down, expecting to see torrents of blood, to see his guts exposed to the world. But this wasn't what he saw at all. It took him a few confused, uncomprehending moments to finally realize what had frightened Officer Enriquez.

Erasmo's vision flickered as he felt his hold on consciousness waver. He stared down, attempting to convince himself that his eyes were simply deceived by the darkness and the shadows. But the officer's flashlight lit up his black sweatshirt, and there was no mistaking what its illumination revealed.

His clothes were covered with tiny white handprints.

The officer moved the shaking beam of light away from Erasmo until it settled on a spot in the middle of the road. A pink container, the one Erasmo had brought with him, lay crushed, the asphalt around it stained with baby powder.

"My God," the officer whispered.

The beam from the flashlight slowly traveled from the pink bottle to where Erasmo sat on the side of the road. As his eyes followed along with the light, Erasmo saw the wavy, smudged lines left in the asphalt by the white powder. The lines began exactly where he'd fallen, in the middle of the tracks, and led directly to his position in the grass.

The officer held the light once more on Erasmo's marked clothes. "My God," he said again. "They dragged you. . . ."

"No," Erasmo whispered, shaking uncontrollably as he stared down at the haphazard pattern of small handprints.

Officer Enriquez made the sign of the cross and began to back away.

"No," Erasmo said again, his head slowly shaking from side to side. *"No!"*

He swatted furiously at his sweatshirt, desperate to get their handprints off him. Puffs of white powder swirled in the night air as his hands hammered at his belly and chest. He glanced up and saw Officer Enriquez running away, head turned over his shoulder to give Erasmo one last look. The officer's face, a fleshy mask of fear, was the last thing Erasmo remembered seeing before darkness overtook him, an oblivion he remained in until the EMT roused him with the brilliance of her penlight.

Erasmo now clearly remembered what had happened that night.

He'd gone mad.

Had he been so scared to learn the truth of an afterlife . . . to feel the genuine caress of dead souls against his own skin, that his traumatized mind immediately tried to erase it? Even though he was about to die, deep shame erupted in his heart. All those years of wanting to believe, and when he was finally shown the truth, his mind had cracked from the strain.

Blood continued to cascade down Erasmo's face, while Leander shrieked incoherently. But the screams and the blood and the blade digging into his throat seemed far away, as if this were happening to someone else.

The unintelligible screams in the background were deafening, and now broke through in a single, clear sentence.

"You're *dead*!"

The knife began to slide across his throat. Erasmo thought of his star-crossed father, of his dying grandmother, of the pact he made with his friend, of that night at the Tracks eight long months ago. He took in a deep breath and whispered a desperate prayer to the universe.

And then, almost immediately, a thunderous crack filled the room, and his prayer was answered.

CHAPTER 33

"FREEZE!" A VOICE yelled from behind Erasmo.

And even through his fear, he realized that it was a voice he knew.

"Do you really think that I'm scared of *you*?" Leander said to the owner of the voice. He bared his teeth, the overhead light bulb casting shadows over his sallow face. "I've seen the *real* face of fear! You're nothing but a plodding sack of flesh."

"Put the knife down NOW or I will shoot!"

"Kill me if you want," Leander said. "You'll be doing me a favor."

"Step away from him and put the knife down! This is your last warning!"

"No!" Leander screamed. "I need him to get rid of her! She won't leave me alone—"

Without warning, Erasmo and the chair he was tied to went flying, knocked over by a massive force. He landed sideways, his left cheek now resting against the cold pavement of the shed's floor, but he could see now who his savior was.

Torres, her fists a blur of speed and power, was engaged in a vicious brawl with Leander. Her gun lay on the floor by

Erasmo's face. She must have dropped it when she shoved him out of the way.

Erasmo watched in horror as Leander unleashed a savage roundhouse that landed square on Torres's cheek. Her knees buckled, and Erasmo screamed and begged for anyone . . . anything . . . to help her. Leander cocked his arm back, and this time his fist struck a dazed Torres in the middle of her face, flattening her nose as blood erupted from her nostrils.

He struggled violently against the ropes, shifting his weight in every direction, but remained frozen in place. Erasmo scanned the floor for the knife. Leander must have lost it in the struggle. Maybe he could use it to . . . no . . . there it was on the other side of the room, too far away.

Damn.

Erasmo watched as Leander walked away from Torres and picked up his knife, staring down at it solemnly. His head then slowly rose, eyes bulging and locked on Torres.

She took no notice of this, as her only focus seemed to be staying upright as she wobbled back and forth.

Erasmo sobbed for her, his tears mixing with the blood still cascading down his face. He cried desperately for this woman he barely knew. This woman who had somehow tracked him down, who had inexplicably cared enough about his negligible life to risk her own.

He shrieked and begged as Leander sauntered back across the room, stopping directly in front of Torres.

"I don't want to do this," Leander said as he raised the knife, "but I need him to get rid of her. And you're getting in the goddamn way—"

With a sudden and unexpected ferocity, Torres charged Leander, tackling him to the ground, their bodies landing hard on the concrete floor. They rolled around frantically, each one trying to gain leverage over the other, until Torres managed to straddle Leander for a fraction of a second.

That was all she needed.

Torres brought down a thunderous hammer fist on Leander's face. His head rocked backward, hitting the floor. She then unleashed a flurry of blows with both hands, each landing with power and accuracy on Leander's rapidly deteriorating face.

"Kill me," he croaked. "I'm tired of being afraid. Please."

"I wish I could," Torres said, cocking her right fist all the way back, "but then I'd be no better than you."

She brought her fist down one last time, and Leander finally lay still, bubbles of blood forming on his lips.

Torres jumped off Leander and ran to Erasmo. She stood over him, her blood dripping down onto him and coalescing with his own.

"The ambulance will be here any minute, Erasmo. Just hold on, okay?"

He opened his mouth to thank her, to ask her how she found him, to tell Torres that he loved her. But before any of that could be said, his eyes were drawn to the space above Leander's body. Somehow, the air shimmered and rippled, as if it were a pool of glistening water. The air and light began to stretch, contorting and bulging until it began to form a familiar shape. It was the outline of a young woman. The form continued to morph and coalesce, until Erasmo knew that it could only be one person.

Sandra Rosales.

She peered down at Leander with wary, watchful eyes, her thick waves of onyx hair falling around her face. After a few moments, Sandra floated down closer, as if she wanted to examine him from close range.

Erasmo saw that she was wearing neither the black dress she'd been buried in nor the outfit she had on when she died. Instead, she was wearing a pristine white dress that undulated and flowed around her in every direction, as if it were very much alive.

Seemingly satisfied with her inspection of Leander, Sandra rose from his body and slowly turned her head to Erasmo.

Now faced with the full force of her strength and love and fury, he wept uncontrollably. As tears poured from him, he mourned the life she had lost, and marveled at her tenacity, how she'd fought her way back to this existence to stop this monster from hurting anyone else.

"You can rest now," Erasmo whispered. "You did it."

Sandra graced him with a gentle smile, her eyes kind and generous and infinite, an image he would carry in his heart forever. Before Erasmo could say anything else to her, Sandra slowly began to dissipate, her form collapsing in on itself, until she had disappeared, leaving this world for whatever awaited her next.

"Did you say something?" Torres asked, oblivious to the miracle that had just appeared behind her.

Erasmo tried to answer, but before he could, his head slowly floated away from his body, and the world went a deep, rich black.

CHAPTER 34

BEFORE ERASMO EVEN opened his eyes, he knew that he was lying in a hospital room. The steady beep of the IV machine, the feel of the flimsy gown against his skin, and the bed that was definitely not his own made where he was abundantly clear.

But even with the knowledge that he was in a safe place, Erasmo found himself terrified to open his eyes. He wasn't entirely sure why he was so fearful, but nevertheless, he passed the time by lying as still as a corpse.

It wasn't until he heard a rustle in the room that he first considered opening his eyes. Then there was even more movement around him, and he had no choice.

As soon as his eyes fluttered open, Erasmo immediately knew what had been terrifying him so.

He'd been afraid of waking up alone.

Torres and Rat peered down at him, both wearing twin expressions of concern.

"Dude, you're awake! Thank God. Let me get the doctor —"

"No . . . I . . . I feel okay."

"Good," Torres said. "The doctor said that you lost a lot of blood but should recover fine. You're going to be left with a nasty scar on your forehead though."

"That's okay," Erasmo said, meaning it. "I was never going to win any beauty contests anyway."

"Here," Torres said, handing him a cup. He sipped the water at first, but then quickly poured the whole thing down his arid throat, immediately feeling better. Except, of course, for the stabs of guilt sliding into his gut.

"I need to get out of here and check on my grandmother. What if she needed something? What if—"

"I went by this morning," Rat said. "She's doing great. I told her you got sick while you were at my house and were going to spend a few days with me until you got better. I promised her you'd call when you woke up."

A surge of relief coursed through Erasmo. He looked Torres over. She looked very much as if she'd just fought off a murderous lunatic. Her fists were wrapped with bloody gauze, and a large splint was affixed to her nose. But she was okay.

"How did you know?"

She shook her head. "I don't think this is a good time to go over all of that. We should at least get the doctor in here—"

"No, please. Tell me."

Torres tugged at the bandages on her hands, wincing as she considered how to start.

"Well . . . it started with a call from your buddy here."

Rat nodded, ashen-faced.

"I got scared when you didn't come back from the store. It should've taken ten minutes. After an hour, I knew in my heart something was wrong, so I called her."

"Normally, I'd have brushed it off," she said. "A young man going off on his own for the night isn't exactly going to raise any alarm bells. But you're not just any young man . . . and you've been involved in some pretty crazy stuff lately. So I went to the store Rat said you'd gone to. When I found your Civic deserted in the parking lot with its door wide open, that's when I started to worry."

"Thanks for calling her," Erasmo said to Rat. "If you hadn't, I'd be dead for sure right now." He turned back to Torres. "But how did you . . ."

"I sat in that parking lot for a while mulling everything over. All I really knew about you was what happened at the Ghost Tracks and your involvement with Leander. I tried to consider who might want to hurt you but kept drawing a blank. Leander had been cleared of any wrongdoing, and Travis was dead. My instincts were screaming at me that I was missing something, but I just couldn't figure out what. But then . . ."

"Then what?" Erasmo asked.

"Then," she said, "I started thinking about our last conversation. And all of a sudden, I knew. I knew who had you."

"How?" he asked.

"Well . . . you'd mentioned that Leander told you how Sandra had been killed by a blow to the back of the head. But here's the thing. We *never* told him that when we questioned him. All we mentioned was that she died of blunt force trauma. The exact location of the injury was a detail that we chose not to publicize. So the only way he could have known that . . ."

"Was if he'd done it himself," Erasmo said.

"Exactly. I sped over to Leander's house, but he wasn't there. I decided to try my luck at Travis's, since it was vacant, and a place Leander might think to use. When I got there I heard noises coming from the shed out back. You know the rest."

"Damn," Erasmo said, incredulous at all the things that had to happen just right so that he could live. If Rat hadn't called when he did, or if Torres had brushed it off, or if she hadn't realized the mistake Leander had made, he'd be on a slab in the morgue right now. Erasmo shuddered at how close he came to death.

"How the hell," Rat said, smiling at Torres in awe, "are you so damn smart?"

"I just wish that I'd been smart enough to figure it out sooner," she said. "We know everything now though. I went back to the neighbor who provided Leander's alibi and leaned on him pretty hard. Turns out he's on parole and occasionally did drugs with Leander. Leander threatened to tell the neighbor's parole officer about the drugs unless he lied about what he saw. And then when I questioned Leander, he spared no detail. In fact, he wouldn't shut up about it."

"What did he say?" Rat asked.

"A lot," she said. "The short of it is . . . he got aggressive with Sandra after they got back to his place. She tried to leave, but he wouldn't let her. During the struggle, she fell and hit the back of her head against the stone fireplace in his living room. The story matches up with her injuries."

"Jesus," Rat said.

An uncomfortable silence fell over the room as each of them considered just how wrong they'd been about so many things.

"There's one thing I don't understand," Rat said. "Why did he invite us over that night if he knew her body was under the bed? And why the hell did he have it there in the first place?"

"I wondered that too," Torres said, her skin now looking pallid. "Leander said that he was desperate to get Sandra to leave him alone. He'd done some research and read that spirits sometimes yearned for their physical bodies. So he thought that if he reunited Sandra's spirit with her physical form, maybe this would please her, and she'd stop terrorizing him. So he stole her body from the cemetery and took it to his house.

"When was this?" Erasmo asked.

"Actually, just a few days before you went over."

"That sick son of a bitch," Erasmo said.

"He also said that was the reason for the ballerina outfit. He thought that Sandra would like it and have mercy on him."

"Is that," Erasmo asked, "when she . . ."

"Yeah," Torres said. "Leander claims that shortly after dressing her body like that, her spirit appeared to him wearing the exact same thing, frightening him. That's when he called you in a panic."

Erasmo felt nauseous, and from the looks of Rat, he did too. A pure, deep hatred for Leander welled inside of him, and he was grateful that Torres had pummeled him the way she had.

"As far as why he had you over, Leander genuinely thought that you were going to help get rid of her spirit. It never occurred to him that you'd find the body. He thought you all would just be downstairs all night. But then he got drunk and made the huge mistake of running all over the house."

"Damn," Rat said.

"What about his cousin Travis? Did he have *anything* to do with this?" Erasmo asked.

Torres grimaced for a moment, weighing her words before she spoke.

"I should mention that Leander told me everything about the night at Travis's house." After a brief pause, Torres added, "How that guy Billy killed him."

"Oh," was all Erasmo could manage to reply.

"Leander said," she continued, "that he tried to blame Sandra's murder on Travis because it was well known in their family that he'd done some terrible things. He figured if he could get the cops to look at Travis, they would see what a bad guy he was and take him for the real murderer."

Torres turned to Rat and said, "It's the same reason he hired you to follow Travis around. Leander was hoping that you'd witness some of his transgressions and tell the police about it. All Leander was really hoping for was some dirt on Travis. He couldn't believe his luck when Billy took him out."

"What about the earring?" Rat asked, incredulous. "How did Travis have it?"

"Oh, he didn't," Torres said. "Not really. Leander took it with him that night hoping to plant it somewhere in the house, planning to call the cops with an anonymous tip. During all the chaos, he had a chance to throw it through an open window into Travis's room."

"Billy killed an innocent man," Erasmo whispered to himself, struggling to comprehend the ramifications of what Torres had just said. "Travis had nothing at all to do with Sandra's murder."

"Well, it's true that he had nothing to do with the murder, but Travis wasn't innocent. The forensics team at the scene found evidence inside his shed, blood splatters on the wall, that come from multiple different sources. Whatever Travis was up to, it was pretty damn bad."

"Guess that particular sickness runs in the family," Rat said.

"Could be," Torres said, "or maybe they're just weak-minded, entitled, violent assholes."

Another silence fell over them as Erasmo struggled with what to say next.

"I'm sorry we lied to you," he finally uttered, his voice unsteady. "We were scared. . . . I was scared . . . of what would happen if you found out we were involved in Travis's—"

"I understand why you lied," Torres said. "I'm going to try to keep that part of his confession quiet, or at least advocate that it's the rantings of a lunatic. There's no physical evidence of you two being there. And I'm the only one who knows about that report from his neighbor, so I think it'll be okay."

She then paused, appearing somewhat confused, before finally continuing.

"The only other thing," Torres said, "is that Leander keeps screaming that Sandra's going to come for him . . . begging us to protect him from her. That's the part I don't understand. Maybe he's angling for some kind of insanity defense."

"He's not insane," Erasmo said. "At least not in the way you think. His mind couldn't handle what he saw, Sandra's ethereal form, and it broke him."

Torres stared at the floor, the muscles in her face tense.

"I . . . I told you once that I wanted to believe," she finally said. "But it's really hard to. I just can't wrap my mind around something like this . . . a spirit terrorizing her murderer. How can it be real?"

Torres began to say something, but then thought better of it.

"Go ahead," Erasmo said. "It's okay."

"Well," she said, "for example, I've been thinking a lot about what you claim happened at the Tracks. About those children that you said saved you. But we know the *real* history of the Tracks. We know for a fact that there weren't any children that died there. So how . . ."

"I've been thinking about that too," Erasmo said. "And I'm not sure that what I'm about to say is exactly right, but I think that it could be close."

"What is it?" Rat said, leaning forward.

"I think . . . I think that we all willed it to happen," Erasmo said.

"I'm not following you," Torres said.

"There are over one point five million people in San Antonio. Not all of them believe, of course, but a large number of them do. And with so many people believing in this story over the years, I think it's possible that we *made* it come true. I think that, as a city, we wanted to believe this legend so much, that we collectively conjured those spirits that haunt the Tracks. Every group of friends that ventured out to them on a cold Halloween night, every dusty car that rolled over those tracks, every loner who had nothing else to do but head down there and believe that he was being saved . . . each of them contributing to the miracle that's there now."

The room stayed silent as the three of them mulled over what he'd just said.

"Wow," whispered Rat. "That's a wonderful thought. I really hope it's true."

"Me too," Torres said, looking like she meant it. "In any event, I think you're right about Leander. Whatever it was he thought he saw broke him in a terrible way."

Erasmo touched the thick bandages wrapped around his forehead.

"I think what I experienced at the Tracks broke me too. I just didn't know it."

"Well," Torres said, her broad face warmly looking down on him, "do you know what the good news is about being broken?"

He shook his head.

"You don't have to stay that way."

Erasmo's lips trembled and hot tears slipped down his face.

"Are you sure?" he asked.

"I promise," she whispered.

Torres took his hand in her gauze-wrapped hand and held it until he eventually drifted off to a long, deep, warm sleep.

CHAPTER 35

"WHEN YOU SAID you had an idea for a business," Erasmo said, eyeing the Facebook page Rat had created, "I didn't think this was what you meant."

"Dude," Rat said, eyes gleaming, "it's going to be awesome."

"I don't know. . . . I'm still not sure, man."

"Look, we don't have anything else going on right now. Neither one of us has any money for college. What else are we going to do? This will be our job in the meantime until we save enough cash. Not to mention . . . your grandmother is still in the fight of her life. We need to help her out as much as we can."

"Why don't we at least hold off while I apply for some more jobs. Maybe I'll get hired somewhere," Erasmo said.

"Dude, we have to strike while the iron is hot! Not only are you the guy from the Ghost Tracks, now you're *also* the guy that the cops had to save from getting murdered."

"Well," Erasmo said, "when you're advertising as an investigator, that's not really a great thing to be known for."

"Nevertheless," Rat said, undeterred, "interest in you is at an all-time high, and we need to capitalize! The problem with the Craigslist ad was that we weren't thinking big enough.

Starting today, we're going to flood social media until everyone in San Antonio knows that we're for hire."

Erasmo almost objected again but in his heart knew that Rat had already won him over. The truth was if it meant giving his friend something positive to work toward, Erasmo would have agreed to just about anything.

But that wasn't the only reason, of course. Over the last few days, his mind kept returning to how lucky he was to still be alive. But had it truly been just luck? He'd been on death's doorstep and had been miraculously saved at the last possible moment. There must have been a reason that he was chosen for salvation. There *must* have been. And it was up to him to find out what it was.

"Hey," Rat said, looking a little apprehensive. "There's something that I've been meaning to ask you. I don't want to make you uncomfortable by bringing it up or anything, but . . ."

"Go ahead," Erasmo said, curious.

"Have you given any thought at all to the fact that Billy was right about everything in his prediction for you?"

"What do you mean?" Erasmo asked, even though, in truth, he'd already thought about it a great deal.

"Well, when we first met him, he said that your face would be slashed open, and that you would be screaming with blood pouring down your face. And he also said that Travis would never stop hurting people, and Torres said that—"

"I got it," Erasmo said.

"So what do you think it means?" Rat asked.

"I think that it means," Erasmo said, "that this is a question for another day."

"Okay, fair enough," Rat said, shrugging his shoulders. "So . . . back to our new business. Are you in or what?"

Was he? Erasmo considered the idea one more time before answering his friend. He had no idea if helping clients sort out fantasy from reality and risking himself to save the truly afflicted was his actual purpose. But it sure as hell seemed like he should try to find out.

"I'm in."

"Yes!" Rat said. "Now all we need is a name."

They sat in silence, pondering the possibilities.

"How about," Rat said, "the ER Detective Agency? Get it? Erasmo and Rat?"

"Dude, people will think we always end up maimed and in the hospital with that name."

"Well . . . that wouldn't be inaccurate."

"Funny guy," Erasmo said. "What else you got?"

"How about . . . RAT (and partner) Detective Agency?"

"Try again."

"Wait, I got it!" Rat yelled. "San Antonio Paranormal Investigators!"

"Uh . . . SAPI?"

"Yeah! C'mon, man. It kind of suits us."

Rat typed the name, a huge grin spreading over his face, and punched the Enter key.

As Erasmo left Rat's house and stepped out into the late-afternoon light, he thought about what the next few months would bring. He might meet frightened clients who were merely jumping at shadows. It was possible he'd encounter genuine disturbances that tested the limits of his knowledge and skills. Maybe he'd even witness events that would forever alter his perception of the physical world. So many wondrous possibilities, and he'd be confronting each one with his best friend at his side. As an invigorating gust of wind swirled around him, and warm sunlight splashed on his face, Erasmo Cruz couldn't imagine anything he wanted more.

CHAPTER 36

ERASMO WATCHED WITH great satisfaction as his grandmother raised the gleaming can of Coors Light to her lips, took a long sip, and closed her eyes as she savored the taste. In the weeks since her treatment had started, she'd found that having a beer in the evening sometimes helped take the edge off the side effects. He'd paid a neighbor to buy a case for him and, as he watched the relieved look on her face as she took another sip, considered it money well spent.

The effects of her illness and treatment had already become gut-wrenchingly obvious. His grandmother's hair was thinning at a rapid rate, and her skin was sallow and loose. But what frightened him the most about her appearance was that she looked exactly like what she was . . . a very old and very sick woman.

"Can you at least try not to look so worried?" she asked after a particularly long sip.

"Sorry, Grandma." He almost smiled. She'd always been able to read his expressions effortlessly.

She took another long swallow, never taking her tired but observant eyes off of him.

"The next few months are going to be rough," she said. "For both of us. But I promise you this, Erasmo I'm going to fight like hell to live. I don't want to die for so many reasons that it hurts my heart to even think about. I want to see what your life becomes. I want to see you use your gift to help people. I want to live because I enjoy seeing the good parts of your father in you, and it comforts me to know that because of you, his life meant something. And I want to live long enough to see you truly happy one day."

Erasmo didn't know how to respond to any of this, and he felt shame that his grandmother had such a clear understanding of his loneliness.

"But," she said after another long sip, "I also want to say this. What happened with your parents was terrible. That hole in your life will always be there, and there is nothing you can do to change the past. But you can shape your future. Some people get born into a large, wondrous family filled with joy and love. But others, Erasmo, aren't so lucky, and have to go out into the world and find their own family. No matter what happens to me, that's what I want you to do. Go out into the world and find people out there who you love, and who love you, and make them your own. Promise me."

"I promise, Grandma."

"Good," she said, a satisfied look on her face. "Oh, by the way, I think that you're off to a damn good start of finding your people with that friend of yours, Rat. He genuinely cares about you, and that's hard to find in this world. Hold on tight, and don't ever let go."

"I won't," he said. He sat quietly by his grandmother's side until she finished her beer, closed her sunken eyes, and slipped into a deep and sudden sleep.

After tucking his grandmother in, Erasmo walked back to his room, took *A Practical Guide to the Supernatural and Paranormal* off the shelf, and stared down at it. He'd been attached to this book for so long and had learned so much from it, but something in his gut told him that it was time to let go and forge his own way.

Erasmo reached under his bed and took out the cardboard box. He was about to drop the book inside but felt a sudden urge to read Dubois's words again. For old time's sake. He flipped the book open to the very last entry, one he knew well, and allowed his eyes to flow over the words.

Hope

I've begun to fear that I have wasted years of my life. In all of my travels, and research, and experiences, I have not been successful in obtaining the only thing I wanted: to hear my sweet Emma's voice one last time. I have sought out and begged witches and warlocks and brujas and shamans and others with mystical abilities to summon her spirit. And while I have seen many shocking and extraordinary things, they have all failed to bring her back.

I was about to give up and spend what's left of my years as a teacher, imparting the knowledge I've learned to those who might find it of use. But then something strange happened. One might say a miracle. I received a letter from a gentleman I met in my travels. He claims that he has come across an old man who is astonishingly proficient at summoning the souls of loved ones.

I almost told him that I no longer had any interest in such matters. In truth, I have grown so melancholy and weary due to the many disappointments over the course of my quest, that the prospect of enduring another is almost too much to bear.

But even the slightest possibility of speaking to my daughter continues to haunt me.

Should I continue to carry even a flicker of hope in my heart? My rational mind says that I shouldn't, and yet, I feel its warmth grow inside me even as I write this. Hope is truly everything, and without it, there seems little reason to go on. And go on I must.

My bags are packed, and I am excited to embark on this trip. The only cause of concern is that my friend has warned me that this old man's price for his services is exorbitantly high. In fact, the highest I've come across: a blood sacrifice.

I'm not sure of the exact nature of this demand, but I am confident that I'll be able to work out an arrangement once I arrive there. I am off, my heart full, and I sincerely hope that the next entry in this journal will truly be wondrous.

Erasmo turned the page and read the book's last sentence.

John F. Dubois was never seen or heard from again.

His heart twinged, as it always did when he read those words.

After putting the book away, Erasmo reached into his backpack and pulled out his new journal. At the time, it had just seemed like an impulse buy he'd made while shopping for his grandmother. But now the journal emanated a robust, magnetic power. He held the book in his hands, enjoying the cool, supple feel of the tan leather, and opened it to the first page. After a few moments of thought, he placed his pen to the cream-colored paper and began to write.

My name is Erasmo Cruz. I start this journal at the age of 17 and hope to one day finish it as an old man, having lived an eventful life, full of love and wonder and family. I've already experienced my fair share of darkness and know that more is surely coming. But my wish is that this journal will be one of hope and discovery . . . a chronicle of our attempts to help those who need it the most. I will use this book to share everything that I learn of the supernatural and the occult, but also what I learn about myself in the process.

While I see now that it's impossible to ever truly "let go" of the past, I've come to understand that it is possible to lighten the weight of it, and let it serve as a remembrance as you forge your own future. And in these pages, I hope to capture that journey.

Let's start with something close to home, shall we?

The Ghost Tracks

Erasmo spent the next few hours working on his first entry in the journal, scribbling furiously as he recounted the legend of the Tracks, his experience there, and what he'd hoped he had learned from it. When Erasmo finally finished, hand cramped and head heavy from exhaustion, he felt soothed and unburdened, as if he'd just confessed his greatest sins. Perhaps he had.

He slid the journal onto the shelf above his bed and was about to bury himself under the covers when a beep arose from his laptop. Erasmo grabbed it from his nightstand and saw that there was a new email in his inbox titled: *Need Help – Urgent.* He opened it, his mouth losing all moisture as he read the message.

Mr. Cruz,

I have a very particular problem that I hope you might be able to help me with. I guess I should first say that, despite what I'm about to tell you, I am perfectly sane. Up until a few days ago, I was living a happy, contented life. But now everything has changed.

Time is working against me, so if you can help, please respond immediately. As far as what I need help with, I'm not even quite sure how to say it, other than this.

My brother disappeared over twenty years ago. The authorities searched everywhere, but he was never found. But now, unbelievably, he's back. He showed up at my front door a few days ago. And it is without a doubt him. Even his birthmarks are the same. I should be happy. Except for this.

He hasn't aged a single day.

And then last night, in the garage, I caught him doing something truly abominable.

Please respond immediately. I need help stopping him. He's dangerous. And he's very hungry.

Yours,

Eric Reynosa

Erasmo read the message several more times, multitudes of questions erupting in his head. He gently closed the laptop and picked up his phone, dialing Rat's number. His friend picked up on the third ring.

"Hey," Erasmo said, "it's me."

He paused, thinking of what exactly to say to his friend, and finally decided on words that felt right and true as they left his lips.

"I think we've got something here."

ACKNOWLEDGMENTS

First, I'd like to thank each and every person who purchased a copy of this book when I was trying to get it published. The overwhelming support I received from my siblings, aunts, uncles, cousins, friends, coworkers, acquaintances, and even people who I'd never met was truly humbling and the best part of this entire process.

Thank you, Dad, for encouraging us to read when we were little, and especially for letting me read your copy of *Lonesome Dove*.

Thank you, Lynda and Grace, for your unwavering support, for putting up with countless hours of me grumpily staring at my laptop, and for allowing me to prattle on endlessly about this book without ever showing an ounce of boredom or annoyance.

Thank you, Adam Gomolin, for believing in *The Ghost Tracks* from the beginning, and for all of the feedback that helped turn it into the book that it is today.

Thanks to the Castro brothers, for their many years of support and friendship.

Thank you, Patrick Delaney, a fantastic author everyone should check out, for providing valuable feedback and insight, as well as for being a great friend and supporter during this process.

Thank you, Mr. Fox, for your many invaluable contributions to the book.

Thank you, Ryan Jenkins, for a fantastic copy edit and for fixing all those ellipses.

And lastly, thank you, Martin, who I still miss tremendously, for providing inspiration to me even all these years later.

GRAND PATRONS

Carlo X. Lopez
John R. Soto
Teresa J. O. Kelley

INKSHARES

INKSHARES is a reader-driven publisher and producer based in Oakland, California. Our books are selected not by a group of editors, but by readers worldwide.

While we've published books by established writers like *Big Fish* author Daniel Wallace and *Star Wars: Rogue One* scribe Gary Whitta, our aim remains surfacing and developing the new author voices of tomorrow.

Previously unknown Inkshares authors have received starred reviews and been featured in the *New York Times*. Their books are on the front tables of Barnes & Noble and hundreds of independents nationwide, and many have been licensed by publishers in other major markets. They are also being adapted by Oscar-winning screenwriters at the biggest studios and networks.

Interested in making your own story a reality? Visit Inkshares.com to start your own project or find other great books.